HOME FIELD *advantage*

A BLUESTONE LAKES NOVEL

JENN MCMAHON

Copyright © 2025 by Jenn McMahon LLC

All rights reserved.

Cover Design: Melissa Doughty | Mel D. Designs

Editing: Caroline Palmier

Developmental Editing: Salma's Literary Services

Proofreading: Erica Rogers

No part of this book may be reproduced in any form or by any electronic or mechanical means, including information storage and retrieval systems, without written permission from the author, except for the use of brief quotations in a book review.

Without in any way limiting the author's exclusive rights under copyright, any use of this publication to "train" generative artificial intelligence (AI) technologies to generate text is expressly prohibited.

This is a work of fiction, created without use of AI technology. Any names, characters, places or incidents are products of the author's imagination and used in a fictitious manner. Any resemblance to actual people, places, or events is purely coincidental or fictional.

A NOTE FROM JENN:

Hello friend.

Thank you so much for picking up book two in the Bluestone Lakes series. This little fictional town has become so real to me. The same way these characters hold a special place in my heart.

Through this series, you will find second chances and found family. Bluestone Lakes is an ideal location for those looking to escape everyday life or whatever problems you're facing back home. In our secluded town tucked between the mountains with a lake as far as the eyes can see, you will find peace and solitude during your stay. However long that may be..

If you want to see more, you can visit the town website. This will be updated regularly *wink wink* as the series progresses.

Click here to visit Bluestone Lakes

While this book was created to be light and easy to read—I understand there are some things that may be triggering to

A NOTE FROM JENN:

someone. My goal is to respect that before you dive into this story.

I wanted to make you aware that this book you has explicit language, alcohol consumption, and explicit sex scenes.

This book also contains a character with Obsessive-Compulsive Disorder (OCD).

Please know that it is complex and the character in these pages is not a template or diagnosis guide, just one story. OCD doesn't look the same for everyone, and I don't claim to capture every version of it. This is one story among many.

If you recognize yourself in these pages and are struggling, please know you are not alone and help is available. Reaching out to a trusted professional or support network can make a difference.

I hope I handled these topics with care and that you end up swooning through this book the same way I did writing it.

As always, my Instagram DM's are always open for your reactions, favorite moments and to chat as you read!

xo, Jenn

For the ones like me and Poppy—who can't escape the storm inside your head. Who apologize for simply existing. Who carry the weight of feeling like you're too much and never enough at the same time. Who think love might never come because you feel broken.

Let me tell you a secret:
You are enough. You are not broken.
And you're worthy of a love that stays—even on the loudest days.

HOME FIELD ADVANTAGE

BLUESTONE LAKES
BOOK 2

PROLOGUE

DALLAS

The bases are loaded in the bottom of the ninth.

We're so close that I can taste victory on the tip of my tongue. Something we've never had before. In my four years of coaching the San Francisco Staghorns, we've never had a shot at going to the biggest championship game in the league, let alone making the playoffs.

That's not the only reason for the pressure weighing heavily on my shoulders, though.

This game will determine if I get to keep my job as head coach.

Do I have a backup plan if we don't make it? Nope.

Should I? Probably.

With one foot on the top steps of the dugout, I rest my elbow on my upper thigh as I watch, without blinking, each of the players on the team. The same ones I played alongside years ago. My shoulder throbs from the memory, but I shake it off.

My friend, and head pitcher, Mitch, takes his stance on the pitcher's mound. The next batter from the Atlanta Strikers takes the field, and the crowd goes wild as he waves his hands in the air to encourage cheers from the stands. Once he gets into position, the stadium quiets down, or at least it does to me while I hold my breath.

We're up by one run.

One fucking run.

If we don't strike out here, we could lose the game.

There's a runner on third base with a lead off the bag, ready to run. Mitch looks to Tyler, standing on third, who's ready in position in case he tries to advance for a steal at home plate. It's a risk if the runner attempts it, but I wouldn't put it past them to tie the game.

With eyes back on home plate, Mitch throws a strike.

Everyone still has eyes on third base to make sure he doesn't get the steal.

Another throw. Another strike.

It all comes down to this.

We just need *one more* strike to win this.

"Come on, please make it," I mutter under my breath as I watch intently as he winds up, and everything begins to move in slow motion. I stop breathing, afraid that if I even blink, it will throw off the ball or some shit. The ball releases from his grip, flying rapidly, and I send a silent prayer that the batter swings and misses.

But as my luck would have it, the opposite happens.

The crack of the ball connecting with the wooden bat echoes, and I follow the ball as it soars through the outfield and over the fence.

Releasing a long, drawn-out exhale, my head falls in defeat.

We just lost our spot in the playoffs.

My team played a hell of a season, so losing my job isn't their fault. But to the team owners and fans, everything falls back on me and my ability to coach them. Every season for the last four years, we've won just enough games to scrape by for even a shot at the playoffs, but we always fall short.

Looking up, I see the Atlanta Strikers and the coaches flood the field with their arms in the air, shouting and celebrating their victory, while my team's disappointment is painted on every face.

These are not just players to me.

They're my brothers, and their success is my success.

"Heads up, boys," I shout across the field as I step out of the dugout.

Even though I have no room to talk since my head was down just moments ago, I know they're just as devastated as I am over this loss.

My feet drag me to the field, where the players line up to congratulate the other team. I do the same by meeting the Strikers coach before following my team into the dugout to grab our things. We filter through the door leading to the locker room. The only sounds are the rustling bags, the light thump of cleats, and my heart pounding in my chest.

I hate this for them.

I hate this for me.

I'm the last to enter behind everyone, and as soon as I do, my eyes lock with the owner of the Staghorns. Clark Harris stands there, leaning against the wall, with a sympathetic smile. He knows he has to fire me today, and the pain of doing it is etched on his face.

Before I took this job, which followed the abrupt end of my career, he was my mentor.

He was *my* head coach.

He was like the dad I never had.

I tip my chin with a silent greeting before he places a hand on my shoulder. "We need to talk."

Forcing a smile, my lips form a straight line. "Never a good thing, huh?"

He shakes his head.

Clark never beats around the bush, and I love him for it. Except right now, my stomach is in knots, and I'd rather be anywhere else but here.

"We can talk after you finish up with the guys and get

changed," he says, then turns to leave me there with my spiraling thoughts.

If I were optimistic, I'd imagine him telling me that he isn't going to fire me, and instead give me one more chance, one more season, to figure out this coaching thing. Especially since he didn't ask me to meet in the privacy of his office. I would be grateful, accept it, and work harder than ever before.

But my life tends to lean toward adverse outcomes, if I'm being honest.

The team is all changed, and with their heads down low, they all sit on the benches scattered around the locker room.

"You all played a hell of a game," I say, clearing my throat. "If you all play the way you have over the last few months, I have no doubt that we can win the title next year."

They nod in unison, but no words are said back.

"We have a chance next season. A big one, especially with the advantage that we have a lot of home games on that schedule. We know how this field works. We know every patch of dirt, weird bounce, and the way the sun glares. This field is ours and belongs to us." I pause, looking from Mitch to Tyler and then the rest of the guys. "And next year the championship will belong to us too."

A round of cheers erupts from the locker room, and I force a smile. I didn't exactly lie to them. They *do* have a chance next year—it's just probably going to be without me.

I give each of them a mix of handshakes and high fives before leaving them to head to my office off to the side. I take a moment to scan the photos along the wall through the years that showcase my journey here in San Francisco. Stopping in front of my desk, I read the block which bears the inscription *Dallas Westbrook – Head Coach* on a small gold nameplate. I run my fingers along the title I never wanted, but when my world crashed around me it allowed me the opportunity to keep baseball in my life.

And now I have to say goodbye to it.

A throat clears behind me, and I snap my head to find Clark standing in my office and closing the door behind him. "Hell of a game today."

I nod, but remain silent.

"Unfortunately, I'm at a crossroads," he continues. "While we always try our best to come out of a game with a win, sometimes the other teams surprise us when they swing and hit it out of the park."

"It was an impressive game on both ends."

"It was. But that's not why I'm here."

I swallow, gesturing for him to take a seat, and he waves me off.

"You're like a son to me, Dallas. You were the greatest pitcher I've ever coached. Probably the greatest of all time."

"It was a short time," I add.

"Things haven't been the best since you were forced into early retirement, and I think we jumped too quickly offering you the role of head coach."

"I haven't been at my best, and the team deserves better."

He shakes his head. "Could you use some work? Sure. We all could. But you *are* the best, even though I know you struggle to believe that."

This time, I don't respond. I assess his features, searching for the lie, to see if he's sugar-coating something with me for the first time. The fine lines and wrinkles from his old age show nothing.

"I appreciate that," I finally say, choking out the words.

"And I want you to understand I'm not here to fire you," he says.

My eyebrows knit in confusion.

"I'm offering you a break because I know when one is necessary. You have what it takes to coach this team, but you never had the chance to get over how your career ended. And that's on me. I didn't want to lose you, so I pushed you into this position before you were ready."

My stomach flips, and I feel like I want to throw up right at his feet, while simultaneously wanting to kiss him for this chance. "What does this mean?"

"Coach James will take over for the offseason training. We can figure out what to tell the press. I want you to take some time to focus on yourself and get your shit together. We can figure out your next steps after that. No decision has to be made right this second, and I won't allow you to make another impulsive one for the sake of keeping this team in your life."

This is…unexpected.

"Thank you, sir."

"First, stop calling me sir," he warns with a finger to my face. "Second, you got this. I know you do. There will be no more strikeouts. Only home runs from here on out."

I let his final words settle as my shoulders relax.

No more strikeouts, only home runs.

The words have more meaning than just baseball, and the both of us know it. Everything in my life is just a never-ending streak of strikeouts. I don't intend for it to be that way, but like he said…I need to take the time to focus on myself for once. I wish I could tell him right now I'll take the offseason to get my head on straight and come back stronger, but that would be impulsive. That could potentially just lead to another situation like this, but worse.

"Thank you, Clark." I nod, swallowing past the emotions. "Mostly for never giving up on me."

"Never," he says, offering me a grin and a firm handshake before walking away.

My eyes stay stuck on him as I try to force myself to believe everything he just said.

That it's not a dream.

That I'm not fired, but instead given a second chance.

"I think I saw your daughter roaming around the family waiting area outside the locker room," he says, just as he's about to leave my office. "You better go get that sweet girl." And then he walks away.

Inhaling and exhaling one more time, I exit into the long hallway that leads from the locker room to where the families gather after games.

"Daddy!"

Snapping my head toward the small voice, I crouch down quickly as my daughter leaps into my arms. A full smile fills my face as she wraps her arms around my neck, burrowing her head into my neck.

"Hey, bug." I laugh.

She pulls back, keeping her arms around my neck. "I'm sorry your team didn't win, Daddy." She wrinkles her nose as if disgusted by the game's outcome.

I mess her hair with my hand. "It's all good," I lie, refusing to let my emotions show in front of her. "Where's your mom?"

"Right over there." She turns to point where April, my ex-wife, stands with one shoulder against the wall at a safe distance to allow us this little moment, as if she knew Sage was precisely what I needed. Once our eyes meet, she presses off the wall and approaches us with a sympathetic smile on their face.

"Hey. I'm sorry about the game," she says.

I shrug a shoulder, trying not to let her know how much it's already affected me in the short time since it's been over.

"Not to jump into anything when you're already down about it, but…" She wrings her hands together like she's nervous. "We need to talk."

"Not you, too," I groan.

She tilts her head and raises a brow in confusion.

"Clark"—I blindly gesture to the locker room I just came out of—"he also had a word with me right before this."

"Right." She nods.

"Can I have a word with you, too?" Sage asks, looking up at me.

"For you? I'll give you as many words as you want."

"I want a bazillion," she emphasizes.

I poke her nose with my index finger. "Then a bazillion words you get. And if it's okay with Mommy, maybe we can get a post-game treat? That always fixes everything."

"Can it be ice cream? Please!" she pleads, hands clasped together.

I cross my arms over my chest. "Depends on what kind?"

"Cotton candy! Duh!" She giggles.

"Then we can *definitely* get ice cream." Sage dances where she stands, and I look up to April. "If that's okay with you?"

April nods but remains silent as she turns to walk down the hall. Sage takes my hand as we follow out into the parking lot. She skips the entire way to my car. Once I have her buckled in her seat, I close the door and face April.

"You want to talk now or later?"

"I really hate to do this now," she says, the words coming out painfully, like she *really* doesn't want to have to do this. "But I've been meaning to talk to you about it for the past month. I didn't want to put more on your plate with the busy end of season schedule, but now they need an answer."

"Who needs an answer to what?"

She averts her gaze briefly, and I know her enough to know she avoids eye contact with me when she's nervous.

"I was offered a new job opportunity," she spits out quickly.

"That's great?" I question, unsure what has her so nervous. "Are you going to accept?"

April finally looks at me again. "I'd like to. But it requires moving to Wyoming. They want me to help get the new obstetrics team up and running at the new hospital. It's a *huge* opportunity for me, and an honor to even be asked. The other hospital on the opposite side of Cheyenne has outgrown their department and can no longer keep up with the demand. It's only temporary."

Did she say Wyoming?
What the fuck?

When I don't respond right away, she continues. "It's not my favorite idea to move out of San Francisco and uproot Sage's life, even if it's only temporary."

Just as I'm about to open my mouth to ask more questions, the conversation I had with Clark circles my head like a movie replay that was meant to come into focus at this very moment.

A second chance to get my life together.

"I'm sorry to spring this all on you. I just need to give them an answer," April finally says. "But we have to discuss Sage."

"Take the job. I'm coming with you."

CHAPTER 1
DID YOU SEARCH FOR SMALL TOWNS TO LIVE IN WYOMING?

DALLAS

"You know, I didn't believe you when you said you were moving out of state," Mitch says before taking a pull of his beer.

"Same," Tyler adds. "I just thought it was some sick joke after that season-ending loss."

Shaking my head, I huff out a laugh. "I'm still not sure how I feel about it, even after weeks of figuring out the details. But when April said she had this opportunity, I jumped on it too. I need the time away from San Francisco to get over my shit without everything hanging over my head."

"I'll be honest," Mitch starts, pausing nervously as he looks down at his hands on the bar top. "I felt like you jumped quickly into the coach position." He looks up and holds his hands up in defense before even giving me a chance to say anything. "Not that I didn't think you were gonna kick ass at the job. You just didn't allow yourself enough time to get over what happened. I know that had to be devastating for you."

"Agreed," Tyler adds.

"If I were to lose baseball," Mitch continues, "I would be a mess. Someone would have to pick me up out of bed every morning." He laughs to lighten the mood.

I nod because he's right. "I think losing baseball, or at least… losing the opportunity to play, just snowballed into everything else crashing down around me. I just needed something else to focus on when things with April…"

Mitch scoffs. "Let's be honest, your marriage was never going to last regardless."

"Agreed," Tyler says.

"Then I was delusional to think things would look up with the head coaching position," I continue, ignoring his comment about my failed marriage. "Only for that to also crash and burn."

Mitch rolls his eyes. "That didn't crash and burn. This is all only temporary, according to Clark. It will be good for you to get this time away."

"Yes." Tyler nods in agreement.

Mitch turns his chair to face him. "Are you just going to agree with everything I say and repeat after me?"

He nods and starts laughing. "You're a wise old man, so I'm just being smart to agree."

"Call me old one more time," Mitch warns before relaxing in his chair. "I'm only two years older than you."

While I may be their coach, these two have been my best friends since the beginning of my baseball career. Mitch, Tyler, and I all attended the same high school in South Carolina and met at tryouts in junior year. Tyler, a freshman at the time, asked if anyone had an extra glove because he'd forgotten his. Mitch gave him one, and then we all fell into hysterics that this guy shows up to baseball tryouts without a glove. We all made the team and have been inseparable since.

"Anyway…" Tyler ignores him and focuses his attention on me. "Did you find a place there?"

I shake my head over the brim of my beer bottle. "I'm not living in the city."

"Where the hell are you going to live?" Tyler asks.

After losing that game and my conversations with Clark and April, I left the stadium feeling every emotion swarming me. I held it in for Sage while I took her to get ice cream, but after that, I sat in my Tahoe in the parking lot of April's apartment complex, staring through my front window until the street lights turned on, thinking about everything that led me to that moment. Thinking about every reckless and impulsive decision I ever made without thinking things through.

The one constant good thing in my life is Sage. But I feel like I fuck that up more often than not, especially when it comes to being a good father to her.

I've never had the opportunity to fully be there for her the way I should've been as a dad. I struggled with my erratic schedule, and my marriage ended because of all of it. April hated that baseball always came first and that I couldn't change the drive in me to be the best there was. I was so caught up in my dreams that I never once realized how much it was affecting the people around me.

"I can't go from living in one city to another," I answer honestly. "I found a small town less than an hour from Cheyenne, where she's going to be, called Bluestone Lakes."

"That sounds..." Tyler starts.

"Oddly therapeutic," Mitch finishes for him. "Is this one of Clark's many getaway recommendations?"

I laugh, shaking my head. "I found it online."

Tyler spits out his drink and can't hold back his laugh. "You just found this place online? Did you search for small towns to live in Wyoming?"

"Actually...yeah."

That only makes him laugh harder. "This just made my day."

"I'm being so serious. Do you guys want to see it?"

Mitch nods. "Duh. Don't leave us hanging here."

Reaching for the side pocket of my jeans, I pull out my phone, open the saved website on my browser, and tilt it to face the guys. Tyler reaches over and swipes to see more.

"That's it?" Tyler raises an eyebrow. "Coach, there's one picture on that site."

"Off the map is what I need. I spoke with a woman named Nan—"

"I'm sorry…what?" Tyler asks, shocked.

"I know. I thought it was strange, too. It's even listed on the website as *Nan*."

"I don't think I like this anymore," Mitch adds.

"I was nervous, too, but Nan made me feel a little more at ease, ensuring everything would be set up in my rental before I arrived. And…I'm going to have Sage with me."

Both of their eyes widen simultaneously.

After sitting with my thoughts for as long as I did, I ended up going back up to April's apartment after Sage went to bed to figure out how this would work for the three of us. Sage was the most essential factor in the plans. April spent years with me putting my job first, so now it's her turn for a big opportunity while I take the necessary break that has been given to me.

After hours of discussion, we came to the conclusion that I'll take Sage full-time instead of having her every other weekend, as per our current agreement.

"We were both concerned with the school situation. Once I stumbled on the website, I got the phone number for the school in town. Which took forever, might I add, because this website has next to nothing on it."

"You could say that again," Tyler scoffs.

"After hearing about what they have to offer compared to her current school, it was an easy decision for us after that."

"Are you concerned with her switching in the middle of the school year, or the short time that you're going to be there?" Mitch asks.

"I was, but we talked to Sage about it, and strangely enough, she's so happy about the adventure. Besides, this move is only a six-month contract."

"And how do you feel about it?" Mitch raises an eyebrow.

I shrug. "You know how I am. I roll with the punches and figure it out as I go. I'll adjust."

"I think this will be good for you two," Tyler says.

"I've spent far too long not putting Sage first. I missed out on so much. I missed my chance at being a good dad," I continue before they press the issue. "I'm choosing to believe this is all a sign from some upper universe that I'm getting a second chance at it."

Emotions sit thick in my throat, so I avert my gaze from my best friends. I land on a family sitting in a booth near us. A mother, father, and daughter about the same age as Sage sit there, smiling, happy, and laughing. The dad has two French fries tucked into his upper lip and makes walrus noises while his daughter laughs so hard that tears spill out of the corners of her eyes. The mother stares at them with a wide grin that reaches her eyes.

That right there is a family.

That's what a good dad is.

I can't remember a single time when my family looked like that.

"You *are* a good dad," Tyler says, shaking his head. "That little girl loves you."

"For once, I agree with him," Mitch chimes in, tipping his head in agreement. "What will you do when you come back? You'll still coach, right?"

His question forces my gaze away from the family moment I invaded. "Clark told me not to make any decisions until closer to the season starting."

Tyler brings his hand to his chest and gasps. "You? Making rash decisions? Blasphemy."

I smile while Mitch and Tyler both start laughing.

They know me a little too well.

"I think this will be good for you," Mitch says.

My chest feels tight, and I rub the ache away before taking another sip of my beer.

"I want to believe that, too."

CHAPTER 2
I'M HERE FOR A FEW MONTHS.

DALLAS

Bluestone Lakes is a sixteen-hour drive, and since I haven't been sleeping the best anyway, I figure I'd push through the night so Sage could sleep for most of the trip. Initially, the plan was for April to fly into Cheyenne with Sage, and once I had things ready, I would come pick her up afterward, but Sage wanted no part of getting on a plane and preferred the idea of a road trip.

This whole thing still feels surreal, and I'm on the fence about being ready.

I thought the drive would help me understand this move and what's led me to this point in my life, but it hasn't. Instead, I find myself constantly questioning every rash decision I've made and my future. Specifically, if I even want to continue coaching. Baseball is the only thing I've ever known. It's been the only constant in my life. I remember the first time I stepped onto a baseball field. The smell of freshly cut grass, the sound of the ball hitting the bat, and the adrenaline rush as the crowd cheered.

But what would my life look like without it?

Bluestone Lakes represents a new beginning, a chance to leave behind the uncertainties and disappointments that have plagued me. And strangely, near the end of our long drive, I find myself looking forward to this new chapter in my life. An opportunity to embrace who I am without baseball.

My Tahoe slows when the welcome sign comes into view before me.

Welcome to Bluestone Lakes.

My eyes scan the space before me for the first time during this drive. It's still early in the morning as the sun barely creeps over the horizon. Mountains in every direction nestle along the skyline without a cloud in sight. The urge to pull over and take it all in is strong, but I'm close to hopefully getting some coffee in my system and meeting this mystery woman who will hand me the keys to my rental.

Reaching behind me, I give Sage's leg a little scratch to lightly wake her up. In the rearview mirror, I watch as her eyes open slowly, assessing her surroundings. My SUV jolts lightly when I hit a little crack in the one-lane highway.

"Are we there yet?" Sage asks groggily, rubbing her eyes and stretching her arms over her head. "Mr. Marshmallow and I are ready to be there."

While most kids have one comfort item they cling to at a young age, Sage has two. She has a thin blanket that we used to swaddle her as a baby, which she calls a nanny, and a plush white bunny rabbit she calls Mr. Marshmallow. It's not exactly the whitest in color anymore, as Mr. Marshmallow has seen better days, but it brings her comfort.

"We're here."

She sits up taller, looking out the window, and at the same time, we pass a ranch. Beautiful horses line the fence, sitting adjacent to the road. I keep the SUV slow so that she can get a good look at them. Watching intently in the mirror and keeping my eyes between her and the road, her face lights up with wonder. It makes me both emotional and happy because I love seeing her like this, and fucking hate that the feeling plagues me

17

that I've missed out on watching her enjoy so many other wonders before this.

"There are so many horses, Daddy!"

"That is a lot, huh?"

"Is this where we're staying? Can I ride a horse? I want to sit on top of that pretty white one. Looks like a princess."

I chuckle from my seat. "We're not staying on the ranch, bug. But this is the town we're staying in. I'll do some research and see if they offer rides, so we can check them out one day."

"I hope they do," she says, craning her neck to keep looking at the horses while I pass them. Then she faces forward again, kicking her legs up and down with happiness etched all over her face. "This is so fun already."

I soak up every ounce of happiness she's radiating, because, quite frankly, I'm nervous. Having Sage with me once a week is very different from having her full-time. The time she's with me is usually packed with something fun and ditching her usual routine: ice cream trips, movie nights, or dinner at her favorite chain restaurants. It's all fun and games. I'm not even sure I know what her day-to-day routine looks like now that she's older than she was when I still lived with her.

"Do you think they have a liquid zoo here, too?"

I choke. "A what?"

"A liquid zoo. You know the places with all the sea creatures inside tanks for us to walk around and look at."

"An aquarium?"

"That's it."

"I have no idea," I say flatly, because where does she come up with this stuff?

"At least I know they gots horses. That's just as good."

"That they do."

I look from the road to the rearview mirror, and she looks deep in thought.

"Hey, Daddy?"

"Yes?"

"Are you going to play baseball here in this town?"

My chest tightens. Even my daughter knows that baseball's my life. The tone of her voice is full of worry, though. It's filled with the question of *are you going to be around while we're here?* and that fucking stings.

"I'm not," I answer honestly, glancing again at her through the mirror. "That okay?"

She smiles, not knowing I'm watching her. "Yeah. It's all right. But what about coaching? You're the best in the world."

Far from it, kid.

"No plans to coach here, bug."

"Okie dokie," she says before looking back out the window and seeing the buildings coming into view.

I notice the second sign I was told to look for. *Welcome to the Heart of Bluestone Lakes*, this one reads. I can already tell this is a very welcoming town. Nan's directions instruct me to meet her at a small bakery, located a little past the sign called Batter Up.

Less than a minute later, I spot the bakery sign. An older woman, who appears to be in her seventies, sits on a bench on the sidewalk. Her pure white hair and retro-style glasses frame her face while the rest of her looks like she just stepped out of *Boogie Nights* at a local club.

Interesting.

I park my Tahoe in one of the spots on the road and hop out to meet her.

"You Dallas?" She raises an eyebrow.

I nod, adjusting the brim of my baseball cap to expose more of my face to her. "Yes, ma'am."

"We aren't doing that *ma'am* shit." She waves her hand in the air, and my eyes widen at how bold she is, having never met me before. She stands up, looking from me to my Tahoe. "What the heck is with these out-of-towners coming here with fancy whips?" she mutters while digging into her pocket for a set of keys before handing them to me. "How was the drive to town?"

"Long." I exhale. "I most definitely need some coffee."

"Cozy Cup is the place to go!" She smiles, and it's a stark mood change from just seconds ago. She points at the building next door. "And how convenient for you, it's right here."

"Thank you…" I trail off, hoping she gives me a real name.

"Nan. You can call me Nan."

"Nan?"

"Everyone in town calls me that, and since you're about to be a part of this town, get used to it," she rattles off.

"I'm only here for a few months."

"You're still here, boy," she says with an index finger in the air like she's making a point. "If you live under the roof of one of our homes, even for a short time, you're part of this place."

I swallow, feeling an uneasiness creep into my gut. Yes, this is only a temporary place for Sage and me, but the last thing I want to do is get used to it. We're just here to escape the city, figure out my shit, and for Sage to finish out the school year.

"Right," I settle on. "Thank you."

She looks back at my SUV as if she's looking for something. "Where's the girl you said was living with you?"

I gesture to my SUV. "She's in the backseat."

"Well…" Nan says, making her way to the back door and opening it without an invitation. I should be taken aback, but there's something about her that screams friendly and safe, even when I don't know a thing about her. Call it a gut feeling or whatever. "Hey there, kid."

"Hi," I hear Sage say as I make my way to where Nan stands. "Who are you?"

"I'm Nan."

"Like a grandma?"

Nan barks out a laugh. "You can say that. I'm everybody's grandma 'round here."

"That's really cool."

"Hungry?" Nan asks.

"I'm always hungry," she says, unbuckling her seatbelt from her car seat and getting out of the backseat. Someone steps out of the bakery door and onto the sidewalk. Sage scrunches her nose as if she's sniffing, and her eyes widen. "It smells like sugar out here. My tummy loves sugar."

Just as I'm about to open my mouth to tell her we'll stop after I get some caffeine in me, two boys who look to be about eight or nine years old barrel past us on the sidewalk. One with a baseball bat in his hands, the other with a bucket of balls.

Nan throws up her hands. "Whoa. Austin and Archie, slow down, will ya?"

They both skid to a stop, walking slowly back to Nan. "We're sorry, Nan." One of the boys says first. "We didn't mean to run into you guys," the other adds.

"It's all right boys. Just be careful. Where ya headin'?"

"The barnyard."

"All right. Get along now. Stay off the ranch and pick up all the balls when you're done."

"Of course, Nan," one says.

"We're sorry, again," the other adds before glancing at me. He's about to turn around and stops, doing a double take.

The way he's looking at me tells me he knows exactly who I am. It makes me uneasy because I don't want to be recognized here. I adjust the brim of my hat and look to the ground, avoiding eye contact altogether.

"Do I know you?" the same boy asks.

"Archie," Nan cuts in. "Don't make the new fella in town uncomfortable now."

He gives me one long, hard stare again, until realization hits him.

He knows *exactly* who I am.

"Have a good day," Archie says, turning on his heel to catch up to his friend.

Nan shakes her head. "The twins don't mean any harm and never cause trouble. Unfortunately, they're just boys who love baseball but have no means to play it."

"What do you mean they have no means to play?"

"Well, they have a field set up by the ranch where they can play, but we haven't had someone willing to step in to coach the kids since the last one quit a few years back."

"So they just need a coach?" I ask with a raised brow.

She nods, eyeing me with so many questions.

"Oh my gosh, Daddy!" Sage jumps up and down. "You're the best coach in all the lands. You should definitely be the coach here."

My daughter's right.

"I can do it." I shrug.

I should want to take back the words as soon as they leave my lips since I told myself I'd leave all things baseball in San Francisco, but these kids seem to need help. Sage thinks I should do it. Baseball saved my life over and over again growing up—a safe place to land when the world around me was chaotic.

And I also feel like it could give me something to do.

"You want to coach the kids?" Nan asks, her brows furrowed.

"Why not?"

"But you're leavin' eventually."

I shrug. "We can figure it out later."

I always do.

Sage whines, cutting off the conversation. "I need food."

"And I need coffee." I smile, crouching down to pick her up.

Standing and facing Nan, I extend a hand to give her a shake.

"Thank you for helping me find a place."

"It's no problem." She waves me off. "Listen, Cozy Cup might be a little busy this time of mornin'. They also don't have snacks there. Here in town, we go there for coffee, and then Batter Up for the treats. Why don't I take Sage into Batter Up and get her a treat while you grab that caffeine? I know the owner of the bakery and can get her in and out."

Does this woman know everyone in town?

I wonder if she's like the mayor or something.

"I don't know," I say hesitantly.

"Daddy, I'll be just fine. And looks," she says, standing on the sidewalk with one arm pointed to the bakery and one arm to the coffee shop, "they are so close to each other. And Nan said I'll be in and out because she knows people."

Nan nods. "I know everyone. And I'm practically glued to this town. There's nowhere I'd run off to."

This is crazy.

But Sage is right, the shops are really close. She will be in and out.

"Are you sure?" I ask Nan.

"Yes, Daddy! Pretty please with sugar on top? My treat belly is screaming right now that it needs something immediately."

I look from her to Nan and then next door to the coffee shop. "Okay," I agree. "I'm right next door when you're done."

Nan places a hand on my shoulder and smiles. "Welcome to town, Dallas."

CHAPTER 3

TIME TO TURN THIS DAY AROUND.

POPPY

I look down at my watch and note I'm running eight minutes behind.

"Shoot," I mutter, getting out of my car and hustling into my sister's bakery.

"Whoa," Lily says when she notices me rushing through the front door, hands in front of her, signaling me to slow down.

"Lily, I'm so late for work," I spit out.

She looks up at the clock on the wall. "You don't have to be there until eight thirty."

"I know," I groan.

"It takes thirty minutes to drive from one end of Bluestone Lakes and back again. Not to drive down the street to the school," she says and I don't miss her slight eye roll.

I swallow, straighten my spine, and take a calming breath. I don't want her to think I'm crazy. Well, I'm not crazy. I just prefer a strict routine because I thrive on punctuality and staying organized.

My alarm went off this morning at five o'clock, as always. It may be early for others, but there's something so peaceful about being awake before sunrise, and I've found that it's also when

I'm the most productive. I often accomplish some of my best work during these early hours.

I follow the same routine every morning, which helps me maintain my sanity. I wake up, make a small cup of coffee to get energized, review my detailed class plan, and finish with a thirty-minute yoga session on my back deck before getting ready for work.

However, this morning my coffee maker refused to work. I spent too much time trying to fix it, which caused me to lose track of time. When I realized how much time had passed, I had to abandon the coffee situation to focus on the day's lesson plans, only to discover that I hadn't prepared everything.

All of it threw me off balance—and I hate it.

It makes me feel anxious, and I don't like feeling like I'm not in control.

"Just...had a rough morning," I finally tell Lily, hoping she doesn't ask more questions.

My family doesn't know what I struggle with, and I've gotten really good at hiding it. I prefer to keep it that way to avoid questions or having them walk on eggshells around me. No one knows how many times I check the light switches in my house to make sure they're all either up or down, or how I have to go back and reread texts five times to make sure I didn't say anything wrong.

She shrugs and turns to arrange the baked goods on the display. "That's on brand for me but not for you." And then she stands up and looks at me again. "Wait. Are you okay?"

I nod quickly. "Yep. Do you have any of those chocolate chip muffins you made last week?"

She smiles widely. Baking is the way to Lily's heart, and loving the things that she makes is the key to her happiness.

"I made a special batch this morning."

"I will definitely take two of them."

"You got it." She bags my muffins for me. "Nothing for the kids today?"

Smiling, I shake my head. "No, we have a birthday today. I offered to bring treats, but her mom wanted to make cupcakes."

Being a teacher has been a dream of mine since middle school. I've always been good with kids, and I had a few babysitting jobs in town throughout high school, which I loved every second of.

"They're lucky to have you," Lily says, passing me my bag of muffins. "I know I tell you that all the time. But it's worth reminding you again since you said you're having a rough morning."

My heart warms while the smile on my face stretches.

Being with my students Monday through Friday for a good chunk of the day makes me feel like I'm a big part of their lives during their first-grade year. I feel like it's my duty to protect them, care for them, and help them grow so they're ready for the coming grades. They're not just students to me, they're like my own kids, and I want the best for them.

"Thank you, Lil," I reply, looking around the bakery. "Where's Blair today?"

"She's off. Griffin took her for a ride around the lake on the horses."

I smile thinking about the two of them.

Blair came into our lives when she moved into town after finding her politician husband cheating on her. She needed to get far away from San Francisco and found her way here. She moved next door to my brother, Griffin, into his old tiny home and got a job here at the bakery with Lily. She's the only one who's ever been able to pull Griffin out of his constant grumpy state.

Now the two of them are in love, and I consider her one of my best friends.

"That sounds sweet," I say before looking down at my watch. "Shit. I really have to go now. I'm already super late."

"Take a deep breath, Poppy." My sister laughs. "You've been

in here for two minutes, and driving to the school will take another four and a half minutes. You have plenty of time."

I blindly gesture to my side. "Except I have to head next door for a large coffee. My pot took a crap this morning, and I'm already going through caffeine withdrawal."

Her hand flies to her chest with an exaggerated gasp. "Not caffeine withdrawal."

"Shut up." I laugh.

"Oh, hey," she says in a normal tone. "Did you hear the news that Nan's big 'celebrity'"—she lifts two fingers on each hand, signaling air quotes—"is moving here today."

"No?"

"That's the morning buzz here at Batter Up Bakery."

"Do we have any clue where they're moving?"

My stomach somersaults, and my heart rate picks up. There are many rental properties available, but the reason for the nerves is because there's one right next door to me, too. Don't get me wrong, I wouldn't mind a neighbor. It's just…I'm not ready for a "celebrity" of some sort to move there and bring a commotion with them.

What kind of public figure is this person?

Will the press follow them

The uncertainty makes me feel uneasy despite having no clue if they're actually getting the place next to me. I just don't like change and the feelings that come with it.

Because I enjoy my quiet lot on Poplar Street.

No significant other.

No kids of my own.

No pets.

It's me, my routine, and my quiet.

From the outside, it might look strange. A twenty-five-year-old who's never really been in a relationship or doesn't own a pet to keep her company. Even my family stopped asking questions a long time ago. They've accepted who I am and how I've prioritized my career.

"No clue," Lily says. "But I'll text you if I hear anything."

"Thank you." I nod. "I'm going to head out before I'm late. Need to stop next door."

"Yes. You said that." She laughs. "Get out of here. Love you."

"Love you most." I smile at her and turn to leave.

When the cold air hits my lungs, I attempt another calming breath. This is too much for one morning, and I feel entirely out of control.

I need to get it together.

The light chime of the bell dings as I enter the Cozy Cup coffee shop next door to the bakery.

I internally groan at how busy it is before looking at my watch. I don't have time, but Lily is right. The school is around the corner, and I need this coffee to make it through the morning.

Everything is fine. I'm fine.

My friend and coffee shop owner, Autumn, works fast. She always has because this place gets packed in the morning. It's the only *good* coffee in town. If someone's in a pinch, they can stop at the gas station to grab a cup, but it will never be as good as this.

Tapping my foot lightly, I feel my patience running thin.

It's no one's fault but my own, I remind myself.

"Yeah, I made it," a deep voice says directly behind me.

The sound travels down my spine, and I feel a shiver run through me. It's most definitely not a voice I've heard before. Not that I've listened to everyone in town speak before, but after Lily dropped that news on me, it has my brain going right to the voice of said celebrity.

"I'm exhausted. It was a long drive." A pause. "Uh huh." Another pause. "Yeah, I met with that woman named Nan? She gave me the keys to the place, so I'm all set."

This time, the hairs on my arm stand tall. The voice coming from behind me—and I'm talking *right* behind me—is so close that if I stepped back, I would probably bump into him. It's the person moving to town.

I let my eyes fall closed. I fight the urge to turn around and see who this person is and if I recognize him from somewhere on TV.

"Excuse me," he says with a tap on my shoulder.

My eyes fly open, and the contact has me stepping forward and swinging around to face him. His eyes widen only for a moment at my abrupt turn, but then quickly soften as he stares at me.

"I have to go," he says to the person on the phone and hangs up without waiting for a response.

He doesn't take his eyes off me as he clicks end on the call and shoves it into the back pocket of his jeans. It's hard to distinguish the color of his eyes with the baseball cap sitting low on his head. Almost as if he's trying to remain incognito.

Seconds pass. Or minutes? Hell, maybe hours, that we both stand here facing each other. I can't understand why my feet won't move. Why won't my head turn to look away? Why is breathing hard all of a sudden?

Who the hell is this man?

"Are you okay?" he asks, bending down slightly and leveling with me.

I didn't realize until he had to bend down how tall he was. He's gotta be six feet tall. Clean face, no hair peeking out from under his hat, and now, he's wearing a wicked smile that could melt me right here on the spot.

And that's the thought that snaps me out of whatever this is.

I don't think about men like this.

Ever.

"Yes," I answer the question I vaguely remember him asking, and I turn around to see that Autumn is waiting at the register for me to order with a sinister grin across her face.

"Shut up," I whisper to her through gritted teeth and school my features. "Good morning." I smile widely as if that didn't all just happen.

"Morning, Poppy," she says, my name a decibel higher.

I roll my eyes.

"What can I get you this morning?" she asks.

"I'll have…" I pause, forgetting what I always order. I want to scream at the way this morning is going for me. I have never felt more out of control than I do at this moment.

Autumn cuts through my thoughts. "A large iced cold brew with one pump of vanilla, two pumps of pecan flavor, and milk?"

I nod once, release a breath, and watch as she moves behind the counter to make my drink.

"Excuse me," the man says again.

I'm not startled this time, but I turn slowly to face him. That same smile stretches wide across his face, and it's doing things to me I can't control. It's making my heart race, and words are strangely hard to find.

"I'm new in town," he says, answering my thoughts. "Is this the only coffee shop?"

"Yes," Autumn answers defensively, and I feel her moving around behind me to keep the line going.

"Well, okay then." He laughs.

A deep laugh that fires down my spine, right to my gut. It's hot. It's intoxicating. It's…

I need to stop.

I straighten my spine. "It's the best coffee shop in Bluestone Lakes."

He raises an eyebrow. "Noted. And your name is…Poppy?"

I nod.

"Poppy," he repeats, and *my god*, hearing it out of his mouth is like an out-of-body experience. I shake my head, knowing he picked up on it, but I brush it off.

"I can see it," he says.

"See what?"

"Poppy. If I recall correctly, it's a flower associated with beauty." He winks.

Oh. My. God.

Is he...flirting with me?

"I'm Dallas, by the way," he continues.

My cheeks turn bright red, and I know that without having to look in the mirror, because they feel hot. I spin around, and simultaneously Autumn slides my iced coffee across the counter. I tap my card on the chip reader and sidestep the man without glancing at his face again or saying another word to my friend.

"Hey," he calls after me. Reluctantly, I spin around but still refuse to look him in the eyes. "Maybe I'll see you around?"

Meeting his stare, my breath catches as he winks again.

"Yeah, maybe," I reply, pushing the door open to head to my car.

Once settled inside, I use my breathing techniques to settle myself. Inhaling for four seconds, holding it for four seconds, exhaling for four seconds, and holding it again for four seconds.

Then I repeat my mantra, which reminds me that *everything is fine, I'm fine*, before looking at the clock on my dashboard: Ten minutes. I have ten minutes to hustle to school and get this day started.

I don't feel any better than when I left my house in a rush.

And nothing this morning helped that feeling.

CHAPTER 4
YOU DON'T EVEN KNOW ME.

DALLAS

"Ready to go, Sage?" I shout down the hallway that leads to her room on the opposite side of the house as mine.

"I'm putting my shoes on now."

"Need any help?"

"Nope. Gots it!"

I laugh to myself as I finish cleaning up the pan I used to make scrambled eggs this morning. We haven't taken a trip to the grocery store in town yet since we got in two days ago, and today will be the day we stock up on all our favorites.

Nan filled the kitchen with the basics for us, which shocked me. I knew the place would be furnished as it's a rental, but I hadn't expected the generosity of having eggs, milk, bread, and other basic essentials we might need to get started with.

I still think it's weird calling her Nan. I wish like hell I knew her real name. I had to save her number in my contacts as Nan, and it's just…odd. Maybe it's just that I never met my grandparents or had anyone to call that. Then again, this town feels a bit off. It's nothing like I expected it to be.

After I spent the last couple of days getting everything unpacked and putting together Sage's room, this place is starting to feel a bit more like a home, and Sage is falling in love with every aspect of the house. Especially since she got the bedroom she's always dreamed of. My daughter wanted a princess theme set up, and who am I to tell her no? She now has a room with light pink and light purple scattered around every square inch.

Waiting for Sage, I make my way to the back sliding door to look outside.

The sun is over the mountain, illuminating the sky. A bright blue looks painted across the mountain backdrop. This property doesn't have a single tree on it compared to other houses around us, only expanding on the views in every direction. It's taking some getting used to as opposed to the congested city views I've been used to.

At first, I didn't know how I'd feel living in a small ranch-style home located on, what appears to be, a quiet street, but this morning I woke up and a sense of calm and acceptance washed over me. Maybe it's that everything is done, minus the grocery shopping, and it hit me hard that this is really happening. Sage seems happy already, and that alone makes me happy.

"I'm all ready," Sage announces, entering the kitchen.

Turning around to face her, I smile. Her light blue eyes, which she got from me, shine in the dimly lit kitchen; her dark brown hair is pulled back into a messy ponytail.

"Let me fix your hair quickly."

She groans. "It's fine, Daddy. Besides, you don't know how to braid it."

"I'm going to learn, bug. I promise." And I mean that. I've known for years that she prefers her hair in a braid. Since I never had her for long stretches, I never had enough of a chance to practice and really learn. "But for now, let's fix the ponytail."

This, I know how to do. I pull the band from her hair gently, raking my fingers through to flatten the flyaway hairs. Scooping it in my hands and replacing the hair tie in the same spot she had it before.

Her hands come up to feel my work, and she nods in approval. "Perfection. Where are we going again?"

"The grocery store. We need to get you snacks and lunches for when you get home from Mom's. You start school on Monday."

She jumps up and down. "I can't wait for school! Do you think I'll make all the new friends? Bestest friends?"

I laugh. "I have no doubt. You're the coolest kid in the world."

She smiles proudly. "All right, let's go get all the snacks."

"And food."

"Whatever you say."

She loads herself into the Tahoe, and we take the short drive to Main Street, where Nan said everything is located. This town really does have a charm to it. It's the kind of quiet magic you don't notice at first, but grows on you fast. When you make eye contact with someone walking on the sidewalk, they smile and lift their hand in a wave. Every single person I've come across makes you feel like you matter, even if you have never said more than three words to them.

There's a type of rhythm to this small-town life.

It's slow, but steady.

It hits differently here, in a way that you don't get lost in the crowd. You don't feel like an outsider. It's a place that makes you feel like you belong.

Even if it's only for a short time.

Parking my truck, we make our way into a place called the General Store. It's enormous and expands almost the whole street. From the outside looking in, it feels like a one-stop shop for everything we're going to need.

"Do you think they're going to have ice cream here?"

"Probably," I answer, making our way inside.

"I hope they have gallons of it. A full tank." I bark out a laugh at that. "Oh, and what about my favorite cereal with those colorful marshmallow pieces?"

"I'm sure they do."

Grabbing a shopping cart, we begin making our way through the produce section. I grab some fresh fruit and vegetables. Sage loves fruit, mainly with a side of whipped cream, but vegetables? Nope. She won't touch a leafy green—typical kid.

As I move down the aisles, I skip the one filled with candy, but when my eyes scan the aisle, I have to do a double-take. Because the strawberry blonde hair I haven't been able to stop thinking about since our run-in at the coffee shop is scanning the shelves.

She captured my attention in a matter of minutes, and I couldn't bring myself to look away.

In the same way that she is right now.

Poppy made me feel like the old Dallas Westbrook for just a moment.

After my marriage ended, I turned into the guy who shamelessly flirted with any woman because that's who I am. Was. That's who I *was*. Because now, I'm a divorced father in a new town, just trying to get my life together. I can't allow any kind of relationship to happen again.

But the past couple of nights, whenever my head hit the pillow, I couldn't stop the wandering thoughts. Mostly, they were of the same hair I'm staring at now, flowing down her back when she faced the counter of the coffee shop. So long that I imagined how it would feel wrapped around my hand, even though she had this look of innocence about her.

She definitely looks young, and I hate myself for thinking these thoughts. She seems younger than anyone I've dated before. Which already means she's off-limits to an old, washed-up thirty-five-year-old like me.

Do you know what the worst part of the whole interaction was? I don't think she knew who I was at all. And I consider that the worst part because it makes me more attracted to her. I can be myself. I would know she's not after me for the exposure of being with a sports celebrity. I don't have to let my past or job weigh on me. At first, I thought her eyes went wide because she knew me as the previous starting pitcher of the San Francisco Staghorns, who turned into a head coach and was plastered all over the media.

Her eyes told another story.

The most stunning ones I'd ever seen—a perfect mix of blue and green—are now staring at me from the opposite end of the aisle. Her lips parted in shock as if she's just as taken aback to see me as I am her. Why? No clue. This is a small town. She said it herself, insinuating that we're bound to run into one another.

"Daddy, can we get these?" Sage asks up ahead toward the next aisle, forcing my gaze to pull away from Poppy.

Looking back at Poppy once more, she's no longer standing there.

"Yeah," I answer, not even knowing what I agreed to.

Now I'm moving along the grocery store on autopilot because Poppy has successfully distracted me again.

We overstock the refrigerator and pantry before taking the first trip to meet April so that Sage can spend the weekend with her. I can only imagine how difficult it will be for April to only see our daughter on the weekends now. I know first-hand that being a parent while chasing your goals and dreams in a career is challenging.

The thought tugs at my chest, making me feel guilty in a way. I never put in the effort I should have, and Sage deserves better.

The drive isn't bad at all, which also proves that this arrangement will work for us. It's about an hour-long trip back and forth since we found a meeting spot that's conveniently halfway for both of us. By the time I make it back into town, the sun has set behind the mountains, and the light blue skies have given way to a deeper ocean blue. When I turn onto Main Street, a neon barstool over the corner bar flashes ahead, tempting me to slow down.

I could really use a drink.

I park my Tahoe in front of Seven Stools, and inwardly laugh. This whole town has an interesting flair to it, that's for sure.

Looking down, I realize I'm wearing a pair of jeans and a solid black T-shirt, deciding it should be enough to fit in with the crowd here. The last thing I want to do is draw attention to myself so I blindly reach behind me to see if I left a baseball hat on the floor.

Bingo.

I place it over my tousled, messy hair, and thank the universe above that it's not my dark green one that says *Staghorns* on it.

Entering the bar, the sound from inside quickly thrums in my body. The music is loud and energizing, a mix of classic rock and country, as I make my way to an open bar stool, taking note of the fact that this place only has seven stools. I smile to myself at the clever marketing. The smell of grilled meat and beer fills the air, and I can feel the energy of the place pulsating around me.

"What can I get you?" the bartender asks.

I scan the area and try to understand what's happening and why they have a mini stage set up in the corner.

"What's all this about tonight?"

"This is karaoke night," he tells me, pointing to the corner. "See that woman over there? She organized this whole thing a few months ago, so we made it a weekly thing here."

Turning toward where he points, I spot her.

"Nan," I say before turning back to face the bartender.

He raises an eyebrow. "You know her?"

"She's the one who gave me the keys to my new place," I say.

"Ahh." The man grins.

With a lopsided grin, I avert my gaze to my hands on the counter, adjusting my baseball cap to ensure I stay as hidden as possible.

"Guess I should introduce myself then, huh?" He extends his hand across the table. "I'm Griffin."

"Dallas," I say, returning his handshake.

"Oh my god," another bartender says. I glance up and see his hand covering his face.

"Don't say it," I warn, feeling uneasy at the sudden attention. I'm used to being recognized, but don't want to feel it here.

Griffin looks at us, very confused. "What am I missing?"

The guy leans in, staring at me, but whispers behind his hand. Not quietly, either. "That's the head coach for the San Francisco Stags Major League Baseball team."

"Was," I cut in, keeping my voice low. "*Was* the coach."

Clark kept things pretty tight-lipped when it came to the media. There was no official announcement of me leaving and someone replacing me for the off season. He wanted to leave it in case I decided to come back and keep my position. I don't know why I just told him I *was* the coach. I think it was the wrong thing to say, because I still am. However, I'm not coaching right now.

"Nooo.." The guy winces.

"Since when are you a baseball fan?" Griffin asks him.

"I root for the underdogs." He shrugs. "And the Stags were…" He pauses before leaning in to whisper to the man again. "They suck."

There's a ping in my chest because everything falls back on me. Do they suck because of how I've coached them the last four years? Probably.

I nod in response to that, not knowing what else to say.

"So what brings you to Bluestone Lakes?" Griffin asks.

"Your website is very welcoming."

The one off to the side barks out a laugh, and Griffin laughs under his breath.

"Ah, Dallas," Nan says before I can respond to anyone, swinging an arm around my shoulder. "You found the best bar in town. Have you settled in nicely?"

"Dallas?" the woman beside her practically shouts, and I cringe at how loud she's saying my name. "You're...you're the head coach for the Staghorns. I'm from San Francisco, too. What brings you all the way out here?"

"Hell if I know," I answer, not wanting to explain it to these people who clearly know who I am. I knew this was a bad idea. Within minutes of being here, I've been recognized twice. And what the hell are the chances of someone from San Francisco being here, too?

I think deep down, I just didn't want anyone here to know who I am.

I wanted time with my daughter without people finding out who I am. It would only bring attention to the media if word got out outside of Bluestone Lakes.

I'm about to shrug out of Nan's hold on my shoulders and find a way to leave discreetly when a glass of amber liquid slides in front of me. "On the house."

I offer a quick nod. "Thank you."

"You got it," Griffin says. "And hey, for what it's worth... Welcome to Bluestone Lakes."

Nan glances down at me, giving my shoulder a light squeeze. "You're gonna like it here," she whispers before I watch her leave to tend to the karaoke machine.

"So, you do this every weekend?" I ask Griffin.

He shakes his head. "Usually it's during the week, but it's my sister's birthday and she *begged* me to have it tonight, too."

"Is this your bar?"

He nods. "I also would like to put it out there that I don't know a single thing about baseball. No offense."

I laugh. "None taken. It's honestly kind of a relief."

He opens his mouth to say more, but the other bartender slides up beside him, wiping his hands with a dish rag before extending his hand over the bar. "I'm Tucker, by the way. Big fan. *Huge* fan. I love the sport. And you. Yeah, I love you," he rattles off in rapid succession before turning to look at Griffin with a face lit up brighter than a Christmas tree, while he bounces where he stands. "Oh my god, it's Dallas Westbrook."

"Tucker," Griffin warns. "You sound like a nutcase right now."

"How is that different from any other time?" the female who said she was from the city cuts in. "I'm Blair, by the way. You'll get used to Tucker. Don't worry."

"Wait." I pause, and stare at how familiar she looks now that she's told me her first name. "Are you Blair…Andrews? Like, formerly married to ex-mayor Theodore?"

She points a finger at my face with a warning. The same way I did earlier. "Don't say it." She softens her features. "I live here now. Moved on a whim to get out of the city after he cheated on me, which I'm sure you heard about…" She pauses, and I nod. "I needed to get away from that life. Now I'm with this brute." She gestures toward Griffin.

"I'm not a brute. Not anymore, at least."

I laugh at the exchange taking place. These people seem like good, nice people. I can tell Tucker is an interesting character, but he also seems fun.

"I'm sorry for my abruptly rude response before when you asked me what I was doing here," I say to Blair. "It took me off guard that people sixteen hours away, in a small town, recognized me."

Blair waves me off. "Please. No need to be sorry, I understand. When I first moved here, I didn't want anyone to recognize me either because I didn't want to be known as the woman who was cheated on by the mayor."

"That, I understand."

"You're famous," Tucker cuts in. "Of course, people will recognize you."

"Tucker has a point." Blair laughs. "Where did you move to?"

Tucker leans on the bar, resting his chin on his knuckles. "Yeah, where did you move to?"

Blair swats his arm with the back of her hand. "Cut it out, stalker."

"I didn't move here." I shake my head. "Well, I have, but it's only temporary." She tilts her head to the side in confusion, and I release a sigh. "I'm just here for a little while to get my head on straight outside of the city."

Griffin nods repeatedly as if he likes what he's hearing. "This is the best place for that."

"Nan got me set up on Poplar Street. Nice place. There aren't very many people around, though."

"You're going to find that anywhere you go here." Blair laughs.

"My other sister actually lives on that street," Griffin adds. "So I know you have some good neighbors. She keeps to herself and stays focused on her job, so you probably haven't seen her around yet."

I look at Griffin and can't help but wonder who his sister is. The longer I stare, the more his features start to resemble a certain someone I can't get out of my head. But it can't be. She has this strawberry blonde hair that's permanently ingrained in my head, while he has a darker brown color. Maybe it's this single glass of whiskey he offered me that's already getting to me. Or perhaps, it's me conjuring her up in my thoughts again because I can't stop thinking about the woman I met for less than ten minutes.

The music cuts out with a piercing screech, and we all snap our heads to Nan. "Sorry, y'all. Promise I ain't trying to blow this place up," she shouts before getting the cord right, and music starts bumping through the speakers again.

"Sometimes I think she is," Griffin mutters, but doesn't bat an eye. Clearly, he's used to her antics.

"Unfortunately, they don't have baseball here." Blair shrugs. Being from San Francisco, she probably knows how big of a deal it was for me from all the media. "At least I don't think so."

Griffin shakes his head. "No, we don't have anything. No big leagues. No little leagues. I know the kids like to play out at the barnyard, though." He shrugs.

"So I've heard. Nan was telling me when I got into town, and I kind of, sort of, agreed to coach them."

"You, what?" Blair laughs. "You do know coaching kids is wildly different from coaching adults?"

"Wait, can I play?" Tucker raises his hand like he's in a classroom. "Oh, oh, oh. No, I can help you coach if you want. I'm great with kids."

"That's because you *are* a kid," Griffin deadpans.

"Twenty-three, Griffin. That's an adult, last I checked."

"Semantics."

"Oh my god." Tucker beams. "We should start an adult league, too. Pick a night during the week and get together. All the guys, hell, even the girls can play. You know, a fun night out. But you gotta go easy on us," he says, pointing a finger in my direction. "Half of us don't know how to swing a bat." He nudges Griffin at his side.

Griffin grumbles something under his breath and rolls his eyes.

"We should do it," Blair joins Tucker in his excitement. "I bet Lily would be down, too."

"Dallas." Tucker leans in close, looking left and right before locking eyes with me as if he has a really big, important secret to share with me. "If you had one shot. One opportunity. To seize everything—"

"Oh, Christ." Griffin rolls his eyes. "Let the poor guy breathe for five minutes before shoving baseball games down his throat. He just told us he came here for a break."

If I didn't like Griffin before, I do now.

"Thank you." I raise my glass to him. "But it's really no problem. Baseball has been part of my life since I first learned how to walk. I sort of like the idea of getting together and playing with you guys if it's something you want to do."

Tucker fist pumps the air. "Yes."

A bell over the door chimes, and Griffin turns to glare at Tucker. If looks could kill, he's stabbing Tucker in the eyes. "I swear you plug that shit back in every night just to piss me off."

Tucker chuckles with his hand over his mouth.

Then he looks over my shoulder, and I follow his gaze. The music cuts out in my mind, and whatever Griffin just said fizzles out. The people around me fade into nothing as I stare at the long hair I was thinking about just moments ago, cascading down her back. A smile spreads on my face as she greets a friend in a hug with her back to me.

She looks…different tonight.

The two times I saw her before this, she was wearing jeans, a T-shirt tucked in, and a pair of sneakers. Tonight she has on a short blue flowy skirt that sways around her thighs with every small move she makes. She has on a pair of dark brown cowboy boots with white leg warmers sticking out of them. She stands with one hip popped while she engages in conversation with the other person. I let my gaze travel to the loose-fitting pink sweater that sits off one of her shoulders.

She touches the woman's shoulder as if to say *I'll catch up with you* before looking to the ground and making her way in my direction.

Seeing her again was a confirmation of everything my brain had been thinking.

She's *the* most stunning woman I've ever seen.

Finally, she lifts her head, and our eyes connect. She almost stumbles over her next step but fixes herself quickly, not allowing the smile on her face to falter or show shock. Every nerve ending in my body is on high alert, and now my heart is racing as if I just did sprint work on the field during practice.

"Hey, Pop," Griffin greets her.

She keeps her gaze locked on me for a second longer, and I want to reach out and beg her to sit with me. Beg her to tell me everything there is to know about herself so I can figure out why I'm so wrapped up in this mystery woman.

Then she looks away, and I release a breath.

I didn't realize I had stopped breathing, but here we are.

"Hey Griff." She smiles at him. "Busy night tonight?"

"You know Nan does the most." He laughs.

"She really does."

"Have you met the new guy in town?" Griffin asks her, gesturing to me.

She turns to face me. Her eyes lock with mine again, and I'm instantly unable to form a coherent thought.

Dammit. I need to get it together.

"Can't say I have," she says, shifting her body to face me. I raise a brow, and the corner of my lip twists into a grin. "I'm Poppy. Nice to meet you."

"Dallas," I say, taking her hand in mine and refusing to break eye contact.

"Griffin," Tucker calls. "Someone's got a question, and I don't feel like I'm qualified to answer it."

Griffin sighs and says something back, but I can't tell you what it was because I'm lost in Poppy's trance. I'm still shaking her hand, refusing to let go. Her touch is a blend of fire and ice. Because while it feels warm and comforting, she sends an icy, sharp buzz through the rest of me.

Staring at her, I stand from my stool and tower over her enough that she needs to lift her head to maintain eye contact. She tries to pull her hand back, but I don't let her, tightening my hold on her. Her cheeks pinken when I step closer and bend down until my lips graze the shell of her ear. With my eyes over her shoulder, I breathe her in, forgetting we're in a room full of people. A warm, comforting scent hits me. A mix of vanilla and honey forces me to close my eyes and soak it into memory because she's intoxicating.

"Are we acting like I didn't meet you at the coffee shop the other day, Poppy?" I whisper.

Her name out of my mouth tastes good.

She nods, but I stay close to her ear, not letting her hand go, sensing her chest rising and falling from our proximity.

"That's really disappointing."

She pulls back but doesn't release her grip. I'd hold her hand all night if she let me. Her eyes widen, and my smile grows. She looks so innocent. But fuck, I can't get over her beauty.

Her face relaxes and morphs from shocked to somewhat sassy when she smirks at me. "Did you want me to randomly remember a stranger I met in the coffee shop for less than ten minutes?"

Shaking my head in disbelief, I grin, tugging her close. Her body almost collides with mine, and her hand lands on my chest to help find her balance. Again, I seem to forget this is a packed bar in a small town. The worry that people might talk isn't even on my mind. All I can think about is...

She looks from her hand and back up to me, pulling it away as if she just set her hand down on a hot stove.

"I remember." I wink. "You're kind of unforgettable, Poppy."

She scoffs, taking a step away from me. "You don't even know me."

Taking a seat on the stool behind me, I level my eyes with hers again. Unable to break the contact for a second, I reach for my glass and take a long pull. She stares at me, full of uncertainty, and I can tell she doesn't know what to think about the new guy in town.

I don't blame her. I shouldn't be thinking about her this way.

"I'd like to get to know you," I say, despite what my inner thoughts are screaming.

She averts her gaze, looking around the bar. I don't know if she's looking for someone to save her or if she's meeting someone. That makes me irrationally jealous.

"Are you meeting a boyfriend?" I ask curiously.

She shakes her head.

"No, you're not meeting a boyfriend? Or no, you don't have one?"

Please tell me it's the latter.

She looks down at her hands nervously, not giving me an answer. As much as I'd love her not to have a boyfriend, I must guard myself here. It's a fine line I'm walking. I shouldn't be flirting with the beautiful local, who has me saying things I shouldn't be saying. Who has me thinking things I shouldn't be thinking. Who has pulled me into her orbit without an ounce of effort.

When she lifts her eyes to meet mine, I know with certainty that despite how much I want to stay away, I'm completely and utterly fucked.

CHAPTER 5
SO IT'S WORKING?

POPPY

Dallas is most definitely flirting with me.

And it makes me feel so out of my element.

Truthfully, I don't know how to feel about it. This doesn't happen often for me, and it's mostly because I don't get out enough to allow the opportunity to present itself.

Seeing Dallas again feels like an earthquake I never braced myself for, and it's a weird and new feeling for me. I thought about lying, telling him I have a boyfriend, so he can keep his distance, and I could protect myself from the inevitable. But the way he looks at me with such intensity, it's hard to deny that I want him to keep looking at me like this.

My brain may be swirling with doubt and questioning every intention of this man, but I can't deny that I *like* this feeling. I can like this and still be in control, right?

"No boyfriend," I say.

The corners of his lips twist up even more as if that's the answer he wanted. The grin on his face forces one on mine, and I try to bite away my involuntary smile at him.

"I'd love to buy you a drink then. Maybe get to know you a little bit."

Turning to face the bar, I rest both elbows on the bar top and check out what Griffin has stocked. I've never been much of a drinker, but when I do, I'm picky about it. As a teacher, I'll always have this fear of going out in town, and the parents of one of my students judge me for my choices.

Will they think less of me for being out in a bar like this?

Will they go to the principal and accuse me of being an unfit teacher?

It weighs heavily on me more often than not. I grew up in this town, and everyone knows who I am, but that doesn't stop the negative thoughts. The only reason I'm even here tonight is because it's Lily's birthday party, and she and Blair begged me to come out after our dinner we had before this.

I've gotten better about not letting the fear of judgment hold me back.

Looking back at Dallas, I decide to let him buy me a drink.

"One drink." I hold up my index finger.

"One drink."

Tucker passes us, and Dallas flags him down.

"What can I get you, coach?"

I raise a brow in his direction, but don't ask why he's calling him that. Dallas shakes his head, looking down at the bar top. He and Tucker both laugh. I feel like I'm missing something here.

"I'll have another round of whatever Griffin poured before," Dallas says, tipping his head in my direction. "And whatever she's having."

When I look at Tucker, it's his turn to lift an eyebrow. I quickly fire him a glare, silently telling him to *shut up*. "I'll have my normal. The Moscow mule."

Tucker scoffs. "That's not your normal."

I narrow my eyes again.

"Oh, yes. That's very scary—I mean, normal. Very normal," he says flatly before moving to make our drinks.

Closing my eyes, I inhale slowly. He's right. It's not my norm.

Nothing about this night is. But my therapist and I have discussed this, and I need to do it. Letting go of my control in every situation and allowing life to…happen.

Easier said than done.

It's weird that I'm deciding to make the change with Dallas of all people—a stranger in town—but I have to start somewhere.

A strange silence stretches between us, though. I'm not sure if Tucker's comments have made him second-guess this drink, or if it's because I don't know what I'm doing. Either way, it has me assuming the worst.

Flirting is foreign to me.

Engaging in casual conversation over a drink with a *really* hot man is foreign to me.

As Tucker returns with our drinks, I straighten my spine and muster up whatever confidence I have to get through this. I take a long sip and finally turn back to face Dallas, letting myself sit on the open stool beside him.

"So, how old are you, Dallas?"

He winces. Almost as if he didn't want to bring up this topic, and of course, I hit him with it first. "I'm thirty-five."

Jesus. I knew Dallas seemed older, but I was not expecting him to be ten years older than me. I lift my drink to take another long sip before my brain starts spiraling with all the doubts about even talking to a man like him.

"Where are you from?" I ask, not ready to tell him how young I am.

I mean, I'm twenty-five and I'm an adult, but I don't know how he would feel if he learned that I am ten years younger than him.

He shakes his head. "I'm originally from South Carolina. I grew up in a large coastal town before moving to San Francisco after college. So, Bluestone Lakes is a culture shock for me, to say the least."

I chuckle at that. "We're definitely different from the rest here."

"Have you lived here your whole life?"

"Born and raised," I answer proudly, lifting my chin and grinning. "It's home for me. My family and my job are here. And the best part? You get the most immaculate views in every direction, no matter where you are."

His eyes bore into mine as if taking in everything I'm saying and trying to process something in his head.

"I can tell…about the views," he says, pausing again. "My favorite has been the coffee shop and this bar."

"That's…" My voice trails off because…is he talking about me? I feel my cheeks heat up when I don't even know the answer to my own question. Instead, I clear my throat. "So, why did Tucker call you Coach?"

"I'm, uh…" He pauses, adjusting himself in the seat before straightening his spine. "Well, I coach a baseball team. Did? Do? I don't know anymore."

"Not just any team," Tucker cuts in like he's been eavesdropping. "This guy coaches the San Fran Stags, baby!"

"Would you keep your voice down?" Dallas whispers, but he's also laughing.

Tucker is very dramatic, and you can't help but laugh at him. He drives me crazy, but he's like a brother to us.

"I don't know who they are," I admit.

Dallas angles his face to look at me fully, and his smile stretches so wide that it forms a crinkle around his eyes. It makes me blush, and my stomach fills with butterflies. Even if I know nothing else, one thing about him is that his eyes can make me melt on the spot. They're the color of dark chocolate—smooth, rich, and dangerous.

"Thank god," Dallas murmurs.

I spit out a laugh, snorting, and quickly thank the heavens I wasn't currently taking a drink.

Dallas almost frowns in response, and I instantly feel hot with embarrassment.

Was that too obnoxious?

Does he think I'm weird now?

"Sorry," I say.

"For what?"

"That was...really obnoxious. And, like, was it that funny? Nothing was funny enough to laugh like that."

And now I've taken my awkwardness to the next level and want to crawl into a hole. I'm not the type of girl to get nervous like this around a man because I always know it's going to lead to nothing.

Why can't this be like every other conversation with a friend I've had?

I angle my head down, facing my drink, when Dallas reaches up, brushing the curtain of hair falling out of the way and tucking it behind my ear. The delicate touch of his fingertips as he trails them along the side of my face, around my ear, and down my neck sucks all the oxygen out of my lungs.

"I'd love hearing you laugh like that anytime, Poppy."

My name out of his mouth sends shivers through my body, but that statement, paired with his deep, gruff voice, makes me feel like I'm back in middle school when I liked a boy and my stomach would flutter when he smiled at me.

The smile on my face comes naturally. "That was clever."

He shrugs casually, angling his body to face me more fully. Giving me his full attention. "Seems to come naturally when I'm talking to you."

"Wow. You have all the right things to say, huh?"

"So, it's working?"

"Depends on what you're trying to do?"

He doesn't immediately answer but lifts his glass of bourbon to his lips. Locking eyes with me as he takes a long sip. My cheeks ache from smiling so hard.

Is he trying to...take me home?

My stomach flips with that thought because I've never gone home with a man before.

I mean, I've never even had sex before or done…anything really.

Okay, well, I kissed some guys back in college after that one short relationship that built the walls I put up around my heart, and started my fear of going further with anyone. I didn't think I was good enough for anyone. Constantly felt like I was doing something wrong. Even kissing, was I even doing it right? I'll never know because I stopped, so the doubts didn't consume me and ruin my life.

"I'm trying to keep that smile on your face," Dallas finally answers.

Is there a tally for how many times my cheeks can turn a shade of pink or red tonight? Because I can't remember the last time I ever smiled this hard outside of the classroom, playing games with six- and seven-year-olds.

"So, since I've just made it my goal to keep you smiling"—he grins at me—"tell me what kind of things make you happy. Where is your happy place?"

The question catches me off guard because no one has ever asked me that before.

I'm not about to tell him that organizing my spice cabinet in alphabetical order, or perfect vacuum lines in the carpet, make me happy. He's going to bolt out of this bar quicker than an Olympic track star. So I settle on surface level. The truth of the things that *do* make me happy.

"It's the little things that make me happiest. I like calm mornings doing yoga on my back deck, and quiet nights with a puzzle."

He nods. "I like that."

"My happy place is definitely Bluestone Lakes."

"Come on, Poppy. Give me something more than your hometown."

I laugh. "I mean the lakes themselves. The ones you passed

on your drive into town. They span miles and miles, as far as the eye can see. Sometimes I like to go there and feel the peace and quiet of the lake."

He stares at me for a moment, with wonder in his eyes. "I'll have to make a point to head out there one day."

"You should." I nod. "How about you? What makes you happy?"

"Baseball." He holds up a hand, a playful grin on his lips. "Before you ask, yes, it's my only real hobby. It's all I've ever known."

"I wasn't going to ask," I say, holding my hands up and laughing. "Is that why you coach? Or did coach? I'm not sure from your previous answer."

He sighs. "I was the head coach for a major league baseball team."

I can tell by how he says it that it's a sore subject. I see how his smile stays on his face, but it's no longer wide and bright.

There's a dull ache behind it.

"That sounds like kind of a big deal."

He shrugs.

"And you used the past tense. So are you no longer coaching?"

He averts his gaze to the bottles lined up behind the bar and shakes his head.

"I'm sorry. That was probably a sore subject. I didn't mean to bring it up."

He faces me again, offering me a lopsided grin. "There you go again."

"I'm sorry?"

"And again." He laughs, and I remain silent, lips forming a straight line. "I don't know what you're sorry for, Poppy."

"Just didn't want to bring the mood down."

"There's no way you can bring the mood down, even if you try." He winks. "Besides, it's only temporary unemployment. Just have to get my shit together before I go back."

This time, I don't ask for more.

This time, I opt not to pry into his personal life and all the reasons he's here.

But my brain locks on the four words.

Before I go back.

Meaning he's not planning to stay. And there's no reason that should sting. Even with this conversation, he's still nothing but a stranger to me. So why do I hate the thought of him not staying here and missing out on a chance to get to know him more?

This was only a casual drink, I remind myself.

I don't do relationships or want one.

He checks all the boxes for someone who's looking. Older and more experienced than I am, not just in the bedroom but in life. My brain can't help but go to thoughts about him finding out I'm young *and* still a virgin.

He seems laid-back and spontaneous, but if something were to spark between us, would he end things the moment he finds out I have a strict routine I follow to keep me sane? And when things stray from my normal, I get too overwhelmed and shut down. Or that I have little everyday quirks that I worry would cause judgment when others find out?

Shaking my head from the wandering thoughts, I look to Dallas sitting on my left. He's staring at me. I don't think he's stopped for more than a few seconds all night, and it lights me up more than it should.

Yep. He checks all the boxes.

But he can't check mine. The boxes need to remain unchecked here.

Standing from my stool, I finish my drink and stick out my hand for a handshake. Dallas looks down at it and back up to meet my eyes.

"I have to head out. I have to be up early."

"So soon?"

I nod. "We agreed to one drink."

"If I had known I was going to have such a good time

listening to you talk, watching you smile, and hearing your laugh, I would have asked for a minimum of five drinks."

I blush. *Again.*

"How about your number?" he asks. "I'd love to take you out."

The question throws me off guard. It shouldn't, because I had a good time with him tonight.

"I'm not sure it's the best idea," I admit.

He takes my hand in his, and his large palm engulfs mine. He stands, forcing my head to tilt up and keep eye contact. Then he tugs me just enough for me to step closer to him. My heart skips a beat from the movement, but also from the intensity of his cologne hitting my senses. It's a blend of earthy wood and cinnamon. He leans down, bringing his head over my shoulder and his lips to my ear. I can't help but suck in a breath.

Him being so close.

His hand in mine.

His breath in my ear.

It's so much all at once.

"I *really* hope to see you around then," he whispers. "Sooner rather than later."

"Maybe," I reply with the same response as the last time I saw him in the coffee shop, as I step away from the heat of him before he consumes me like flames ignited by gasoline.

"It's a small town." He winks.

"It is, isn't it?" I smile before turning on my heel and walking toward the exit, away from the inferno of a man.

But walking away does nothing.

I feel the heat of him everywhere.

Dallas is only here briefly, but I have a strange feeling he will do whatever he can to break through the walls I've put up to guard myself.

And I'm not sure I can let him.

CHAPTER 6
HE PREFERS MURDER.

POPPY

"Good morning, Julia," I say, greeting the receptionist at the school office. "How are you today?"

"I'm good, Poppy. Thank you for asking." She passes me my mail over the counter. "Your new student starts today."

My smile grows as I take the papers from her.

We rarely get new students, but when we do, I get overly excited about welcoming another child into the fun world I create inside my class.

Being able to dive into my craft world to put their name on their cubby and desk makes me so happy. There's something about watching the other students welcome and celebrate them, too. Since most of my students are six and seven, they're at that age where everyone is their best friend.

"Her parents are coming in later to complete the rest of the paperwork, but I gave you what I have so she can get started."

"Great."

"I will schedule a parent-teacher meeting for the end of the school day tomorrow if that's okay with your schedule."

I nod. "Thank you again," I say, leaving the office to make my way to my classroom to prepare for the day.

Filtering through the few papers in my hands as I walk, I try to organize them in priority order so they're ready to put them where I need them on my desk. A bump to my shoulder makes my steps falter backward, and a hand grips my upper arm to steady me. Looking up, I'm met with Ben, the school principal, whose lips twist into a full smile when he realizes it's me.

"Hey, Poppy."

"Oh, hi." I smile back politely. "I'm sorry, I wasn't paying attention to where I was going."

"All good. Are those papers the information on the new student coming today?" he asks, adjusting himself to catch a glimpse of the paperwork.

I angle the papers so he can see them, too.

"Ahh, yes." He nods repeatedly. "I was excited to hear she was placed in your classroom. There's no better teacher we have here to welcome her with open arms."

To others, that might seem like a professional compliment.

But I've known Ben for a good part of my life. He transferred here when his family moved to Bluestone Lakes during his senior year of high school. Since he first laid eyes on me, he's done nothing but flirt with me. My problem is that he also flirts with everyone else in town. So I've become immune to him and his "compliments."

When I finally trust someone and let them into my world and who I am, it won't be someone like Ben, who I have to worry about flirting with someone else. For some strange reason, I had those similar flirty vibes from Dallas at the bar last week. It was hard to deny the butterflies swarming my stomach with how he talked to me, but the more I thought of it, the more it made me wonder if that's how he talks to everyone.

"Appreciate that," I settle on, shaking the thoughts from my head and returning a smile to Ben. "I'd better go get everything ready."

"See you at lunch?" he asks.

"Maybe." I shrug, trying not to fall for his antics. "Have a good day, Ben."

Spinning on my heel and not letting him get another word in, I continue toward my classroom. When I step in, I look around and see that everything is the way I left it, and that always makes me feel relieved. After placing the papers in a neat pile on the corner of my desk, I pull my planner out of my bag and place it flat in the center of the desk. I place a red, blue, and black pen, as well as a sharpened pencil, across the top. When I glance at the clock, I notice I still have three minutes before the day really begins.

Pulling out my notepad that has my name across the top, I begin making small boxes on the left-hand side of each line. There's something about checking off something on a list that tickles my brain in all the best ways. I've become a person who will make lists for anything and everything. Whether it's things to do in the classroom, house cleaning to-do lists, or obviously, the regular shopping lists.

I start listing all the priority stuff to do today.

1. Straighten up the drawing table
2. Order more dry-erase markers
3. Print worksheets for the telling time activity

After I finish, I check the dry-erase markers on the board and ensure the caps are arranged with their labels facing the same direction. Today, I pull out the green one and write my morning welcome message on the whiteboard.

Welcome to Miss Barlow's class, Sage.

Stepping back, I smile proudly at the straight line of letters I made across the board and the perfect bubbly curve of each letter.

It's the little things that bring me a boost of serotonin and make me smile.

People tend to throw the term "obsessive-compulsive disorder" around like a personality trait, saying things like "I'm so OCD because I like my desk neat." But it's so much more than that.

The bell rings across the speaker, signaling that the students are entering the building. I quickly grab the wipes from the table by my front door, wipe down the desks, and position the chairs just right for each student before they filter in.

"Good morning, friends," I say cheerily.

"Good morning, Miss Barlow," they say at different times while settling into the routine.

I scan the children huddled in the corner where the cubbies are situated, but I don't see her yet. They hang their backpacks on one hook and their winter jackets on another before tucking their lunch boxes into the bin assigned to their spot.

Then, my new student walks in.

Sage doesn't have a smile on her face and looks nervous, which I expected. She's wearing black leggings and an oversized pink leopard-print shirt, with her jacket already draped over her arm.

As I crouch down to Sage's eye level, I make sure my smile is warm and my voice is gentle. "Good morning. I'm Miss Barlow. I'm so, so happy to meet you."

"I'm Sage," she says, eyes everywhere but on me, one hand plays with the end of her low ponytail resting over her shoulder.

I take one of her hands in mine, and she finally looks at me. "It's okay to be nervous. I get nervous, too. Especially when big changes happen."

"You do?"

I nod, keeping a reassuring smile on my face. "Always. But we're going to have so much fun today." Holding her hand in mine, I stand as I guide her to the corner. "I have a cubby over here for you. Later today, I'll make you your own nameplate for it."

"I can put my stuff in here?"

"Yep. This one is all for you."

She looks from me to the cubby before removing her backpack and placing it on the hook to the right, then unzipping it to grab her lunchbox and putting it in the bin.

"I like having a cubby," she says with a smile. And my heart warms at the quick comfort in her face as she looks around the room. "This classroom is a lot nicer than my old one. It's colorful."

"I'm glad you like it, Sage. I have a desk set up for you, too."

"You do?"

"Of course." I chuckle lightly at how cute she is. "I put it closest to my desk for now. This way, if you need anything, I'm right there."

"That makes me feel a whole world better."

"Good," I say through a laugh.

She makes her way to the open desk, and I take my place in the front of the classroom.

"Waterfall, waterfall," I announce to the room.

The kids all raise their hands and say, "Shhh," as their hands fall in a waterfall down the front of them.

"Excellent job. Today is a very extra-special day. We have a new friend in class. Everyone, help me give Sage the biggest warm welcome."

They all turn to face her, and her cheeks turn a shade of pink. Then, all the students shout their greetings—a mix of hi, welcome, and hello—while they all wave.

"Hi." She raises a hand in the air shyly to return the greeting.

"You all remember how nervous you were on the first day of school, so we're going to do our best to use our kind words to make this a great day for her."

"Sage, will you be my new best friend?" Ally says from the desk next to her.

"Sure." Sage beams, and they both high-five before facing me again.

I spend the next few minutes settling into our morning

routine, which the classroom seems to thrive on. We review the calendar, the day of the week, and the month before discussing the weather. After that, we do a quick review of spelling words that were covered throughout the week.

Sage fits right in, as if she's been a part of this class since day one. I watch her to learn more about her and ensure she's picking up on things.

When I wrap up, we go around the classroom and let each student introduce themselves to Sage. As each of them says their name, their favorite snack, and a fun fact about themselves, I notice Sage's fears melt away in front of my eyes.

"Do you want to tell the class a little about yourself?" I ask Sage.

She nods, standing the way everyone else did. "I'm Sage. Which you all know." She giggles, and the rest of the students follow suit. "My favorite snack is weird, but I really like croutons dipped in Caesar dressing. But I like what I like." She shrugs.

"I want to try that," one student shouts.

"That's not weird at all. If it makes you feel less weird, I eat my bread from the inside out," another says.

"I do, too." Sage smiles with wide eyes. "That's so cool."

Seeing and hearing them all interact and make Sage feel welcome is everything I could have hoped for this day. While she feels less nervous, I do too. She fits right into the crazy crew I've come to know over our first few months of the school year, and I know we're going to have a great year together.

"What about a fun fact?" I ask Sage.

"Hmm." She brings her fingers to her chin, deep in thought. "I have lots of fun facts. But I *really, really* love doing puzzles."

"I *love* puzzles," I say, grinning from ear to ear.

"I wish my daddy was good at puzzles to do them with me. He prefers murder."

My face falls, and I'm positive all the color drains from my face. For a six-year-old, that's a heavy topic to carry. Julia said her *parents*—plural—were coming to sign paperwork later.

Oh, my god. Was her father a murderer?

No. If he's coming here, he can't be.

My insides crumble, and I can't help it when my brain goes to the worst-case scenario. Would he come after me? Would he go after her? Is that why she's in this small town and we haven't heard about anyone else moving here? Are they hiding?

Irrational thoughts cross my head, as it's not something I can control if I try. I feel my heart rate pick up, and I know I need a moment to gather myself.

She's six. She can't mean that. Right?

"We're going to break for independent study," I announce to the class, but even my voice sounds hoarse. "You can either go to the reading corner on a beanbag chair, the magnetic tile station, or the coloring table."

The students cheer as they all jump from their chairs to where they want to go.

I can't seem to stop staring at Sage with so many questions. I don't want to make her more nervous by asking what she meant by that comment. But I know I have to address it as soon as possible because she can't be saying those things in the classroom.

The longer I watch her at the coloring table, the more I wonder about her.

She wipes the table before opening the coloring book in front of her. Then, she organizes the crayons with all the pointed ends facing the same way in rainbow order. She uses precision as she colors, staying within the lines and avoiding mistakes. Her tiny tongue darts out in concentration. With one accidental draw outside the lines, she flips the page, exhaling and starting anew on a clean one.

A smile touches my lips, and I know that this will be an excellent year because I know exactly how to make this change smooth for her.

CHAPTER 7
THE SQUIRRELS ARE A LITTLE DIFFERENT FROM BACK AT HOME.

DALLAS

> **TYLER**
> I'm hurt

> **MITCH**
> Here we go.

> **TYLER**
> No. Don't try to stop me. Westbrook moves states away and forgets about us. Like we're the scum on the bottom of his shoe. Like we mean nothing to him. NOTHING.
>
> He promised to keep us updated on all things at all times.

> **MITCH**
> *eye roll*

> Fuck. Sorry guys. It's been an adjustment moving here. The town is the polar opposite of city life, and I've just been spending time with Sage.

TYLER
> You just had to throw her name in there. You know I can't be mad at you when you mention her.

> *eye roll*

TYLER
> If you both keep rolling your eyes like that, they're going to get stuck there.

> Also, I'm going to be coaching again…

My phone rings with an incoming video call from them in our group chat, which Tyler named *The Wolf Pack*. I don't understand it, or him, but we roll with it.

Mitch must have been the one to click the call, because his face is the only one I see.

"Are you kidding me? You're coming back?"

I shake my head. "No, I'll be coaching here."

"Whoa, whoa."

Tyler answers, moving each of their faces into two boxes. "You coming back, coach?"

"No," Mitch answers for me. "He's coaching there. I'm waiting for him to tell me what the hell is going on."

I sigh. "You're the only two who aren't allowed to judge me for my rash decisions. But the day we got here, we met Nan, who gave us the keys to the place. Two boys went running past us, nearly knocking me over. And Nan mentioned how they don't have a team and need a coach. I said yes almost instantly."

"You? Coaching kids?" Mitch scoffs.

I laugh. "It's no different than coaching you two."

"I take offense to that." Mitch feigns hurt. "Tyler is the child of the group."

"I'm still stuck on the part with the woman named Nan," Tyler chimes in.

"See?" Mitch laughs. "But to remain serious here, weren't you supposed to be there to get your shit together? You know, take a break from baseball?"

He's right.

The more I think about it, the more I question if I made a mistake.

Baseball has never been just a game or sport for me. It's something that makes dreams feel real, where things make sense. Standing on the pitcher's mound, rounding the bases, holding a bat in my hand, all of it makes me feel like me. It was my safe place to land when the world around me was unsteady. I don't know what the family life of the kids here in town looks like, but I know what mine looked like.

A father who died when I was young, and a mother who bounced from boyfriend to boyfriend. I had to practically raise myself as an only child because she was never around.

Baseball was all I fucking had.

Mitch and Tyler know this. I'm not about to dig up emotional trauma on this video call, though.

"It's kids. It's not professional baseball, and it's something to keep me busy here."

They both remain quiet.

"What?"

"It's just…" Mitch pauses, releasing a long, drawn-out sigh. "You're coming back, right?"

I don't even have to think when I reply, "I'm coming back to San Francisco. Yes. What I do when I get back is still up in the air."

"Okay, no more serious shit. One, you're going to be an awesome coach for those kids. Two, have you met anyone yet?"

Mitch rolls his eyes. "Real slick with the question that's been plaguing you."

"I'm looking out for his needs."

I laugh. "If you must know, I met someone. But before you even ask...no, it's not anything serious. Obviously. We just had a drink together. And I won't be answering any more questions about it."

That's a lie. Or is it?

It's not a thing, but it didn't end up being nothing, at least not to me. Since that unexpected night at the bar over the weekend, I've been unable to shake off thoughts of her. I've found myself at the coffee shop every morning since then, hoping I run into her just for a chance to say even a few words to her—an opportunity to see a smile on her face.

What the hell has gotten into me? I find myself in a state of confusion, trying to make sense of these newfound feelings. Hence, asking them not to press me for more questions.

"Hell yeah." Tyler fist bumps the phone.

I hear the school bell chime, and they must hear it too. "Are you at the school?" Mitch asks.

"I'm in the car line now picking her up from her first day of school."

"Aww," Tyler coos. "A car pickup dad."

"Fuck off." I laugh. "Keep going the way you're going, and you're next."

"I wrap it up every time, Daddy."

"You make me sick," Mitch says to Tyler.

"Listen, I have to go. Sage is getting ready to come out. I'll text you guys later."

"Wolf pack out," Tyler chants, and I click end call.

I've been nervous about today since I picked up Sage from her mom's last night, so laughing with the guys was just what I needed, even if they didn't know it. Last night, as my head hit the pillow, I could only hope she didn't have the worst first day of school here.

I hope my decision to stay outside the city was the right one.

Hoping like hell I didn't make yet another mistake.

That's why I'm the first one waiting in the car pickup line since there are no buses in town. Also, I had to fill out some last-minute paperwork for her that I missed. The receptionist in the office set me up with an appointment tomorrow after school hours to meet her teacher. I called April, and she's going to drive into town so she can meet her, too.

Exiting my car, I see kids start to filter outside the building. I round the front and lean against the hood of my car. Adjusting the brim of my baseball cap, I cross my arms over my chest as I wait for Sage. I spot her seconds later, hand in hand with an adult.

She's smiling.

I feel like I can breathe again, seeing that happiness written all over her face. She's skipping, laughing, and grinning up at her teacher.

When she turns and spots me, that smile only grows.

"Daddy!" She lets go of the teacher's hand and runs to me. I crouch down to her level, opening my arms for her. She practically leaps into me, and I almost lose my balance. "I missed you so much!"

"I missed you too," I say into her hair that's now…braided? That's not how I sent her to school. "How was school today?"

"It was the bestest day!"

She pulls back, gripping the straps of her backpack, and her teacher comes to stand next to us. I stand up, extending my arm to greet her. "Hi. I'm Dallas."

"Rachel," she says with a nod, taking my hand.

Sage scurries off into the back seat of the SUV, and I stuff my hands in my pockets. "Today was good?"

She laughs lightly. "From what I heard. I'm not her teacher, though. I'm a classroom aide who helps Miss Barlow in the afternoon a few days a week."

Miss Barlow.

That last name sounds so familiar.

"Well, thank you for walking her out."

"Of course." She blushes and turns to walk away.

Jumping in the front seat, I turn around and see Sage already buckled into her car seat. Kicking her feet and staring out the window toward her new school.

She's so happy, and I can't help but channel some of that to me.

Is this how she always is after school, though?

During the short drive home, I only think about how I've never picked her up from school. Guilt for missing out on so much of her life hits me like a punch to the gut. After my injury, I shut the world out because I felt like my life was over and there was nothing to live for.

I should have *lived* for Sage.

Instead, Clark gave me a coaching position, and I lived for baseball again.

I chose that.

Tears threaten to spill over as Poplar Street comes into view.

But I don't allow them to reach the surface.

I don't ever allow my emotions to show, even alone.

"Yay! We're home," Sage shouts from the back seat.

Home feels like a foreign term. It hasn't felt like home in our short time here in town. I keep telling myself it's temporary, putting up that mental block so I don't get attached.

This isn't home.

But I don't tell my daughter that.

"So, how was your day, Sage?" I ask eagerly, sliding a bowl of sliced oranges and strawberries across the table. With extra whipped cream, just the way she likes it. "Did you make any new friends?"

She throws her arms out wide. "All of them are my best friends now."

I raise an eyebrow. "All of them, huh?"

"I don't remember all their names, though," she says, with a mouth full of fruit. "Just know they are all my bestest friends."

I laugh. "Do you like your teacher?"

"I loooooove her, Daddy. So much. She put me at a desk right by her in case I had questions. I told the class my favorite snack, and we got to color! My favorite ever." She beams, her eyes sparkling with the excitement of a new adventure.

"Wow. You love coloring."

"Next to puzzles, it's my fav. And guess what?" I raise a brow but let her continue. "Miss Barlow likes puzzles, too! She said she would bring me one she finished already for me to do here at home."

"That's very nice of her."

She stabs a strawberry with her fork, swiping through the whipped cream. I can tell she's excited because she keeps talking through her mouthfuls of food. "You know how I feel about puzzles."

Tilting my head to the side, my stomach swirls because I *don't* know. How do I not know this? I mean, I know she loves coloring and activity pages, but this is new information for me, and I fucking hate it.

"Remind me again?" I smile, hoping she doesn't think I'm the worst dad.

"Relaxation time," she says, drawing out the word to emphasize it. "Oh, and we also learned to stop, rock and roll."

"Huh?"

"You know, that thing we need to do if there's ever a fire. *Stop, rock and roll.*"

Shaking my head, I laugh. "You mean stop, *drop,* and roll?"

She shrugs nonchalantly. "Same thing."

I'm about to ask more about her day because I'm already

loving this after-school time with her, but there's a knock on my front door.

"I'll get it," Sage shouts, jumping off the chair and hustling for the door.

"Slow down, bug. We don't know who it is."

She opens the door, and I come up right behind her to see Nan standing at the front door.

"Oh, hi, Nan," Sage says with a wave.

"Hey there, kiddo." She lifts a little white paper bag in her hand with the words "Batter Up" written on the side in pink ink. "I brought my girl a first day of school treat."

My girl.

My heart flutters in my chest at the kindness this woman is showing to someone she just met only days ago. It's a small gesture to welcome my daughter and me to town. It makes me feel at ease that we have these people around us during our time here.

"For me?" Sage sparks up at her comment.

Nan nods. "Only the best treats we have in town come from the local bakery."

"Treats? Oh my god." She turns around, looking up at me with pleading eyes and hands in prayer. "Is it okay if I have some? I know I just had a snack, but my other tummy is ready for more."

"Other tummy?" I laugh.

"Yes. The treat tummy. It's empty and needs something sweet."

Shaking my head in disbelief, I glance over at Nan, who's laughing behind her hand. "Do you want to come in?"

She doesn't answer but crosses the door's threshold, entering as if she's been here a hundred times before. She goes to the kitchen with Sage in tow, rummaging through the cabinets for a small plate. I'm mildly taken aback by it, but intrigued by this strange woman and who she is in town.

She finds one, stuffs her hand into the bag, and pulls out a piece of crumb cake larger than my hand. My eyes widen, but I don't stop her. Sage is beaming with happiness right now.

It's all I've ever wanted to see from my little girl.

Nan slides the plate in front of Sage, and she dives right in. Nan then takes the second seat at the small table across from her. "How do you like Bluestone Lakes so far?"

"I love it." She emphasizes the word. "The squirrels are a little different from back at home."

Nan chokes. "The squirrels?"

"Yeah, the ones back home are mean. I think I once heard one growl like a tiger!" She puts her hands up, curling her fingers like claws. "The ones I saw when we were by the school just stay on the trees."

"Interesting observation, kid."

"I agree," I add.

"Anyway," Nan continues. "How was the first day of school?"

"So good," she says with a mouth full of food and eyes in the back of her head. Almost as if she's talking about the crumb cake and not just school. "I already have a boatload of best friends."

"A boatload, huh?" Nan laughs.

"All of them."

"Well, that's great to hear, kid. And you like Miss Barlow?"

"How did you know that's my teacher?"

Nan scoffs. "I know everything in this town. Did you know her sister owns the bakery and made that special treat just for you?"

Sage's eyes widen even more. "That's so cool. I love my teacher so much. She likes puzzles just like me!"

"She most definitely does," Nan confirms. "She gets lost in them all hours of the night. We always know where to find her after seven in the evenin' if we need her."

"I could too. But I have a bedtime."

Nan leans in, keeping her voice low. "Me too, but don't tell anyone."

Sage doesn't say anything back; she keeps going to town on her treat. Nan swivels in her chair and eyes me up and down as if seeing me for the first time. It's a kind of uncomfortable feeling, if I'm being honest. She looks like she's ready to scold me or judge me. I can't tell.

She stands up, coming to stand on the other side of the door frame, mimicking my stance as she leans against the opposite side. We both watch Sage as she gets lost in her own world. Bopping her head side to side as if some happy music is playing while she eats.

"You got a cute kid, Dallas."

Crossing my arms, I turn my head to face her. "I do."

"So, I heard a rumor."

"Yeah?"

"Tucker says you're starting a fun little adult league thing at the barnyard at night."

I nearly choke in laughter. "He did, did he?"

"Yep. He won't stop talking about it. He's kind of obsessed with you, if you haven't noticed."

"Can't say I have. Don't you think it's getting a little cold here to be playing outside?"

"Nonsense. We're used to that type of weather around here. Only thing that's ever stopped this town before was snow up to my tits. Otherwise, you say the word and we're playin'."

My hand covers my mouth to cover the laughter that wants so badly to erupt. This woman is certifiably insane. She has to be. That's the only logical explanation.

"Come on, Dallas. It would be fun for you to have some friends around here. Besides, you seem like the extroverted type that needs people to talk to or you'll go insane."

"You know me that well already, huh?"

"I have a keen eye for things. I see everything." She winks.

She's not wrong. That's definitely who I am, even though I'm trying like hell to only focus on my daughter. I could use some friends around town while I'm here.

Tucker seems wild, but I can tell he means well.

Griffin sounds a lot like me, and I know we will get along just fine.

And Poppy? We can be friends.

I internally laugh at myself, because who am I kidding?

You don't think about your friends the way I think about Poppy.

CHAPTER 8
SO, POPPY IS MY NEIGHBOR, HUH?

DALLAS

I glance at the clock on my nightstand and see it's just after six in the morning. Groaning, I get out of bed. What's the point in trying to go back to sleep when Sage has to get up and ready for school in an hour?

As I wait for my coffee to finish, I make a mental checklist of what I want to get done today while Sage is at school. I think I'll head out to the ranch, visit the barnyard, and see what I have to work with. If it's enough, I'll discuss this with the school before I meet with Sage's teacher later to ask about spreading the word and starting this thing for the kids.

Even with my doubts, I can't let it go.

Stepping onto my back deck with my mug, my coffee steams in the cold air. I stretch out the stiffness in my shoulders from lack of sleep, and the wooden boards are cool under my bare feet. Winter has definitely settled in here, but I've always liked the cold. The scent of pine and damp air fills my lungs as I close my eyes and inhale deeply. There's a fresh feeling in the air here. It's not smoggy like the city and doesn't smell like fumes from buildings or cars.

The quiet feels more than good, it feels calming.

Movement draws my eyes to my neighbor's deck. At first, she's just a shape in the dim light—a silhouette moving with slow, deliberate grace. I almost look away until the glow from the porch light brushes over her hair. Strawberry blonde hair, nearly copper in the low light, spills over her shoulders as she moves through a slow stretch.

Everything in me stills.

Poppy?

The realization slams into me. She's facing away from me, but I recognize the shape of her body. It's been permanently ingrained in my mind since our first meeting.

The woman I haven't been able to shake from my thoughts, the one whose laugh has haunted me every time my head hits the pillow, is my neighbor?

How did I not know this?

How is this the first time I'm seeing her?

Her back is to me, lost in the kind of concentration that makes it clear she has no idea she's being watched. She shifts into another stretch, arms lifting, spine curving, and my chest tightens with the ease of her movements. It's a sharp contrast to how she carried herself at the bar. This is less playful and more peaceful. You can tell just by watching her that this is her true self. The one that doesn't come out when there's music, people around, and alcohol involved.

She said this was something that makes her happy, and it shows.

I should look away.

I should go inside and give her privacy.

The logical part of my brain tells me to shout "good morning" across the lawn, joke about small worlds, or acknowledge this twist of fate.

But I don't.

Instead, I stay quiet, standing there with my coffee, facing toward her house and watching her.

Then, she spreads her legs and bends down until I can see her face through her legs.

I freeze with my mug halfway to my lips as her gaze lands on me instantly. Her lips part slightly as the flicker of recognition hits when her body snaps up, and she sucks in a sharp breath.

She had no idea either.

The air between our homes stretches tight, charged with something I don't quite understand. Both of us stand there, still and staring. Words sit in my throat, thick and useless.

Say something, dammit.

Instead, I smile over the brim of my coffee mug.

But just as quickly as she found me, she breaks the stare, straightening her spine and stepping inside. The sliding door closes behind her, and I exhale, running my hand through my hair.

So, Poppy is my neighbor, huh?

"Daddy, I'm up!" The soft voice coming from inside, and the creak of the floorboards, remind me I don't have time to stand out here and process whatever the hell just happened.

With one last look at Poppy's empty deck, I head back inside.

This just got a lot more interesting.

CHAPTER 9

OR HOW A HOT BASEBALL COACH
WATCHES YOU DO YOGA.

POPPY

"You're here earlier than usual." Lily laughs, glancing at the clock in the bakery.

I round the counter and collapse into a chair, letting my head fall back as I stare at the ceiling. My heart has been racing since this morning, when I finally saw the man living in the once-vacant house next door. I'm torn between the excitement of a potential romance and the fear of disrupting my routine.

"I met my new neighbor," I say to the ceiling.

"Oh, that's great!"

My head snaps up, and I shoot Lily a glare.

"No. Not great." She shakes her head, raising her hands to make an X. "Bad vibes."

I groan. "Not the worst vibes, but not the best neighbor."

"Loud music? Plays with car engines all day? A barking dog?" she teases.

"None of the above."

"Well, spill."

I sit up, resting my elbow on my thighs. "You know that guy I was talking to at the bar on your birthday?"

"The one you have yet to tell any of us about?"

I nod.

"The one we've been dying to know about but haven't asked about because we're, you know, respectful. But also really nosy."

I roll my eyes.

"Blair," Lily calls into the kitchen. "Poppy is here and ready to talk about the hot baseball coach!"

Blair bursts through the double doors. They swing and slam against the wall before she hops on the counter, ready to hear whatever I have to say. Her dramatic entrances never fail to amuse me.

"Tell me more," she coos.

"Stop that." I wave a hand. "You're making it more than it is."

Lily raises an eyebrow. "Are we?"

I sigh, sinking back into the seat, knowing I shouldn't have brought this up with them.

Yet again, my head isn't on straight this morning.

My morning routine was going perfect today, too. I woke up when my alarm went off, and my coffee pot didn't break down. My plans for the students today were ready, and I was eager to do all the fun things with them. I even started a mini list of everything I want to accomplish to cross off throughout the day.

Although it was freezing outside, my yoga session was smooth and grounding.

Until I caught my neighbor watching me through my legs.

In nothing but sweatpants and a T-shirt that clung to his ridiculously built body. I want to put emphasis on the T-shirt, because *my god*, it hugged every curve of muscle on his body. Is the man immune to winter weather? It's freezing in the mountains this time of year. His hair was a tousled mess, as if he had just rolled out of bed and done nothing but run his fingers through it.

And damn, if it didn't throw me off balance.

Once I went back inside, I kept repeating to myself, *you can't control everything,* because it's true. I can't. No matter how much

I wish I could, I just freakin' can't. I knew there was a chance that he would be moving next door to me, as it's one of the rentals available. But when I didn't see him his first few days here, sitting outside or moving boxes inside, I just assumed Nan set him up elsewhere.

"Well," I mutter. "The guy you two think is hot? He's my new neighbor."

"It's okay if you think he's hot. I thought your brother was hot when I moved next door to him." Blair shrugs.

"First, ew." Lily grimaces at Blair before facing me again. "Second, I agree with the first part of that statement. It's okay if you think he's hot."

I shake my head. "I don't do relationships, nor do I want to get involved with someone Nan considers a celebrity."

"He's kind of a big deal," Blair remarks. "At least he was back in San Francisco. He was the starting pitcher for the Staghorns. They're a major league team. And then something happened. I have no clue what because I never followed sports like that, but he stopped playing and took over as head coach."

"Ohh, a head coach," Lily murmurs, waggling her eyebrows.

"The team is awful," Blair huffs out. "Like, really bad."

"Is that what has you all out of sorts and here earlier than usual?" Lily asks. "It's not like you."

She's right. It's not like me to be off my schedule.

She might not know the extent of my routine and how structured I am, but...new things are scary for me, so I like having a plan. I'm not good when things change at the last minute.

Which is why I got ready and left my house earlier than I normally would, determined to maintain my routine and avoid another run-in with my dangerously attractive neighbor. Now, I need to add a new thing to my daily list.

Avoid the hot neighbor at all costs.

Can't wait to check that one off.

"I didn't know he was my neighbor until this morning," I admit. "I didn't put two and two together when Nan was rummaging on the property next door for a few weeks, or when I saw a black Tahoe parked out front. We always know when someone's new in town. Like everyone knows about it." I look at Blair because she was once the new person in town. "No offense."

She holds up her arms. "None taken."

"I should have known it was him. And I was doing morning yoga on my back deck the way I always do, and he was standing there—watching me."

Lily practically growls. "That's so hot."

Throwing my head back, I groan. "It's not hot. It's annoying."

Blair scoffs. "Hot and annoying are not mutually exclusive. Your brother was hot and annoying."

I rub my temples, already regretting getting here early. "I was having a great morning. I was feeling all the zen. Then, bam. He's standing there, staring at me. And not in a normal, friendly neighbor way. It made my skin heat up and my brain short-circuit."

Instantly, I regret saying that much because I never open up like this about men with anyone. It's a rare moment of vulnerability that I'm not comfortable with.

Blair and Lily exchange a look.

"That's hot," Blair confirms.

"So what did you do?" Lily asks.

My brows furrow. "Nothing?" What did she expect me to do?

Lily's eyes widen. "You didn't even say anything?"

"Wait, did he say anything?" Blair asks.

I press my lips together, reluctant to relive this morning.

"Poppy," Lily says. "What did he say?"

I exhale, letting my eyes travel to the tile floor to avoid seeing their faces. "He smiled."

Blair gasps. "You're *so* done for."

"Game over," Lily adds before the two high-five, forcing my attention back up.

"Stop it," I groan. "I can't do this. Am I mildly fascinated by him? Sure. In a way that someone might be when a bear comes into town."

"Or how a hot baseball coach watches you do yoga," Blair interrupts.

I level my stare in her direction before continuing. "My only focus is my job and my students. Today, I have a meeting with my new student's parents, and since my day started on the wrong foot, I'm anxious about this meeting. Oh, and did I tell you what the student said to me that makes me not want to meet her father?"

"What?" they say in unison.

"She said—and I quote—my dad likes murder."

Blair freezes, and Lily's eyes go wide.

"Yeah. It's going to be a fantastic day."

"Sarcasm aside…" Lily chuckles. "What's your plan?"

"Plan?"

She shrugs. "Are you planning to avoid him forever? Are you going to put together a welcome basket for him? What's the plan here?"

"The murderer dad?"

Lily rolls her eyes. "No, Pop. Your new neighbor who has you all worked up."

I scoff. "Absolutely not."

Blair smirks. "What if he shows up at your door looking all hot and broody again?" She gasps. "And what if he has that smile when you open the door?"

Standing from the chair, I cross my arms over my chest. "Then I'll hand him a frozen pizza, say welcome to Poplar Street, and call it a day."

Lily sighs, letting her back fall against the wall. "Romance is dead."

Blair hops off the counter, laughing. "It's just getting started, Lil. And it's all going down on Poplar Street."

"I hate you both."

"No, you don't," they say together.

Exhaling sharply, I round the counter again. "I have to get to work. Thank you for the lack of advice this morning. Forget I said anything."

"We won't." Lily smiles, wiggling her fingers in a wave.

Leaving the bakery, I get in my car for the short drive to work.

Opening up to them wasn't the best decision. It makes me more curious about Dallas and forces me to replay the entire morning.

What if I just said good morning?

What if I didn't run inside like a coward?

What do I do if he actually knocks on my door one day?

I feel my cheeks heat at the thought of seeing him standing there the way he was on his deck. The vision of seeing the smile on his face makes my stomach swirl in a way I'm not familiar with.

Dammit.

Maybe Lily and Blair weren't completely wrong.

CHAPTER 10
YOU MET MY FAVORITE TEACHER, HUH?

POPPY

The bell signaling the end of the day rings over the school's loudspeakers, and the kids all hustle to grab their things and filter out the door. Nervous energy courses through my body as I know my meeting with Sage's parents is in a few minutes.

I pull out a fresh piece of paper from my notepad and make a list of things to discuss with her parents for the meeting.

1. *Classroom schedule*
2. *Special schedule for the week*
3. *What we're currently covering in class*
4. *Ask about murder*

"I'm going to bring the kids outside to meet their parents and then take Sage to the library while you have your meeting," Rachel says.

I nod, still looking down at my list.

"Are you nervous, Poppy?" She laughs lightly.

I nod again, this time repeatedly.

Walking over to me, she places a reassuring hand on my shoulder. "I know we don't do this often, as we don't get a lot of new students, but you're an amazing teacher. The kids love you. The parents will love you, too."

I still can't find the right words to respond because she wasn't in the classroom when the murder comment was made. It seems irrational to think that her father might come here and try something, but I don't know what to expect. After just two days with Sage, I still barely know her.

"I saw her dad yesterday when he picked her up." A devilish grin spreads across her face as she fans herself. "He's hotter than sin, Poppy. Whew."

My eyes widen. "He's what?"

"I know we shouldn't say things about our students' parents, but it should seriously be illegal how good-looking he was." She shakes her head. "I'm going to hell for this. I'm sure of it."

I can't pinpoint why *this* is easing some of my tension, but Rachel has a personality that can do that. I'm so lucky to have an aide and friend in my classroom like her. She doesn't know what I struggle with internally, but she's the calm to the storm in my brain most of the day.

Laughing, I shake my head. "You probably are for talking about a *married* man like that."

"I'll take it to the grave with me," she says. "Oh, and did you hear the rumor around the school this afternoon about someone stepping up to coach the kids for a baseball team. They're going to fix up the barnyard."

"I know they didn't have a coach, but didn't know someone finally stepped up."

"Yeah, this guy is apparently feeling some type of way over the fact that the kids don't have a team here in town."

My mind immediately goes to Dallas. He's a former head coach of a major league team. It has to be him wanting to start things up here for the kids. The idea of seeing him around school and with the kids makes me feel uneasy, but also warms my heart that he wants to do that for them. After our night out, the way he watched me on my back deck, and the conversation with the girls, I'm beginning to feel my heart flutter more and more when he comes to mind.

"Anyway, let me get out of here with the kids. I'll take Sage to the library for a bit until the end of your meeting. I'll see you when I get back," Rachel says before following the students to meet their parents for end of the day pickup.

As I inhale and exhale, I push Dallas out of my head and move around the room to push in all the desk chairs and tidy up the drawing station. My students are generally good about putting away their supplies, but our methods differ. While they tend to toss everything into a bin, I have to come back and organize the crayons neatly.

A light knock on the door has my head snapping that way.

"Is this Miss Barlow's classroom?" a woman asks, not fully stepping into the room.

"It is," I say, standing straight, brushing my hands down my shirt to ensure it looks okay. "You must be Sage's mom."

"I am." She offers me a friendly smile, stepping into the room. Sage most definitely gets her beauty from her mom because she's beautiful. "You can call me April."

"You can call me Poppy," I say, extending my hand in greeting. "The secretary told me both parents would be here today. Is it just you?"

She rolls her eyes. "He's here, but in true fashion, he forgot to finish filling out a form for Sage, so he had to stop in the office."

"Perfect." I chuckle, grabbing the papers I had prepared for the meeting and making my way to the table where the kids usually color. It's a smaller table, as it's designed for kids, but it's the one I use during parent-teacher conferences. "We can sit here and wait for him to finish up."

"Great," she says, taking a seat. "Is Sage getting acclimated nicely? I've been nervous about how she would transition into a new school."

"I understand those feelings, and it's normal for you to feel that way. I'll tell you with confidence, there's no need to be nervous, Mrs. Westbrook. Sage is transitioning perfectly. She's so bright, funny, and smart."

Her shoulders fall with relief as the nervousness leaves her body with my assurance. "That's all I want for her."

"Before your husband returns, I wanted to ask you about something Sage said yesterday. I'm sorry if it's too personal, but I wanted to ensure everything was okay."

She waves her hand in the air. "Oh, he's not—"

A knock on the door interrupts her, drawing both of our attention. The atmosphere in the room shifts. My eyes go wide, and my stomach sinks. I think my soul leaves my body when I see Dallas standing in the doorway.

"Did you get everything handled?" April asks him.

He doesn't reply or move. He stands there with one hand on the door frame, staring at me with lips parted in shock, his eyes narrowed in confusion. My heart pounds in my chest, and I feel frozen, papers clenched between my fingers as I realize that I not only shared a drink at the bar with the father of one of my students but also a married man. A married man who is said to have a penchant for murder!

Oh my god, is this really happening right now?

And how in the world did I not put two and two together?

If I weren't trying to remain professional at work, I would swivel my chair to the side and vomit into the trash can because this cannot be happening right now.

Apparently, Rachel isn't the only one going to hell.

Dallas shakes his head as if snapping out of whatever was going through *his* head and makes his way into the room, keeping his head to the ground. "Yeah. I took care of it."

April beams, clapping her hands together, oblivious of the tension in the room. "Perfect. Here, take a seat and meet Miss

Barlow." She pushes the seat next to her out for him. "We chatted briefly while you finished in the office, and she said Sage is transitioning nicely."

He reluctantly sits down, making the chair feel much smaller than it is. His body is most certainly not made for these types of chairs.

Once he settles in, he leans forward on the table, intertwining his fingers, and slowly lifts his gaze to meet mine. I suddenly can't breathe. The flirty man I met at the bar is long gone, replaced by a serious and stoic version of Dallas. Forcing myself to breathe before I pass out, I look away and focus on the papers laid out in front of me.

I straighten my spine to maintain a professional composure. "As I said before, yes, Sage is settling in nicely. I think she has about eighteen new best friends." I laugh nervously, looking down at the papers in front of me. "However, there was something she said yesterday that I was just about to ask your wife—"

"She's not my wife," he cuts me off. My head snaps up again, instantly connecting with his. The corners of his eyes crinkle as his lips twist into a smirk. "We've been divorced for a while now," he adds.

I know I shouldn't feel relieved, but I can't help it because now I don't need to feel guilty about ogling over a married man. The problem is that he's still the father of one of my students, still making him completely off-limits. I simply can't. But it's hard to deny the way he makes me feel. It still is, especially with how he looks at me from across this small table, while his ex-wife sits beside him.

"Is Sage okay?" April cuts in. "What did she say?"

Clearing my throat, I turn to face April. "We were doing introductions around the classroom. Each student told a little about themselves, and Sage took a turn. The last thing was to give us a fun fact about yourself. She said she loves doing puzzles."

"She does." April smiles. "She's always loved them. She can tackle a 500-piece puzzle at six years old in two days."

"She told me that you planned to bring one for her one day," Dallas chimes in.

I nod, trying to avoid eye contact because I did tell her that.

That's when it hits me: I've been so focused on Dallas sitting right in front of me that I didn't even consider that he's my neighbor. Dallas is my freaking neighbor. Oh my god. This means Sage lives right next door to me. Or does she live with her mom? I have so many questions, but it's not my place to ask them. I don't want to learn anything more about Dallas than I already have.

Except, there's one thing I need to know to bring me some peace.

"After she told us about liking puzzles, she continued to say that she wishes her dad were good at puzzles." I shift my focus from April to Dallas. His eyebrow knit in confusion. "She said you prefer murder. And listen," I say quickly, "I don't judge anyone by what they choose to do. I just want to make sure my students are safe at home." I rattle out the words quickly as if to defend my accusations. My cheeks heat with the grin that spreads across his face, and I want nothing more than to crawl into a hole now.

April smacks his arm with the back of her hand. "I told you to stop watching those murder mystery shows when Sage is in the room, Dallas."

Dallas keeps his eyes fixed on mine, not reacting to April's smack on the arm while his smile grows. It causes my stomach to somersault with guilt for even thinking her father was a murderer. Granted, I didn't know her father is Dallas. The comment would throw up a red flag for any teacher.

"I'm sorry," I admit, letting my shoulders fall in relief. "Like I said, I just want to ensure my students are safe."

April reaches across the table, taking my hands in hers. I look from her to where our hands connect, and I wonder if she feels how clammy and shaky they are from this entire meeting.

"I appreciate that so much, Miss Barlow."

"Please, you can call me Poppy."

"Poppy." She nods. "I'm so happy I could make it into town for this meeting. In an effort for full transparency…" She pauses, looking to Dallas for confirmation that she can continue. He nods. "We *are* divorced. Dallas and Sage are here in Bluestone Lakes because I took a job opportunity in the city. But it also keeps me away from my daughter temporarily." I can feel the emotions building with each word out of her mouth. "It's another reason I was so nervous about this change for my girl."

"Wow. I'm sorry. I had no idea."

She shakes her head. "There's no need to be sorry. I just wanted you to know about her life outside of school. I wanted to give you a little background about our situation. I won't be able to make many meetings or school functions."

I nod in understanding. "If it's okay with you, I can keep you in the loop on our classroom app." I slide the paper with the login information for both of them. "Normally, we only see one parent in it, but I'm happy to add you so you know what's happening with updates and even some photos I take in class and send through the app every so often."

"That would be…amazing. Really amazing, Poppy."

"And this is how we can get in touch with you?" Dallas asks quickly.

His question throws me off guard. Does he want to get in touch with me? I mean, it's bad enough that he knows where I live. But this? I'm not sure how I feel about that.

"Yes. And my number is on the papers you received, too." I want to palm my face because why did I just tell him about my phone number? "Do you have any questions for me?" I ask, clearing my throat.

April shakes her head. "This covers it for now." She chuckles.

"I'll probably have one at some point, but right now I'm just happy to hear her first few days were great."

Offering her a smile, I briefly review the remaining topics I wanted to discuss from my meeting list. I mostly keep eye contact with April to avoid stumbling over my words. I already feel slightly better that I managed to address my entire list, even if it made me uncomfortable the whole time.

The classroom door opens, and Rachel drops Sage off, signaling me with a wave that she has to head out for the day.

Once Sage spots her mom, her eyes widen momentarily before she shouts, "Mommy!" and runs into her arms, where April sits.

"Hi, baby. Surprise!"

"You're here. This really is the bestest day ever now." Sage beams.

"Is it?"

Sage nods. "Daddy made me pancakes for breakfast before school. Then, I colored the most *epic* picture during drawing time. And Miss Rachel, let me pick a snack at the cafeteria just now on our way back from the library!"

April laughs. "That sounds like an epic day."

Sage turns to face her dad. "Hi, Daddy. You met my favorite teacher, huh?"

Dallas smiles at his daughter before looking at me. I know I'm blushing at her compliment and Dallas's picture-perfect smile. He stares at me for longer than I wish he would, which is unsettling but also makes goose bumps pebble across my skin.

"I did," he replies.

That's my cue. I need to stop looking at him and force myself to resist the pull of his eyes on me. My heart shouldn't race uncontrollably at the mere sight of him. I should be able to breathe steadily, without the suffocating sensation of everything being trapped in my chest. I should not feel a fire in my gut, but ice cold on my skin.

"Thank you again for coming in today," I practically choke

out, stacking my papers and going to my desk on the opposite side of the room. "I'll see you tomorrow morning, Sage."

"I can't wait!" She fist-bumps the air.

"Want a bite to eat before I head back to the city, baby?" April asks her.

"Yes!"

April looks to Dallas. "I'll drop her off after we eat if that works for you?"

He nods.

Taking Sage's hand in hers, they reach the door. "Thank you again, Poppy. We'll chat soon."

"Anytime." I smile, and they walk out.

After carefully stowing the papers away in a file folder, I look up to find Dallas where we left him at the table. He's still standing there with his hands in the pockets of his jeans, staring at me with such intensity as if he has a million and one questions floating through his head.

I feel stuck behind my desk, uncertainty coursing through me. I want him to break the silence, to say even a simple thought that could dissolve the thick air between us. Another part of me desperately wishes for him to leave the room, to escape this feeling.

"So..." he says, looking to the ground before his feet move in my direction across the room. With each step, my nerves grow. He stops before me, forcing me to tilt my head up, and I'm met with the most piercing gaze. "You're my daughter's teacher."

"Yes."

"And you're my neighbor." He smiles as if the memory of this morning sparked something.

I swallow, fighting down the shiver so my voice doesn't break. "Seems that way."

"Interesting."

Our eyes remain fixed on each other as if he wants to say more. Breaking the stare, I turn on my heel to avoid making this more awkward than it has been. "Thanks again for coming in for this meeting. You have a very adorable daughter."

"I'm glad I did."

I straighten my spine, putting on my professional face in an attempt to show that he's certainly not affecting me right now.

"I had something else I wanted to talk to you about," he adds. My body freezes up, and I remain silent, waiting for him to say more. "You braided Sage's hair."

"I'm sorry. Her ponytail fell out when we were on the playground. She told me she prefers her hair in a braid, so I put one in for her before we returned to the classroom. I'm sorry," I say again, trying to defend my reasoning.

Dallas laughs, and it vibrates through my body.

I raise an eyebrow and tilt my head in question.

"There's absolutely nothing you need to be apologizing for, Poppy. I'm not mad."

"You're not?"

He shakes his head. "I wanted to say thank you. So, I guess it's not a question, but more of a thanks."

"I—Uh. Sure. Anytime."

"She also mentioned something to me yesterday." He takes one more step closer to me, his earthy wood scent engulfing all of my senses, knocking me off kilter, but I remain steady.

"Yeah?"

"She said you would bring her a puzzle for her one day."

I swallow. "I did."

"And now you know where we live."

"I do."

His eyes scan my face as if trying to memorize every detail. It's unsettling, yet it ignites a fire in my gut with how he looks at me. I know I shouldn't want more since he's off-limits, but I can't deny how he makes me feel things I'm not accustomed to.

We both stand there in silence, staring at each other for longer than necessary. The way his eyes stay laser-focused on mine tells me that there's a whole lot more he wants to say, but isn't.

"I'll be seeing you around then, Miss Barlow." He winks and walks away.

I don't take my eyes off him as he leaves, closing the door behind him and leaving me alone in my classroom. I close my eyes and take a calming breath.

"You're most definitely going to be seeing a lot of me, Dallas Westbrook," I murmur to an empty room. "Whether I like it or not."

CHAPTER 11
GO, BASEBALL!

DALLAS

"Daddy, do I get to play too?"

"I don't see why not. This is just a bunch of us getting together to have some fun."

Tucker has successfully recruited a "team" of sorts to play ball down at the barnyard, and it's our first night getting together.

I won't lie, I'm excited to get a baseball in my hands again and maybe swing a bat. I might not be able to play professionally with my shoulder injury anymore, but this is something I can do.

Pulling into the dirt lot that Tucker gave me directions to, I take in the sight in front of me. Sitting on the edge of the ranch next to the wooden fence lining the property, there's an open field that serves as the unofficial baseball field.

The barnyard.

It's not much at all—overrun with uneven grass and dirt—but from what I understand, the kids love it. To them, this is a professional baseball stadium. The bases are flattened cardboard boxes, and the footpaths to each base are carved out by endless sprints from the kids running the bases. It's rough around the edges with all the overgrown weeds, but it's alive with imagination.

Tucker spots me, jogging up to greet me halfway from my SUV to the field. He opens his arms, grinning from ear to ear, and spins around. "Well, what do you think?"

"Man, if Tyler and Mitch could see where I've ended up."

His eyes widen. "Are you talking about Tyler Goodman, the most epic third baseman ever to play the sport? And Mitch Holden, the second"—he leans in close to whisper—"because you're the first. Duh. Best pitcher in the Major League?"

"Yep."

His hands come up to the side of his head as he starts pacing in front of me. "They're amazing. I'm obsessed with them. And you. Oh my god. This is amazing. Can they come out here and play?"

"I'll talk to them." I laugh at how much of a fan he is, with how far outside the city of San Francisco we are.

"Wow, that's just so cool. I can't get over it. Tell them I said hi. Anyway, what do you think?" He gestures to the field they call the barnyard.

"It can work."

He rests an arm on my shoulder. "That's the spirit." Doing a double take, he spots Sage, who's now standing next to me after switching from her sandals to her sneakers in the backseat. "Who's this?"

"I'm Sage. I love baseball."

Tucker beams with excitement. "Me too." He leans in close to me, still staring at her. "Where did she come from?"

"That's my daughter."

"No shit. I didn't know you had one of those."

"Yes. I have one of those," I say through my laughing fit. "She loves baseball, so I thought I'd bring her to hang out with us. If that's okay?"

"I gotta be honest with you, I'm not good with kids. Mostly

the little ones because they're too delicate for me. Oh, and I curse a little. Well, a lot."

"Daddy does too," Sage cuts in. "Just the other day he was unclogging the toilet, and he screamed sh—"

Covering her mouth with my hand, I stop her. "He gets the point."

"Yep. I like her. She can hang with us."

Tucker takes Sage's hand and leads her to the field where everyone else sits. Mostly faces I know, some I haven't met yet. I can't help but scan every face to see if Poppy is here. I don't know if she's the sports type, but I can't help but hope.

My head has been a mess of thoughts for the last week after learning that the one woman I can't stop thinking about is Sage's teacher. Not that I was going to try to pursue anything, as my time in Bluestone Lakes has an expiration date. But it's hard to deny her effect on me after the last few times I was around her.

I've spent the last few days trying to steer my thoughts in another direction and letting myself be consumed by the one thing that has never let me down.

I couldn't stop thinking about saying yes to coaching the kids.

Even with every doubt, every question, there has been a constant tug in my gut telling me that I *should* be doing something about this.

So I met with the school secretary, who was enthusiastic about something starting in the town again for the kids. The roadblock isn't the money involved for equipment and other things, because I have that. I *want* it to go toward this. The issue was that the season would just be starting before I leave here to return to San Francisco. Meaning, someone would need to take over after the first game of the season.

Even with that, I still said we need to do it.

Me leaving would be a problem for a later day.

"Dallas Westbrook," Nan announces. "Took ya long enough. Let's play ball."

"Maybe we should introduce him to everyone first, Nan," Griffin says to her, before greeting me with a handshake. "Good to see you again. I know you've met Tucker."

"Duh. I'm his biggest fan," Tucker announces proudly. "And we're best friends now."

Griffin shakes his head, then gestures to Blair on his left. "You've met Blair." I nod, and then he gestures to the woman next to her. "And this is my sister, Lily."

"Well, I've heard *all about you*, but seeing you in person is… wow." She shakes her head, eyes wide.

"Lily," Griffin warns.

I'm not sure what to make of her comment.

How has she heard about me, and from whom?

If I had to take a guess, it would be between Tucker and Nan.

"Sorry. Yes." Lily blushes, extending her hand in greeting. "I'm Lily. I own the bakery in town. And I actually met Sage the morning you guys got here."

"Oh yes, you did!" Sage beams. "Now I want some of your special sugar."

"Well…" Lily walks to the bench, picking up a white bag. "I didn't know if you would be here or not, but I brought this with me *just* in case."

"I love you so much," Sage shrieks, reaching into the bag and pulling out a giant chocolate chip cookie.

That's the thing about kids. You can weasel your way into their hearts with just about any kind gesture.

I'm smiling at the interaction, but it falls quickly when realization smacks me in the face. Nan said Sage's teacher's sister owns the bakery. Lily is Poppy's sister. Which means, Griffin is Poppy's brother. Which means…

"Wait. Are you my teacher's sister?" Sage asks the question in my head.

"Is your teacher Miss Barlow?"

"Yep. I love her sooo much."

Lily laughs. "Yep. She's my sister. You must be the new girl in her class. She talks about you all the time."

Poppy talks about my daughter?

Is Poppy who Lily heard about me from?

"Did you know she likes puzzles just like me?" Sage asks Lily.

Lily nods. "She *loves* them."

Griffin takes the time to introduce everyone else. The only other two I haven't met yet were Levi and Autumn. I briefly remember Autumn from the coffee shop, but never knew her name. Tucker chimed in about how Levi works with him in construction here in town.

All the other details are a blur because I can't get my mind off the one person who isn't here.

Poppy Barlow.

"Is this everyone?" I ask, hoping my question doesn't give away that I'm looking for her.

Griffin nods, extending his arms out. "This is our crew. It's kind of a nutty bunch, but they keep things interesting. Poppy is the only one missing. She doesn't get out much." He shrugs casually like it's no big deal.

"She doesn't?"

I don't know what makes me ask as quickly as I do. Maybe it's because I'm standing in front of her brother, more curious about her than ever. A part of me wants a reason to talk to her about something, anything, just for the chance to get to know her better. I keep finding myself *wanting* to connect with her when I usually don't.

I can't understand why I'm so drawn to her, but I have to remind myself that my stay in Bluestone Lakes has an expiration date.

Griffin shakes his head. "If she comes out, it's like a big deal."

"It's like an *alert the media* type of moment." Tucker barks out a laugh.

"We playin' ball or what?" Nan says, standing on home plate

with a bat in her hand. "I have recorded soaps I gotta catch up on after this."

"Daddy." Sage tugs at my hand. "What are soaps?"

"I think they're some kind of TV show."

"Sounds boring." She wrinkles her face before skipping over to the bench with her little bag of treats in hand. "Go, baseball!" Sage cheers.

"That's the spirit," Nan shouts.

Everyone moves around, taking random bases, and Tucker puts me on the pitcher's mound. There aren't enough players to make two teams, and since this is really just for fun and messing around, everyone is on the field with rotating turns batting.

It feels good to stand on a pitcher's mound again, even if it is just a flattened cardboard box.

Throwing the ball lightly overhead, Nan swings and, to my surprise, hits it. Hard. Past everyone in the field.

"Nan," Tucker screams, running for the ball. "You aren't supposed to be good."

Nan jogs the bases. For an older woman, she's got some quick feet on her. "Ah-ha." She laughs. "You underestimate me, Talkative Tucker."

"Go, Nan! Go, Nan! Go, Nan," Sage cheers, jumping up and down from the first base sideline.

"What can't that woman do?" I say through my laughter, shaking my head.

"She's a wild one, that Nan," Lily says, now standing next to me. "She can do everything and anything."

Everyone moves to the bench, grabbing water from their bags.

"I'm water hungry," Sage says.

"Does that mean thirsty?" Tucker asks.

"Yep."

"Look at me, learning kid language. I'm basically a pro now. I can babysit any night for you, Dallas."

"I'm not a baby," Sage huffs out, narrowing her eyes.

"Kid sit?"

Sage thinks about it for a second and shrugs. "Sure."

"I wouldn't go that far," I deadpan.

Lily nudges my side. "So…you're the guy who moved next door to my sister."

"I am."

"She told me."

"She did?"

Lily nods, and then silence stretches between us before she leaves my side to go grab water.

I want to ask more, but what? I don't even know how I'm feeling about the whole thing. I'm struggling to wrap my head around the fact that I'm really attracted to her, but she's also my daughter's teacher.

Does that make her off-limits?

This urge comes over me that I *need* to talk to her.

And it needs to happen tonight.

I haven't had a sip of alcohol tonight, but my judgment is a cloudy mess.

Which perfectly describes my life. I've just been a string of fuck-ups, one after another.

Which has me wondering if my pull to bring baseball into Bluestone Lakes is driven by my need to fix all the things I've screwed up. Baseball has brought a lot of good into my life, but it's also been the reason a lot of other things in my life have crumbled.

If I do this, I would be setting a team up for the town to have long after I leave.

But it would also give me a reason to come back here every so often.

Maybe to see Poppy.

But what would I do if I came back here in a few months and she had a boyfriend? How would that make me feel? My fists tighten around my steering wheel because I can't stand the thought of that. Not that I have a right to feel this way.

After questioning myself if she's off-limits or not, I realized that whatever chemistry I felt with Poppy needs to stay stuffed down. These thoughts I've been having need to get the fuck out of my head to avoid issues for Sage at school. The one thing I don't want to screw up any more than I already have is Sage.

When I turn onto my street, I realize the radio has been off the entire ride home, and the quiet hits me hard. Sage fell asleep almost immediately after putting her in the car. It feels like the world is holding its breath with me when I slow down and stare at Poppy's house as I drive by. Her porch light casts a yellow glow, begging me to step up and knock on the door to make things feel normal again.

Begging me to clear the air and get ahead of any weird feelings.

Begging me to lay my eyes on her again.

Pulling into my driveway, I throw the car into park. I inhale and exhale before letting the freezing air hit my lungs. I stand there, staring across the yard at her place as my breath makes a cloud of smoke in front of me. I should talk to her tonight. Otherwise, I won't be getting any sleep.

Picking Sage up, she barely stirs when I bring her inside. It was a struggle to keep her awake long enough to brush her teeth. But she did it and had her eyes closed again the minute her head hit the pillow.

Staring down at my daughter, I brush her hair away from her face and lean in to press a kiss to her forehead. "I love you, bug."

Pacing my living room, I question if I should go and talk to Poppy quickly. I check the camera app on my phone to make sure it's connected in case Sage wakes up and needs me. I don't plan to be gone long, and will be right outside the house.

Making my way across the yard, my stomach swirls, and my

palms feel sweaty as I step onto her porch. Her house is the complete opposite of mine. It resembles a cottage-style house with white siding, a white picket fence, and a colorful assortment of floral baskets hanging under the front window.

Lifting my hand to knock, I pause.

Just knock. Don't make this weird.

Maybe this is a bad idea? I shouldn't be here right now. I should leave and go home. I don't need to talk to her, get to know her, or smooth things over. I step back, staring at her door again before turning on my heel and retreating down the steps.

"Dallas?" Poppy says, forcing me to turn around quickly. I didn't even hear the door open. "Are you okay?"

I'm stuck where I stand on the little walkway leading to the street, and I swear the air just jumped twenty degrees. She's only wearing a pair of black sweatpants and a sweatshirt that's about three sizes too large on her, but I barely register the words out of her mouth because I'm taken aback by how stunning this woman is.

"Dallas?"

My name from her lips again snaps me from my trance. "Yeah?"

She steps out of her house and onto the porch, closing the door behind her. The light makes her look like an angel in the night. *Fuck my life.* "Is Sage okay?"

My eyes fall to the grass as I walk back to her porch, staying on the walkway but close enough to converse with her. My heart hammers in my chest at her asking about my daughter. When I gaze back at her, Poppy has her arms crossed over her chest before leaning on the porch railing. I knew this was a terrible idea. I should never have walked over here in the first place, because seeing her again only makes the reason I'm here harder to ignore.

"Is everything okay?" she repeats.

"I wanted to talk about our meeting at the school."

She remains silent, as if she wants me to continue.

I clear my throat, and my nerves spike. "I don't want things to be awkward for us. We shared a drink and I had a really good time, only to learn you're Sage's teacher. The last thing I want is for things to be...well, awkward."

She still says nothing, just continues watching me with curious eyes.

"I came here to keep things simple. I guess I wanted to ensure we're on the same page. But now that I'm standing here, outside your house, I can't stop thinking about how this would be a hell of a lot easier if you weren't...you."

She stands straighter, lips slightly parted as if I'd surprised her.

Fuck, I surprised myself, too.

It feels like minutes have passed, eyes locked on each other, while my racing heart doesn't let up for one second. My palms feel even more clammy than before, and even with the chill in the air, there may be sweat on my eyebrows.

"I...I mean. I'm just. We can't. I'm Sage's teacher, and I'm..." she fumbles over her words before her voice trails off as if she wants to say something but can't bring herself to say it.

"A professional?" I raise an eyebrow.

"That too." She blushes, turning her face to the side to avoid eye contact.

I nod repeatedly, choosing not to press her about what she wanted to say but didn't. Instead, I offer a comforting smile. Something that's not hard to fight back when she's around, as her presence could bring even the strongest man to his knees.

The only thing I've learned from walking over here is that I'm weak for her, even though she clearly stated that I barely know her. I *recognize* that I'm weak for my neighbor—for my daughter's teacher. I'm weak for her, knowing that I will be leaving.

I retreat a few steps backward but don't take my eyes off her. Ready to say precisely what I was thinking before even deciding to try to dull the flame by coming over here. It wasn't my intention, but seeing her, I can't help myself.

"Just so we're clear, Poppy," I murmur, keeping my gaze locked on hers. "I still haven't stopped thinking about you since the day I moved here. And every single thought I've had is very *unprofessional*."

She sucks in a breath before I wink and turn on my heel to head back to my house.

Poppy Barlow is the most unexpected thing to show up in my life. And damn if I don't want to explore it more.

So much for keeping it stuffed down.

CHAPTER 12
THAT BASEBALL DADDY IS SOMETHING ELSE.

POPPY

> **LILY**
> How's the plan for avoiding your neighbor going?

> Great. Going on two whole weeks now.

> **LILY**
> You can't avoid him forever.

> **BLAIR**
> I think he's really into you, Pop.

> I can't allow that to happen. He's off-limits.

> **LILY**
> Oh, please. *eye roll*

> **BLAIR**
> Off-limits can be so fun!

When I open the car door and step outside, the cold air hits my face, shaking my body. The temperature in town has dropped significantly in the last few weeks as winter fully sets in. I've officially had to move my early morning yoga sessions into my living room because the frost coating the back deck doesn't help me relax like yoga should.

But it's helped ease my anxiety of coming face-to-face with my neighbor again.

After he showed up on my porch and admitted he would have continued flirting with me even if he knew who I was, my brain went haywire trying to figure out how to deal with this.

Dallas Westbrook is hot.

I'm not talking casual hot; I'm talking all-consuming, rigid muscles, incredible smile, and bold personality hot. Being near him in any capacity only fills my body with a strange craving to be closer to him. I *know* I need to stay away because he's the parent of one of my students, and if I were to allow myself to get closer to him, he's only going to break my heart when he learns about who I really am.

Dallas seems spontaneous, like he's up for any adventure at the drop of a hat.

As I step into the general store for my Saturday morning grocery trip, the heat hits my face, and I welcome it with a smile while brushing off the thoughts of my neighbor. I barely make it to the produce section when Nan spots me.

"Pretty Poppy." She beams, using one of the nicknames she has for some of us in town. It's cute because it's very Nan. She's named most of us—Pretty Poppy, Grumpy Griffin, Lovely Lily, and newly added, Talkative Tucker. "How unlike you to be here at exactly nine o'clock on a Saturday morning for grocery shopping."

I prop my fist on my hip, tipping my head to the side before giving her a knowing glare. "Nan, you know this is my weekend routine."

"Very predictable." She laughs. "That's why I'm here."

I narrow my eyes, wondering where she's going with this.

"We haven't seen you around karaoke night in a few weeks," she says.

"You know I don't frequent the bar like that."

"But you can."

"You're right, I can. But I also don't want to." I laugh with a shrug. "You know my job has always come first for me, and the last thing I want is a parent seeing me and tarnishing my reputation because they saw me have a drink or something."

My anxiety spikes just saying it out loud. My entire family knows that, including Nan. Even if she's not a direct line of the Barlow family in any capacity, she knows I love my job. It's my entire personality at this point.

"I understand," she says in a more somber tone. "I just miss my Pretty Poppy. And love to see you have a good time and let loose every once in a while."

Placing a hand on her shoulder, I offer her a reassuring smile. "I'm happy, Nan."

"Are ya?"

The question throws me off guard.

I've worked hard for the things I have in life, and I love the path I've chosen. I've never felt like anything was truly missing. Would I like to have a relationship someday? Yeah. It's been on my mind more often than not lately. It's something I've been working with my therapist to overcome after my last boyfriend in college broke up with me. Everything I was always afraid of came to light the day he broke up with me. He told me I was too much for him, and that I prioritize my career and routine before him, among other things that I don't want to let come into my head again.

I spiraled, but therapy saved me.

I can't help the way my brain functions.

I've learned that it doesn't make me crazy, though, it makes me…me.

But being with someone isn't the end-all, be-all for happiness, is it?

"Miss Barlow!" I hear just as I open my mouth to reply to

Nan. Snapping my head toward the small voice, my smile grows. "What are you doing out of school?"

"Hi, Ally." I laugh. "You know I don't live there, right?"

Her eyes widen briefly before she breaks into a fit of hysterics. "I knew that. I was testing you."

"I bet you were, silly goose."

"Hi, Miss Barlow," her mom, Mindy, says behind her. "So nice to see you again."

"Same to you. How are you two today?"

"Fantastic!" Ally shouts. "I gots cinnamon crunchie cereal!"

Her mom shakes her head before looking around us as if she doesn't want anyone else to hear what she's about to say. Nan picks up on it, stepping closer and adjusting herself so her ear is close enough to listen to the tea—such a Nan thing to do.

"Have you seen the new guy in town?" She grins, keeping her voice low before waggling her eyebrows. "I just saw him in the cereal aisle and almost forgot what I was there for." She fans a hand in front of her face. "It should really be illegal for someone to look as good as that man does."

There's only one new man in town who fits this description. The thought of running into him after successfully avoiding him since he showed up on my porch makes the hairs on my arm stand tall and my stomach twist. My palms feel clammy on the shopping cart as I tighten my grip, forcing myself to listen to whatever she's saying.

"I just know he's not going to be on the market long," she adds. "And I'm so mad I look like I just rolled out of bed."

"You did just roll out of bed, Mommy," Ally chimes in.

"What did I tell you about giving away my secrets?" She chuckles with her daughter.

"That baseball daddy is something else." Nan laughs, crossing her arms over her chest but keeping her eyes fixed on me. It feels like she's waiting for a reaction from me.

"Baseball daddy?" Mindy questions.

Nan nods. "Head coach for some fancy major society team in San Francisco."

"Nan, it's a Major *League* team. Not society," I correct her.

"Same thing," she waves her hand in the air.

"Ohhh," Mindy coos. "The head coach for a major league team? Wow. Maybe I should return to the cereal aisle to give him my number if he's still there." She winks.

My stomach churns again, and my heart rate picks up out of…jealousy? I don't know, but I feel a protectiveness creep into my pores over the way she's talking about him. Not that I have a single right to feel this way. I've made it clear that he and I are to remain professional, and I know I can't allow myself to get into a relationship.

Then again, Dallas and Mindy would be ideal for each other.

They're around the same age and both single parents, so they have a lot in common, right?

"Speak of the devil," Nan says.

Mindy and I turn our heads to where she's looking and find Dallas and Sage walking toward us.

"Ally," Sage shouts before jogging to meet us. "I see you twice in one store!"

"Coolest thing ever." Ally beams. "Did you get the cinnamon crunchies?"

Sage shakes her head. "I got the rainbow marshmallows!"

Both girls cover their mouths and laugh together.

"*Miss* Barlow," Dallas drawls out, and I swear I could melt right here in front of everyone, hearing my name in any form out of his mouth. "It's nice to see you again."

Dammit, I feel the same way, and I most definitely shouldn't.

So much for avoiding him.

I nod in response, offering a tight-lipped smile.

"We were just talking about you," Mindy says in a flirty tone.

My eyes drift to where she places her hand on his shoulder. It's covered in a black sweatshirt with bold letters that read *San Fran*, but I know she can feel the broad, rock-hard muscle underneath the fabric. I know it's there because I couldn't stop staring that night at the bar.

"Yeah?" Dallas raises a brow, focusing his eyes on mine.

"I was tellin' them about your job as a baseball daddy," Nan cuts in.

My eyes widen, and Dallas nearly chokes before facing Nan. "What?"

"Did I say that out loud?" Nan winks.

"Nan was just telling me about your job," Mindy says. "I think that's amazing. I'm a *huge* baseball fan."

Dallas still doesn't look at her, but instead faces me again. He looks at me as if he's watching the most intense sports game in history, and if he blinks, he'll miss it. It's a look that sucks all the air from my lungs because I like how he does it. I like how it makes me feel to be seen by someone like him.

"Is that so?" he answers.

"We should meet up at Seven Stools one night for a drink and talk more about it. I'd love to hear more and get to know you," Mindy says, stepping closer to him.

Finally, he gives her the time of day by turning his gaze on her. "Did you have a day in mind?"

What?

Poppy, you have no right to be jealous right now.

"What about Friday?" Mindy asks.

"I can't, I have plans that night."

"Saturday?"

"Also have plans."

"Oh." She giggles. "You're a busy guy. What are your big plans?"

Like she has a right to know.

"Nothing big, honestly." He shrugs. "I just plan to sit on my back deck and hope my neighbor emerges from her house so I can talk to her. It's been a couple of weeks, and I want to make sure she's okay."

My. Jaw. Drops.

I hear Nan choke beside me because she knows he only has one neighbor in direct view of his back deck. I hold my breath, watching Mindy to see if she pieces together what he's saying. The last thing I need is a mom like Mindy, who's heavily involved in school activities, to spread the word around town that I'm involved in anything with the parent of one of my students.

When I'm most certainly not.

"Oh. That's adorable how much you care for your neighbor. Listen, I'm free if you don't want to be alone when you do it. I'm great company. Besides, I think our daughters are new best friends at school."

"I'll be in touch." He smiles before turning to face me again.

The two of us stand there, staring at one another as if we have a million things to say. Words unspoken as Ally and Sage say their goodbyes, and Mindy writes her number on scrap paper to hand him before leaving to the checkout. Nan moves to stand between us, bouncing her gaze back and forth from me to Dallas out of curiosity.

"Well, well, well." She crosses her arms over her chest. "Now that she's here, Dallas, it looks like your Friday and Saturday plans are canceled."

"I used a permanent marker on the calendar hanging in my kitchen, Nan," he answers her, still looking at me. "So I'm going to keep those plans in hopes I get to see my neighbor again."

My lips part as I take in everything he's saying. How in the world is he still this flirty, bold man after I told him I needed to remain professional?

I can't. I can't. I can't.

"Well, I'll give you two a minute or twelve to talk," Nan says, tossing her arm around Sage's shoulders. "I'm going to show Sage the best ice cream flavor on the planet."

"COTTON CANDY!"

Dallas gives Nan a knowing look before she covers her

mouth with her hands, chuckling, and guides Sage toward the frozen section, leaving Dallas and me alone.

"What the hell was that, Dallas?"

His grin grows. It's wicked and hot and so sexy.

Christ, what's wrong with me?

"If a rumor started in town that I was dating one of my students' parents, it could hurt my career," I continue. "Not that this is. You know. We're not dating and all. But…" I ramble, letting my words fall off my tongue when he steps closer to me.

His hand reaches the side of my face before he brushes a loose strand of hair from my eyes and behind my ear. His touch is featherlight and lasts only a few seconds, but I feel it throughout my entire body.

"It's a good thing I don't date anymore then." He winks.

Aside from Dallas being Sage's dad, the main thing preventing me from letting things progress beyond a surface-level friendship is that I'm afraid I'll start seeing someone in town, and they'll run at the first sight of who I am deep down. And because it's a small town, people will talk. Before I know it, everyone is talking about the girl who organizes her spices from A-Z, has to have her plates and glasses arranged a certain way in the cabinets, and gets easily overwhelmed when furniture isn't aligned correctly. These are just a few things that make me, me, but I always worry it will drive someone away.

But I can't push someone away who's already only here temporarily, can I? Before I get to give it any more thoughts, a voice cuts through.

"We're back," Sage announces, cutting through my racing thoughts. "They have gallons and gallons of ice cream flavors here. This is definitely my favorite store."

"Gallons," Nan adds sarcastically.

"Oh, Miss Barlow. Did Daddy tell you how he burned the pizza last night and said a bad word?"

"What did he say?" Nan encourages.

"He said—"

"Nope. Okay. Moving on," Dallas says, covering her mouth with his hand, and they start laughing.

Letting my eyes bounce between the two of them, I can't help but feel the smile on my face grow.

"I have that puzzle for you, Sage." Her eyes light up. "Maybe I can drop it off sometime this week if you're going to be home."

She looks up at Dallas. "Am I, Daddy?"

"Yes."

"You should probably exchange numbers so you know everyone is decent," Nan interrupts.

"Nan!"

"Fine by me." Dallas shrugs with a grin before pulling out his phone and handing it to me. I look at the phone and back up at him before taking it, and I see that the phone app is already open for me.

He makes me forget my phone number all of a sudden.

"I guess…I'll text you when I plan to come by," I say, handing him back his phone.

My phone buzzes in my back pocket, and I take it out to see a text.

UNKNOWN NUMBER:
It's me.

Smiling down at the text, it feels like the weight of the world is in my palm. A line of communication with the neighbor whom I wanted to steer clear of, but am now having second thoughts about.

Do I want this?

Do I want to explore this, knowing he's here temporarily?

"I'll put her number in your phone," Sage says to Dallas, pulling the phone from his hand. "I know how to spell Miss Barlow's name now."

She clicks away with her tongue poking out in concentration, and I take the opportunity to watch Dallas watch Sage. He looks at her like she's his whole world. And it makes me feel like I'm missing out on so much. Not even realizing that the fear of relationships will hold me back from *this*. Experiencing someone looking at me like I'm their whole world.

Nan clears her throat, breaking Dallas's trance from watching his daughter and mine from watching them.

He turns to face me. "Well, we'd better get going."

I nod, wringing my fingers nervously in front of me.

"It was good to see you outside of school," Sage says first. "I can't wait to see you again tomorrow for the puzzle. And the next day for school. And the next day, and the next day. Every day with Miss Barlow! Yes!" she rattles off, her voice growing with each word, as if she's realizing at the same time the words leave her lips.

I laugh. "Yes, I'll see you then."

Looking at Dallas now, my nervous system strikes again. He brings his bottom lip between his teeth as a lopsided grin forms on his face. I feel weak, like my legs are going to give out beneath me at any second.

"It was good seeing you, Poppy. I'm glad we ran into you this morning."

"You too."

These are the only two words I can manage without fumbling over my words.

Dallas winks and takes a few steps backward, facing me before shaking his head, smiling, and turning on his heel to walk away.

I feel my cheeks heat on their own.

"Well," Nan says beside me, forcing me to face her. She has her arms crossed over her chest and a knowing grin. "Looks like Pretty Poppy has an admirer in town."

"Definitely not."

"I saw the way he looks at you, girl."

"How did he look at me?"

She stands there, assessing me. "He looks at you like you're the answer to everything."

CHAPTER 13
I'M ONLY HERE FOR THE SNACKS.

DALLAS

MITCH
Good luck tonight, Coach.

TYLER
Oh, that's right. He's coaching the kids tonight. Fuck yeah.

TYLER
Don't show them my text. It has a curse word.

No shit.

TYLER
Don't say that in front of them.

MITCH
Ty, respectfully, shut the fuck up. Hope you have a great practice, Dallas.

TYLER
Anyway, don't forget to keep us updated.

Thank you, guys. Heading in now.

"I'm so glad you asked me to tag along."

"Tucker, you invited yourself." I scoff.

"But if I didn't, you'd still want me here. For moral support and all."

Sage tugs at my arm. "What's moral support?"

"It's—"

"Encouragement," Tucker chimes in. "In case your dad needs a reminder that he's the best."

"Oh, I can do that!" Sage jumps up and down. "I got all the moral support."

We all laugh as we enter the doors of the elementary school gym. The town was eager to get this started after I offered, and told us we could use the gym for some indoor practices after school while we wait for the weather to warm up. Everyone was just as adamant as Nan and Tucker about practicing in the cold, and they all claimed to be used to it. I'm not, though.

Since it's the first practice, I thought inside would be best anyway for some basic introductions, a little game of catch, and learn how to swing a bat.

I don't know a thing about the athletic abilities of these kids.

What the hell am I even doing here?

Taking in the space, it's much larger than I expected for an elementary school. The entire area is about two basketball courts wide, with bleachers retracted against every wall. I try to suppress my laugh when I see a massive bulldog painted on one of the walls with the words *Bluestone Lakes Bulldogs* written under it. I never would have expected the school to have a bulldog as a mascot. Then again, I don't know what I expected.

My thoughts trail to Poppy—the way they always do lately. The last time I was inside this school, it was for a meeting where I found out she was my daughter's teacher.

Is she still here or has she left for the day?

A small part of me hopes I run into her because I haven't seen her since the last grocery trip I took with Sage.

Scratch that, a huge part of me hopes I do.

As I cross the gym, I count the number of kids who showed up. There are nine of them, and their parents, waiting to play. They are dressed in mismatched sweatpants, and most of them are either wearing superhero T-shirts or glitter.

I can't help the smile on my face because this is exactly what I need.

Whether these kids have played before or not, I hope to provide them with an opportunity to learn the game and perhaps fall in love with it, just as I did at their age. And hell, a chance to keep myself busy enough so I'm not sitting with my racing thoughts.

A few heads turn when they spot me. Two boys I remember, Austin and Archie, are the first to jump up from their seats simultaneously, their eyes lighting up.

"Is this really happening?" Archie asks.

I nod. "It's really happening. Are you ready?"

"I was born ready!" He leaps in the air, picking his glove up off the ground. "Where do we start? When do we play at the barnyard? Can I pitch?"

"I want to catch," Austin adds.

"I'm a killer outfielder," another girl adds.

I laugh. "Whoa there, we have a few things to do first before we get started."

"Fine," Archie grumbles.

"I think the first order of business is getting to know each other, and then from there we can start with the basics to see what we need to work on for future practices. To start, my name is Dallas."

"Westbrook," Archie adds for me. "I knew you looked familiar that day I saw you on Main Street. But I couldn't figure it out then."

"Are you famous?" a girl who looks to be a little older than Sage asks.

Archie looks at her. "He's the head coach for the Staghorns. *The* Dallas Westbrook."

"You know your baseball."

"I live and breathe baseball," he emphasizes. "I've been following you since you were drafted as a starting pitcher. I want to be a pitcher just like you when I grow up."

And that right there is confirmation that this is what I need to be doing.

I didn't understand it a few minutes ago before walking in here. I wasn't supposed to be standing here with a clipboard in my hand and coaching a group of kids when I could barely coach adults to win a game to put us in the playoffs.

But I said yes—the way I always do. Too fast. Too eager.

Just another impulsive Dallas Westbrook moment I can add to my list.

But his response makes me feel like, for once, I've made the right decision.

I get the chance to be a part of this kid's future when it comes to baseball. Hopefully, be someone who can help him learn the game and new skills the same way Clark taught me all those years ago.

"I was so sad when I learned you retired early from your injury," he continues. "Are you okay now? To coach us and all?"

I nod. "I'm ready," I offer the best answer I can. I'm not ready to bring up the pain of losing my ability to play to a group of kids.

A young boy with his hat backward raises his hand. "Is this the real sport? Or is this more like gym class? Because I'm only here for the snacks."

"Or is this like that time I joined the cookie seller club and never got a sash?" a girl with glittery shoes asks.

I clear my throat. "It's as real as it gets, kid."

"I'm Tucker," he says at my side. "You can all call me Tuck. I'm going to be assisting coach here."

I give him a side eye because we never agreed to that.

"And I'm Sage," she chimes in. "This is my daddy, and I love baseball, too."

I watch her as she walks over to the girl who just told us she would be a killer outfielder and introduces herself. My daughter is so bold and brave. She's open to opportunities and making friends. She reminds me so much of myself, and I hate that it's taken me so damn long to see it.

After we go through a round of introductions, the kids all grab their gloves. I hope I can remember their names by the end of practice. "Okay, let's get this started. Since we're inside, we'll focus on the fundamentals, such as catching. I brought some tennis balls to start. Now let's form two lines."

The kids scatter around the gym like a group of cats in a bathtub.

"Two lines," I shout again, gesturing with my hands like an airline marshal.

This is going to be harder than expected.

When they finally form two lines as best they can, I look around. Most of them are ready to go. Except I have one spinning in circles and another lying on the ground.

"Gabe, I'm going to toss you the tennis ball. Put your glove out in front of you to catch it."

He nods in response, but when I let the ball out of my hands as lightly as possible, he leans forward dramatically, and it hits him in the forehead.

"You tried to kill me!" Gabe shrieks.

Tucker laughs off to the side, and I give the kid a knowing look before grabbing another one and tossing it to Sammy, the girl with the brightest glitter shoes I've ever seen. But she misses it completely, moving her glove just before the ball would have landed safely inside of it.

"You throw like my baby cousin," she huffs, stomping her foot and crossing her arms over her chest.

Coaching isn't new to me.

But coaching these kids? I feel completely fucking out of my element.

I decide to let them play catch with each other, standing off to the side and watching as they run around, chasing balls in twelve different directions.

I notice Tucker watching me from the corner of my eye and do a double-take.

"You know, you can stop staring at me like a butterfly that's going to fly away."

He laughs, and it echoes in the gym. "You're nothing like a butterfly. More like a bear. You're like a bear we don't normally see in town."

"I…have no idea how to take that."

Just as he opens his mouth to respond, the gym door behind us opens with a creak. We both turn to find Poppy walking in. My eyes trail over her body without skipping a beat. She's wearing a pair of slim-fit jeans and a T-shirt covered by a yellow cardigan hanging over one shoulder. Once I reach her face again, the sounds of the kids shouting and their sneakers scuffing across the court are drowned out by the smile on her face.

God, she's beautiful.

It's not the first time I thought this, and it won't be my last.

Her hair falls in loose, natural curls, and she tucks some behind her ear as she walks in our direction.

"I'm sorry," she says. "It sounded like someone was being attacked as I was heading out for the day, and I thought I would check it out."

Gabe runs to stand next to me, entirely out of breath. "That was me, Miss Barlow. Coach tried to assassinate me with a tennis ball."

Poppy's eyes widen, and Tucker barks out a laugh. "Pop, this is the most interesting afternoon of my life. I'm so glad I was asked to be an assistant coach because this is going to be the new highlight of the week for me."

"You? Assistant coach?"

I roll my eyes. "He wasn't actually asked."

"Now *that* I believe." She laughs.

And the sound echoes off the walls, vibrating through me. It wasn't loud in the sense that everyone could hear it, but it shook me. Hearing her laugh will always have that effect on me. I want to bottle it up and listen to it whenever I feel I need a smile.

But she stops herself quickly as soon as she sees the corner of my lips twist up. Her cheeks turn pink, and I want to take her face between my hands and beg her never to stop laughing like that.

"Are you okay, Poppy?" Tucker asks her, dipping to her eye level with a hand on her shoulder. "Why are your cheeks all red?"

"Dammit, Tucker," she says through gritted teeth.

"Oh," he says before looking between both of us. "Ohhh! Wow. I mean. Cool. Great."

"No, no. Nothing is going on between us, Tuck," she defends, pointing a finger in his face. "So don't start any rumors around town."

He winks. "Got it, Poppy."

She groans. "I'm being so serious. Dallas is just my neighbor, and I'm Sage's teacher."

And there it is again. The reminder right from her lips that she's off-limits.

I'm about to open my mouth and ask her how her day was, anything to hear her keep talking, but there's a tap on my arm. Looking down, I see Ethan with the backward baseball cap next to me.

"Coach, is it snack time yet? My blood sugar is basically crashing."

My eyes widen. "Oh my god, Ethan. Are you diabetic or something? Why didn't you say anything?"

"No, but I have the metabolism of a horse. Or so my mom says." He shrugs. "I don't know what it means, but I just really like snacks. My dad says that all kids my age are like this. And then my parents argue for about one whole minute about how I can't live off snacks. But little do they know, I *can* live off snacks. I need them to survive."

I stare down at him in disbelief as he rambles through his words.

Poppy and Tucker are both giggling behind their hands next to me, and the weird tension from before is gone.

Thank you, Ethan.

"There's a bag on the bleachers for you," I say, and he scrambles off.

"Seems like you have your hands full with this coaching thing, huh?" Poppy says.

I look around the gym. Kids are throwing tennis balls in all different directions, and others are playing with the plastic bats I brought, so we don't mess up the gym floors with real ones. They're using them like their lightsabers. One kid is even running around the gym with a bat between his legs, as if he's riding a horse. And then there's Ethan trying to negotiate snack time like he's part of a hostage situation.

I nod in response. "I've coached adults before, never making it to the championship game. But I think I've made it."

Poppy tilts her head to the side in question.

"Are you going to coach us or what?" Archie shouts from across the gym, interrupting my thoughts.

I lean in so only Poppy can hear. "I've made it to the championship game of patience."

"I'm not sure you're going to win that either," Tucker mutters.

She rests a hand on my shoulder, the friendly touch igniting the fire within me. "Welcome to elementary school."

And with those parting words, she takes her hand off of me —and I fucking hate it—before she walks away. I stare because I can't help it. I've been drawn to her from the moment I saw her, and this isn't any different.

The urge to run after her is strong, but I have a team to coach.

If that's even what you want to call it.

"Are you okay?" Gabe asks. I had no idea he was even standing so close to me. "Your face is doing something weird."

"I agree," Tucker says, adding fuel to the fire.

I clear my throat and avert my gaze from the door Poppy just left. "All good."

"Oh good," Gabe says, sounding relieved. "Because you look like my dog when my dad brings home a rotisserie chicken for dinner and starts drooling all over the kitchen floor. What a mess that is to clean up."

This is going to be an interesting season.

CHAPTER 14
ARE YOU REGRETTING COMING TO THIS DINNER YET?

POPPY

"Thank you for picking me up."

Lily waves me off from the driver's seat. "Please. It's fine. You can't help that your car won't start."

I sigh, letting my head fall back on the passenger seat's headrest. I could have avoided this if I had just turned off the interior light last night when I got home. I'm so mad at myself for not remembering. But when I pulled into my driveway after having dinner at my parents' house, Dallas was pulling Sage from the backseat of his SUV, likely after another one of their baseball practices. She was asleep in his arms, and I found myself in a trance watching him and how careful and protective of her he was. He held her like a porcelain doll he didn't want to drop, then moved easily to unlock his door without even startling her.

When he closed the door behind him, switching the porch light off, I stayed there for another few minutes just staring, thinking about how attracted to that man I am. There's no use trying to fight how he makes me feel. I told myself it's because he lives close by, and I see him in this light that others normally wouldn't.

I witnessed how he cared for his daughter like a creep from my car.

I witnessed how he coached those kids despite them being a hot mess.

I witnessed him smile more times than I can count.

"Who's all going to be there tonight?"

Lily laughs. "It's Griffin's yearly winter dinner party, Poppy. So our normal crew. Nan *obviously* invited herself. But Tucker has befriended Dallas now that they're coaching together, so I think he'll be there with his daughter."

"What?" I practically shout, sitting up higher in the seat. "I mean…what?" I repeat a few decibels lower.

"Whoa. I didn't expect that reaction to the hot neighbor being invited to dinner at Griffin's house. But now I want to know more."

"There's nothing to know."

"Your reaction tells me that's a lie."

"Lily…" I exhale, trying to find a way to explain this to her. "We can't be calling him the hot neighbor anymore."

"We call it like we see it."

"Okay, fine. But Dallas is…he's different. I can't deny that I'm attracted to him, which is a new thing for me. As you know, I don't do the whole relationship thing. But Sage is my student, and my career comes first. Besides, Dallas is only going to be here for a few more months."

"Perfect amount of time to lose your virginity. Finally," she draws out.

"Lily!"

"What?" she laughs, pulling onto Barlow Drive toward Griffin's house. "Listen, I know you don't allow yourself to get involved in relationships because you hate the small-town talk. You hate the idea of people knowing your business, and if things don't work out, you'd be walking on eggshells."

I remain silent because she's right.

To an extent.

She doesn't know the real reasons why I avoid relationships.

"He's not staying," she continues, putting the car in park in the driveway and turning her body to face me. "There's no harm in allowing yourself this time. It won't take away from your job, and since it's mostly just physical attraction for him, you won't have to worry about your heart getting involved."

That's what I worry about the most.

I don't know what sex feels like or the impact it has on two people together. I'll never admit this to my sister or anyone, for that matter, but I don't even know what an orgasm feels like, as I've never attempted to give myself one. I just don't know how, and it feels weird to me.

"You're overthinking it," Lily says, as if she's reading my mind. "Take it one day at a time."

That's always been easier said than done because I'm always over analyzing everything to try and keep some resemblance of control in my life.

"Yeah, you're right," I admit.

"Now, let's go inside and enjoy this night together," she says with a hand on my shoulder.

I nod and offer her a weak smile.

My sister might be right, but what happens if I give Dallas all of me, I fall head over heels for him, and then he leaves? Then I'll be left picking up the pieces of what I feared all along. Even though I *know* he's leaving, would I be left feeling like I wasn't enough?

Feeling like I wasn't enough to make him stay?

***

"Did you want me to set up the boom box?" Nan asks.

Griffin glares at her. "What do you think?"

"You're a changed man. I was hoping you were open to some music tonight. But I guess not."

"You guessed correctly. This is just dinner, not karaoke night at Seven Stools."

"Can be one in the same and you allow it."

"I think the boom box is a great touch," Tucker chimes in. "Good friends. Good music. Good mood," he draws out the last word.

"Speaking of good friends," Lily asks. "Where's your new bestie?"

"He'll be here. He would never let me down," he says with conviction.

My insides continue to swirl with nerves, but the last few minutes have been laced with anticipation, too. I hate that I find myself *wanting* to see a man. Is this what having a crush feels like? Jesus, I need to get a grip.

The doorbell rings, and everything in my world pauses. I stop breathing as my head turns toward the hallway leading to the front door. Lily leaves to answer it, while I don't move from where I'm sitting on the stool in the kitchen.

I force myself to relax my beating heart, but it does no good, because seconds later, Sage emerges with a stuffed rabbit in her hands that looks like it's seen better days. She seems nervous as she scans the room. When her eyes land on me, she lights up. She smiles wildly and comes rushing over to me, wrapping her tiny arms around my waist where I sit.

"Miss Barlow," she almost whispers. "I'm so happy you're here."

I put an arm around her shoulder as she tightens her hold on me. She's definitely nervous to be around new people and is clinging to the comfort of a familiar face.

"Who's this you brought with you?" I ask, noticing the small stuffed rabbit in her hand.

"Daddy told me this is a dinner party with friends. And Mr. Marshmallow, beside you, is my favorite friend, so I thought I would bring him with me. He also makes me feel less nervous around a lot of people. But I don't need him anymore now that you're here."

I breathe out a relieved sigh. As much as Sage finds comfort in me, I think I see it in her, too. I remember being her age and having a stuffed animal, which was my comfort item. It went everywhere with me.

"I'm so happy you're here," I say.

Lifting my eyes, I find Dallas staring at the two of us from the archway connecting the hallway and the kitchen with a wooden slab with various meats and cheeses on it in his hands. He's rooted there with his eyes laser-focused on the two of us while Tucker says something to him that he's most definitely tuning out. My breath hitches with the intensity of the stare, but I don't allow him to see the effect he has on me. Scanning him from head to toe, I notice he's wearing dark wash jeans and a dark green checkered flannel. I never once pegged Dallas for the type of wear flannels, but seeing it on him and how he has the sleeves rolled up just enough to showcase his strong forearms isn't helping right now.

I bring my bottom lip between my teeth, but catch myself. However, Dallas catches the move before I can stop, and the corners of his lips twist into a grin as he averts his gaze to the ground, shaking his head while making his way in my direction.

Dammit.

"Daddy, look who's here." Sage beams, bouncing where she stands.

"Hey, Poppy."

Two words. A simple greeting that has me practically melting in my seat with how he says them.

I'm about to open my mouth to say something—anything—but Nan steps between us.

"Cheese!" she shouts. "Griffin, charcuter-daddy brought a cheese board! This is what I was saying you were missing. There's nothin' like a wooden slab filled with meat and cheese."

She takes the tray from his hands. "Extra points in my book for this, Dallas."

"Oh, hell yeah," Tucker rushes over to where Nan places the board down. "Extra points for me, too. Even though you were on the verge of being capped out with me."

"You put a cap on your people points?" Nan asks.

"In my defense, Dallas hit max the day I recognized who he was. And then he hit infinite numbers as time progressed." Tucker shrugs.

"The math isn't mathin' for me, but okay," Nan says, popping a cubed cheese in her mouth.

"His math never adds up for me either," Griffin says, shaking his head. "I often wonder how the books at Seven Stools are correct."

"There's girl math, and then there's Tucker math. It doesn't make sense, yet it makes all the sense," Blair adds.

"Damn straight," Tucker says with a mouthful of cheese.

Dallas laughs, and I can't help but do the same. "Are you regretting coming to this dinner yet?" I ask him.

His laughter fades, yet he maintains his signature grin across his lips, focusing all his attention on me. Goose bumps ripple across my skin as he looks me up and down.

"I knew you would be here."

I blush. "That's not really an answer."

He shrugs. "I knew you would be here, so I don't think I could regret coming tonight. I've been waiting for another chance to see you again." He leans in over my shoulder, just enough to keep his voice down, but not enough that anyone would catch on. "I came outside last night to see you, but you had already gone inside."

I rear back to look him in the eyes and my lips part, knowing I was caught creeping on his private moment, bringing Sage inside. My cheeks flame even more than before.

He leans in again. "I like it when you watch me."

I clear my throat, turning away from Dallas so he doesn't see what he's doing to me with every word out of his mouth.

What do I even say back to that?

The last thing I want to do is say the wrong thing and scare him away before this has a chance to be anything.

"Ready to eat?" Griffin announces.

Relief floods me that I didn't need to come up with a reply. I jump from the stool and lose my footing. Dallas grips both of my arms to balance me. His warm palms hold me steady, and I look up at him. The room stops moving around us, or at least that's what it feels like. Everyone who was just here is gone. It feels like it's just the two of us now. Not my family, my friends, or Sage. I don't move, I can't move. With every stare, touch, and word out of his mouth, I sink deeper into my feelings. They fight to reach the surface and for more, while I fight to keep them stuffed.

"Are you good?" he asks.

I nod, looking anywhere but into those captivating brown eyes.

We all move effortlessly around the kitchen island to prepare our plates before bringing them to the oversized table Griffin has set up in his dining room. I feel Dallas's eyes on me with everything I do.

And I like it.

Dammit. I r*eally* like it.

"Can I sit next to Miss Barlow, Daddy?" Sage asks while Dallas follows her with a plate of food for both of them in her hand.

"It's up to her."

"Of course you can," I smile, taking my seat. She sits beside me with Dallas on the other side of her. "And hey, you can call me Poppy while we're not in school. But only outside of school, okay?"

"Are you sure?"

"I'm sure."

"Thank you, Poppy," she whispers, cuddling herself into my arm to give me a side hug. "I love that name. It's so pretty." I look down at her and smile. Sage has imprinted herself in my heart, as all my students typically do, but I think it's different with her since I've been seeing her so much outside of school.

When I lift my head, I find Blair staring at me. But her face doesn't tell me she has questions or is ready to scold me. Her eyes are soft, and they tell me she approves of whatever is happening here. Little does she know, this is how I am with my students. I love and protect them as if they were my kids. But her look only reminds me that he's not staying here, and that realization sends a sharp pain to my chest.

"Everyone hold hands," Nan announces. "We're going to go around the table and say everything we're thankful for."

"This isn't Thanksgiving, Nan," Griffin grumbles.

"Can't I be thankful for the people in my life and all of us getting together finally? It's been too long."

Griffin rolls his eyes. "And we have to hold hands to do this?"

"God forbid you hold my magical hands." Tucker rolls his eyes.

Griffin glares at Tucker. "How are we related? Honestly."

"I have magical hands, too," Sage chimes in. "I can color with them for hours!"

Tucker's eyes widen. "Wait, I want to color with you. I love coloring."

"You would," Griffin murmurs under his breath.

"I have a coloring table and everything in my room. Daddy set it up for me."

"Your dad is awesome!" Tucker says, excitedly punching the air before taking Griffin's hand in his. "Now, hold my hand like you love me, Griffin."

"Anyway," Nan draws out. "Let's begin so we can eat."

"I'll start," Blair says. "I'm thankful for the people around this table right now. Each of you has changed my life in ways I could never begin to thank you for. Finding home here in Bluestone Lakes has become more than expected."

"I love you, sweetheart," Griffin says, leaning over and kissing her cheek. "I'm not good with words like you, but I'm thankful for the same thing."

"Boring," Tucker drawls out. "I'm thankful for the same thing."

"I hate you." Griffin laughs.

"Let me finish. I'm thankful for the people around this table, specifically the Barlows. You already know I'd be lost without you. Thank you for opening up your family to me. I know we're already family." Tucker chuckles. "But now we're more like brothers and sisters, and I love you guys more than you know."

Tucker rarely allows himself to get emotional, but when he does, I want to wrap my arms around him. He had a really rough childhood, and my parents' taking him in helped him overcome so much. He's changed.

Nan clears her throat. "I'm going to piggyback on that. I'm not related to a single one of you, but you've welcomed me into your lives—except for Griffin most days—and you all have brightened my life more than you know."

Sappy Nan has a tear ready to form in my eye, but I blink it away.

"We love you, Nan," Lily says next to her, giving her hand a tight squeeze. "I truly can't figure out what I'm thankful for. Is it weird to say my bakery?"

"Not at all," I tell her, squeezing her hand on my side.

"The bakery has given me something to hold onto. Something I'm proud of. Something that has brightened my days and brought me immense joy."

"It brings us joy, too," I say.

"Is it my turn?" Sage whispers to me on my opposite side.

"Go for it."

"I'm very thankful that you all invited me and Daddy here tonight. But I'm very, very thankful for my daddy. He's the best and gives the best warm hugs, even if he doesn't know how to braid my hair. He's my superhero, and I hit the biggest home run with him as my daddy."

I look up to find Dallas gazing at his daughter with a flat expression. Not quite a smile, but not quite a frown. It seems as if he's processing this information as if it's being told to him for the first time.

"I love my daddy the mostest. And Miss Barlow, too. Oop. I mean Poppy," she adds, facing me. "She loves puzzles just like me. I want to be just like her when I grow up."

I swallow, fighting the emotions that threaten to reach the surface. Sage had slowly been tugging at my heartstrings, and I believe that just pushed me over the edge.

Lifting my eyes, I find Dallas already looking at me, his expression flat yet filled with so many questions, want, and need. It's an uneasy feeling to have him looking at me the way he is, without a smile. My stomach nearly bottoms out at the thought, and I instantly feel sick.

Did I do something wrong?
Have I said the wrong thing?
Is he mad at me for her response?

Averting my gaze to my plate, I smile, trying not to show the table that my thoughts are racing or that I feel completely out of control in this situation. Lily must have caught on just enough that she forced everyone to dig into their food without the need for me to tell everyone what I'm thankful for.

Right now, the answer is her.

Everyone participates in conversations around the sound of forks clicking on plates, while I maneuver mine along the edges of my plate, forcing a smile on my face.

These feelings? These irrational thoughts?

This is exactly what I was afraid of.

CHAPTER 15

CAN POPPY READ ME A BEDTIME STORY FIRST?

DALLAS

Dinner has come and gone in a complete blur.

I can't stop replaying my daughter's words as I push food around my plate, every so often putting pieces in my mouth while I smile and laugh at the conversations around me. I couldn't even tell you half of what was said because my mind is on two people at this table.

"Dallas?" Tucker asks.

"Ya?" I say, snapping out of inner thoughts.

"I asked if you thought we had a shot at a winning league this upcoming season?"

"Are we coaching the same team?"

"Yes. Future champions, baby!"

I shake my head. As hesitant as I was about accepting Tucker's help to coach the kids, he's actually been really great. I like to think it's because it's quite literally a kid himself. He's goofy, relates to the kids, and makes the practices go fast. He claims he doesn't know how to handle children, but they listen to him. Which is more than they do for me.

Archie straight up told me "You suck at coaching," and he's right.

I do.

In every aspect of the word.

But the whole team needs work. This town has been without baseball for so long that most of them don't know what they're doing. Which I expected going into it. I'm eager to help them fall in love with it the way I am, but also know that it's okay if they don't love it the same way.

Regardless, it's something for them to do.

Something for *me* to do.

"I need to make it to one of these practices you got, just to see Talkative Tucker in action." Nan laughs.

Tucker sits up, lifting his chin proudly. "I'm the best assistant coach this town's ever seen."

"You're the only assistant coach this town has ever seen," Griffin adds.

The whole table erupts into a fit of laughter, including Poppy. This is a nice change, considering she's been quiet and has kept to herself most of this meal. It's had me mildly on edge if I'm being honest.

It makes me wonder if I'm the cause.

"I still can't believe you got this up and running again," Nan says. "I know we talked about it, but I didn't think it would actually happen with you only being here a short time."

My chest tightens with her words. It's the same thing I've repeated to myself since agreeing to coach these kids.

Am I crazy for doing this?

Who the hell is going to take over when I go back to San Francisco? I'm scheduled to leave right after the season even starts.

I didn't have all the answers, but I knew in my gut I needed to do this.

"My daddy is the bestest!" Sage adds.

There goes my heart again, beating a mile a minute. All I've ever wanted in life was for my daughter to be proud of me after constantly feeling like luck wasn't on my side. Since stepping

135

foot in Bluestone Lakes, I've never felt luckier than I do here. I'm at peace, even without baseball. I have everything I could ever want.

Looking over at Poppy, I question if that statement still rings true.

Maybe I don't have everything I could ever want because I don't have her.

And fuck, do I want Poppy Barlow in the worst way.

Sage yawns at my side, resting her head on my arm. "I'm tired. My belly is so full that it's making me sleepy."

"Do you want to get going, bug?"

She nods repeatedly.

I look at Griffin, who's looking at Blair like she's hung the moon. I open my mouth to announce our departure, but can't help but revel in their love momentarily. Tucker told me that Griffin used to be the town grump. Everyone hated talking to him because he never smiled and was in a constant state of misery. Seeing him now, there's no trace of that anymore.

Clearing my throat, I stand from my seat. "We're going to head out. Sage is tired."

"Of course." Griffin stands, rounding the table to meet me. "Thank you for coming tonight."

"And thank you for the cheese board," Nan adds.

I laugh. "Anytime. Thank you for having us. I think we needed to get out of the house a little bit and do this."

"You're welcome anytime," Griffin says before turning to Sage. "You too. Oh, and hey, do you like horses?"

Sage looks to me for reassurance, and I shrug. "I think I do. I've never seen them up close."

Griffin barks out a laugh, bending at his waist before crouching down to meet her level. "Well, you're welcome to Barlow Ranch anytime to see the horses."

"Oh my gosh. That would be so, so fun. Can I, Daddy? Can I?"

"I'll set something up with Griffin."

"Yes!"

"Hey, Dallas," Lily says, standing quickly. "Do you think you'd be able to give Poppy a ride home since you live right there?"

"You hate driving people home, huh?" Blair chuckles.

Lily shrugs, and a mischievous grin forms on her face. "It worked last time."

"Lily," Poppy warns.

"What? He literally has to drive past your house to get to his."

I have no clue what the subcontext of this conversation is, but it sounds like Lily has done this before. "It's no problem, Poppy. As long as you're ready to go."

"She's ready," Lily states matter-of-factly.

Poppy stands and, at the same time, lets out a yawn. "I am getting tired."

"Is your belly so full that it's making you sleepy, too?" Sage asks.

"Yes. I'm so full."

"We can drive you home then." Sage nods.

Poppy smiles at Sage before lifting her head to look at me. Our eyes lock, and it ignites everything inside me all over again. It's starting to drive me insane how *one* look from her, and she has me ready to get down on my knees for her, give her the world, and then worship her like she deserves.

My cock stirs to life with that thought, but I force myself to stop.

Not here. Not now.

I clear my throat. "Ready?"

"Ready," she says, grabbing her purse and saying goodbyes.

As hard as it is to control myself around Poppy Barlow, I remind myself that I'm just offering her a ride home.

She lives next door to me.

That's it.

The drive is too short.

I get that it's a small town, but couldn't I have gotten lost or something? *Anything* to continue to feel her all around me in my SUV. Her honey and vanilla perfume lingers in the closed-in space, and I'd like it to stay here for good.

Driving past her house, she snaps her head in my direction.

I smirk, pulling into my driveway. "A true gentleman walks a woman home."

"Can Poppy read me a bedtime story first?" Sage says from the backseat.

"I think she wants to get home, Sage."

"Pretty pleassseeee?"

Poppy's elbow nudges my arm resting on the center console before she leans in close enough that if I lean over and press my lips to hers—

"I'm okay with reading her a bedtime story if you're okay with it, Dallas."

And fuck, my name on her lips.

I need more of it.

What the hell has gotten into me tonight?

"Of course," I say before meeting her over the console, even closer than before. "If you wanted to come inside, you could have just said that." I wink and pull away before doing something in front of Sage in this car.

Poppy blushes, tipping her head down as she brushes a loose strand of hair away from her face. The small move reminds me that this is a terrible idea. She's too young for me, and the last thing I want to do is hurt her when I leave. But dammit, I can't help myself and the pull my body has toward her.

"So that's a yes?" Sage asks, climbing out of the car while Poppy rounds the front. Poppy smiles at her and nods her head. "Yes!"

She grabs Poppy by the hand—a hand *I* would like to hold—and drags her up the front porch. They wait hand in hand while I take the keys out, and the sight before me makes my heart skip a few beats. Sage bounces excitedly and looks up at Poppy like she put every star in the sky.

No sooner do I unlock the door than Sage tugs Poppy in and through the house to her room. I hear her telling her all about her stuffed animals and her collection of books that she can choose from. Poppy's laughter flows through the house.

It's addictive and beautiful.

Everything about Poppy is.

I decide to leave them alone for the bedtime story and go to my bathroom to catch my breath. Having Poppy inside my house is making me tense. It's not even about her reading Sage a story; it's more about her being in my space. She's been a temptation, and I'm not sure I can fight it off any longer. The need to press my lips to hers and confirm if they are as soft as they look is overwhelming. I crave to make her laugh so I can hear it on repeat. I want to strip her and taste every inch of bare skin she's willing to let me devour.

Pressing a palm to my jeans, I will my cock to stay down. Now is not the time to be having these thoughts. It's damn near impossible not to think about this though when she's here. In my house. Reading a bedtime story to my daughter.

"Fuck," I growl before running my hands through my hair and pulling at the ends. Exhaling, I finally have it in me to leave my bathroom.

As I make my way down the hall, I hear Sage giggle and Poppy's voice carry through the house, forcing my steps to slow.

"Clumsy Gloria fell on the turtle," Sage says through a deep laugh.

"The tortoise trotted off with a huff and a grumble, muttering, I'm not a rock," Poppy says in a very animated voice.

A smile tugs at my lips as I stop in the doorway of her room, listening in. It's not the first time I've invaded their private moment. This time feels different. This time feels more intimate. A bedtime story is a big deal for kids. I should know because most of the fights leading up to my divorce were because I wasn't home in time to read one to Sage.

Guilt consumes me with the thought.

My jaw clenches at the reminder, but I'm snapped out of my pity party when I hear them laugh. With one hand on the door frame, I lean in to get a small glimpse of them. I swallow, feeling the air sucked from my lungs as I stare. Sage is cuddled under her blankets with them nestled under her arms. Poppy sits next to her with her back propped up against the headboard and her legs crossed together close to the edge of the bed.

"The end," Poppy reads, closing the book.

"That was such a good one. It was sad in some parts," Sage says, sitting up in bed. "They were so mean to her because she was clumsy. But she made new friends. Like I did when I moved here!" She beams.

"You've made some great friends here."

She pauses, looking from the book to Poppy, and I hold my breath, waiting for the next thing out of Sage's mouth, but it's not what I expected her to say.

"I think you're my greatest friend, Poppy. I really love you so much."

"I think you're one of my best friends, too, Sage." She bops her nose with her pointer finger. "I think it's time for you to go to bed, though. We don't want your daddy mad at me for keeping you up late."

"He won't be mad. He rarely ever gets mad."

Poppy smiles, and it hits me right in the chest. Not just the smile, but the way she interacts with Sage. I know she's her teacher; it's what they do. They're kind, compassionate, and caring. But this is different. She's not being paid to do this. She's doing it because she genuinely cares about Sage.

Stepping into the room to make my presence known, I clear

my throat. Both of them snap their heads in my direction. Sage's face lights up, and it's my favorite thing ever.

Poppy moves to stand from the bed. "I was just getting ready to head out. We finished Clumsy Gloria."

"Wait, one more thing," Sage says, sitting up on her knees in bed and facing me. "Daddy, can Poppy put my hair in a braid before she goes?"

I look from Sage to Poppy, letting her answer because I don't want to keep her longer than she wants to be here.

I mean, I do, but for selfish reasons.

"My hair gets messy when I sleep without one. It's like a rat's nest, my mommy says." Sage laughs, and Poppy does too.

"How about I teach your dad how to do it so you can have one every night?"

I swallow, because I *have* wanted to learn. I hoped to find a video on the internet to teach myself, but it slipped my mind until now.

"You'd do that?" I ask Poppy.

She stares at me for a beat before she nods.

Grabbing her brush from the dresser and Sage's hair tie sitting next to it, Poppy sits on the edge of the bed as Sage positions herself on the floor, sitting between her legs. I take a seat next to Poppy, and the energy shifts, feeling like an inferno.

"The first thing you're going to want to do is brush out any knots," Poppy explains and begins to brush her hair. My eyes bounce between the back of Sage's head and Poppy's face. I can't not look at her. "Once that's done, you're going to want to separate the hair into three sections."

"I love it when someone plays with my hair. Soooo relaxing," Sage says, causing Poppy to chuckle.

"Me too," she answers Sage before turning her head to face me. She opens her mouth to say something, but she pauses when she notices my gaze is already locked on hers. Her eyes trail the features of my face and linger a second longer on my lips.

Does she want me to kiss her?

Because I will.

"Uh. Yeah. Three sections. Even sections," she practically stutters nervously.

I rest a hand on her thigh, silently telling her she doesn't need to be nervous with me. But it startles her. Hell, it startles me with the zap I feel under my palm. It runs through my body rapidly and makes my head feel dizzy.

What the hell?

"What happens after the three sections?" I ask.

"Right," she says, focusing back on Sage's hair, who is completely oblivious to the tension swirling in the room. "You're going to cross the outside section over this big middle section. Which now puts the outside as the new middle."

I watch as she does the steps she mentioned before dropping her hair and placing two hands on her lap. Facing me, she smiles, and I eye her curiously.

"Let's switch spots. I'll talk you through it, and you can practice as I teach you."

"Good idea," Sage adds with a clap of her hands. "You're gonna make the best braid."

Sage scoots forward, keeping her back to us as Poppy and I stand simultaneously, almost butting heads.

She giggles, taking a step back. "Oops. Sorry."

I grip her upper arms with both hands, steadying her, and lock my eyes on her, giving her a knowing look. Her eyes widen because she knows.

Leaning into the shell of her ear, I keep my voice low. "I don't know who ever made you feel like you have to apologize for everything, but they need to be castrated. Immediately."

I pull back, but keep my arms in place, maneuvering her so we switch places. She's so close that her body is mere inches from mine, and the heat radiating from her is intense. It's electrifying. It's…exhilarating.

It's also made me realize that this is the first time, probably in my life, that I haven't acted on impulse when it came to a woman. Because if I had, she would've been in my bed weeks ago. We wouldn't be sitting in my daughter's room and braiding her hair because she'd be flat on her back in my bed right now.

It's a wild and new feeling.

Bluestone Lakes is changing me, slowly and surely.

It's making me want things that shouldn't be in the cards for me.

I know for a fact I'm playing with fire, saying these things to her and touching her the way I am.

I'm playing a dangerous game.

But I've always loved the rush that comes with it.

CHAPTER 16
CAN YOU SHOW ME?

POPPY

I've been braiding hair since I was little, whether it was mine or Lily's. However, sitting next to Dallas and teaching *him* how to braid his daughter's hair is making me forget every single step.

I want to be so pissed at Lily for pulling this stunt and not driving me home. Not too long ago, she did the same thing with Blair when she asked Griffin to drive her home since he also lived next door to her. Her mission was to successfully bring them closer.

I knew that was her motive.

And it worked.

I'm in Dallas's house.

I read Sage a bedtime story, and now I'm sitting here braiding hair.

Disrupting my nighttime routine should stress me out at the moment, but strangely, it doesn't. I feel calm around Dallas, despite how my body reacts around him. His touch is gentle and soft, yet it sends shivers down my spine. His voice is reassuring, yet hot. With every smile, laugh, or touch, my stomach flips, making my breath catch in my throat, leaving me unable to form sentences.

There's so much I want to say to keep him at arm's length.

I've never felt a pull to open up to a man before, but it makes me want to lay it all out there. Let him decide if getting involved with me and my overthinking brain would even be worth it to him.

I release a breath and take a seat next to him. He now sits behind Sage with her hair in his hands.

"Like I mentioned, you're going to divide the hair into three sections. Then you cross one of the outside sections over the middle."

"Like this?" he asks as he does it.

"Yep. Now that's your new middle. Then you'll cross the opposite outside section over your new middle."

"Criss-cross-applesauce," Sage singsongs.

He smiles at her as he tries to do it, but loses his grip on a section. I reach over his forearms to hold the piece. With my eyes fixed on the back of Sage's head, I can sense the shift in Dallas's gaze. He's no longer looking down; all his attention is on my face. I don't need to turn my head to know; my body can feel it.

"Can you show me?" Dallas says. "Like, guide my hands where they need to? Because this is where I always screw it up."

Lifting my head to look him in the eyes, I'm stunned silent when I realize he's mere inches from my face. I can feel his breath on my skin. His eyes dip down to my lips as my mouth parts, ready to say something, *anything*. His tongue swipes across his bottom lip, and that does it. A strange and new sensation floats to the sensitive spot between my legs.

What kind of power does Dallas Westbrook possess that he can make me feel this way with just one look?

"Yeah." I swallow. "I can show you."

He tips his head over my shoulder, grazing the shell of my ear. "Thank you," he whispers, even though we haven't even so much as formed a braid in Sage's hair yet.

With his large hands under my small ones, I don't say anything as I guide them where they need to go. One section over the other, before grabbing the other section and putting it over that one, repeating the pattern under a loose braid that forms in her hair. It's not the best, but it's also not the worst I've seen for someone's first time doing it.

Taking my hands away, my body already misses the heat of his skin. "Then, when you reach the bottom of the braid, you take the hair tie and secure it at the bottom."

"And that's it?"

I nod. "Yep. You did it."

"He did it?" Sage reaches behind her, blindly feeling the braid in the back of her head. "It's perfection!" Dallas grins down at Sage as she stands, putting herself between his legs and wrapping her arms tightly around his neck. "I love it so, so much. And I love you, Daddy."

I watch intently at this intimate moment between them. Dallas's arms visibly tighten around Sage with her words as if they were words he'd wanted to hear her whole life.

"Okay. Now it's time for bed, Sage."

Sage holds up a pointer finger. "Wait, one more thing," she says, before shuffling around the little drawing table on her desk.

I chuckle, and Dallas gives me a playful side eye. We both know this is how it goes with kids. They'll do anything to put off going to bed.

Sage lifts a few papers in her hand, organizing them just right as she stops in front of me. Lifting them, she hands them over to me. "These are for you. I wanted to draw stuff about baseball so you can learn and love it as much as I do. Since we love puzzles so much, we can now love baseball together."

Together.

With each word out of her mouth, whether now or in the classroom, I fall for this little girl more and more.

She spent her time coloring me these pictures and sharing her favorite things with me. I can't help but swallow, fighting back the emotions because I know my students love me. They all express it in different ways. While many of them share their life outside of school with me, never has a student done something like this. Little things like this mean the world to me.

"Thank you, Sage." My words barely above a whisper. "I still have that puzzle for you and will bring it over later this week. If it's okay with your dad."

Dallas nods.

"That would be so epic." Sage smiles from ear to ear.

"I'm going to read through them when I get home. I'm so excited to learn about baseball."

She frowns. "What about your puzzle?"

"I'll read through these after I do some of that. How's that sound?"

"I love it."

"Now off to bed, bug," Dallas says.

Sage jogs into bed, diving under the covers and bringing them all the way up until they are tucked right under her neck. Lying on her side, she nestles into the pillow. I'm standing in the doorway, feeling like I should leave. This moment is very personal to them, and I'm staring because I can't tear my gaze away. He tucks the blankets under her legs on both sides, as if to make it snug as a bug. Then he brushes the few loose strands of hair from her braid out of her face. They stare at each other for a beat before he leans down and presses a kiss to her forehead.

My heart melts.

"I love you," he whispers to her.

"I love you, too, Daddy."

As soon as Dallas turns to leave her room, his eyes find mine, and I quickly turn around as if I've been caught staring. The last thing I want is him thinking I'm a creep for not leaving for their moment together.

My body jumps slightly when I feel his hand on the small of my back, though, guiding me out of her room and into the hallway. He doesn't remove it until we're in his living room. The contact burns my skin right through my shirt, and I want him to keep it there. I want to feel his hands all over every part of me if it makes me feel like that again.

He removes his hand, and I stop, scanning the space when I notice a small puzzle being worked on at the kitchen table. He doesn't follow me as I make my way to it, running my fingers over it and smiling.

"I meant it when I told her I would bring over a puzzle for her, as long as it's okay with you." I turn to face him, and he's standing where I left him, keeping a safe distance. I can't tell if it's for himself or me. "We can...uh...figure out a time for me to drop it off."

"You want to come back over again?" He smirks.

I shrug, as if he doesn't have a pull on me. As if he hasn't tilted my universe in his direction. "For the puzzle."

"For the puzzle," he repeats. "Only to bring it over, right?"

The energy in the room builds with every passing second. Want. Need. Desire. A burning flame in my gut that says I can do this, that I want to do this. That it's okay to want this.

"Dallas," I breathe out, breaking the silence.

He takes two quick steps toward me, hands cupping both sides of my face, forcing me to look up at him. And when I do, my heart begins to hammer loudly in my chest. With eyes boring into mine, I practically melt.

He must see the effect he has on me written all over my face, and his features soften, and that signature smile stretches across his face.

Is he going to kiss me?

He's so close.

Do I want him to kiss me?

Standing here, with his hands on my face, being this close to me—yes.

He opens his mouth to say something, but pauses. Eyes searching mine as if he's looking for something, anything. I don't know what's going through his head right now, but everything in me feels tingly and on edge. The good kind of on edge. A feeling I want to keep feeling.

"Poppy," he says, in a whispered plea I feel against my lips.

He's so close. God, he's so close.

"Yes?"

His eyes fall closed at the same time he releases the hold on my face, taking a step back. I instantly miss the closeness and warmth radiating off of him. The cold creeps in, and I fight back the shiver that runs through me from the loss of contact.

I've never wanted anything like this before.

I've never craved a man's touch.

"It's my turn to say I'm sorry." He shakes his head, averting his gaze. "You made it very clear that you want things to remain professional, and I'm crossing every line here."

I open my mouth to protest, but the words don't come out.

Fear races through me because this is the *exact* thing I've been afraid of with getting into any form of relationship. It's a crippling feeling to think one thing, but feel another. To believe that the man standing before me could want me, but to instantly feel like I'll never be good enough.

Did I do something wrong?

Maybe I shouldn't have come inside and read Sage a book, then proceeded to teach him how to braid his daughter's hair.

I should have gone home.

"I'm going to go," I finally say, barely able to get the words out as I hike a thumb over my shoulder and beeline for the front door.

He nods, shoving his hands in his pockets.

And without another passing glance, I walk out of his house.

CHAPTER 17
YOU SHOULD STAY.

DALLAS

TYLER

How come we always have to be the ones to ask for the updates?

MITCH

Ty, he's probably busy.

TYLER

So you're saying he's too busy for us now?

MITCH

Goodman...stop.

TYLER

No. I'm hurt, and my feelings are valid. Coach moves to a middle-of-nowhere town where there's probably nothing to do and forgets about us.

MITCH

Leave him be.

TYLER
> Fine. I'll leave him be the same way he left us hanging.

> I'm sorry I haven't checked in. *eye roll* I've been mildly preoccupied.

TYLER
> Ugh. Fine. I'll let it slide because Sage is also number one in my book.

> Yes. Because of Sage…

TYLER
> That sounds very vague. I'm no longer mad at you, so you can continue to explain that part.

MITCH
> Normally, I'm not one to egg on our golden retriever friend here, but I also need to know more.

> She's unlike any woman I've ever met before.

TYLER
> I…didn't expect that update.

MITCH
> Wow.

I sigh, staring at my phone in my hands.

He's right. This is a big deal. After everything, I said I was going to be more focused on being present with Sage. My priority is supposed to be *her* because I was never there the way I should have been after the divorce, because baseball was everything to me.

But I can't help myself anymore when Poppy is around.

I can't help but become wrapped up in her, too.

Since the dinner at Griffin's, it's been a struggle to hear Sage come home from school all week and hear her talk about the fun things she did in class, and how much she loves her teacher. Or how they laughed and danced in class to an alphabet song they found online.

I want to see Poppy laugh.

I want to dance with her to anything and everything.

When she was here last week, reading Sage a bedtime story, I held back because I didn't want to move too fast for her. I didn't want to come off too strong. I've been pissed off that I held back, even though it was probably the right thing to do.

There's no denying that I wanted to press my lips to hers and see if she tastes as good as I think she does.

Something I wanted to do the night she was here.

Something I can't help but feel like I *should* have done.

Would it be the worst thing in the world if I allowed myself to act on the thoughts I have about Poppy? To explore these feelings that I can't seem to deny when she's around?

She cares about Sage.

She taught me how to braid my daughter's hair.

Something was there between us.

I put my phone face down on the counter, leaving the conversation with the boys at that, because how do I explain something I haven't figured out myself? All I know is the truth I sent them.

Moving to turn the coffee maker on, Sage enters the kitchen.

"Morning, Daddy," she says with Mr. Marshmallow in one hand, rubbing her eyes with the other. "I'm starving."

"Good morning, bug. What do you want today?"

She giggles. "It's Sunday, Daddy. That means we get the epic breakfast day."

"Ohhh." I laugh. "You want the new Sunday special, huh?"

"Yep. My breakfast belly is ready for all of it. Mr. Marshmallow's tummy is grumbling too."

"One Sunday special coming right up."

"Can I play that block game on your phone and try to beat your high score while I wait?"

"Of course. But you'll never beat my high score."

"That's what you think," she teases as she swipes my phone from the counter.

It's wild to me how kids know how to work technology more than I do most days. It shocks me a bit because Sage isn't usually the kid who likes to sit on the tablet and play games, or watch television, for that matter. She's more of a creative kid. Always drawing, coloring, or making up games in her room with her stuffed animals. Her brain has fascinated me since she's been living with me. I knew she was special, but seeing her in her element daily, I notice it much more.

I move easily around the kitchen, grabbing the pancake mix, eggs, bacon, sausage, and strawberries to slice up. On our first Sunday here, I made her a mini breakfast buffet in the kitchen. It's become our little Sunday tradition on the weekends she stays because April has to work a certain number of weekend shifts.

I successfully juggle all the breakfast pieces at once, taking the last pancake off the griddle and placing it on a plate. Moving everything to our small kitchen table, I feel the ache in my shoulder again. It's a constant pain that comes and goes, but when a flare-up happens, it's almost debilitating. I wouldn't call it that this morning, but the change in the weather here probably isn't helping.

"I'm going to grab some medicine quickly," I tell Sage, grabbing my mug of coffee to take with me. "You can start making your plate."

"Yummm," she says, stabbing a fork into a pancake and bringing it to her plate.

I head to the bathroom connected to my room, grab an ibuprofen to take before it gets worse, and then take a moment to do a few shoulder stretches I learned in physical therapy.

Once I enter the kitchen, I'm stopped dead in my tracks when I see Poppy standing there with wide eyes that rake down my bare chest. I tighten my grip on the mug because I feel it slipping through my fingers under the weight of her stare.

It's the same way I look at her every time I see her.

She shakes her head as if to snap her out of whatever daze she was in, quickly turning her head to the side and covering her eyes with her hand. "Oh my god. I'm so sorry."

"There's nothing to be sorry for, Poppy," I smirk, entering the kitchen fully and grabbing a plate. I don't even bother going to grab a T-shirt, because even though I told myself I should stay away, I love how flustered she is right now. "Do you want some breakfast? I made plenty."

Poppy looks at me, to my door, and then back to me as if questioning what she should do next. My eyes narrow in confusion, and her nervous body language forces me to replay the last time we were together.

Did I do something wrong?

Is this confirmation that she *did* want something to happen between us?

No, that can't be it.

She made it clear she wanted to remain professional.

"No. I don't want to impose. I'm just here to drop off the puzzle. I sent you a text asking if now was a good time to come over, and you said yes." Her eyes trail me up and down, and it sends blood rushing to the one place it should not be rushing to right now. "So I came right over."

Turning to face Sage, she beams. She has my phone, which means she responded to Poppy. Lifting her chin in the air, and a smile so wide that her eyes are almost shut. I can't be mad at her for it; I just wish I were a little more prepared.

"Stay. Stay. Stay," Sage begs with her hands together in prayer. "Pretty please. Daddy makes the best pancakes."

"It does smell great, but I should get going."

"You should stay," I say quickly before she runs out like she did the last time she was here.

Poppy looks from me, to Sage, to the food scattered across the table before her emerald eyes find mine again. The hairs on my arms stand tall, and my body shivers with chills. I can't remember a single time when a woman looked at me that made me feel this much, this intensely. I want to blame it on witnessing every little interaction she's had with my daughter. I want to blame it on the sparks I remember from touching her as I guided her out of Sage's room that night.

But it's all her.

It's all Poppy.

There's no use denying it anymore.

Fuck everything I've said about how I can't do this, because I want to do this.

When someone feels something this strongly, it's the universe pushing you in that direction; your gut is waving the green flag that this is right.

"I'm not opposed to begging," I say with the corner of my lip twisted in a lopsided grin.

"Okay," she whispers. "I'll stay for breakfast."

"Yay!" Sage says, bouncing in her seat with a mouthful of pancakes. "You're going to love all of it. It's so good."

She takes a seat across from Sage. I only have two chairs at the small table, but I don't mind standing. Besides, it'll give me the opportunity to look at Poppy.

"I brought you this puzzle," she tells Sage, handing it over to her.

"A thousand pieces?" Sage asks. "That's a lot. It's going to take me five hundred days to finish this."

Poppy laughs. "No, it won't. I promise. Your mom told me you can finish a five-hundred-piece puzzle in two nights. I believe in you."

She chuckles. "Do you do a lot of puzzles, Poppy?"

"Every night."

"Every night? That's a *lot* of puzzles."

Poppy laughs. "I don't finish it all in one night, most of the time. I keep it on a small table in my living room, which is specifically designed for puzzles, and every night before I go to bed, I work on it a little at a time. Plus, it relaxes me. I have trouble turning my brain off most of the time, so focusing on a puzzle with either a TV show in the background or music helps me turn off my brain for a bit."

"Wouldn't it be so cool if there were a switch on the side of our head, and we could just flip it on or off whenever we wanted to? On. Off. On. Off," Sage says, pretending to flip an imaginary one.

"That would be great." Poppy chuckles, prompting Sage to laugh, too. "Since that isn't real, puzzles do the trick for me."

"Sometimes I have trouble turning off my brain, too," Sage admits. Alarm bells ring in my head because she's never told me this before, and April has never mentioned this.

I stand there, with my plate in my hand, chewing on the piece of bacon I made as I listen in on this conversation. It's the first time since being in Bluestone Lakes that Sage has really opened up more than just surface level.

This conversation has only ignited some dad-guilt in me.

Guilt for all the years I put baseball before her.

Guilt for not taking more initiative to learn the things that go through my daughter's head.

So. Much. Fucking. Guilt.

"Dad, can I be excused to go do this puzzle in the living room?"

"Of course," I choke out, clearing my throat. "Do you need help?"

"No. Besides, you don't know how." And with that, she skips off with the box in her arms.

My mouth hangs open in disbelief, and Poppy covers her mouth in a chuckle.

"I'm sorry for laughing. It was just so funny how she said that."

An involuntary grin forms on my face.

"Sage likes you," I say, even though that's the last thing I want to say.

Poppy bites her bottom lip, and her cheeks pinken. "I like her too. You raised a really great kid."

I wince and don't bother hiding the guilt in my face with her words. Poppy notices, tipping her head to the side in question.

I've never openly talked to anyone about the guilt that eats me alive. I've never talked to anyone about how much it destroyed me when I lost baseball. I've never let anyone see the side of me I want to show Poppy right now. Not Tyler or Mitch. Not April. Not Clark. Taking the seat that Sage was sitting in, I lean forward on the table, bracing myself for the vulnerability I'm about to share with her.

"I wasn't always there," I admit. "April did all of that. I was a shit dad who put my baseball career before my family. I just—"

"You don't need to explain yourself to me," she interrupts, reaching across the table and placing her small hand on top of mine. I don't back away. Feeling her touch is all I want right now. "Whether you were there or not, she's lucky to have you now."

I swallow, letting the guilt settle in my gut. Letting the comforting words from Poppy ease the racing thoughts of how much I've fucked up in my past with Sage. But it also reminds me that the whole purpose of us being here is to fix that.

"Thank you for that, but there's so much more to it."

She's silent this time.

"I know that you know I was the coach for the Major League team in San Francisco. The Staghorns." She nods. "Well, prior to that, I played. I was the starting pitcher, and our team was so close to a championship game. I've had the goal to make it since I was young. I wanted all the titles. MVP. Rookie of the year. Hall of Fame. Baseball was my entire life."

"Was?"

I huff a laugh. "I guess you can say it still is. But I was in a car accident." I swallow, feeling more vulnerable than I ever have. "I ended up hurting my shoulder, and it was enough to end my baseball career."

"I'm so sorry."

"You're killing me." I groan while letting my head fall back.

She laughs, forcing my head to snap up. There it is. The sound I've been desperate to hear again.

I needed *that*.

"To be fair, that's a valid answer when someone tells you about a thing that was taken from them," Poppy says defensively. "While I do say sorry often out of fear of disappointing people, I feel this time was justified."

I nod, wanting to dig deeper into the meaning of her words, but not wanting to pry.

"Well, you're not the one who chose to get in the car with someone who definitely shouldn't have been driving."

Her eyes widen.

"Yeah, it's not one of the most intelligent decisions I've made."

The memory of the night creeps in every so often, like it is right now.

"I knew it wasn't smart to get in the car with the guy. He was a good friend of my teammate, Mitch, and even he was skeptical. But the guy assured us he was fine. Standing steady on his feet, claimed only to have two beers and was good to drive us a few blocks home."

"But he wasn't fine."

I shake my head. "He ran a red light, and another car slammed into the side of the car I was in. I knew then, with the pain radiating through my shoulder, that I was fucked. But it could have been a lot worse if the other car hadn't tried to slam on their brakes before impact."

"Dallas," she whispers, unable to find the words as many people are when I tell them the story.

"Don't say the words, Poppy." I smirk, and her cheeks pink. "It's actually the reason I'm here in Bluestone Lakes."

"Huh?"

"After the accident, I continued playing for a little over a year. I hid the pain from trainers, my coach, my family, and my teammates. I was terrified of losing the game I grew up playing and loved. I was afraid to know life without it. After everyone found out, I was forced into early retirement. The game was over. Playing was no longer an option for me. I wasn't ready to accept that yet, so when the opportunity arose to coach the same team I was forced to leave, I said yes without a second thought. I wasn't thinking about my family, Sage, or anyone else but me."

I swallow past the ball of emotions lodged in my throat. The memory strikes a nerve, and I fight to keep it in check because the last thing I want to show Poppy is that I'm a weak man.

"I jumped into that role without getting over my loss of the game. It only snowballed into all these feelings I couldn't comprehend. I was a shit coach. They deserved better than me. I was an even shittier dad because I still wasn't there for Sage when I should have been, because I still decided to put the game first. I—"

I stop myself there because I feel like I've said far too much. I didn't beg for Poppy to stay and have breakfast with us for me to dump all my past trauma on her lap.

But weirdly, it feels good to get that out.

It feels good to have someone listen to me.

"On the night of the accident, I wasn't thinking about anything other than a big game we had coming up when I got in the car, so my brain was in overdrive. Just as it was when I said yes to coaching the team. Hence why I'm here. To get out of the city and clear my head a little bit."

"I can relate to that a little bit."

"The big game?"

She blushes. "Total honesty here? I don't know much about sports."

"You wound me, Poppy Barlow," I say with a hand to my chest.

She laughs again. "More so about the brain being in overdrive. Except mine is like that *all the time*."

Leaning forward on the table, to bring myself as close as I can, despite the table between us. "Is it in overdrive right now?"

She bites down on her bottom lip and nods.

"I can relate to *that*."

She cocks her head to the side. "How so?"

"Sitting here, with you, is sending my brain spinning, Poppy," I admit. "You've been doing that since I first met you in the coffee shop. There's something about you, and you've flooded every thought in my head since then."

She swallows, eyes wide. "Since the coffee shop?"

I nod. "And every time I've seen you after that, it has only intensified. Then, when I found out you were Sage's teacher…" I shake my head, reliving the memory and how shocked I was to see her sitting there. "It should have forced the thoughts out of my head. Knowing I'm older than you should have stopped the thoughts. Knowing that I'm not the man you deserve should have stopped them. I'm working on controlling this impulsive behavior I seem to have, where I act before thinking things through. But I can't fucking stop with you. I know it's wrong, but if it helps ease *your* racing thoughts, just know it's driving me crazy, too."

"Dallas. You shouldn't feel those things for me."

"Why? Is it because of Sage and you being her teacher?"

She shakes her head, wringing her hands in her lap and nervously looking anywhere but at me. "Because I'm not who you think I am."

"You're not a criminal, Poppy."

A light laugh bubbles out of her, and she finally looks at me again. "I wouldn't be a teacher if I were. But I'm different from a lot of women you've been with."

Her features soften with the last words out of her mouth.

I'd love nothing more for her to elaborate, but I fear I've said too much this morning and don't want to push her into dumping her thoughts on me the same way I just did.

She sighs. "My brain works differently than most people, and sometimes it consumes my life."

I don't say anything and keep my features blank, letting her know she can continue if she's comfortable to do so, or end it there.

"I...uh." She pauses, looking down at her watch. "Should probably get going."

I nod.

She's holding back, and it's understandable. I'm an outsider who doesn't belong here.

Even though I just opened up parts of myself to her that I don't allow others to see, I feel myself holding back, too. I don't want to act quickly with her.

She's different.

In a good way.

I know, deep down, I'm too reckless for her.

And the last person I want to be reckless with is Poppy.

CHAPTER 18
SOUL SISTERS

POPPY

LILY
We need to talk

Is everything okay?

And did you rename this group chat?

LILY
I felt it was right since we're soul sisters and all.

Aww, Lil. That's so cute.

LILY
I know, right? Okay. Listen, you're not going to like this, but tomorrow night you're coming out.

BLAIR
And you can't say no.

Just remember how cute we are with this new chat name.

There's a winter storm tonight.

HOME FIELD ADVANTAGE

LILY
It will be gone by tomorrow morning.

BLAIR
We've been watching the weather.

LILY
And Nan is hosting a winter party at Seven Stools.

Griffin allowed that?

BLAIR
What can I say? He's a changed man.

LILY
Please, Poppy. We really want you to come.

Absolutely not. You know I don't like going out like that. Besides, I'm busy tomorrow night.

BLAIR
Come on. The whole town will be there.

And that's what I fear.

LILY
The parents of students don't care if you have a life outside of teaching. The other teachers are always there, and no one bats an eye.

Fine. But I'm driving to avoid you setting me up with a ride home again, and I'm not staying long.

CHAPTER 19
I'M NOT MOST GUYS.

POPPY

My head's been a mess of emotions since Lily texted me about this party tonight at Seven Stools.

I do *not* want to go.

I agreed to go just to end the conversation. Neither Lily nor Blair understand what I go through because I haven't allowed myself to open up to anyone other than my therapist about how my brain works.

I love my sister. She's been my best friend all my life, and I hate that I can't allow myself to open up to her about who I am. I should be unapologetic about my life. I should be able to discuss it openly without fear of judgment. She's my sister. So she can't judge me for it. Except the little voice in my head screams, *please* don't do it.

It's a terrifying feeling to be vulnerable with someone. It feels like standing in front of them without the usual armor you wear to protect yourself. There's no mask. No rehearsed lines. No shield. It's raw and exposed. It's not knowing if the other person will hold whatever you say gently or crush it.

Deep down, I knew Lily made a good point about other teachers going out all the time. She always makes valid points.

My struggle is allowing my brain to catch up that it's okay to allow myself to get out and enjoy myself outside of being a teacher.

Sometimes I wonder who that even is.

Oh wait, I know. The girl who organizes her spice cabinet three times a week and loses it when things don't go as planned.

I groan out loud in my kitchen, swiping my grocery list off the counter. It's almost nine in the morning, which is the time I always go to the General Store for my weekly trip.

But as soon as I open my front door, I see that the storm hit overnight harder than expected. My car is covered in a thick layer of snow to the point that all you can see is the outline of it. Not a single part of my car is visible. I've been so stuck in my thoughts that I didn't even notice the weather outside the window this morning.

And it's *still* coming down.

Attempting to take a calming breath, I dig through my closet and find my snow shovel tucked away in the back corner next to my brush to clean off the car. I grab my jacket, and when I swing it around my body to put it on, the hood gets caught on the doorknob. Emotions bubble to the surface because when you're already on the verge of freaking out that something isn't going to plan, one minor inconvenience is enough to tip you right over the edge.

Normal people would have closed the front door, put on a comfortable pair of sweatpants, and settled into the couch with a good book and called it a day. A sign from the universe saying, *yeah, you're not going to the store today.*

Not me.

I need to do this.

I step outside, and the cold sends a shiver down my body, but I fight it off. Making my way to my covered car to start brushing the snow away. "Should have put your car in the garage, Poppy," I mutter.

The snow is heavy and thick. I don't think my car is going to make it down the road, even if I do get it cleaned off.

I need to do this.

"What are you doing?" I hear a voice call from across the lawn.

No. No. No. I suck in a sharp breath, staying focused on cleaning off my car and pretending I didn't just hear Dallas shout from his front porch. That last thing I need is for him to see me as such a frantic mess.

Because that's what I am right now.

My body is moving with a need to make this happen.

It's trembling with the thought that I won't make it to the store today, and I'll have to do it tomorrow. I feel crazy, but I know I'm not.

I hear footsteps crunching in the snow behind me, only making me more frustrated.

I don't want him to know.

Why won't the snow stop so I can get this cleaned off?

"What are you doing?" he repeats, this time right behind me.

Looking down at the ground in defeat, I close my eyes, fighting back the tears threatening to break free.

Finally, I spin around to face him.

He's bundled in a puffy winter jacket and a beanie on his head. God, does this man ever not look good? In the snow, his chocolate brown eyes reveal hints of amber, like fire buried beneath the surface. His eyes don't just watch me curiously; they linger as if they know more than I'm ready to say.

"I'm cleaning off my car to head to the General Store," I finally say.

"I don't think your car is going to make it, Poppy. Let me take you. It's coming down pretty hard still, but I have four-wheel drive."

He doesn't ask me why I need to go.

He doesn't make me feel stupid for needing to go right now.

He's simply offering me an alternative.

If I didn't want to cry a few seconds ago, I do now.

"I don't want you taking Sage out in this."

"She's with her mom for the weekend. I drove through this on the way back earlier this morning, and it's not that bad on the main roads."

"Not so bad?" I scoff, looking around with my arms out. "It's everywhere. It's up to my ankles."

He smiles, and dammit, it makes me weak. "The roads aren't as bad as the driveway. It seems that Bluestone Lakes works hard to keep everything running smoothly here. Which is a good thing."

I look from him to our street, and I do see that it's not as deep with snow as my driveway. He's so casual about all of this. What I would give to be as carefree and able to adapt to change so easily.

"I really can take you, Poppy. It's not an inconvenience to me. I want to help you."

"I need to go now," I breathe out, finally looking back at him. "I mean…I'd like to go now. I don't have a lot of food left from my last trip, and I want to get stuff in case the storm gets worse."

He nods. "First, I'm going to need you to put on a real jacket. It's cold out here. Go inside to grab one, and I'll bring my SUV over."

He doesn't wait for any response from me as he turns on his heels and walks back to his house in the snow. I open my mouth to protest, but nothing comes out. I'm stuck where I stand, still in shock that this man doesn't think I'm crazy for needing to get this done in the middle of the biggest winter storm Bluestone Lakes has gotten in years.

When he skips up his front porch steps and disappears into his house, that's when I finally head into mine and do as he asked and grab myself a thicker jacket.

But when I close the door behind me, every emotion I fought to keep stuffed down breaks free. My back rests against the door, and I slide down, bringing my knees to my chest. I cry, and I cry hard, which seems so silly. This is just a damn snowstorm. It's only a trip to the grocery store.

I have some stuff in the pantry, right?

I can make do for another twenty-four hours, right?

I groan because it's moments like this that are beyond embarrassing.

I feel so stupid.

I feel like I wasn't thinking it through and only thinking about how I *needed* to get to the store as part of my routine. I could have—should have—let it go. I knew this storm was coming; I could have gone yesterday before it hit. I could have had more control over this situation, but I didn't.

Now, Dallas will be back any minute to drive me through this mess to get a few things.

Reluctantly, I stand up and grab my jacket from the coat closet next to my front door. The knock at my door sounds almost as soon as I slip it on. I stand there, zipping it up, not ready to face him yet. I know my eyes are puffy and glassy now. I know he's going to see right through me.

He's going to ask questions that I'm not prepared to answer.

Swinging the door open, Dallas looks from the ground to me. His face contorts in confusion as if he can read every emotion written all over my face.

Damn him for being so observant.

He opens his mouth to say something, but it falls short when the soft humming sound of my heater running cuts off. I snap my head to my living room to see that my table lamp next to my couch has also turned off.

"Is that…"

"The power went out," Dallas groans, cutting me off. "Dammit."

My head falls back, my eyes flutter closed, and I go back to hating myself for these emotions coursing through me.

Why can't I stop crying?

"I'm actually okay with not going anymore," I say through

nervous laughter. "I don't know why I thought it was a good idea."

"Do you have any firewood for the fireplace?"

"I do, but you really don't need to do that. I can take care of it. I have a solid thirty minutes before the frost sets in."

He laughs, and it forces a smile on my face while easing the tension inside me.

Something I didn't know I needed from the most unexpected man to enter my life.

"Can I ask you a question, Poppy?"

The tone of his voice is unnerving. I feel my body tense, but nod in response.

"Have you ever allowed anyone to take care of you?"

That…isn't what I'm expecting. I tilt my head in response, confused by why he's asking me this.

"I only ask because I'm free right now. Sage is with her mom, and when I offered to take you to the General Store, I sensed the hesitation in your voice. And now I want to help you get your fire started, and you don't seem like you want help with that either."

"I'm not—"

"Poppy, let me do this," he says quickly. "I *want* to do this."

"You want to start a fire for me?"

He smirks. "There's a lot I want to do, but it's a start."

I've never been the type of girl who is good at asking for or accepting help of any kind. It's the part of me that likes control over how things are done. I wouldn't say I'm a controlling person, because that's not who I am. But there's a certain way I like things done that works for me.

This is only starting a fire, though.

"The firewood is in the garage, to the right of the door," I tell him.

Dallas smiles, ripping off his jacket and placing it neatly over the back corner of the couch before making his way to the garage.

I shrug off my jacket, placing it where I took it out moments ago, lining it up neatly with the others. I don't tend to be crazy over people coming over and where they put things for their short time here, but with my current state of mind, I would feel better without his jacket resting on the back of the couch. Picking it up, the earthy smell of his cologne hits my senses, and I find myself inhaling it to memory as I drape it over the back of the high-top chair sitting at my kitchen island.

Dallas comes back with a towel that he must have found in the garage, tucked under four wooden logs in his arms. The sleeves of his solid black flannel shirt are rolled up, exposing his forearms. The muscles protrude, and damn, he's hot. There's no other word for Dallas Westbrook. I mean, there's probably a lot more words if I had time to think them through, but that happens to be the only one that comes to mind.

Moving quickly in front of him, I move the fireplace screen out of the way for him. He places the four logs, resting on top of the towel, on the ground, being careful not to get any wood on the carpet. My heart races at how much care he's putting into ensuring things remain neat. Kneeling beside the fireplace, he tucks his head in to look inside. While he examines it, I grab a lighter from the end table next to the couch for him to use.

"Have you ever used this thing?"

"No," I admit, chewing on the inside of my cheek.

"But you have wood, and know how to start the fireplace up?"

My cheeks turn fire engine red as I shake my head again. "Griffin drops the wood off for me. To be completely honest, I have no idea how to use this thing. I wasn't even sure it was a functioning fireplace. It's mostly decoration for me."

He laughs, picking up a log and placing it inside the fireplace.

"Why are you doing this?" I ask.

He keeps stacking the logs in perfect formation before brushing his hands over the top of them to remove the dirt.

Anxiety churns in my gut waiting for his response, and then he turns to face me.

"Why not?"

"I mean, is this just you being a friendly neighbor?"

"A friendly neighbor." He raises an eyebrow, and it sounds more like a statement than a question. Then he shrugs. "Sure. Let's go with that."

I stand there, stunned. I have no clue what to think about the way he just said that. It makes me think there's more to this. Do I want there to be more to this thing happening between us that neither of us is acknowledging? Yes. Considering the state of my brain a few minutes ago, this is a crazy revelation.

"I'm a friendly neighbor, Poppy," he continues when I don't reply. He stands from his spot on the ground, erasing some of the space I put between us, but also keeping a safe amount of distance for both of us. "But that doesn't mean I want to be friends."

"Dallas," I breathe out.

"You know…to be completely honest and all." He winks before reaching down and grabbing the lighter that was still in my hand.

If there's one thing about Dallas, it's his confidence in the way he talks to me. He knows what he's doing, and he's willing to do whatever it takes to get it.

It terrifies me.

I wonder if I told him all the parts of me I keep hidden, if he would run.

Would he stay?

Would he still act the way he is now?

There's nothing more horrifying than saying "Here I am. This is the real me. Please don't turn and walk away."

"Dallas," I say, just above a whisper, and he snaps his head around to face me. "I'm not like other women you've dated or been with before," I repeat my words from the last time I said this so he remembers.

171

"I know."

"I'm really different."

"I know."

My chest feels tight, like my heart is inching closer to the surface and ready to burst free from my ribcage. My palms feel sweaty, and I try to brush them on my jeans.

Don't cry. Don't cry. Don't cry.

"I was diagnosed with obsessive-compulsive disorder a few years back," I finally admit. It feels like a foreign language coming out of my mouth as I don't think I've ever said it to anyone other than my therapist. "But I'm in therapy for it and everything. We're working on making it not take over my life anymore," I rattle off quickly, as if to defend myself. "It makes me feel a little crazy sometimes."

Dallas pauses, as if he's absorbing everything I have to say.

There's no disgust in his features, though. He's simply processing.

He feels so far away from where he stands near the fireplace, like there are miles between us. He closes the gap, he's in front of me, lifting my chin to meet his stare with just his finger—a feather-like touch.

"That doesn't make you crazy, Poppy. It makes you human."

I exhale a breath I didn't realize I was holding.

I never knew how much I needed to hear something like that. I'm certain my therapist has said those exact words. This feels different. Coming from Dallas, everything feels different.

He must sense the shift in my body, the way it relaxes with his words. His fingertips trail along my jaw until he's tucking a strand of hair behind my ear. "The most beautiful thing about you is who you are. Besides, everyone's a little crazy in their own way." He laughs. "I don't know enough about your past, and I don't know if there was someone who made you think this way, but Poppy, you shouldn't hide who you are because of it."

A tear breaks free, and Dallas quickly swipes his thumb to brush it away.

"I feel like I've had this most of my life," I admit. "I've always had weird quirks that I thought were normal—lining things up, organizing them, or ensuring that all the light switches are either up or down. I've always been the type of person who, when I can't stop thinking about doing something, I have to do it. No matter what it takes. In college, I knew I wanted to teach first grade. I was willing to do whatever it took to get there."

"I can relate to that."

Dallas makes me feel safe enough to let the walls come down in front of him. There's this pull in my chest to let him see all the parts I've kept locked away from the world. I want Dallas to understand me, and with everything I've just told him, he hasn't so much as flinched. He's not judging me or running away.

His steady presence makes me feel like I can keep sharing more.

Like I don't have to carry all of this on my own anymore.

"I had a boyfriend at the time," I continue. Dallas stiffens at my words, even though it's in the past. "He basically said the way I prioritized my career and daily routine was just too much for him. He made me feel like I wasn't enough. And maybe I screwed up. Maybe I should have put him first—"

He holds up a hand to stop me. "No."

I tilt my head to the side in question.

"First of all, fuck him." That forces a weak laugh out of me. "Second of all, if he cared about you in any sense of the word, he would have pushed you to be the best you could be. He would have pushed you to see the success you craved. It makes my blood boil right now that you've spent all this time thinking you're less than what you are because of that."

All this time, I've been terrified of being vulnerable with anyone.

Dallas is showing me that it's not a weakness. It's the courage to be seen as you truly are.

When it's met with care, the way he is doing right now, it's like the weight of the world has just lifted off my shoulders. It feels like exhaling for the first time in a long time.

"I guess, because of that, I thought most guys wouldn't want to deal with something like that."

I try to look away, emotions ripping through me like a tornado.

He grips my chin, forcing me to keep looking at him.

"I'm not most guys."

I swallow, not even sure how to process that.

It's not like it's new information for me. I *know* Dallas Westbrook is different.

So much different.

"If I were like other guys, I would have kissed you by now. I would have had you in your bed and on your back ten minutes ago, forgetting your own name."

"Dallas," I whisper, letting my eyes flutter closed.

There's so much more I want to say, but all my words stay stuck in my throat.

I want him to kiss me.

I want to feel his body on top of me.

I want things I've never felt before, and only from him.

Just as I'm about to admit any of that to him, the lights turn on, and I hear the heater start running again. We both look around before we turn back to one another. The air between us is thick. There's so much I want to say, and so many unspoken words linger on his tongue. I can tell by the way his eyes darken with each passing second.

"I should go see if everything is up and running again at my place. I had a load of laundry in the washer when the power cut out," he says before leaning down, his lips dangerously close to my skin. "And before I finally dare to act on everything I just said I would do."

I smile, thinking about all of it.

The feeling of his lips on mine, and him taking me to my room.

I'm not ready for any of it.

But I want to be. I want to lose everything to this man in front of me.

He lets his lips graze my cheek as he pulls away, not fully pressing them to my skin, but it's enough to make my body shiver and my heart pound in my chest.

"I'll see you soon, Poppy."

And as he walks toward the door, he gives me one more passing glance and a wink before closing the door behind him. As it clicks shut, silence engulfs the room. For once, it's not heavy or crushes me like a ton of bricks.

My thoughts aren't spiraling.

There are no voices in my head telling me I'm not enough.

Dallas didn't try to fix me. He didn't show me pity. He just saw me for me. I didn't realize how loud the war zone in my head had been until he quieted everything.

For the first time in a long time, I don't feel like I'm drowning.

I'm just breathing.

And it has everything to do with Dallas Westbrook.

CHAPTER 20
AM I JEALOUS NOW?

POPPY

Walking into Seven Stools tonight feels different.

There's a lightness in me after the conversation with Dallas earlier today.

I didn't want him to leave, but his leaving is exactly what I needed to understand the power behind his words.

I was able to finish laundry, vacuum, and wash my bedding—all with a smile on my face.

He brought calm into my day, and it's carrying over into tonight.

He didn't leave because he thought I was crazy; he left because he understood.

Something no one else does. I mean…not that I've allowed anyone the chance.

I wonder if I opened up to my sister or even Griffin, if they would be as accepting as he was? Such a stupid question, because my siblings love me no matter what. However, it's not something I want to find out right now.

Tonight is Nan's winter party at Seven Stools. The town successfully cleared the roads enough to get everyone here. And I'm pretty sure *everyone* is here. I'm willing to place a heavy bet that Nan had something to do with the urgency of getting the roads cleared for everyone. Griffin is probably covered in hives over it because he hates crowds like this, even if he knows it's good for business.

Taking in the bar, it feels like the storm outside was brought in here. Paper snowflakes that Nan definitely cut herself hang from the ceiling, speckled with glitter. She's set up the karaoke bar in the corner, complete with sheer white drapes and twinkle lights, creating a backdrop for anyone brave enough to get up and sing. In the other corner is a small display of mini water bottles with custom labels across them that say *melted snowman* on one end of the table, and a mini hot cocoa bar situated on the other.

Party planning is kind of Nan's thing, and she's damn good at it.

Everyone here is familiar to me, being it's a small town, but it's the set of chocolate brown eyes locked on me that has my pulse beating rapidly in my chest, thrumming like a bass drum. Dallas doesn't blink or look away. It pulls at something beneath the surface, screaming that I want him in a way I haven't allowed myself to want something before, making the world around me narrow to a single face, a single breath that's not yet mine.

The longer I stare, the deeper it claws at me.

He's dressed so casually tonight. Where half the town is dressed in jeans and button downs, he's wearing his signature T-shirt that might as well be painted on his skin—showcasing every hard-earned muscle on his upper body.

Gravity pulls me in his direction, demanding to feel his hands on me in some way, shape, or form.

But I'm snapped out of my bubble when Lily finds me, wrapping her arms around me. "I'm so happy you're here. Eek! This is truly going to be the best night ever now. I mean, look at this place," she says, throwing her arms out to showcase the bar. "Nan outdid herself here."

"She really did. I've never seen it look this festive."

Scanning the room again, my eyes land on Dallas. I look from him to Lily and back to him. Lily notices, nudging me lightly with her elbow. "Oh, yes. I see our hot neighbor is out tonight."

"He's *my* hot neighbor." I laugh, but then choke on my own words because where did that come from?

She must pick up on it because she raises an eyebrow. "So we're finally admitting he's hot?"

"He's all right."

"Whatever you say. Anyway, he told us a few minutes ago that he wouldn't miss it when he found out the whole town would be here."

"Yeah?"

"I guess that he thought the whole town meant *you* would be here."

"I don't see why he would think that."

"Tucker told him." She laughs, and I stay silent. Lily eyes me curiously. "And with the way that man is staring at you, I can see why he wouldn't want to miss out on seeing you. Even *my* skin is burning from the intensity of it. I'm surprised you're not on fire right now."

Oh, but I am, Lily. I am.

"I guess I'll go say hi?"

"You better do more than just say hi, Pop." She laughs. "I'll go get us a drink from Griffin."

We part ways, and I don't make it two more steps before a voice stops me in my tracks.

"Poppy?" Turning around, I find Ben grinning, with a glass of whiskey hovering close to his mouth as his eyes trail my body up and down. "I didn't expect to see you tonight, but I'm so happy you're here."

"Hi, Ben," I say, returning the smile.

"I must say, you look gorgeous tonight, Poppy."

Hearing him say my name makes my skin crawl because I know this is his way of flirting with me outside of school when we're working. It's never made me uncomfortable before because I've never felt anything toward him. I still don't. I've been immune to his light attempts at flirting, and now it makes me feel sick over the way his eyes travel my body.

I know I'm just as safe here as I am at school because this is my brother's bar, but I still hate it.

"Thank you," I finally reply, averting my gaze in hopes he picks up on my disinterest.

"Let me buy you a drink?" he says in a questioning tone as he places one hand on my shoulder.

Absolutely not.

"Thank you, but my sister is grabbing me one." I point somewhere in the direction of the bar, scanning the area and looking for Lily to be my saving grace right now.

"Then maybe you can save me a dance tonight?"

I don't answer him while I still look for my sister, but my eyes latch onto Dallas over Ben's shoulders. There's venom in his stare as he leans one elbow on the bar, his jaw set in a sharp line. But he's not looking at me, he's looking at the back of Ben's head.

Is Dallas jealous?

"I'm actually here with my sister and friends tonight," I reply, still staring at Dallas.

"Well, I'll be here all night if you change your mind." He winks and turns to walk away.

I watch him retreat, only to look back at Dallas and see that he's no longer watching me. He's now engaged in a conversation with Mindy, who's laughing next to him, likely over something he's said. She's standing so close, and I trail their movements. He stands there with a drink in one hand and his elbow resting on the bar top. She has her hand on his forearm, and he doesn't seem to be making a move to back away.

Is he into her?

Are they flirting with each other?

Am I jealous now?

Yes. I'm irrationally jealous. I've told him we had to keep things professional, but so much has changed. I felt the shift earlier today when I opened up to him. He's holding back because he respects my boundaries. He seemed to understand.

Lily returns with a drink for me, and I welcome it, sipping it through the straw as if the liquid is the air that I need to breathe.

"Jesus, Pop." She laughs. "I don't think I've ever seen you finish a Moscow mule that fast before.

She's right. I feel dizzy from drinking it so fast.

"You said it's a winter party, no?" I smirk at her. "Anddd you told me I need to have some fun tonight. So this is me having fun tonight.

"There's my sister. I've been waiting for this side of you to come out for a long time. You've kept it hidden for too long, babe."

Again, she's right.

Now's not the time to tell her why, though. After everything today, I feel the urge to open up to her, too. I'm mildly addicted to the free feeling I've felt all day of not hiding from the world. While I still am in a sense, putting it out there to Dallas seemed to flip a switch inside of me. I want people to see me for who I am, the way he did. I want my sister to understand why I've been this way for so long.

"Let's get you another." She drags me to the bar, and of course, it's almost directly next to where Dallas and Mindy stand. The hairs on my arm stand tall being this close. I can't help but watch him out of the corner of my eye.

Tucker wipes the bar top in front of us. "There's my favorite cousin."

"Tucker," Lily warns.

"Oh, hey. I didn't see you there." He chuckles.

"Liar."

I laugh at the two of them before holding up my drink, signaling I'll take another.

"So it's that kind of night, huh?" Tucker nods his head repeatedly in approval. "Anything for you, Poppy."

While we wait for our drinks, I can hear Mindy's laughter echo around me. It feels like all the sound has drowned out to nothing but their conversation.

"We should get together outside of school sometime," Mindy says.

"Maybe."

"Is your wife around?"

It's odd that she's asking that particular question. It makes me feel even more disgusted by the whole thing. If you're going to flirt with someone and have your hands all over them, you should at least determine if they're married.

I see movement from the corner of my eye as he holds up his hand. "No wife."

"Oh, that must be so hard," Mindy says in a sympathetic tone. "You have my number. You know, just in case you need anything or help with Sage. I mean, you can always use it if you need some company, too."

He shifts next to me, and I feel it before I see it. His eyes are on me, but I refuse to look and acknowledge it. Dallas leans on the bar with both elbows now, facing me, knowing I'm standing inches from him. I don't want to see the look in his eyes. I don't want to get myself trapped in his orbit while Mindy stands right there.

But I feel him turn away again.

'I'm good," he says to Mindy. "But thank you."

And then he walks away.

Not even waiting for a response from her.

No passing glance in my direction.

Tucker slides out drinks across the bar, and I take another long sip, turning my body to Lily. She has a smug grin on her face.

"What?"

"That man fucking wants you."

"Oh, Christ. Nan is on top of the bar," Lily says, laughing so hard you can barely understand her.

Blair and I look up and see she's standing there with a microphone in her hand while the music from the karaoke machine blasts through the speakers. Griffin is shaking his head on the ground behind her, and if smoke could come out of someone's ears literally, it would be fuming right now. I can tell he's nervous that she's going to fall face-first off the bar.

Nan sings the lyrics of "Can't Fight the Moonlight", at the top of her lungs.

My stomach hurts from laughing so hard at this point as she continues, shaking her hips as if she's a twenty-year-old working at the *Coyote Ugly* bar.

She brings her hand to her ear, signaling for everyone to join her in the last part. *"Can't fight the moonlight."* And the entire bar erupts with the final words of the chorus. She points to where Lily, Blair, and I stand. "Get up here, girls."

I shake my head, waving my arms to say no while Blair jumps up and down with her arms in the air, ready for this moment.

"I think I said it already, but it's worth saying again, this is the greatest night ever," Lily shouts. "Let's go!"

"Hell yeah," Blair says in approval, making her way behind the bar. She pauses to give Griffin a pair of puppy dog eyes that beg for him to help her on top of the bar. He visibly groans, but helps her up anyway after pressing a kiss to her forehead.

She moves in sync with Nan, swaying their hips side to side with their arms around each other. Everyone is having the time of their life watching them up there.

Lily tugs at my wrist. "Let's go up there, Pop."

"Oh no. I can't, Lily."

She turns to face me. "Poppy, you're having the most fun I've ever seen you have. If you're worried that other people will see you up there and say something about you being a teacher, you truly have nothing to worry about. Besides, I just saw the fourth-grade English teacher beeline it for the bathroom, covering her mouth to puke. No one gives a shit."

I do. I say to myself.

Glancing around the bar, she's right. The way she always seems to be. No one cares right now. Everyone is dancing, grinding their hips against each other to the music as if Seven Stools is a nightclub all of a sudden.

The last thing I need to be doing is dancing on a bar.

But it's my sister.

It's Blair

It's Nan.

It's my brother's bar.

It's all in good fun.

You know what? Screw it.

This time, I'm the one to grab Lily by the wrist, guiding her behind the bar for Griffin to give us a boost, too. I can tell by the look on his face that he hates everything about this, but obliges us anyway. He helps Lily first, and she quickly joins Blair, moving and swaying their hips with the beat as Nan continues belting the words of the song.

"Well, this is a first," Griffin says with a smile.

"Don't start," I joke back, lifting myself to join them on the bar.

Music thrums in my chest, and my hips sway on their own. I feel lost in the music, and I love it. For the first time, there's no negative thoughts flowing like a raging river through my head. It feels good. It feels free. Lifting my hands in the air, I close my eyes. Feeling the music reverberate through my body, I can't help the huge smile that takes over at how much damn fun this is.

Nan keeps singing, her words louder and louder as the energy in the room grows. They love this. *I love this.* When I open my eyes, they immediately connect with an intense stare from Dallas on the other side of the bar. We stay locked in that moment as I move my hips in a way I've never moved them before, letting my hands trail down my neck, down my body, until they find their place on my hips, still moving and swaying.

I don't know who I think I am right now, but I'm addicted to the way he's looking at me.

He's looking at me like I'm the only woman in the bar.

He's looking at me like I'm the answer to everything.

The only thing missing from his stare is his signature smile. There's nothing but a hard set in his jawline, likely grinding his molars together. It's the same jealousy as before, written all over his face. It's not until he averts his gaze to his left and then back to me that I do the same.

Ben is watching me, and it instantly makes me feel uncomfortable. Did he see that mini performance I just put on for Dallas to see? He had to have. *Dammit*. It felt so good having Dallas watch me, and letting the music seep into my skin, that I didn't even think about Ben being in the room.

I'm ready to jump off the bar and hide because I don't want to give Ben any more ideas about flirting with me more, but I'm saved by the music ending. Griffin helps guide each of us off the bar, and I can tell he's relieved the song is over.

I quickly excuse myself to the bathroom. Once inside, I splash some water on my face and look at myself in the mirror to see if any of my mascara has rubbed off under my eyes. Even with the heat blasting to keep it warm from the winter weather outside, I'm shocked I don't look like a sweaty disaster after that.

When I exit the bathroom, my body collides with someone. Their hands grip my forearms, and I instantly hope it's Dallas when I look up, but I know it's not.

My body knows it's not.

"There you are," Ben says. "I was looking for you."

"Yeah?" There's a nervous squeak to my voice. "Sorry, I had to use the restroom."

"I was wondering if you'd be up for that dance I asked about earlier tonight."

I swallow, looking around to see if anyone else is here. Ben isn't that type of guy, but he's had some drinks in him. My gut is throwing up all sorts of red flags for this situation, as I feel backed into a quiet corner in front of him.

"I don't think that's a good idea. You know, since we work together and all."

He takes a step toward me, and I try to move back, but a wall stops me. "Come on, Poppy. You know the gym teacher and the fifth-grade science teacher are dating. It's a small town, so it's inevitable that some people might be together and work together." He reaches up to tuck my hair away from my face, and I flinch. "You can't help who you fall for."

"I just don't think it's a good idea, Ben."

"Oh, stop. It's fine."

"She said it's not a good fucking idea, *Ben*."

My head turns to the voice, and Dallas stalks down the tiny hall toward us.

"Ah, Dallas." Ben lights up. "My man! How are you?"

Dallas stops next to us, eyes bouncing between us, and I can tell they linger a little longer on me, ensuring that I'm okay. "I'd be a lot better if you weren't cornering Poppy here in the hallway," he says to Ben, but doesn't take his eyes off me, as if I'll disappear if he does.

"It's not like that." Ben laughs, oblivious to what's happening here. "Poppy and I go way back. Don't we?"

I shake my head, but Ben doesn't notice.

"Oh!" Ben continues to Dallas. "Let me buy you a shot, Dallas. I've been wanting to for a while now, as a welcome to town kind of thing. And because you're...well, you're Dallas freaking Westbrook."

"Why don't you run off and do that," Dallas tells him.

"Oh, hell yeah," Ben says, running back to the bar and leaving us alone.

Dallas repositions himself across from me, the same way Ben just was. My back is still pressed against the wall, but the discomfort from before is gone. It's been replaced with a calm. It feels like I can breathe again.

"Are you okay?" he asks flatly.

"I'm fine."

His molars grind together as he glances down the hall. I feel the effects of the alcohol mixed with his presence through every inch of me. I'm not even thinking when I reach up, running my fingers along the sharpness of his jaw, forcing him to face me again.

"This is all hard and tight. Are you angry?"

"Yes," he says quickly. *Too quickly.*

We stand there in silence. Gravity pulls my body off the wall, putting us closer than we were before. I have to angle my head up to get a good look at him.

"I'm okay, Dallas. But curious minds would like to know… were you jealous?"

Damn, alcohol mixed with a clear mind is making me bold.

He grumbles some kind of denial under his breath, but I can't make out what it was. He leans in, letting his hand fall to the wall over my shoulder, leaning down and pressing his lips to the shell of my ear. "Do you really want the answer to that?"

He pulls back, locking eyes with me again. Instinctively, I bite down on my lower lip, which forces him to look down. My breathing picks up—labored and uneven. I couldn't even form a coherent answer if I tried because everything about this man stirs up new and strange feelings in my body.

He's still close. So damn close that I wonder if he will kiss me this time.

Please. Do something. Anything.

I nod, answering the question he just asked.

"I'm trying really hard to be a gentleman here."

I know I want this when I shouldn't. I want to feel his lips on mine and taste whatever is on his tongue. It's wrong because I'm

Sage's teacher, and it's so unlike me. Panic surges at the thought, but I keep everything under control the way I always do.

"And I'm trying really hard to be professional," I say back.

He stays silent, just staring. The two of us are in this tiny hallway with no one else. My back to the wall, his one arm caging me in. If anyone rounded the corner and caught us, it would look exactly as it seems.

Two people fighting to remain in control and not cross the boundaries.

But my head is screaming, *kiss me, dammit.*

He's still frozen in place, heat radiating off of him, refusing to break the intensity of the stare. The longer he looks at me like this, the thicker the air feels around us. I'm ready to break. I'm ready to end this inner fight with myself. It's the first time anyone's ever looked at me like they're obsessed with me—intoxicated with me. And I know it's not the alcohol.

What if I just leaned in?

What if I initiated it?

He's trying to respect my boundaries, and I'm now saying screw them.

I push up on my toes, resting my hand on the side of his face. A move he's done with me before. He leans into my touch, and he knows. He knows I want this. I can see it in the way his eyes darken like the storm outside. I trail my hand down until it's on his neck, feeling his pulse pound rapidly under my touch, and then he presses his forehead to mine.

"Not here. Not like this," he whispers softly.

I pull away, letting my back fall into the wall as if it would give us some space. Fear crushes me like an elephant sitting on my chest. I went too far. I'm too much. He knows the most vulnerable parts of me, and now I've scared him away.

Then he surprises me when he takes my face in his hands, holding me in place, his thumbs brushing the apple of my cheek.

"Is this okay?" he asks.

I nod eagerly. It's more than okay. His hands are the reassurance I need right now. His lips are the confirmation I want, but I won't push it.

"The first time I get a taste of your perfect, soft lips, it won't be in this tiny dark hallway at a bar, Poppy. When I say not here, that's what I mean. Trust me when I tell you this, I will have my taste of you. There isn't a part of you that I don't want to taste." My breath hitches at his words. "But you're in control here. I may be stopping it right now, but next time—"

A group of girls comes barreling out of the woman's bathroom, laughing, and it pulls us both away as if we've been caught.

He rubs the back of his neck. "I'm sorry."

This time, it's my turn to smirk at him, reversing the roles.

He's smiling, and it's exactly what I've been looking for all night. *That smile.* I side-step him, retreating down the hallway. But before I round the corner for the bar, I turn around one more time, and he's still standing where I left him.

"Next time," I say, grinning.

He shakes his head, still smiling from ear to ear.

Not here. Not like this.

I turn around and make my way through the crowd with only one thought on my mind.

Don't you dare fall in love with him, Poppy.

CHAPTER 21
I'M PLAYING WITH FIRE.

DALLAS

I never thought I'd be the person to hold so much restraint.

Now, because of it, I'm pacing my living room after getting home from Seven Stools. I turn the TV on just to hear something, only to turn it off again because it doesn't help take my mind off Poppy. I told her I wouldn't kiss her, not like that, but my skin is still crawling with the need to taste her.

I should have fucking done it.

I feel like I can't breathe or even think straight.

Coming to a halt at my front window, I look outside and across the lawn to her house. Her front porch light glows a soft yellow, illuminating the snow still sitting on the ground around the porch. A light is on in her living room, telling me she's home —she's awake.

What would happen if I went over there right now?

I wouldn't be able to control myself around her anymore.

That's the only answer I have.

Without thinking, I put on my jacket and boots, closing my front door behind me. I walk across the yard in ankle-deep snow because I can't wait another minute to see her again.

Poppy is the high you crave with every fiber of your being.

You need it more than your next breath, even though you know you're going to crash in the end.

I lift my hand to knock, but it opens before I have the chance.

"Dallas," she breathes out softly, almost as if she's been waiting for me.

As my eyes trail up her body, my breath catches in my throat. She has a smile on her face—a welcoming and friendly one. Alarm bells ring in my head that I shouldn't be here. I need to stop putting myself in these positions with her before I cross a line that she will despise me for.

I'm playing with fire.

But I'll gladly burn myself over and over again with her.

She steps back, opening the door wider, allowing me into her space. And I follow, because I'm learning that I'll follow Poppy anywhere.

There's a shift in the air the moment I cross the threshold of her front door. It's something I can't quite explain. It feels like exhaling after you've been holding your breath for so long. It's not about the decorations, the furniture, or the lighting. It's deeper than that. It's like my nervous system recognizes the space before my mind does. The stillness wraps around me, but it doesn't feel cold. It feels warm like a thick blanket.

It feels like…home.

Poppy disappears down the hall without a word. My eyes settle on the corner setup she has, with a lamp hanging over a table and a single chair. A puzzle is scattered across it as if she just recently started a new one. Walking over to it with the comfort her space brings, I pick up a piece, assessing what she's started. The one piece I picked up is the missing puzzle piece for a small corner section she's been working on. Smiling, I put it in, letting it fit perfectly.

When she returns with a cardigan over her T-shirt, I clear my throat as if I've been caught.

"I thought you weren't any good at those?" Poppy smirks.

With a smile growing on my face, I shrug. "I've been practicing with that puzzle you brought over for Sage."

"You what?"

"I figured if it's something you like to do, that I could learn to like it, too."

"And?"

"It's oddly therapeutic. I don't hate it," I say with a chuckle.

"That...makes me oddly happy," she admits.

Damn, the hold she has on me tightens. I don't move from where I stand because if I do, I'll end up throwing her over my shoulder, finding her bedroom, and having my way with her like I've been so desperate to do.

"Listen, Poppy. I didn't mean to intrude on your night like this, but I wanted to talk about earlier at the bar."

Her lips part, and her eyes widen, but she catches herself, schooling her features to remain neutral. "You don't have to explain anything. I get it. Alcohol sometimes makes you say things you don't mean."

Is that what she thinks?

Does she think everything I said about it not being the right place, the right time, was because of alcohol?

She averts her gaze, making herself busy by folding the blanket she had on the couch and draping it neatly over the back corner.

"Poppy," I say her name a little louder this time, begging for her attention to be back on me. Begging her to look at me.

She spins around, eyes meeting mine, and they're...glassy?

No. It can't be.

"I understand, Dallas."

"Poppy," I say her name much softer this time, meeting her where she stands. "Is that what you think?"

She closes her eyes, chest rising and falling as she sighs.

"It's fine, Dallas."

And then it hits me. I think back to everything she's admitted to me. I know very little about how her brain works, and when she told me all there was to know about herself, it didn't scare me or make me want to run. I remember a few friends from college who also struggled with the same thing she does. One of them was particular about needing stuff in a specific order, and another always feared that we judged them for their quirks.

It doesn't scare me.

Poppy doesn't scare me.

Reaching up, I rake my fingers through her long hair because I can't help but touch her in some way whenever she's around. "It's not fine. The last thing I ever want you to think is that I said those things because of some whiskey in my system."

"But—"

I cut her off with a finger to her lips, soft under my touch. The same ones I want my mouth on. "I didn't drink tonight, Poppy. I was already drunk on being in the same room as you, watching you dance, and laughing with your friends. I'm inebriated in the best way possible, without a sip of alcohol."

Bringing my other hand up, I cup her face with both hands and tilt her head just right so she stays focused on me. Her skin feels soft under my touch, but it burns every part of my body. Our heart rates are pounding erratically but in sync. I can tell from how it feels under my hand.

"Is your brain in overdrive right now?" I breathe out, dangerously close to her lips.

She nods her head in my hold.

"Talk to me."

"I...uh. This. Right here. You did this before."

"Holding you?"

"Yes."

"And what about it?"

"I thought"—she closes her eyes—"I keep thinking you're going to kiss me when you do this."

I bring my face closer to hers, letting my lips graze just barely above hers. Fuck, I already know she's going to taste so sweet.

This is dangerous. I'm playing with fire. I'm going to get fucking burned.

I also no longer give a shit.

Because if Poppy wants this, then I'll give her everything.

"Is that what you want me to do, Poppy?"

With her eyes still closed, refusing to look at me, she practically moans. She *moans* at the tone of my voice. And it goes straight to my cock, with nothing but a pair of sweatpants to keep it down.

She doesn't move an inch from the hold I have on her face, so I let my thumb caress the apple of her cheek. She finally looks at me. Emerald green eyes bore into mine and filled with so much fire.

"I didn't think I did. I tried hard not to want it. This isn't who I am, but to answer your question…yes. I do, but also understand if you don't want this."

I've pictured this moment since I first laid eyes on her at the coffee shop. I've played this moment in my head many nights when my head lay on the pillow and I couldn't fall asleep.

Every glance, every touch, every breath held was mutual. Just two people circling the same gravitational pull, waiting for their orbits to align.

She doesn't move. She doesn't pull away.

My heart is beating so loudly that I swear she can hear it.

She stares at me, waiting on bated breath for my next move, and looking at me like she wants to be undone by me.

God help me. I'm so gone for her.

"Fuck it."

Leaning in slowly, her breath catches. My stomach swirls with anticipation as her eyes flutter closed, and that does it. I press my lips to hers, keeping both hands on the sides of her face.

The world around me explodes.

But not even the fantasy of kissing Poppy prepared me for this.

It's not fireworks or sparklers in the night. This is a kiss that sits on the edge of the fault line, splitting me wide open, shaking the world around me.

Her lips are soft and sweet. The tiniest sound coming out of her tells me she's waiting just as long for this moment. Almost like a relief that it's finally happening.

I want more.

I want everything she's willing to give me.

I let my hands slide into her hair at the same time her fingers grip at my shirt, pulling me closer, keeping me there like she's afraid I'll pull away.

Not a chance in hell.

For the first time in my life, I know what it feels like to kiss someone and know it's right.

Her body melts into mine, and I deepen the kiss as my tongue grazes her bottom lip, urging her to open up for me. And she does. It takes everything in me not to lift her, wrap her legs around my waist, and pin her to the back of her front door.

This isn't a curiosity between us.

This is inevitable.

She pulls back, breaking the kiss apart and barely breathing. I press my forehead to hers, and she stares at me with those dark emerald eyes.

She's looking at me like I just changed her entire world.

But I think she just changed mine.

CHAPTER 22
THIS NEW COMPANY YOU'VE BEEN KEEPING MUST BE RUBBING OFF ON YOU.

POPPY

"Would you believe me if I told you I'm *still* sore from playing baseball two nights ago?" Lily says, stretching her arms over her head.

"I believe it." Blair laughs. "I've never seen you play as hard as you did. Nan had to keep reminding you that it wasn't a real game, nor was it professional baseball. But you refused to listen."

"I'm a very competitive person."

"Like previously stated, it's not even a real game."

I can't help but laugh with them, even though I wasn't there. It's very on brand for Lily to treat it as if it were a professional game. It feels good to hang out with Lily and Blair for a chill night in. It's been so long that I can't even remember when it was just the three of us. Tonight, Blair invited us over for dinner, where she was making Griffin's signature dish—chicken parm.

"I think it's cute that you're all getting together for baseball nights at the barnyard now," I say.

"Cute would be you coming." Lily nudges my arm at my side.

"We do invite you every week," Blair adds.

"You know that sports in any capacity aren't my thing."

Lily scoffs. "And you think they are mine? I don't have an athletic bone in my body, but it's really nice to get out and have fun with everyone. You know, it's not even a real game, or as bad as you think. Even Dallas takes it easy on us, being a professional baseball star and all."

Turning my head away from both of them, I try to stuff down the tingling feeling in my stomach at them bringing up my neighbor. My very hot neighbor. My older neighbor, who kissed me a few days ago and tipped my world off its axis.

"Plus," Lily continues, oblivious to my shift in thoughts, "it's always a guaranteed fun night with Nan and Tucker going at it."

"They fought over pretzel twists this week. I don't understand how the General Store doesn't know these two by now and just always keep stock of it," Blair says.

Lily barks out a laugh. "I'm convinced they do it to fuck with the two of them. You know they're laughing their asses off every time those two walk in fighting over pretzels."

Blair points to Lily. "Okay, that I believe."

"What I can't believe is that you somehow convinced Griffin to play," I add.

"No convincing was needed from me," Blair says. "I'm pretty sure Tucker did all the work for us in that department. Apparently, he's very persuasive."

"Speaking of, where is he tonight?" I ask.

"He's helping at the bar tonight."

"During dinner hours?" Lily gasps with wide eyes.

"I've told you already, he's a changed man."

Prior to Griffin and Blair getting together, my brother was so grumpy that he refused to work at his own bar during the evening hours because the crowd always pissed him off. It was too busy for him, and he hated dealing with people.

"Yeah, you're right." Lily sighs. "It's been such a nice change from the Grumpy Griffin we've been subjected to for years."

"I agree." I nod, turning to face Blair. "I think you're what he needed all along to get out of his shell, and give up the whole *everyone, leave me alone* facade."

Lily stands from the chair, palms resting on the table. "You know what's always driven me crazy about that and ends up putting me into protective little sister mode...so many people think he was stupid for acting the way he did when Sierra left him for the city. They find it hard to believe he would be that grumpy and go that long without a relationship because of one single girl." She huffs, letting herself fall back into the chair as if she's said her peace.

"I know," I say with conviction. "I hated that people talked about him like that, but they don't know Griffin the way we always have. When he loves, he loves hard and with every fiber of his being. Sierra destroyed him." I look to Blair again. "Not to bring up his past and all, Blair. You know it all anyway."

She nods. "I do, and I'd love to give that Sierra girl a piece of my mind, but also thank her for leaving him. While I hate that you all had to deal with his grumpy ass, I've never been happier and can't fathom knowing this feeling with anyone else."

Lily and I offer her a soft smile.

Their love is the type of love people dream of.

"I think when you believe you're going to spend the rest of your life with someone, and you have a plan in place for that, only for it to be destroyed, it really fucks with your head."

Blair and Lily pause, looking at each other before looking at me with their lips parted.

"Did you just curse?" Blair asks.

I shrug. "I guess I did."

"Wow," Lily draws out. "This new company you've been keeping must be rubbing off on you."

"What new company?" Blair asks in confusion, before her eyes widen with realization. "Are you talking about Dallas? Oh my god, are you hanging out with Dallas Westbrook?"

I shake my head, only half lying because we haven't done

any "hanging out." "No, he just happens to be where I am sometimes."

"Liar," Lily coughs out as if to hide her accusation. "I saw you two emerging from the hallway at Seven Stools seconds after one another last week. I've been wanting to pester you about it, but I've been a good girl and chose to wait." Lily sits up taller in her chair, crossing one leg over the other.

Blair laughs. "God, I love a good girl moment even if this isn't the same context."

"Please don't bring up my brother at this moment," Lily groans. "I've told you a million times that I'm happy for you, but I don't need to hear it."

"What's a good girl moment?" The question leaves my mouth, and I want to take it back. They already know I'm a virgin, but I hate the judgment that comes from asking questions I should probably know the answer to.

"It's mostly a thing in romance books, but when it happens in real life, it's so hot," Lily says, fanning her face.

"It happens mostly in the steamy scenes when the guy tells the girl that she's being such a good girl," Blair adds.

"Or when he's telling her that she can take it. Good god." Lily rolls her eyes.

My insides swirl at the way they both explain it, and I can't help that my first thought is of Dallas when they say all these things. Does he talk like that in the bedroom?

Would he call *me* a good girl?

Oh my god, now I'm thinking about sex with Dallas.

"Your cheeks are fire engine red, Pop." Lily bends over in laughter. "Are you thinking about Dallas calling you a good girl? I've told you once, but he would be the perfect guy to lose your virginity to."

"Jesus, Lily. Way to get right to the point," Blair says.

"I wasn't thinking about it until two seconds ago," I say, in an effort to defend myself.

Lily puts both hands in the air. "Wait. Wait. Wait. Is something really happening with you two? Now would be an excellent time to tell us what happened in that hallway."

"Nothing happened in the hallway." That's not a lie. "But he did almost kiss me."

"Did you want him to kiss you?" Blair asks.

I nod in response, but stay quiet.

"I think you should do it then." Lily shrugs. "There's no harm in it. And he's Dallas. He's hot."

""Well," I draw out, chewing on the inside of my cheek, and both of their eyes widen. "He sort of showed up at my house later that night. And *then* he kissed me."

I keep my expression blank because I hate the way my brain fights me on things like this. I've spent so much damn time going back and forth between wanting it and reminding myself that I shouldn't want it. It's a vicious cycle that I can't freaking break.

When he's not around, I tell myself I don't want to feel these things.

It wasn't until he had my chin in his hands, again, that I wanted him to kiss me.

And he did.

Oh my god, he did.

It was soft, warm, and electric. But also tender and slow. Kissing Dallas opened a floodgate of emotions I didn't know I had. Time stood still in that moment, and for the first time in a long time, I felt good enough again. I didn't think of the future or how everything could end with my heart broken. Getting lost in the feel of his lips on mine and welcoming the tingling in my stomach when his tongue swiped my bottom lip for me to open up for him.

It was everything.

"I want to scream in excitement for you, but by the look on your face, I'm not sure if I should hug you or jump up and down to celebrate," Lily says.

Since opening up to Dallas about my struggles, there's been a lightness in my chest. It's different than talking to a professional about it the way I always have. There was something about the free feeling of it being out in the open with Dallas that makes me wonder how telling my sister would be.

Would she accept me the way I am?

Of course. It's insane to think otherwise.

But why does it feel like I'm standing on the edge of a cliff, worrying that she won't understand, or worse, think I'm broken?

No, she's not like that.

And so the raging war with logic continues.

"There's something you should know," I say out loud. My palms feel sweaty, and I brush them along my jeans to try to calm my nerves.

Lily's face goes sheet white, and I can tell she's also nervous for what I'm about to say.

She's never seen that side of me because I don't allow her or anyone else to. They believe staying a virgin was a choice. They think that I'm not going out or making plans because of my career, and only my career. While a part of it is, it's mostly my brain lying to me, and me believing it, over and over again.

And that's exactly what's happening now.

Maybe Lily will understand—or at least try to. And if she doesn't, maybe saying it out loud will help me stop feeling so alone in this storm I can never seem to escape.

"There's a reason all of this terrifies me, and it's the same reason I'm still a virgin and don't date."

"Is it your job?" Blair asks.

"Poppy," Lily says, leaning forward, resting a hand on top of mine. "Did someone hurt you?"

I shake my head and finally tell them what I've been keeping to myself for too long. "A few years ago, I was diagnosed with obsessive-compulsive disorder. It's not the typical 'I like my room clean' kind of thing. I have a few signature quirks like lining things up, making lists, and needing to keep everything in order, but sometimes I also have tiny voices in my head telling me I'm not enough, and my brain believing them. I've developed a deep-rooted fear of relationships and allowing myself to get too close to someone because I worry they'll leave. I didn't want to hurt myself, so I just never pursued anything."

"Oh, Poppy." Lily sighs, wiping a tear from her eye.

"And I know you're going to be upset that I never told you. I feel silly even hiding it from you because you're my sister. I know deep down you would never judge me, but that voice in my head tells me everyone will. The fear tangled web in my brain has never let me have the courage to open up. But I can't keep pretending I'm fine when I'm not. It's exhausting."

Lily's features soften, and I know she understands. "I don't know the first thing about what you're going through, and I understand keeping this to yourself out of fear of what others may think."

There's a lot she's never told me about what changed her after we graduated from high school, when one of Griffin's best friends left the next day without a word. I'll never push her for it, the same way she's never pushed me, but we both have secrets.

One day, she'll tell me hers when she's ready.

"And you're right. I always thought it was the keeping your room clean thing—which you always had the cleanest room in town." She smiles softly. "I didn't know it was more than that. My heart hurts that you've been silently dealing with this for so long. I hate myself right now, though, because if I had known, I would have never cracked those virgin jokes with you or pushed you to bang your neighbor."

We both laugh at that. Lily makes her way over to me, wrapping me in her arms. "I'm sorry for not telling you."

"I'm sorry you were scared to talk about it, but you will get zero judgment from me."

Blair sniffles next to us. "I'm sorry. I don't mean to be crying this much, but you're so strong, Poppy. Dealing with the raging war in your head alone? I want to hug you, too."

She joins us; a group hug with my two best friends. The two people who I know have my back and would understand me, even when fear tries to tell me otherwise.

My brain is a lying bitch.

Between telling Dallas and now these two, I believe that statement more and more.

It's an amazing, yet strange, feeling when your brain is quiet. That constant buzzing in the background, the tension from always keeping a secret and pretending—it's just gone.

It will never be completely gone, but it's now noticeable enough.

I think this is what healing and moving forward is supposed to feel like.

I pull away from the hug, looking between Lily and Blair. "All that being said, that's why I'm spiraling over the kiss with Dallas. Everything inside me is screaming that he's not here to stay. Things between him and me seem to get more intense every time I see him. I don't know what to do because I really do feel myself falling for him."

"I *knew* there was something there," Blair says with conviction. "I think I've known from the night he first showed up at Seven Stools."

I raise an eyebrow. "You mean that karaoke night?"

Blair nods. "I watched the way he looked at you when you first walked in. It was as if the entire bar emptied out in his head, and you were the only one there. The only one he had eyes on. I didn't think anything of it because, well, you're a catch, Poppy." She smiles widely. "But then, seeing him watch you a dozen times after, the look never left."

I groan, falling back on my chair. "I don't know what to do. One kiss and I'm ruined, it seems. If I see him again, and he kisses me the way he did last week, I'm done for."

"What's your biggest fear?" Lily asks.

I scoff. "That's a loaded question."

"Let me rephrase that...what's your biggest fear when it comes to feeling something for Dallas?"

Everything.

That I'm not enough.

That I'm not like the other girls.

"He's not planning to stay here. He's only in Bluestone Lakes temporarily."

"What if he decides to stay?"

I avert my gaze out the sliding glass doors that overlook the mountains. That's one thought that's never crossed my mind. I don't know enough about his relationship with his ex-wife, or how him staying here would work with Sage. But what if he *did* stay?

"You never know." Lily winks, leaving to bring her dish to the kitchen.

Can I allow myself to take that risk?

CHAPTER 23
MR. GRIFFIN, DO YOU THINK POPPY LIKES MY DAD MORE THAN A FRIEND?

DALLAS

"Great hit, Gabe!" I shout and clap my hands as I watch him swing the bat and hit the ball into the outfield.

If that's what you want to call it.

The barnyard isn't even an official field.

We've had a handful of practices here now, and even with the cold weather, the kids are loving it. They're getting good, too, which shocks me mildly because I had low hopes after our first indoor practice. The kids are no longer using the baseball bats as telescopes, and no one screams murder when a ball is thrown in their direction anymore.

I feel like shit for ever doubting them. All they needed was a little practice and snacks. I feel like I have my own little team now, one that I've built from the ground up.

Sage picks up the ball in the outfield and throws it as hard as she can to first. I love watching the smile on her face when she has a ball in her hand.

Gabe is running the bases still, but he looks like he's ready to collapse halfway down first, running like a T. rex, but then he passes first base, pauses to turn around, and begins to run… backward?

"Why are you running like that?" I shout.

"I'm training my reverse instincts for when a bear tries to attack me during a game."

"There are no bears in baseball, Gabe."

"Yet," he shouts, fist in the air, and picks up his backward pace.

I shake my head. "Why don't you guys take a break and get a drink of water?"

The kids run for the bench, and I notice Archie dragging his feet. I jog up to meet him, wrapping an arm around his shoulder. "What's up, kid?"

"I need more, coach," he says quickly, as if he's been holding that in for so long now. "I need to be challenged. I need to be stronger. I want to make it to the major leagues just like you did."

"You'll get there."

"Not with this team and these practices."

"What are you saying?"

"I'm saying you suck," he says proudly.

I laugh, but only because I know he's telling the truth. Kids always are. A somber feeling washes over me at his words, because I couldn't coach a Major League team, and now I can't even successfully coach a group of kids. I knew coaching wasn't for me; I always have. I wanted to keep it in my life, so I did it anyway.

Now Archie is telling me everything I already knew.

The worst part? I don't fucking know how to fix this and be better for him.

"Grab a drink of water, and we'll figure it out. I know I suck, hence why I'm no longer coaching in the big leagues anymore. But maybe you can help me be better?"

His face lights up. "I help you, and you help me?"

"Yep."

"Okay, you rock, coach," he says, jogging off to the bench for water.

Sighing, I turn around and find Nan making her way toward me. "You're everywhere," I shout.

"I am," she says with a nod. "You're lookin' like you got a team here."

"If that's what you want to call it. I mean, we've graduated from calling it a 'hand trap' to calling it a glove now. So, I guess you can say we're making progress."

Ethan takes that moment to run by with a glove in one hand and a ball in the other, up above his head, screaming, "My arm is a rocket missile!"

"That's a typical practice," I say flatly.

Nan barks out a laugh. "You positive Tucker ain't the one coaching these kids? Because they all weirdly feel like he's rubbing off on them."

"I try to give him as little control as possible."

"You're doing something right."

I rub the back of my neck, looking from Sage to Archie, and around to the other kids. They all laugh and chat together as if they have been friends forever. Some of them probably have, but Sage is now a part of that. She fits right in with these kids, and even if I suck as a coach, I'm so proud of that right there.

Even if I suck as a coach.

My brain immediately goes to the final conversations I had with Clark at the stadium when he told me I needed a break. I knew I needed one, I just didn't expect all of this.

I didn't expect a nine-year-old to confirm that I suck as a coach.

No more strikeouts, only home runs.

Clark's words play on repeat in my head. It's taken me this long to remember them, even though this struck me so hard when he first said them. I felt the words in my chest, and I knew it meant so much more than baseball. It was his way of getting through to me that there would be no more failures or setbacks, and it's time to stop dwelling on the past.

It's only success from now on—only big wins.

Glancing around the barnyard, the make-shift baseball field, and over to the horizon as the sun barely dips beyond the mountains. I feel a tug in my chest. A strong one that tells me Bluestone Lakes is the big win.

That can't be, though.

We have a life back in San Francisco, and when all is said and done, we'll have to go back to it.

"I like it here," I finally admit to Nan. It's not what she asked, but it's what needed to be said.

"I knew you would."

"Is Seven Stools the only place to grab a bite to eat around here?"

"Nah. There's a diner, but you don't want to go there. Swear I saw a rat run across someone's feet last time I was there a few years back. Never again," she says with disgust.

"Damn, okay. I wanted to take Sage out to eat tonight."

Nan laughs. "Go to Seven Stools, boy. You do know it's a restaurant, don't you?"

I shrug. "I guess I just always associated it with being a bar."

"Duh. But that's because you come late at night. It's also a family-friendly place. Take my girl out to dinner. You both deserve it," she says, patting my good shoulder and retreating from the field.

I nod, because we do. I turn to look at the mini team I've built, consisting of kids who share the same love for the sport and are looking for an outlet to play. I came here to get away, but I think, somehow, I found the one thing I wasn't looking for.

People who don't care about my resume and who I am outside of this town.

A neighbor I can't stop thinking about.

Friends who love my daughter as if she were one of their own.

A place to stay.

"We should adopt a dog," Sage says with a mouthful of French fries.

"That's so left field," I choke out, nearly spitting out my soda.

"Actually, it's very home base."

Both of us pause, staring at each other while we let the pun register, and then we break into a fit of hysterics. Sage bends over the table with tears in her eyes, and I can barely breathe. I never knew how much I needed this moment until now.

Memories of the family in San Francisco, the last time I was out with Mitch and Tyler, flood back, almost sobering my laughter. But it does nothing to wipe the smile off my face. That family there—that dad laughing with his daughter—it's something I've always dreamed of but never allowed myself to experience. Life has always moved at lightning speed for me. I missed so much because of it. I spent the moments we should cherish as parents rushing to get to the next thing, only to rush to the thing after that. A constant cycle repeating until one day I woke up, and Sage was six.

This town has slowed me down drastically.

This town has opened my eyes to life moving at the speed it's meant to.

I may have spent the better part of my life making reckless and impulsive decisions, but this one has paid off.

Griffin shows up at our table mid laughter. "Can I get you two anything else to drink?"

Sage nods. "My throat is so dry it's doing the desert dance."

"That's a new one," Griffin says in a serious tone, but the smile on his face tells me he wants to laugh. My guess is he reserves all of that for Blair.

"I'll take another soda, and she'll have water," I tell Griffin.

His phone rings, and he rolls his eyes when he looks at the screen. "My sisters and Blair are going to destroy my house."

The mention of his sister only makes me think of Poppy that much more.

"Is everything okay?" I ask curiously.

He turns his phone to face me, and on it is a picture of the three women sitting on the couch in Griffin's house, posing and laughing so hard that they can barely hold it together. The wine glasses in their hands look like they are going to spill over. My eyes focus on one person, and only one person. The way her long, strawberry blonde hair sits on the top of her head in a messy bun. The sweater that's falling off her shoulder, exposing the delicate shape of her collarbone. My tongue swipes along my bottom lip, wondering what it would taste like to trail my lips along every inch of exposed skin.

She's perfect.

She's the fever I don't want to break.

She's everything I crave.

"You know, Blair said something and I wasn't one hundred percent sure myself until now."

"Huh?" I say, forcing myself out of the daze from the picture on his phone.

He pockets it, and I see the smirk on his lips. "So, Poppy, huh?" He raises an eyebrow in question, and I avert my gaze to the half-eaten chicken sandwich in front of me. "I hate saying it, but Blair was right, it seems."

"We looooove Poppy," Sage cuts into the conversation, oblivious of the tension rolling off of me.

Yes, I have a thing for his sister.

Yes, I kissed her, and it only made those feelings that much stronger.

No, I'm not admitting any of that to Griffin.

"She's the best, huh?" Griffin says to Sage.

"Yep. Mr. Griffin, do you think Poppy likes my dad more than a friend?"

My eyes widen, bouncing between Sage and Griffin. He has the same shocked look on his face. I can feel the color drain from my face with how bold that question is when I don't even know what's really happening between us.

I know I can't stop thinking about her.

I know if given the chance, she would bring me to my knees in an instant.

"Poppy likes a lot of people," Griffin says with certainty. "As far as liking your dad more than a friend"—he faces me, still answering her question—"I think she could. But she struggles to let people in. I don't know why, but she does. If she lets you in enough to see that part of her she chooses to keep hidden, consider yourself lucky." He leans down, close to my ear, so only I can hear. "I know where to find you. Don't fuck it up."

I nod, understanding what he means without asking more.

The parts she keeps hidden, I know them.

She told me everything there was to know about her, and she let me in.

Everything just got a whole lot clearer.

I need to see Poppy.

CHAPTER 24
ASK ME AGAIN, DALLAS.

POPPY

As I stand in the middle of my living room, I look around with a smile on my face. There's nothing that tickles my brain more than seeing my home put together and clean at the end of the night. The puzzle I finished last night is boxed back up and tucked away in the small TV stand I have, the kitchen counters are wiped clean, and the pillows are fluffed. Reaching into the drawer on the end table, I pull out the lighter to light my favorite candle from *Stella Candle Co.*, called *Main Street*, that I stocked up on during their recent holiday collection launch.

A creamy, peppermint mocha scent fills the space, and I've never felt happier.

Looking at the time, I see that it's still early, but getting darker out. I turn on the table lamp to its dim setting for ambiance. First, I pull out my notepad and pen and make a list of what I need to get done tomorrow.

1. *30 minute yoga session*
2. *organize closet and put away laundry*
3. *lesson plans for the week*

Now that that's out of the way, I decide to rummage through the boxes of puzzles to start a new one for the night. I only have one left that I haven't done before, so I add: *order a new puzzle* to the list.

A knock on the door startles me, because I'm not expecting company.

I never am, really.

When I open it, I find Dallas standing on the other side. His eyes down to the wooden boards of my porch before they slowly meet mine. He's dressed for comfort in a pair of light gray sweatpants and a long-sleeved thermal that hugs every muscle on his body. I hug the cardigan I'm wearing over my tank top tighter, because my body is fully aware of him standing there, but I can't find words to come out of my mouth.

I want to ask what he's doing here.

I want to ask if he's okay.

I want to ask if he can kiss me again.

"Are you okay?" he asks.

"Yep. I'm sorry, I'm just a little shocked you're standing here."

His lips turn up into a smirk.

"I mean, I'm not sorry," I say quickly, knowing exactly what that face means.

"Yes, you are," he says, side-stepping me as he makes his way into my house. Normally, this would drive me nuts, but not with him. I want him here. "And it's okay. I sort of dropped by unannounced here. But I brought you something."

"You did?"

I look down at his extended hand, and he has a puzzle for me. One thousand pieces of a baseball themed puzzle. On the bottom are a few fans facing a field, and players scattered across it. But that's not what draws me to it the most. There are mountains in the background. Beautiful mountains paint the sky behind it, and the box is titled *Field of Dreams*.

"You got this for me?"

"I saw it at the General Store yesterday when I was there. I immediately thought of you," he smiles, looking down at the puzzle still in his hands. "So I had to get it for you."

My heart stumbles in my chest—no, it flutters—as if it's forgotten how to properly beat in a regular rhythm, because Dallas thought of me. He remembered, or noticed, or whatever. Either way, he saw me and the things that bring me the most joy and got it for me.

I take the box in my hand, it's nothing but a cardboard box, but it's also someone whispering my name in a silent room. Something that may seem minor to someone feels so loud to me.

Because he remembered.

"Dallas," I whisper, keeping my eyes on the box, afraid I might cry if I look at him.

"Poppy, what is it?"

I shake my head, the tear escapes on its own, and I want to wipe it away, but I don't want him to know that a silly puzzle has made me this emotional. Instead, I turn my face away from him, but he stops me. My chin between his fingers, urging me to look up at him. My eyes are closed, keeping everything put together so he doesn't see me.

But he does.

Dallas sees all of me.

I open my eyes, and there's a serious expression on his face. His fingers don't leave my chin, holding me in place. "I can't seem to stop thinking about you."

"You can't?"

He shakes his head. "You've been the first thought in my head when I wake up and brew my morning coffee, and the last thought I have before my head hits the pillow at night. Most of the time, I find myself thinking about you without meaning to."

I swallow, but everything feels thick in my throat at his admission. "Is that why you're here? Wait, where is Sage?"

"I dropped her off with her mom for the night earlier today," he pauses, assessing my features. "And that's part of the reason why I'm here."

Silence stretches between us with his answer, except for the pounding in my chest. His eyes bore into mine, and my body heats with the intensity of his stare. The air is thick with tension, like a lightning bolt waiting for its chance to strike.

Then it hits me, he's waiting for me.

He's giving me the control I desperately crave.

"Kiss me, Dallas."

"Thank fuck," he practically growls.

He erases the space between us and crashes his lips to mine. It's not soft or careful this time. My fingers grip his shirt as his lips part, stealing every breath I'm willing to give him. My body melts into him, and I feel the kiss down every part of me, making my knees feel weak. He angles my head at just the right amount to deepen the kiss, making me feel like I'm being pulled underwater.

My control slips. I no longer think, I just feel.

I welcome it, love it, *need* it.

When I moan into his mouth, he pulls back. I'm breathless and dazed. My lips feel swollen in the best way, and I feel as undone as he looks.

He looks at my face up and down in silence before moving my head to the side, tugging my cardigan to the side, and peppering kisses down the pulse of my neck. My body relaxes in a way it's never relaxed before. I quite literally *melt* where I stand, but he holds me in place, taking his time exploring my skin.

I want this, I think on repeat.

I reach up, running my fingers through the light scruff of his jaw, and he lifts his head again to face me.

"I'm here because I can't stop fucking thinking about you—about this," he says breathlessly, thumb grazing the pulse his lips were just on. "Since I kissed you, your taste has lingered on my tongue. It's all I can think about at night, alone, in bed."

I suck in a sharp breath, my nerves on high alert because even though I'm inexperienced, I know what he means with each word out of his mouth.

His fingertips trail the same pulse his thumb was stroking; no doubt, he can feel how fast it's beating. Then he trails them along my collarbone, forcing my eyes to flutter closed as he continues down the side of my breasts and my stomach.

"Can I touch you, Poppy?"

"You don't want this," I breathe out, my inner mind fighting with the desire I'm feeling. "Trust me."

He pulls his hand away from the hem of my leggings, back up to my face as if he still needs his hands on me in some way, shape, or form.

He doesn't say anything, he just kisses me again. Softer this time—tentative and careful. Like I'm a glass doll that he's afraid he's going to break. I guess, metaphorically, I am. I know Dallas has the power to break me, but there's also no denying that I want him to.

I can already hear the voice in my head telling me his response, *Seriously? You're still a virgin at twenty-five?*

There's that lingering fear that he's never going to look at me the same again.

But I'm tired of hiding it.

"I'm an inexperienced virgin, Dallas," I admit. "When I tell you that you don't want this, that's what I mean."

I want to curl into a ball at my own admission, knowing something as huge as that has the power to make him walk away. He could be the one to step away any second now and walk right out the door. I fight to stay where I stand, though, not letting him know that saying that out loud makes me feel weak.

But it also makes me feel strong and powerful.

This is a truth I've carried with me quietly for years, and now I'm telling Dallas. Not because I owe him, or anyone, an explanation, but because I respect myself.

"Oh, but I do," he finally says, shocking me to my core.

Taking another step into me to close whatever space I put between us, he presses his body into mine, and our bodies fuse like glue. "I told you I wanted to take care of you, and that's what I intend to do. I don't care that you're inexperienced, and it's not something you should be ashamed of. I won't push you into it either. *Never*."

I release the breath I've been holding since I said the words out loud.

His hips jerk forward, and the feel of him hard against my stomach forces a moan out of me. Virgin be damned, because I *do* want him to touch me.

"Ask me again, Dallas," I practically pant out.

He grins, and his fingers trail the same path they did moments ago. "Can I touch you, Poppy?"

"Please."

"Mmm. You ask so nicely."

In the slowest speed imaginable, he reaches for the opening of my cardigan to expose my tank top underneath. The cold air seeps through the light fabric, and I feel my nipples harden from just his eyes on me. His hands move to cup my breasts, and it's an out-of-body experience having him touch me this way. My breath catches in my throat as he gently massages them before grazing his fingers over my nipples, tweaking the hard peaks through the fabric.

A growl rumbles through his chest as his lips find my neck again. He doesn't stop playing with my nipples, and I swear, the build-up of sensations between my legs is too strong.

It's too much.

"I'm going to learn every inch of your body," he says softly against my skin, one hand leaving my breast to trail down my stomach until he reaches the waistband of my leggings. He runs a finger along the inner part before bringing his hand down between my legs. "I'm going to learn what turns you on, and what makes you moan in pleasure. And then I'm going to do it over and over again."

My breathing comes hard and fast. My hips instinctively buck forward at his touch. I don't know what I'm doing, but I find myself chasing the feeling he's ready and willing to give me. It feels so good—euphoric, almost.

"Playing with your nipples turned you on, didn't it?"

I nod eagerly.

"I can tell. You're dripping right through these tight little leggings."

My eyes widen. "What?"

"You're fucking adorable." He chuckles lightly before applying the smallest amount of pressure to the throbbing pulse between my legs. "Trust me, it's a good thing. There's nothing hotter than knowing how much my touch turns you on."

"It feels really good," I moan, letting my hips roll against his hand.

Why does this feel so good?

The intense feeling of ecstasy rolls through my body with every move of my hip. Dallas isn't doing anything but applying just the right amount of pressure. I can't believe this is really happening, and I don't want it to stop.

"That's it, Poppy. Take what you need from me."

He presses harder, using two fingers to rub circles on the outside of my leggings. This feels wrong, but it feels so damn right. My hands claw at his shoulders, my mouth parts, and he presses his body into mine, not daring to remove his hands from between my legs.

He presses his forehead to mine, and his lips hover over mine as our breath mingles in the air between us. I bite my bottom lip to keep from crying out. It's the most intense feeling. I want to scream, cry, and call out his name. My legs shake under me, and I feel like I'll collapse into a puddle at any minute, but he doesn't let up. He doesn't stop me from moving my hips against his hand.

I feel his body tighten around me while stars begin to dance across my vision. My eyes flutter closed, and my head falls back as everything hits me like a wave crashing on the shore during a storm. His lips move to my neck, and his other hand plays with my breast, tweaking my nipple one time before the thunder rolls through my body—a lightning strike up my spine.

"Dallas," I cry out.

"Yes," he grunts. "That's it. Say my name when you come for me."

Is that what this feeling is?

Holy mother of— "Dallas!"

The feeling doesn't let up. I can't see straight, my legs can no longer hold me up, and Dallas knows it because both arms wrap around my lower back, pulling me flush to him. I miss the feeling of his hands between my legs, but it's replaced with a thick, muscular thigh. My body tingles in a way I've never experienced before. I can barely breathe as my hips roll against his leg.

"Come for me, honey," he whispers against my skin.

I don't know how to make myself do that, but the moment he applies more pressure between my legs with his thigh, I'm sent flying over the edge of the cliff I've been standing on. I moan and cry out in pleasure. I feel soaked between my legs as a rush of new feelings washes over me.

This is it. This is what an orgasm feels like.

Everything begins to subside, my breathing still fast, but steady. I take a step back from him. Almost feeling embarrassed that it just happened, but also feeling sedated. My body wants to collapse and fall into the deepest sleep I've ever had.

I watch as Dallas adjusts himself in his pants. My eyebrows knit in confusion when I notice a wet spot on his grey sweatpants between his legs, away from the one on his upper thigh that I clearly put there.

He looks down and rubs the back of his neck. "Yeah. I'm sorry."

"That's my line."

He smirks, stepping back into me as he cups my face between

his hands. He bends down and softly presses his lips to mine. It's not rushed or hungry; it's confirmation he wanted it too.

It's silently telling me I'm enough.

And for the first time, I actually believe it.

Dallas didn't stay long after that. Not because he didn't want to, but because he needed to change, and I needed a shower. In the short time he did stay after, his hands never left my body in any way while we talked about Sage and the progress he's made coaching the kids in town.

Holding my hand.

Sitting next to each other, arms or legs touching.

Kissing me like the air he needed to breathe.

When he left, I stood at my door, a smile on my face the whole time as I watched him retreat across the lawn to his house.

The smile is still plastered on my face as I lie in bed, staring at the ceiling, thinking about how this night wasn't planned, which should give me anxiety. But I don't feel an ounce of that. I feel relaxed and...happy. I think Dallas has been making me feel that way for a while now, and it's something I struggled to accept.

Even with the relaxation settling into my body, I can't fall asleep.

I can't get him off my mind.

I can't get what happened out of my mind.

I *know* I want more of that.

I just don't know the first thing about what more would entail.

Getting out of bed, I turn the lamp on my bedside table on and pull the notepad from my drawer, along with my laptop. Settling into bed, I cross my legs and begin my research.

I should be embarrassed by typing these things into the internet search bar. The FBI agent who watches me is probably wondering what type of shit I'm up to. I laugh to myself at that thought, but you never know.

I type in *"how to please a man."*

Clicking on the first link, my eyes widen, and I freeze in place. It's not like I've never seen one before, but there's a lot of sweat and nakedness on the page right now. A picture of a woman with a dick in her mouth, another with him using a vibrator on her, and you can see he's getting pleasure from it by how hard he is between her legs.

I close the laptop, realizing it's too much for me. But it's also kind of interesting.

Dallas *knows* what he's doing. I'm sure he also knows what he likes.

I decide to make myself a list of things I'd like to explore. I might be getting ahead of myself here with Dallas and assuming that he would want more, but regardless, there's this strong desire inside of me to feel all of that again with him—only him.

One orgasm and I'm wanting more already.

1. Give a blowjob
2. Try a vibrator
3.

I leave the last one blank because I'm not ready for anything else beyond that. Feeling satisfied with my list, I walk over to put my laptop back in my bag and the list on the table.

I fall asleep instantly with a smile on my face.

And it has everything to do with Dallas.

CHAPTER 25
I WAS HOPING YOU'D SAY YES.

DALLAS

> **MITCH**
> How are the practices with the kids going?

They are getting better.

One told me I sucked as a coach.

> **MITCH**
> That's a lie.

Is it, though? It's definitely opened my eyes to how I should be coaching, and since then, we've gotten a lot better.

> **MITCH**
> That's great. When is your first game? We want to come.

Soon. I think next month. I'll let you know.

> **MITCH**
> That's awesome. I'm proud of you, coach.

> **TYLER**
> And the woman you met?
>
> I'm also proud of you, stud.

> *eye roll* You always seem to have only one thing on your mind.

> **TYLER**
> I'm just curious.

> She's good.

"Daddy, can we have a snuggle fest on the couch tonight?"

"Of course, bug. Do you want to watch a movie or a show?"

"I think I'm in the mood for a movie! Let's watch *Air Bud*. The basketball one this time since I just watched the baseball one last week."

I laugh. "You got it. I'll make us some popcorn, too."

"Ooooh!" she says, jumping up and down in the kitchen. "Yes. Yes. We can make it like an actual movie date! But with blankets and pillows and pajamas!" Her face sombers almost immediately as if something just crossed her mind. "I wish Mommy was here."

Her admission is a knife to my chest. She's been doing so well over the last few months, adjusting to this temporary living situation. So much so that it hasn't crossed my mind as often that she could be struggling with things. And now, my heart hurts for my little girl.

"I'm sorry, Sage. I know this is hard for you and your mom. She misses you just as much as you miss her on the days you're not with her."

The look on her face tells me she wants to cry but won't. I know my girl now. She's strong like the roots of a tree—you can't see it, but she holds everything together.

"I do miss her," she admits. "I know I just saw her yesterday, but she always loves movie nights with me, too. Have we ever had a movie night?"

I swallow, emotions lodged in my throat.

No, we never have.

Because I wasn't always there.

"No, bug." I shake my head, answering her honestly. "And I hate that we haven't. I hate that I was always so busy playing baseball or coaching."

She smiles softly. "That's okay, Daddy. Mommy always used to tell me you were living out your dream. And that hard work gets you to your goals. You and Mommy are the hardest workers."

Dammit. She got me.

Tears well in my eyes, and I can no longer fight them. I don't cry. I don't show emotion like this. The only person in the world who has that power over me is Sage.

"Don't cry." She jogs to me, wrapping her tiny arms around my waist. My hand cups the back of her head, and I hold her to me. I never knew how much I needed this, until this moment. Which makes me hate myself that much more. "I love you so much."

"I love you, too, Sage. So much." I hold her shoulders, separating us just for a moment so I can crouch down to her level. "Your mom was right, and I was trying to live out my dream, and working hard can help you reach your goals. The tears in my eyes are because I'm so upset with myself for not making time for that movie night. Not making more time for you."

"But we are now."

I nod.

No more strikeouts, only home runs.

She skips off to the couch. She pulls the blanket from the back and drapes it over her legs.

"I have one more ask," she says.

"Anything for you. You should already know the answer will

be yes. Unless it's candy. We don't have any, and I'm certain the general store is closed."

She giggles behind her hand.

There's no evidence of the somewhat deep conversation we just had. I'm glad we had it, and I'm glad it's ending with a night on the couch with her.

"Do you think you can ask Poppy to come over and watch *Air Bud* with us?" My body stills, frozen in place. "If that's okay with you," she adds with a shrug.

Is it okay with me?

Hell, after showing up at her house the other night and watching her come undone for me, I'd do anything to spend more time with her at this point. As if I wasn't already thinking about her all hours of the day, she's now permanently ingrained in my brain. A tattoo etched into my skin that I can't wipe off even if I wanted to.

Her admitting to me that she's a virgin should have scared me off. Thinking about it later that night, it *would have* scared me off if Poppy were someone back in San Francisco. I told her I wasn't like other guys, and I'm not. I didn't lie about that, but it's because this place, this town, is changing me.

She is changing me.

Now I want to learn every inch of her skin. I want to know what brings her pleasure. I want to be the fucking first to do it all.

"I can text her and see if she wants to come over," I tell Sage.

"Okay!"

Pulling my phone out of my pocket, I hover over her contact. I'm hesitant, even though Sage and I both want her here, but only because the last thing I want to do tonight is derail whatever plans she has.

> Hey, what are you up to tonight?

The bubble indicating that she's replying lights up our text thread, then disappears. It repeats for another minute or two before my phone buzzes in my hand.

> **POPPY**
> Just doing a puzzle.

> Yeah? Which one are you doing?

> **POPPY**
> This guy dropped one off to me the other day. It's a baseball one, so I thought I would do that one next.

I'm smiling so hard, staring down at my phone.

I've been flirting with Poppy since the moment she turned around at Cozy Cup the day I got here. Even if she's not doing it intentionally, her reply back to me has my insides swirling with rainbows—as Sage would say.

> Oh yeah? Sounds like a nice guy.

> **POPPY**
> Eh.

> That's a shame because I heard the guy was curious to know if you want to come over for a movie night with Sage.

> Her request...if that helps you make up your mind.

I feel like I'm holding my breath, waiting for her response. The reply bubble dances on and off again. My stomach is in knots thinking she doesn't want to come over. I don't blame her, honestly. She has a routine, and I'm attempting to derail it. I put my phone face down on the kitchen counter and put the popcorn in the microwave. The entire two minutes that the bag is popping, I pick up my phone and put it back down.

As soon as I put the popcorn in a bowl, there's a soft knock on my back sliding door. I spin around and see Poppy on the other side of the glass. She's lifting her hand in a shy wave, but she's smiling. It's a breathtaking one, too—like they all are. They stop me dead in my tracks, frozen in place, but also wanting to run to her, wrap her in my arms, and tell her all the things that run through my mind when I see her.

She laughs through the glass and points to the handle of the door.

Oh, it's locked.

When I open it, she doesn't move. She looks up at me, her emerald eyes glistening in the soft glow of the back porch light.

"You came."

"You asked."

I look over my shoulder, and Sage is nowhere to be found, so I face Poppy again. I lean down, with one hand on the sliding door and the other on the frame, and press my lips to hers. She lifts both hands, resting them on my chest as she melts into my kiss. When I finally pull away so we get caught, I'm smiling down at her.

"Way to leave me on the edge of my seat, though," I say, before stepping to the side and allowing her in. She crosses the threshold, and she engulfs every inch of the kitchen—her presence known by my mind and body. One stop through, and she makes a house feel like a home. She brings warmth and sunshine even if it's dark outside.

"You thought I'd say no?"

"I was hoping you'd say yes."

Placing my hand on the small of her back, I guide her to the living room. I remove my hand as soon as we enter, so Sage doesn't get any ideas. Poppy is still her teacher, and I don't want to cause problems for her because I can't control myself.

Sage sits up on the couch, eyes wide. "Poppy! You came for movie night!"

"I did." Poppy giggles, making her way to the couch to sit next to Sage. "I couldn't pass up the invite." Her eyes move from Sage to mine as if there's a double meaning to it. Or maybe I'm reading too much into it. "Besides, I can't remember the last time I sat down to watch a full movie."

"Yay!" Sage dances in her seat. "I asked Daddy if we could watch *Air Bud*, but we can watch something else if you want. You can pick the movie."

"I'll watch whatever you want to watch."

"I'm in the mood for a sports playing dog. I was gonna do the basketball one, but we can watch the baseball one if you like that sport better."

"Which one is a ten out of ten in your opinion?"

Sage grips her chin, deep in thought. "That's tough. The basketball one is superior. But I cried the first time I watched it, and I don't know if I want to be the reason you cry tonight."

"But is it a happy ending?" Poppy asks, and Sage nods. "Then let's do the basketball one since it's superior."

My heart swells in my chest as I watch these two interact. Sage looks at Poppy like she's the moon and the stars, while Poppy looks at Sage like she's the best thing to ever happen to her.

But little does Poppy know, *she's* the best thing that has happened to *us*.

I've spent so long harping on all the things I've done wrong in life. All the reckless and impulsive decisions that ultimately led to everything falling apart around me. Witnessing these two together was the reminder I needed to look around and appreciate all the things going right as well.

The one clear thing...Poppy fits with us.

It's not because she's a teacher and good with kids.

She genuinely fits into our lives.

I grab the popcorn from the kitchen and load the movie on the TV. Sage is cuddled under Poppy's arms. Both of them look like they're about to fall asleep.

"Are you both going to fall asleep after I turn this on?"

Poppy shakes her head, giggling.

"I can stay up all night," Sage says confidently.

I shake my head and put a bowl of popcorn in front of them. Sage pulls it to her lap, keeping it close so Poppy can have some too. I take a seat on the other couch adjacent to where they sit.

The two of them watch the movie, while I watch them.

Twenty minutes into the movie, Sage falls asleep. Her head is across Poppy's lap, and she's raking her fingers through my daughter's hair delicately, not to wake her up. It's in this moment, staring at the two of them, Poppy oblivious to my eyes on hers, that I fall deeper for this woman than before. Deeper than I've fallen for anyone, I think.

I loved April. I wouldn't have married her all those years ago if I hadn't. She was all I'd known of falling head over heels for someone. We both had that sparkle in our eyes when we looked at one another.

This is different.

This is wildly different.

When Poppy is in the room or anywhere near me, everything else around me fades. I continuously find myself bending the hands of time, stretching the minutes as far as they can go to hear her laugh once more. The weight of the world is lifted off my shoulders at the sound of her voice, and the world instantly has more color when she smiles.

It's not just physical attraction anymore.

There's a chemistry between us that no one can deny.

Witnessing this moment confirms it all.

She belongs.

But do I belong here?

That's what I think about as Poppy and I watch the rest of the movie. When it ends, I walk Poppy to the door and give her a kiss before taking Sage to bed.

I've never been the type to be scared of the future because I've always kept my eye on the ball, no matter the pitch, staying focused when life throws me challenges. I've spent my life rounding the bases like it was second nature, moving through life with momentum and confidence. I've always played the bounce off the wall, adapting to the unpredictable.

But Poppy…she scares me.

She makes me fear the future because my time in Bluestone Lakes has an expiration date.

And it's coming quicker than I want it to.

CHAPTER 26
THIS IS ALL MY FAULT.

POPPY

It's Fun Friday today in class—the students' favorite day of the week.

I aim to make every school day a fun learning experience, but today, especially, we let loose. The kids are free to move around the room to different play centers. Each station is set up with various activities to make learning enjoyable. One station features sentence-building puzzles where they can create short sentences like *I like the bear*, with the bear being a photo. Another station has simple addition and subtraction flashcards. The kids absolutely love it. It's highly interactive, and I've been lucky to have an amazing group that gets along and doesn't fight over anything, which is common at this age.

You know, the whole *sharing is caring* thing.

It's a personal favorite day for me because it's my time to straighten up my desk and classroom before the weekend. Otherwise, I'd be home wondering all weekend how much of a mess I'm going to walk into on Monday.

"Miss Barlow?" Sage says, standing in front of my desk.

"Yes?"

"I wanted to give you this. I drew you a picture." She smiles proudly.

"You did? Oh, Sage. That's so sweet."

I extend my hand over my desk, and she hands me the colorful drawing before hiding her hands behind her back and swaying in anticipation for me to see. When I look down, my heart practically stops beating. It's a picture of stick figure people, with two houses on each side of them. A colorful sun is drawn in the corner, with mountains perched in the background. But it's not any of that forcing me to pause. There are three adults in the picture and a small child—I can tell by the height difference that she's created.

In messy and backward letter handwriting reads:

Mommy. Sage. Daddy. Poppy.

Poppy.

A family portrait.

Sage drew me into a family picture in Bluestone Lakes, and my heart doesn't know what to make of it. It's beating so hard in my chest that it feels like it will pound right through the skin. There's a part of me throwing up all sorts of alarm bells that this is bad...very bad. It means I've crossed a line with one of my students' parents and allowed myself to get too close.

I'm her teacher. That's where it's supposed to end.

But my brain sees so much more. A child's drawing that feels like an open door I want to look through. Guilt hits me in the face as I wonder what it would be like if this were my family. One that she wants me to be a part of.

This should feel wrong, but it doesn't.

And that's what scares me the most.

"Do you like it?" Sage asks innocently.

"I love it," I choke out. "I think this will be one I take home with me."

"Yeah?" Her eyes light up. "Are you going to put it on your fridge?"

I nod. "I have a special place for it."

"I love that," she says before skipping off to join her friends at a station.

I can't lie to Sage, and while I'm only stretching the truth, I can't have this in my classroom. I don't want other teachers or a parent of another student to get the wrong idea or think I play favorites after reading too much into this picture.

That's when reality strikes.

I force myself to pause, waiting for the sounds to come—the voice in my head screaming. But it doesn't. It's quiet now. There's a dull murmur, but it's low enough that I can take a step over it. It's mildly disorienting, like stepping onto solid ground after being on a rocking boat.

Lifting my eyes, I watch Sage playing with the other kids. My mind shifts to her dad. I won't say he saved me. That's too dramatic and would be a lie. But I can't deny the truth either. Since he's come to town and into my life, something has shifted. Dallas doesn't fight my chaos; he welcomes it. He hasn't pushed me away, even knowing all the darker parts of me.

And reality strikes me *again*.

Dallas Westbrook hasn't pushed me away. I told him everything—from having obsessive-compulsive disorder to being a virgin—and he hasn't ghosted me. Instead, he invited me over for a movie night with Sage. He didn't try anything, but he didn't need to. His eyes were on me the entire movie, the kiss when I showed up at the back door, and then again when I left, tells me everything I need to know.

I used to believe I would live my life tense, controlled, and tired.

But I'm starting to wonder if I'm now allowed to be more.

Not because he made me feel like more.

Because being with Dallas has helped me see that I already was.

The bell signaling the end of the period rings, pulling me from any more thoughts. Rachel comes in moments later because our next period is outside recess, which ends the school day.

"Do you mind taking the kids today?" I ask her.

"Of course."

"I didn't get a chance to finish cleaning up, and I'd like to get things together so we can get out of here on time today."

"Sounds good to me." She nods. "Is everyone ready to go outside?" she asks the class.

They all cheer and line up by the door, ready to go.

As soon as they're out the door, I circle the room and begin cleaning up. I place all the colored pencils, crayons, and markers in their designated spot before piling the drawing paper all together and wiping down the table. I put all the books back in the mini bookshelf and the puzzles away on the shelf. By then, I make my way to my desk to sit down to finish organizing that.

The phone on my desk rings, and I pick it up quickly.

"Hello?"

"Poppy," Rachel says, sounding frantic. My nervous system is on high alert as I stand from my chair. "Sage fell off the swing and hit her head."

I hang up the phone and run to the playground. My hand grips my badge to prevent it from bouncing all over the place as I fly through the double doors leading to the playground.

"This is all my fault," I mutter.

I never skip outdoor recess, and the one time I do, something happens.

The cold hair smacks me in the face, and the only sound I hear is screams and cries coming from Sage. Snapping my head in their direction, I run some more, my heart in my throat, unable to breathe.

No. No. No.

Sage sees me running to her, and I watch her break down even more. I sit next to her on the bench, completely out of breath as she wraps her arms around me and sobs.

"Shh. It's okay. I'm here," I say calmly, even though my insides are screaming in panic. I look down, brush her hair out of her face, and see the bump already forming on her forehead where she hit it. "You're okay."

"It hurts, Miss Barlow. Is my head bleeding?"

"No, no blood. But you already have a little bump forming. Let's get you to the nurse to have you checked out."

I look up at Rachel, and she nods. "I have the other kids. Go."

Sage doesn't let go of me when we walk to the nurse. I have my arm around her shoulder, and her arms are around my waist as we walk together. I'm terrified she's going to pass out and fall to the ground at any given second.

This is all my fault.

I sit on the chair next to the desk in the nurse's office while she looks over Sage. My leg bounces, and my hands feel clammy while I wait. I know she's okay. She has to be okay. It's just a bump.

"She's going to be okay," the nurse says. "She's just got a little bump. No immediate signs of a concussion. I'm going to call her dad to come pick her up, though."

"I'll do it," I say a little too quickly. "I mean, I can do that. I can call him."

"Okay." She shrugs. "I'm going to grab her an ice pack."

Pulling my cell phone from my pocket, I find Dallas in my contacts and press connect with shaky hands.

"Hey, Poppy," he says with a relaxed voice.

"Dallas," I nearly sob when I say his name out loud, but I

clear my throat. "Sage had an accident on the playground and hit her head. I'm—"

"I'm on my way," he says quickly, cutting me off and hanging up the phone.

I close my eyes, letting my head fall back against the wall behind me.

I need to breathe.

But I can't.

I have to get out of this room.

"Do you have her for a second?" I ask the nurse, and she nods. "I'm just going to run back to the classroom to grab her stuff so she's ready to go."

Once I step into the hallway, I inhale one long breath to try and steady myself. I rush to my classroom and close the door behind me. Alone in the room, panic engulfs me. I claw at my stomach, bending over and letting the tears fall. This is exactly why I stick to my routine, because I feel a sense of control. Could she have fallen off the swing with me there? Yes. But I wouldn't have been so far away. I could have jumped into action quicker.

I stagger my way to my desk, feeling uneasy on my feet.

I can't rid my mind of this panic.

Dallas is going to blame me. Sage is going to blame me.

This is all my fault.

Moments later, there's a light knock on my door. As soon as it opens, I see Dallas filling the frame, hesitant to come in. As soon as his eyes meet mine, though, something in him snaps. He rushes over to me, rounding my desk and crouching down beside me. My lips tremble, and my eyes well with tears spilling down my cheeks. I don't say anything because I can't.

I'm sorry just seems so inconsequential.

"Are you okay?" he asks.

I shake my head, and he reaches for me, pulling me into him. My forehead falls to his shoulder, and my body shakes with sobs. "I'm sorry."

"Shh, honey. It's okay."

"No, it's not."

He pulls back. With one hand on my shoulder and the other taking my chin in his fingers, he forces me to look at him. "Sage is okay. She has a nasty bump on her head, but I promise you, it's not the first one she's ever had." He pauses, making sure his words hit me where they need to. I release a sigh of relief, almost, even if my brain is still telling me otherwise. "I don't know what I would have done if you weren't there."

"But I wasn't," I snap, standing from my chair and brushing him aside to pace the room. "That's the problem, Dallas. I always am. I never miss outdoor recess, but today I did." My words come out louder with each one I say, frantic as I move around the classroom. "Today, I sent Rachel. I wasn't there. You should hate me. I wasn't watching your daughter."

He doesn't respond. He just stands there in silence, absorbing everything I just said. With slow, tentative steps, he closes the gap between us.

"Listen to me carefully when I tell you this, Poppy. You're not to blame. No one is."

And the better part of my mind knows that.

I don't know why I'm still spiraling.

"And I never want to hear you say that I should hate you. There isn't a bone in my body that possibly could."

I stand there, shocked at his admission.

The corners of his lip twist into a grin as he registers the look on my face. Swiping a tear lodged on my cheek away, he presses a kiss to the spot. "And I mean that. I'd stay here for hours if I could to tell you and make sure you know, but I'm going to get Sage home to ice her head some more and rest."

I nod, unable to find the right words to say back.

He leans in one more time, kissing me softly. Confirmation that he meant what he said before turning around, grabbing her bag, and walking out the door.

It's only then that the screaming in my head subsides.

CHAPTER 27
YOU DESERVE TO FIND HAPPINESS IN YOUR LIFE, DALLAS.

DALLAS

I called Tucker to cancel baseball practice tonight because I didn't want to bring Sage with her lingering headache or leave her with anyone. He insisted on handling it and keeping it as scheduled. I don't know what to think about that, but I'm going to let Tucker have this one.

My second call is to April.

I save her for last because I know this one will be longer.

"Hey, Dallas," she says on the other end.

"Hey, April. Sorry to call you while you're still at work, but there was an accident at school today."

"Oh my god. Dallas! What!"

"It's okay. She's okay. I probably should have led with that. I'm sorry."

"You think?"

"She fell off the swing at recess and hit her head. She didn't need to go to the doctor, and there were no cuts. She just has a bump on her head, and there's no signs of a concussion or anything."

When I left the nurse, that was the first thing I asked. From my years of playing sports, I know a concussion when I see one.

I know the signs to look for and when things start to indicate that we need to implement some type of medical intervention.

This isn't that.

"Okay," she breathes out on the other end. "That's good. I'm going to leave now and come there."

"Of course. Sage will love that. We're hanging in tonight, so we will be here."

"See you soon."

She hangs up, and I spend the next half hour straightening up the kitchen and putting her backpack from school away. Just as I'm about to sit down on the couch next to Sage, there's a knock on the door.

"Who's that?" Sage asks.

"Not sure."

When I open the door, I see Poppy standing on the other side, holding a box in one hand and a basket in the other. She's still wearing the same outfit she had on at school—a pair of bright pink jeans and a tucked-in T-shirt with an apple on the front. She hasn't even taken off her work lanyard.

She came right here.

I'm not surprised, given the state of mind she was in when I left her in her classroom. She blames herself, and I hate that. I fucking *hate* that she's blaming herself for this, and I wish I had the right words for her to know she did nothing wrong.

"Hey," she says softly. "I'm sorry to show up unannounced, but I wanted to see that Sage was okay. I brought her some goodies, too."

"You didn't have to do that, Poppy. But she's going to love it."

I step back, letting her in, and Sage notices her.

"Poppy! You're here!" She sits up taller on the couch, and I watch as Poppy assesses her from head to toe. Her shoulders relax as if seeing her was what she needed. "I'm all better now. Just have a bumpy bump on my head."

"That's so great to hear. I brought you some goodies." She

lifts the arm with the box. "I got a six-pack of assorted muffins from Batter Up." Then she lifts the basket. "And I put together a little basket of coloring things for you since I know it's your favorite."

Sage claps her hands in excitement. "This is so fun. My head feels much better already."

Poppy and I laugh simultaneously, because it's always the little things.

I stare at Poppy while she looks at Sage in wonder. She looks at her like she's the light of her life, or maybe I'm reading too much into it.

She just fits.

And it's so much deeper than that for me. Poppy was right to say she's not like other girls I've been with, and it has nothing to do with her being inexperienced. It has everything to do with how I've approached things with her. Did I flirt hard at the start before I knew she was Sage's teacher? Yes. Did I slow down and control myself when I found out? Also yes. All of it's an approach I've never taken before. With April and all my past relationships, it's been physical before it got any deeper.

It's the opposite with Poppy, and maybe that's why I'm feeling the way I do about her.

There's no denying that I'm hooked on her.

She's like a song you can't help but play on repeat.

Her eyes find mine, and they lock there. A smile grows on her lips when she sees me already watching her—drinking her in.

"I'm going to grab us some drinks," I say, clearing my throat. "Poppy, would you like something?"

She nods. "I'll help."

She follows me into the kitchen, keeping her distance, and I hate it.

"She's okay?" she asks almost immediately.

"She is."

Silence in the room stretches. I grab the pitcher of iced tea I made earlier today and three cups from the cabinet. I fill them each and hand her one.

"I don't know if this makes you feel any better, but I was scared shitless. I've never been scared like that in my life. Not after my accident. Not during intense games. Not ever."

She averts her gaze to the floor because she knows the feeling.

"I don't know how to handle this part of parenthood—the unexpected things that happen. I know about head injuries, but it's different when it's your kid. I'm really trying to be a good dad."

Poppy moves forward, palm connecting with my forearm. "But you are."

I offer her a soft, reassuring smile. "I'm starting to feel like one. One day at a time, I'm starting to feel more like a dad than a father."

"It's the same thing."

I shake my head. "If there's one thing I've learned through life, it's that anyone can be a father. But it takes a lot more effort, time, and love to be a dad."

"I don't have experience being a parent, but from the many meetings I've had with them at the school, I think they all feel that way one time or another. There's no rule book for parenting or what to do when things happen. It's just something you have to learn along the way. You're a really good dad, Dallas." She removes her hand from my forearm and looks to the ground before nervously wringing her hands together. "And I'm not just saying that because I like you."

I soak in every word she says because she means them.

Every. Single. One of them.

"You like me, huh?"

She rolls her eyes. "Out of everything I just said, that's what you're stuck on?"

"I'm stuck on every word out of your mouth always, honey."

She blushes at my admission, and I smirk. "But in all seriousness. Thank you for everything. It means everything that you came here today to bring that stuff for Sage. I think she would say the same."

"She means a lot to me."

I close the space between us, wrapping my hand around the side of her neck, and she looks up at me. My eyes trail from her eyes to her lips and the way she opens her mouth to say something, but nothing comes out. But she doesn't look away.

"This place is changing me, Poppy." My admission shocks even me, but I can't take it back. "Being here, it's everything that I needed."

I move closer to her, just a little, letting my lips hover as if waiting for permission to kiss her again and letting her have this control. I wonder if she can hear the thunder of my heart beating in my chest.

She reaches up on her toes and presses her lips to mine.

There's no rush in this kiss, and it's not explosive fireworks. It's slow and tentative. Her fingertips graze my jaw before the tangle in my hair, and it feels like she's anchoring herself to me. So I wrap my arms around her waist, kissing her like maybe my showing up is everything she's needed too.

She pulls away, ending the kiss more quickly than I would have liked.

"We should bring Sage her drink," she says, blushing and hiking a thumb over her shoulder.

"You're probably right."

She grabs two glasses, and I grab mine. When she enters the living room, Sage is immersed in the latest episode of *Spidey and His Amazing Friends*. Poppy sits down right next to her.

Just as I'm about to sit down again, the front door opens.

"Mommy!" Sage says, leaping off the couch and into April's arms. "What are you doing here?"

"Daddy called me, and I wanted to see that you were okay."

"I'm okay," Sage says before brushing her hair back and revealing the bump. "I gots this. But it doesn't hurt anymore."

"Oof. Yeah, you really hit your head hard. You take after your dad with your recklessness, it seems."

Sage laughs and heads back to the couch, and that's when April notices Poppy for the first time. Everything in me is on high alert. I've never discussed another woman with April, and she hasn't seen me with anyone since our divorce years ago. She knows my history and that I was casually seeing women here and there, but she knew my rule was never to bring them around Sage.

"Hi, Miss Barlow," April says to her before facing me and raising an eyebrow.

Poppy stands abruptly. "I'm sorry to intrude here. Sage fell on the playground today, and I wanted to come by and make sure she was okay."

"That's very sweet of you."

Poppy nods and looks at me. "I'm going to head home. Thank you for letting me stop by." She turns around to Sage. "Feel better, Sage."

"Thank you, Poppy!"

Poppy's eyes lock with mine, and I want to pull her into my arms, tuck her under my shoulder, and tell her she has nothing to worry about—that she can stay. That April is here for Sage. I can't read her face to know if she's upset, mad, or anything.

The door closes behind her, and I feel like I'm suffocating already.

April is about to bombard me with questions.

"Did you ice her head?" she asks, shocking me because that's not what I expected.

"Yes."

"Good." She nods and makes her way to the kitchen as if she's been here a hundred times before.

I follow her, waiting for the rug to be pulled out from under me.

Once she's in the kitchen, she turns around to face me. "So, does her teacher come here often?"

And there it is.

"No."

It's not a lie, but the long stretch of silence coming from April leads me to believe she doesn't buy it. I let the tension linger in the air, and just as I'm ready to open my mouth to say something, she cuts me off.

"I like her."

"What?"

"I'm saying I like her. I don't know what's happening between you two, aside from her being Sage's teacher, but I hope you know that I don't care who you date. Even though we didn't work out, I know you're not stupid enough to bring someone around Sage who would hurt her. I know I've only met her once at the conference we had at the school, but the communication on the app tells me she's friendly and a great teacher. I don't blame you for liking her, too, if you do." She shrugs.

That…is not what I was expecting.

"She's different," I settle on, unsure if this is a trap and something that will lead to an argument. "I do like her and care about her."

She eyes me carefully before her features soften. She steps closer to me, putting a hand on my shoulder. "You deserve to find happiness in your life, Dallas. I mean it when I say I don't care who you see, just like I know you don't care who I see."

And she's right. I don't care because I know she will only have Sage's best interests in mind when she brings anyone around her. But her saying it out loud is almost the confirmation I needed. I wasn't worried about what April would think about me being involved with anyone; I was more concerned with the possibility of her judging me. I don't know why. Maybe it's because I've fucked up so much in the past that she would hold it against me.

"So if something were to happen with me and Poppy, you'd be okay with it?"

She scoffs, waving me off. "Dallas, please. I'm okay with

whatever makes you happy. As long as it makes Sage happy, too."

"We're not here much longer, though."

"Do you think you'd want to stay in Bluestone Lakes?"

The question catches me off guard because it's not something I had considered until just now. Would I want to stay here? Can I see myself living here and giving up baseball completely?

"Clark is waiting for a decision from me before we head back."

"Do you know what you'll do?"

I shake my head.

She looks away, biting her bottom lip to fight a smile forming on her lips. "Now probably isn't the best time to tell you, but a few things have come up in the city."

"Like what?"

"Well, for one, they offered me a permanent spot as head of the obstetrics department team," she says proudly.

"April, that's amazing."

"And, I, kind of, sort of, maybe met someone?" she says, but it comes out like a question.

I laugh. "Didn't you just tell me you don't care who I see, and I don't care who you see. It's great that you met someone, April."

"Yeah, I guess you're right. I guess it puts me at a crossroads. I don't know what to do because our life is still back in San Francisco."

"Are you saying you'd like to stay out here possibly?"

She shrugs.

I know she doesn't want to admit it because we've spent our lives around my baseball career. We came out to Wyoming because I wanted her to put her job first for once. I don't want to be the reason she gives up on that.

"Let's see what happens in the next few weeks," I tell her.

"Good idea."

Everything about this temporary stay here in Bluestone Lakes has changed me. If this conversation had happened months ago, I'd be saying "Sure, let's stay." But here we are, standing in the kitchen of my rental, with level heads, as we figure out the next step.

Except now, I can't stop thinking about what would happen if I did stay here.

CHAPTER 28
YOU'RE NOT PLANNING ON USING THAT LIST WITH ANYONE ELSE, ARE YOU?

POPPY

When I'm anxious, I clean.

I don't know what Dallas has told April about us. I mean, I don't even know much about us, other than I want him to keep kissing me, and I fall asleep thinking of the only orgasm I've had in my life from him. I didn't want to stick around and be the reason Dallas argued with his ex-wife for my being there.

As I move around the house cleaning things that are already clean, my head goes to the worst case scenario for everything that happened today. I think of things like April calling the school to tell them about Dallas and me, or her telling him they are going back to the city tomorrow. It's irrational, but I don't know anything about her. All things are out of my control, but things I can't stop my brain from wondering.

I've wiped down the kitchen counters and coffee table already. I grab the stack of notes, checklists, and papers off my nightstand and bring them into the living room to put them out of the way. Then, I grab the dusting rag and solution to wipe down the dresser. Before I can put anything back where it was after I'm done, there's a knock on my door.

Opening the door, I find Dallas on the other side. I look

around him to see if Sage or anyone is with him and notice he's all alone.

"I'm sorry for showing up unplanned, but I wanted to check on you since you left so quickly earlier."

I want to say something witty back about how that's my line—I'm the one who's always sorry. But the only thing registering is that he understands me enough to know that I don't like unplanned things. That he wanted to check on me because he cared.

"I'm okay. I'm just cleaning. Is Sage okay?"

"She's good."

"Where is she?"

He tips his head toward his house. "April is with her."

Taking a step back, I open the door wider and allow him inside. I know he said he's just here to check on me, but it feels like more. My nerves are on high alert because this is where everything falls apart. This is where I learn I'm not good enough for him after I've already allowed myself to fall. Or is this where he tells me he's leaving for good?

He stands in the middle of the living room, eyes on me as I nervously play with my fingers in front of me.

"So, April and I talked briefly."

"Yeah?"

"She had questions about why you were there." There's a long pause as if there's more to the story, so I stay silent. "She likes you."

"She what?"

"She likes you. And the conversation was mostly her telling me that she wants me to find happiness. How she doesn't care who I see, while I don't care who she sees. As long as it's in the best interest of Sage."

Does April think I'm not the best person to be in Sage's life?

The questions racing through my brain not long ago come rushing back. Maybe she sees me as unfit since I'm at a student's house after hours, falling for a parent. She's going to call the school. I knew this was a bad idea.

As if he picks up on my panic, even though I'm trying to hide it, he walks over to me. He grips the back of my neck with one hand, lifting my head and crashing his lips to mine. I gasp at how rough he is compared to how gentle he's always been with me, but Christ, that's the hottest thing he's ever done. He uses his other hand to pull my body flush with his. And I melt—weak in the knees at the intensity of this kiss. There's no reservation or gentleness in this kiss, just raw desperation driven by hunger.

My fingers dig into his skin as I grip his waist, and his lips part, allowing him to deepen the kiss. It's the kind that says *don't leave again*. The power in this kiss doesn't come from dominance. It comes from passion being pushed to the brink and finally breaking through.

He pulls back, lips hovering over mine with one hand still wrapped gently around my neck and the other gripping my waist. "I saw the questions and uncertainty racing through your mind. I wasn't wasting another moment of you second-guessing everything this is between us."

"What is this between us?" I practically pant.

"I wish I had the answer," he says, smiling against my lips. "But you're in control here. I'm following your lead." His hand around my neck moves to the back, tangling his fingers through my hair. "You should know I'm at your mercy, honey."

My body shivers at the way he explains it, sending a throb between my legs, and I can't help but smile.

Dallas Westbrook makes me want things I didn't realize were possible. I envision a future I never thought I could have. I don't know anything about baseball, but I want to run all the bases with him—I think that's called a home run.

"Okay," I say, shyly stepping away from him, only to catch the edge of the coffee table. I stumble, but he steadies me before grabbing the stack of papers from my room, before they fall.

My eyes widen when I see what's sitting on top.

Dallas notices it and does a double-take, setting everything else back on the coffee table but still holding the note. I didn't expect Dallas to come here when I decided to clean.

I try to snatch it from his hands, but he lifts it high in the air. The grin on his face tells me he's read every word on that list.

"So, you made a list, huh?"

My cheeks feel crimson red as I try to jump and snatch the list from his hand. I fail miserably and take a step back. I watch as he takes the list, folds it up, and stuffs it into the back pocket of his jeans.

"You weren't supposed to see that."

"I need you to answer my next question very carefully, Poppy."

I swallow before nodding in agreement.

"You're not planning on using that list with anyone else, are you?"

With my heart pounding in my chest, I shake my head. Of course not, because Dallas is the only man that's been on my mind. I wrote that list with him, and only him, in mind.

"Good." He steps toward me, forcing me to look up at him. I suck in a sharp breath when he brings his lips back down over mine. My entire body is on fire with every move and every breath. "I want to be the only man who will be checking anything off that list of yours. The only fucking man to touch you the way you deserve to be touched. It'll be me and *only* me," he growls. "Understood?"

I suck in another sharp breath. "Yes."

"However, I only noticed two things on the list."

I shrug, feeling embarrassed and stepping out of his hold. "I haven't done anything other than what you've done to me."

The corner of his lips twist up at the same time he raises an eyebrow. "Nothing?"

I shake my head, averting my gaze because this is so embarrassing. Probably worse than telling him I'm actually a virgin.

He grips my chin, forcing me to look at him. "Don't be shy

with me, Poppy. You *never* have to be shy with me. I'll take care of you."

Oh my god.

My core throbs; the feeling of the first time his hands were all over me comes rushing back. Is it crazy that I want him to start checking things off with me right now? He can't stay long, so that's insanity, but Christ, the pressure is building the longer he looks at me.

He must know because he reaches into his back pocket, never taking his eyes off mine, to reread the list.

"Number one, give a blow job." His smile stretches from ear to ear.

Obviously, I've never given one, but the thought of doing it with Dallas excites me more than it scares me. I know he's going to take care of me and ensure I don't feel embarrassed about doing it wrong.

And I want it.

I know Dallas won't push me either. He won't take the first step because he's giving me control. I look to the door, and back to him. My body moves on its own when I take a step into him, hooking my fingertips into his jeans. He hisses at the touch, looking down at where I toy with the button of the jeans.

"You don't have to do this right now, Poppy. I want you to take all the time you need. I want you to be ready."

I remain silent, unbuttoning his jeans and sliding the zipper down. Before I can do anything else, Dallas tosses the list onto the table and grips my chin between his fingers, forcing me to look up with my hands still on his jeans.

"Can you show me?" I ask, before he can protest this anymore.

He gives me a quick nod, not moving, letting me have this control.

I tug down his jeans, and he stands there in just a pair of black boxer briefs. Anticipation swirls between my legs, but fear grips my chest because, without even taking them off, I can tell he's big from how hard he is under the fabric. My tongue darts out, swiping across my bottom lip, which forces a low growl to rumble in his chest.

Which only makes me want this that much more.

"Take it out."

Tucking my fingers into the boxer briefs, I push them down. His cock springing free and a bead of pre-cum dripping from the tip already. I bite my bottom lip as I stare at it, while I involuntarily rub my legs together, craving some sort of friction.

"Wrap your hand around my cock."

His orders are strong and dominant, which only builds the tension in my body. With one hand resting on my thigh, I sit back on my heels and take his cock in my other hand. It's thick and hard with veins protruding around the sides, but the skin around it feels soft under my touch. He sucks in a sharp breath at the touch, his hips moving forward on their own.

"Now you're going to slide your hand up and down."

Slowly, my hand pumps him from root to tip, and he moans. That one moan ignites something in me I never thought I would feel. Where he was once feral for me, I'm finding myself desperate for him. Without further instruction, I press off my heels and lick the drop of pre-cum off the tip.

"Fuck, honey," he groans, eyes rolling in the back of his head as he tips his head back. But it only lasts a second because he needs his eyes on me. "Now open those pretty lips for me. Let me feel your mouth wrapped around my cock."

"I don't want to mess this up," I admit nervously.

"Poppy… You don't have to be nervous with me. You're so fucking perfect that I want to come just from your hand wrapped around me. I can come from just seeing you on your knees in front of me. I promise you, you can't mess this up."

I smile at that, and it turns me on even more that barely doing anything *turns him on* this much. Opening my mouth, I take him in as far as I can.

"Oh my god," he draws out. "Yes, Poppy."

I push a little deeper until I feel him in the back of my throat. A soft gag escapes me, but I don't stop. As much as he's enjoying this, I am too. The need to give this man pleasure is so intense right now. Pulling back, I let my tongue slide across the base.

"That's it."

I move quicker with every move out of his mouth, letting his words of reassurance tell me I'm doing this right, even if I don't know if it is. My one hand still grips his shaft, moving up and down in sync with my mouth. From the small grunts coming out of him every few minutes, I know he likes this.

"You like it when I tell you how good you're doing, don't you?"

I nod, swirling my tongue around the tip while I pump his cock with my hand harder and faster.

"I can tell," he pants, barely able to hold it together. "You're taking me so well, Poppy. Do you feel how hard I am for you?"

I nod repeatedly, answering his question, as I take him completely into my mouth. This time, when he hits the back of my throat, I don't gag. I close my eyes, feeling hungrier than ever to see him come for me. I feel soaked between my own legs at how good this feels–how hot this is.

Releasing my mouth from him, I work my hand from base to tip, looking up at him. "I like it when you watch me."

He growls in response, taking his hand and placing it on the back of my head, tangling his fingers through my hair to hold me in place as I suck his cock. *Yes*, I want to say.

"You're so perfect on your knees for me." I squirm in response to the praise. "You're so turned on by sucking my cock, aren't you?" I nod. "Reach your hands into your leggings and show me just how turned on you really are."

Holy shit.

He pulls out of my mouth, taking a step back and watching, waiting to see how turned on I am. I reach into my leggings, swiping my index finger through my pussy, and moan when I touch my throbbing clit. I've never gotten myself off, but there's something about his eyes on me that makes me want to stay here, letting him watch me touch myself for the first time.

Taking my fingers out, I show him the wetness coating them. "Such a good girl."

"Are you going to come?"

"Yeah, honey. I'm definitely going to come."

I lick my lips, ready to see this man fall apart before me. I pump my hand up and down a few more times before taking him into my mouth again—lingering there for a moment, and that does it. His body tightens, and his abdominal muscles contract.

"Poppy," he warns. "I'm going to come. If you don't want it down the back of your throat, I would stop now."

Truthfully, I don't know what I want.

All I know is I want to see him come undone for me.

I suck him harder, not releasing my mouth, and within seconds, he grunts, cursing under his breath as he comes down the back of my throat. The feeling is so intense, almost like an out-of-body experience. I have never felt so sexy and alive before, and it has everything to do with this man.

"Are you going to swallow for me, Poppy?"

I sit back on my heels, looking up at him with glassy eyes, and swallow everything he just gave me.

"Fuck," he says, barely above a whisper. He leans down, lifting me off the ground to stand in front of him. His pants are around his ankles, and he presses me into him, wrapping his arms tightly around my body before kissing me.

"That was really hot." I giggle against his chest when we pull away.

"That was the hottest blow job I've ever had."

My head wants to tell me he's lying. My thoughts want to throw up a red flag that he's just saying that in a post orgasmic haze. But there isn't a part of Dallas that's lying. I know that–I feel that.

"Normally, this is where I would take care of you," he says, leaning forward, pressing a kiss to the pounding pulse in my neck before he whispers, "this is where I would make you come so hard you're seeing stars."

I gasp, pressing my legs tighter together because I want that.

"But I didn't expect to even be here this long, and April needs to go back to the city tonight."

I nod. "I'm sorry—"

He cuts me off, pressing an index finger to my lips. "This is most definitely not something you should be sorry for. I'm more than happy to help you check this off your list for you." He winks before stepping back and reaching down to pull up his boxer briefs and jeans.

Then he does what I least expect him to do.

He picks up the paper that I scribbled the list on and moves to find a pen on my kitchen counter. He leans over it, smiling to himself as he checks the box I drew in front of the first line.

I blush because it still feels silly for me to have a checklist for this, but at the same time, it's comforting to know that Dallas isn't thinking of me any differently for it. He doesn't make me feel self-conscious about it. He makes me feel seen. He makes me feel heard even when I don't have the words all the time.

But some people don't understand words, while some won't even need words to understand.

That's Dallas.

Standing in front of me again, he leans down for one more kiss. He presses his lips to mine, reassuring and comforting. He doesn't need to make a comment about what he just did to the list, or ask me if I'm okay, because he knows.

He's taking care of me in his quiet, comforting way.

"I'll see you soon, Poppy." And he turns on his heel and walks to the door, but pauses as he opens it and turns back to me one last time. "Oh, and you don't fucking check off number two without me. Understood?"

My lips part in shock as I nod, unable to speak.

"I need your words, honey."

"Yes," I breathe out.

"Good girl," he says in a low, raspy voice with a grin plastered on his lips because he knows what he just did. He knows my body is craving his touch and desperate to feel more after all of that. It just won't be tonight. "Good night, Poppy."

With that, he walks out the front door, closing it with a click behind him.

As I look at the back of the door, two things are certain:

1. I need to order a vibrator.
2. I'm officially at the mercy of Dallas Westbrook.

CHAPTER 29
YOU'VE BEEN DOING YOUR RESEARCH, HUH?

DALLAS

> Did you order something to be shipped to my house?

POPPY

> No?
>
> Dallas! DO NOT OPEN THAT. OH MY GOD.

> Now I'm intrigued.

POPPY

> It's illegal to open someone's mail.

> I just flipped the box around. The packaging isn't very discreet, honey.
>
> Green is my favorite color, too. *wink face*

POPPY

> I'm mortified. This is so embarrassing.

> It's actually really hot.
>
> I can't wait to help you cross this one off the list next.

I'm sitting in my truck outside of the barnyard, ready for practice this week. Sage was better the next day after her playground accident, and everything is resuming as normal.

Just as I'm about to exit, my phone rings. I smile to myself, assuming it's Poppy calling me to ensure I don't open her box that holds a green vibrator. I'm not sure where she ordered from, but their packaging needs some work.

Except, I see Clark's name flash across the screen, and my smile falls. I haven't spoken to him since I left after the last season ended. Not because I don't want to, but I was afraid that if I picked up the phone to call him, I would make a decision before I've thought anything through.

He didn't call me either, presumably for the same reason.

Now that we're creeping up on spring training, it's getting close to me making a decision.

"Hello?"

"Hey, Dallas. Long time no talk," he says on the other end. "How's everything in Wyoming?"

"It's going good."

"How're Sage and April doing?"

"Both of them are doing well. Sage is having a good school year here, and April is liking her job."

"That's great," he says, pausing, waiting for me to say more, but I don't. "I know we're still a few weeks away from making a decision. Time is flying, huh? Anyway, I was calling to see if you've come up with a plan for this upcoming season after all your time away."

Yeah, I've come up with a lot of plans.

I've come up with a lot of plans, but surprisingly, none of them revolve around baseball or San Francisco. My issue is I have no fucking clue what to do anymore. It's not like me to have to think things through. I know what I want, make a decision quickly, and figure it out along the way. That's how I ended up leaving the city.

But now that I'm here, in Bluestone Lakes, everything has changed.

I didn't expect to like the quiet, slow-paced small town.

I didn't expect Sage to fall in love with her school, although I should have guessed she would.

I didn't expect my neighbor to throw a curveball in my life.

I fucking told myself coming here, I wouldn't form any attachments due to the impending expiration date. Well, now I have one. And it's not like any other one I've had before. It's one that I can't see giving up.

One that I don't want to give up.

"I haven't, Clark," I tell him honestly. "I'm not sure of anything anymore."

"Yeah?" I can hear the smile in his voice. He's pleased by this because he was right about me needing a break. "I'm proud of you for not jumping into any decisions and thinking this through. You needed that. We will need to know soon. Not right now, but soon. I'll email you a date I have on my calendar for a meeting with the board here in the city. If you can make it in person, that would be great."

"You got it."

"On a lighter note, you're doing okay? What have you been doing to keep busy?"

I stare out the front window of my Tahoe, look out at the barnyard, and smile. This wasn't what I expected to happen when I got here, either. Now, I see a group of kids tossing the ball around with one another. Sage included, who jumped out of the car as soon as I put it in park a little bit ago.

Not just a makeshift diamond of dirt anymore.

It's a *baseball* field now.

Tonight is the first practice on a field I created for them over the weekend with a bit of help from Griffin.

We built an entire mini dugout for the kids with circle letters over the top that spell out HOME. The weeds have been picked, new benches installed, the wire fence behind the home plate replaced, and they now have real bases instead of cardboard pieces.

"I'm doing good. Keeping busy," I answer honestly. "I have to get going, though. I'll give you a call when I have a plan in place."

"Sounds good. Remember what I said, no more strikeouts, only home runs."

I hang up, tossing my phone into the cup holder and making my way to the field, where the kids are taking everything in.

"Would you look at this, coach?" Archie shouts. "It's a new field."

"And a whole dugout with nice new benches!" Ethan adds. "No more butt splinters."

Tucker pulls up moments later with Nan in tow, making their way to the field with wide eyes, too. I didn't tell anyone I was doing this. I wanted it to be a surprise for all the hard work these kids put in.

"The barnyard got a makeover, huh?" Nan says, knowing I had everything to do with this, but not saying it out loud. "Never thought I'd see the day this space got cleaned nice enough to look like the real deal." She laughs before moving off to the side to take a phone call or something.

"Holy cannoli," Tucker says. "This is so epic. Oh my god. Makes me want to win a championship."

"Yeah!" all the kids shout in unison.

"When is the first game, coach?" Gabe asks. "I got my cannon arm locked and loaded to win."

"The first one is scheduled for a few weeks from now. It's coming up quickly, and I think we're going to do amazing. And now that the weather is no longer below freezing, we can really enjoy the game."

"Cold means nothing to us," Austin chimes in. "Feels like summer."

"Summer? It's still in the thirties," Ethan scoffs. "Meaning, I'm still cold."

"Let's warm up then, shall we?" I announce and toss the bag of equipment next to the bench.

They all spread out, gloves in hand, and partner up to toss the ball around.

Every week that passes, they surprise me more and more. At that very first practice, they couldn't hit the water if they fell out of a boat. Shoulders slumped, eyes down, and some of them were afraid even to speak. I kept showing up for them as long as they showed up for me. Even on the coldest days, they *still* showed up.

And now? Now they move like a team that's been doing this for years.

They aren't just playing the game anymore. They're living it.

I'm a little proud of myself, too, if I'm being honest.

After being told I was a shit coach, I shifted everything. Bringing myself to their level and adapting to what *they* need versus what I *think* they need. Each and every one of them now believes in each other, themselves, and *me*.

I look to my left and see Tucker standing there. His legs are spread, his arms crossed over his chest, and he watches as all the kids warm up. I clasp a hand on his shoulder, startling him out of his daze.

"Oh, sorry, coach. I'm in awe of these kids and seeing them on a real baseball field. This is so cool. I wonder who did all of this."

"I did." He snaps his head in my direction with eyes wide, and I laugh. "I did it over the weekend with Griffin, but don't tell them that."

"First, I'd like it on record that I'm deeply offended I wasn't asked to help. I literally work in construction, Dallas. I thought we were friends." He rolls his eyes and then smiles. "Second, my lips are sealed."

I can't help but shake my head. "Let me ask you something before we get started on practice."

He turns his body to face me. "Of course, Dallas. Whatever

you need. I'm still offended, but you know I'm your guy no matter what."

"You think you can coach these kids on your own when the season starts if I go back to San Francisco?"

"If?"

Car tires crunching on the gravel pull our attention to the makeshift parking lot. A grin spreads on my lips—I can't help it because Poppy emerges from her car.

I turn back to face Tucker, who looks confused. "If."

He still seems unsure until he looks from Poppy and back to me. "Ohhhh. If!" He bounces where he stands like a child who can't contain their excitement. "Tell me something's happening between you two. Oh my god, please tell me. I can be related to you. This is amazing news."

"Shh. Can you chill out? I didn't say anything was happening."

"You said *if*, Dallas. Meaning you're not sure you want to go back. No one stays in Bluestone Lakes when you have the life you have back in the city for no reason. Poppy girl is your reason."

Among other things, Tucker is right.

She's a big reason.

When you feel a connection this strong with someone, you chase it. I've had relationships. I've been married. I've done casual. And nothing has ever compared to this.

She lights up every part of me.

She forces me to slow down when I want to jump.

She's soft and steady.

She's…everything.

Turning around, I see her making her way to where Tucker and I stand. She has her hands tucked into the back pocket of her skin tight jeans with a solid pink long sleeve T-shirt tucked in.

"Nan told me this place got cleaned up. I had to come see it for myself right away."

That one sentence does something to me I didn't expect.

It's six at night, in the middle of the week, and Poppy dropped everything to come here and see this. My heart skips a few beats the longer I stare at her with only that thought in mind.

I open my mouth to say something, even though I don't even know how to respond, but Sage beats me to it. "Poppy! You're here!"

Poppy turns, opening her arms and letting Sage jump into them. My daughter is full of dirt and sweat, and Poppy is wrapping her arms tightly around my little girl anyway.

She looks so good with my kid.

"I wanted to come see the new field." They both release their hold, and Poppy stands. "This place looks amazing! I can't believe it looks like a real field."

Sage giggles. "Do you know what a real field looks like now?"

"I do," she answers Sage, then looks at me. "I've been doing some research, so I know what you and your dad are talking about."

I feel like I can't breathe.

She's admitting to taking the time to learn the one thing that has been a part of my life since I could walk. The thing that has brought me joy for my entire life before Sage was born.

Poppy not only feels like a grand slam in the bottom of the ninth, but she feels like I was given extra innings—one more chance to try and open up my heart to the possibilities for me.

No more strikeouts, only home runs.

Poppy Barlow is my home run. There's no doubt about it.

Tucker clears his throat, as if he can read every thought like an open book. "I'm going to get the kids started on practice. Let's toss this ball around, Sage."

He leaves with Sage, and I'm left staring at Poppy.

"You've been doing your research, huh?"

"Mm-hmm."

"So, have you learned any of the positions or what each one does?"

She shrugs. "I've learned the basics like the pitcher and catcher. I know a little bit about first, second, and third base, too. Outside of that, I have no clue yet." She laughs.

"Do you have plans tomorrow night?" I ask quickly.

"Uh. No, I'm just planning to do my puzzle like I do every night before I go to sleep."

I nod. "Good. I'm coming over." She eyes me curiously, so I lean down, letting my lips graze the shell of her ear. "No more research on your own. If you're going to learn, it's going to be from me."

She nods repeatedly, a blush painting her freckled cheeks. Just as she opens her mouth to say something else, tires screech to a halt on the main road. Loud music blasts from the speakers' bass. We all snap our heads in the direction of the blacked-out Tahoe that matches mine.

It takes me a moment to register who owns that vehicle, but it's clear when Tyler pops his head out of the sunroof in his team jersey with his fists in the air that I know exactly who is here for a visit. He points his finger in my direction and smiles widely. "There he is!"

"Don't leave yet," I tell Poppy and give her hand a light squeeze before jogging to where they parked.

Tyler jumps out of the passenger seat with more energy than I've ever seen from him, while Mitch takes his time getting out of the driver's side.

"What the hell are you two doing here?" I ask just as Tyler wraps his arms around my neck in the tightest hug, patting my back aggressively. "Watch the shoulder, Ty."

"I'm sorry, man. It's just so good to see you. We thought we'd show up in this middle-of-nowhere town and see what has kept you so busy that you can't talk to us anymore."

Guilt pricks me, because he's right. I've been the worst friend because I've been so preoccupied with everything. "I'm sorry. I've been doing a lot around here to keep busy."

Mitch eyes the field. "I can see that. This all looks brand new."

Tyler inhales deeply for exaggeration. "I can smell the fresh wood from the new dugout from here."

"I worked on it over the weekend with a new friend here in town. I wanted the kids to have something." I turn around, facing the field with my two best friends from back home. "Welcome to the barnyard."

"Ahh. I get it. The field is right next to the ranch. The *barn*yard." Tyler laughs, nodding his head in approval. "What's happening here tonight?"

"This is my team."

"Oh, that's right," Mitch says. "I completely forgot you were coaching kids here. Whoa." He pauses, pointing to Archie deep in the outfield, who just threw it to home plate. "That kid's got an arm on him."

"I'm more so wondering who *that* is over there by the dugout," Tyler says, gesturing to where Poppy stands next to Nan. "She hasn't stopped looking over here since I pulled up. Is she single? Do you know who she is?"

I smack his chest with the back of my hand. "Off-fucking-limits, Goodman."

"Shut up! Is that her? Is that the girl you were telling us about?"

"Yeah." I stare at her, smiling like a kid who just got told they can have the lollipop they just finished begging for. The woman who has shattered my sense of normal in the best ways possible. "That's her."

"No wonder you don't talk to us anymore." Tyler scoffs. "I'd be spending all my free time with her, too."

"Ty. You're my best friend, so I'm going to say this in the nicest way possible. But take your fucking eyes off of her."

"What's she like?" Mitch asks.

I pause, not knowing how to explain it. I stare at Poppy standing by the field. Sage has run up to her, handing her some type of weed she picked from the grass as if she just picked the most beautiful flower in the garden. They laugh, and Poppy gives her a hug.

My chest tightens with emotion. If the question was him asking me how I felt about her, I'd probably tell them she's it for me.

"She's different," I settle on. "She's not the type of woman you get out of your system."

Mitch turns to face me, placing a hand on my shoulder. "You're different, too, coach. In a good way. I'm really fucking proud of you."

I swallow, not wanting to get emotional with my best friends.

He's right, I *am* different.

I've been feeling this way for a while now.

Mitch doesn't have to say anything more, because I know what he's talking about. I'm not acting like the old Dallas with Poppy. I'm not making her a temporary stop in my life. She deserves so much more than that.

"SHUT UP! SHUT UP! SHUT UP!" Tucker screams, running to where the three of us stand. "Tyler Goodman and Mitch Holton are here. In Bluestone Lakes. At the barnyard. I think I'm going to fucking pass out."

Tyler leans over, keeping his voice low. "Who does he belong to?"

"The town, but sometimes I question if he belongs to the wolves," I answer, also keeping my voice low. "Tucker, this is Mitch and Tyler." I introduce them because it's polite, but I know Tucker doesn't need it.

He extends a hand, shaking both of my friends' hands. "It's an honor to meet you both. Oh my god, this is the greatest day of my life. I'm a huge fan."

"*Huge fan,*" I repeat, emphasizing the words.

The guys laugh. "Are you helping coach the kids?" Ty asks.

Tucker nods. "Coaching and moral support for our guy here." He gestures to me, playfully punching my good shoulder. "I can't believe you two are here. The kids are going to lose it."

"Introduce us," Mitch says, and follows Tucker to the kids.

When Poppy starts making her way to us, Tyler jogs up to meet them to say hi to the kids.

"Sorry about that," I say when she comes to a stop next to me. "Those guys would be my teammates from San Francisco. Mitch and Tyler."

"It's nice of them to show up to see the new field."

"They're actually here because I've apparently disappeared." She eyes me curiously, so I lean down, whispering for only her to hear, even though no one is around us. "I've been a little busy lately."

"Yeah. You put a lot of work into getting this set up for the kids."

"Not what I mean, honey."

She looks up at me from the side, a shy smile spreading across her lips.

"When my brain isn't focused on Sage and what I need to do with her, or keeping her busy. Every thought I have is consumed with you, Poppy. I'm always wondering what you're doing, how you are, and waiting for the next moment I can kiss you—touch you. It's all I think about."

"I've found myself doing the same thing," she admits.

"Good. I'll be over tonight then."

"But you said tomorrow?"

I nod my head toward my two friends. Mitch has Sage lifted, and her arms are wrapped around his neck, and Tyler is playing catch with Archie. "I have two guys who have missed Sage and will be more than happy to spend some time with her tonight."

I can tell she's nervous by the way she wrings her hands together, looking down at the dirt. So I spin her to face me. With wide eyes, she looks up at me. I say nothing but lean down and press a kiss to her forehead.

"Listen, I know we keep talking about checking the next thing off your list. I told you you're in control, and I meant it. But I want to—no, *I need to*—see you tonight even if it's just to spend time with you. That being said, I understand if you already have plans. I don't want to intrude on them."

"No, I want to see you, too, Dallas. Come over whenever, I'll be home."

I grin. "Yeah?" She tips her chin. "Then I'll be seeing you soon, honey. I'm going to get back to practice."

"Okay."

I give her hand another squeeze before jogging back to the field for practice.

CHAPTER 30
IS THIS WHAT YOU WANT, HONEY?

DALLAS

"Daddy, can we have a movie theater night with Uncle Mitch and Uncle Ty?" she asks with prayer hands and puppy dog eyes. "Pretty please."

"You always fall asleep twenty minutes into every movie, bug."

"I won't this time. I have all the energy flowing through my body tonight. My funcles are here!"

"Yeah, her funcles are here," Ty adds with his hands on his hips.

"Funcle?"

"Yeah. Uncles, but cooler and obviously more fun." Tyler shrugs.

I look to Mitch, who leans back on the couch and shakes his head. "You already know I had nothing to do with that."

"Trust me. Well aware."

"Pleaaaaseeeee," she begs.

"Fine," I say, grabbing the remote and clicking to the streaming service to let her pick the movie. "I'll make some popcorn."

"Yes!" she and Ty cheer in unison.

I swear, he's forever a child at heart. He really should spend some time with Tucker while he's in town because those two are the same person.

Once I enter the kitchen, reaching into the cabinet to grab the package of popcorn to throw in the microwave, a throat clears from the doorway. I find Mitch standing there with a look on his face.

"She's definitely going to be asleep in twenty minutes," he says.

"Yep."

"Are you going next door?" He raises an eyebrow. I give him a knowing look, but avert my gaze. "We can watch Sage if you want to."

"I did want to," I admit. "But you guys are only in town for the weekend, and I haven't seen you in months. Maybe after she goes to bed, we can sit on the back deck and catch up over a beer or something."

He barks out a laugh. "We just drove sixteen hours here on little sleep because we left sometime in the middle of the night. Ty will be passed out the same time Sage is, and I'm going to end up right there along with them shortly after."

"What are you saying?"

"I'm saying you should go next door and spend some time with your girl. At least that's what I assume she is. I know your time here is going to come to an end soon. I also know you well enough to know that you can't get enough of her. She's different, and so are you. You want time with her, and you should go take it."

My time here is going to come to an end soon.

His words hang in the air, and they sting like lemon juice on a paper cut. I've known this is the case. This was always supposed to be temporary—a reset.

But things have changed.

I didn't plan for Poppy to come raging into my life like a tidal wave.

The plan was always to leave and go back to the steady life I've always known. I have a job and a life waiting for me back in San Francisco. And now I'm here, thinking about a future that suddenly feels like a closed door, while another door I never expected swings open.

"You're right. I'd like to go see her."

"Get out of here then," Mitch says, gesturing to the back sliding door. "I'll bring the popcorn out and say you ran next door to drop something off. They'll be asleep before they even know you're gone."

"That means a lot. If Sage falls asleep on the couch, you can leave her there until I get back if you want. The guest bedroom is already set up. Leave Ty on the couch." I laugh.

"That was the plan." He winks.

"And call me if you need anything."

"I won't."

I shake my head, grab the box accidentally delivered to my house, and slip out the back door and walk across the lawn. The only light illuminating her house is the soft glow of her porch light. As I cross her front lawn, I don't see any lights on in her house other than the small one over her puzzle table, but I don't see her. Just as I'm about to lift my arm to knock, the door opens.

"Hi," she says softly.

I use this moment to take her in. She's wearing a pair of sleep shorts with a tank top tucked into the waistband. I spent a little longer checking out her long legs before she crosses one over the other where she stands, wrapping the cardigan covering all of it over her body. When my eyes meet hers, there's a tint of pink on her freckled cheeks.

"I'm sorry, I should have texted to say I was coming."

She shrugs, and a soft smile plays on her lips. "I knew you would come."

I step through the door, wrapping my hand around her waist to pull her closer. Her hands smooth up my chest to the back of my neck as she moves her body close. Her chest presses into me before her mouth connects with mine.

But this time, she's in control.

She's not holding back as she holds my head in place, tangling her fingers in my hair. She's kissing me like she wants to commit me to memory, like she'd been thinking about kissing me since I saw her earlier. She parts her lips, swiping her tongue against mine. A rumble vibrates through my chest as I toss the box in my hand onto the couch and walk us deeper into her house, kicking the door shut behind me with a bang. She guides me, and I follow.

I'm learning quickly that I'd follow her wherever she led me.

Bringing my hands behind her, reaching under the cardigan to the hem of her tank top, I slide them under the soft fabric and up her back, pressing my palms to her skin. She flinches, but doesn't break the kiss. It only makes her hungrier, and before I realize where we are, she backs us into her bedroom.

"Are you sure this is what you want, honey?"

"Yes. More than anything."

I crash my lips to hers, matching her desire, as if something deep inside of me that's remained dormant for so long has been woken up. Heat builds inside of me, my cock stirring to life between us, making me desperate for a taste of whatever she's willing to give me tonight.

Reluctantly, I stop kissing her, taking a step away from her. My fingertips graze along her collarbone and down her arms as I peel the cardigan off her shoulders, letting it fall to the floor around her feet. Goose bumps pebble across her skin, and my eyes land on the swell of her breasts. Her nipples pebble under the fabric, which forces my cock to strain behind the zipper of my jeans.

I take a moment to brush her hair behind her shoulders, giving me a full view of her. "You're so fucking perfect," I tell her honestly. "I'm a strong man, Poppy Barlow. But you…you make me weak. Whatever you want, ask for it. I'll give it to you."

"I don't know exactly what I want, but I know I want you to touch me."

"Where?"

"Everywhere, Dallas."

My hands reach up, cupping both of her breasts in my palms. My heart's racing at any chance to touch Poppy the way she deserves to be touched. I *want* to make her feel good. I *want* to give her anything she's willing to let me give her.

I just want her.

"How about here?"

She nods, reaching up to let the thin strap of her tank top slide down her arm. I take that as an invitation to reach down to the bottom, lift it, and pull it over her head. She has nothing on underneath, and I bite my bottom lip from grinning like a fool. She has perfectly round breasts that have the type of symmetry that defied nature. Her chest rises and falls with every breath, and I can't take my eyes off of them. I take that moment to lean down, taking her hard nipple in my mouth and sucking it.

"Mmhh."

I cup her other breasts with my hand, tweaking the nipple between my fingers. Her legs press together where she stands, squirming, telling me she's feeling it exactly where I want her to. I repeat the same thing on her other breast before I flick my tongue once over the peak. My hands move to her sides, my thumbs still grazing her nipples as I move. With every brush over them, her body jerks a little more.

"So responsive."

I trail my fingers down her exposed stomach before I tuck my index finger into the waistband of her shorts. She looks down at where I'm touching, and back up to me, her breathing picking up with every second that passes. She gives me a silent nod of approval as I slide her shorts and panties down her legs, letting my knuckles graze every inch of skin on the way down. As I stand up, slowly trailing my fingers back up her inner thigh, she sucks in a sharp breath, and I realize I love the way she reacts to my touch.

"How about here?" My index finger grazes just outside of her pussy, barely pressing in, but I already feel how wet she is. "Do you want me to touch you here?"

"Please," she pants.

"I love it when you say please."

Sliding one finger in, I rub small, light circles over her clit. Her body jerks with the sensation. My lips move to her neck, and she tilts her head to the side, giving me more access as I trail kisses down her pulse until I reach her collarbone.

"Oh my god," she whispers. "This feels so good."

I press one finger inside her pussy, and she moans, gripping my shoulders for support. I press in, her arousal coating my finger and knuckles, and I pump in and out of her slowly, letting everything build inside of her. When her lips part and her hips start to buck against me, I press my thumb to her clit.

"You're dripping for me. Your tight pussy is begging for a release, isn't it?"

"Dallas," she moans.

"Did you touch yourself after you sucked my cock the other night?"

She shakes her head, and I narrow my eyebrows. "I've never done that before. Never touched myself."

I pull my fingers out of her, and her eyes widen in shock. I know where her brain is at. It's thinking the worst, and I won't allow it. Gripping her waist with both hands, I guide her to the edge of her bed, where she sits.

"Legs open."

She slowly spreads them, exposing the most perfect pussy I've ever seen. My lips dart across my tongue as I think about all the ways I can devour her. I take my hand, wrapping it gently around her wrist, eager to teach her how to do it—how to touch herself.

"What are you—"

"I'm going to show you how to pleasure yourself, Poppy. I'm going to show you how you can make yourself come."

With one hand over hers, I guide her middle finger right to her clit. Her back arches and her hips jerk forward. I crouch down, letting my thumb guide her finger in circles. Her head rolls back, and her body moves in time with her hand. It's the hottest thing I've ever seen in my life.

"You're doing so fucking good, honey."

She lifts her head, looking at me in a daze. I can tell by the way her lips are parted, the tiny moans she's trying to hold back, and the heat of her skin that she's going to get herself off. And I'm going to watch as she does.

"Is this right?" she moans.

"Yes."

"It feels different—good, but different."

"How so?"

"It's not you. I want your hands. I want you to touch me."

I apply more pressure to the back of her finger so that she can do the same on her clit. Letting our fingers move together, faster. I lean down, pressing a kiss to her inner thigh, and I hear her whisper, "Yes," under her breath.

"Do you want my tongue on this sweet pussy?"

"I—Yes."

"Then beg," I growl. "Tell me how much you want it."

"Please, Dallas. Please make me come."

"That's my fucking girl."

She tries to remove her hand, allowing me space to devour her, but I hold her in place. My tongue swipes through her pussy, and I moan into her. She tastes like she can ruin me—sweet, warm, and dangerous.

And I already know with this *one taste*, I'm done for.

I devour her, swiping my tongue up and down, eating her like a starved bear.

"Oh my god, Dallas. That feels so good. What is happening right now?"

"I'm eating your pussy," I breathe against her skin. "And I don't plan to fucking stop."

I release my hold on her finger, and she pulls back. I wanted her to be able to get herself off, but she tastes too good—too addictive. The moment my lips suck her clit, and my tongue flicks over it, she bucks against me. Practically riding my face where she sits. I can't stop even if I tried.

"I think I'm gonna come."

Taking two fingers, I reach down and drive them into her. Fucking her with my hand while flicking my tongue over her clit. She's close, I can feel her contracting around me.

"Oh my god," she screams out, falling back to the bed. I drive into her harder, finger fucking her until she's ready to see stars. "Yes!"

"Come for me, Poppy." I pump my hand two more times. "I want you to soak my fingers and show me who this pussy belongs to now."

"Dallas!"

"That's right," I groan, sucking her clit one more time and sending her over the edge. She squirms around me, thighs tightening around my head, nearly suffocating me. I'd gladly die this way if this is how I'm going to go with my head between her legs, and my mouth on her pussy.

Rest in peace to me, because either way, Poppy Barlow just ruined me.

CHAPTER 31
YOU KNOW, SHOW ME?

POPPY

I lie there still, staring at my ceiling, trying to control my breathing.

My skin is buzzing, heat radiating off me as I lie naked and exposed to the man whose face was just between my legs. Every nerve in my body is still tingling, and I feel like I could melt into these sheets.

My heart is still racing, but it's slower now, steady.

I felt like I was holding tension in my body all week, since we checked off the first item on my little list I made. I didn't even realize just how much until now.

When I lift myself to my elbows, I see Dallas standing there, smiling. He doesn't say anything, and neither do I.

His silence feels like a quiet trust. He's allowing me this time to process everything. He hasn't run away or told me he needs to leave. He's not eager to run out the door because I wasn't enough. As if he can read my thoughts, he moves to sit on the bed beside me, placing one hand on my exposed thigh.

I place my hand on top of it, letting him silently know I'm okay.

Hell, I'm more than okay. My body is craving more of whatever that was. I feel like a sex-crazed fiend, and I haven't even had the actual sex part of that.

"I promise you, that isn't the reason I came here tonight," he says.

"I know."

"I'm learning quickly that I'm desperate for any time spent with you. If we hadn't kissed at the door, I would have done a puzzle with you. I would have whipped up a snack or something and watched a movie with you. I would have done whatever you wanted to do." He pauses, turning to face me completely. "I lose all control with you, Poppy."

As someone who craves control and consistency, his chaos makes me strangely feel at home. It's a welcome kind of tornado tearing through my life. Where I used to fear this kind of mess, I want it now. I want it with him because he makes me feel comfortable and safe.

He makes me feel like I can be myself.

He makes me feel seen in ways no one else has.

I spent so damn long fearing that someone would think I wasn't enough—that someone would see me for me and run the way my one relationship ran.

I don't feel that with Dallas.

There's no fear. There's no second-guessing. There's no wondering.

It's my brain's way of saying, *he's it for you.*

Lifting myself off the bed, Dallas tracks every move. His eyes are on me as I grip both of his shoulders and bring one leg over his thighs to straddle his lap. My nerves are still buzzing, so when I sit down and feel his hard length between my legs, my body ignites in flames again. I allow my hands to circle his neck until my fingers are intertwined in his hair, pulling him back to look from my chest and up to my eyes.

No words are spoken.

I *know* he's waiting for me.

He's giving me this.

And I want to give Dallas Westbrook all of me.

"Honey," he whispers the nickname, something he's been calling me for a while now, but this time feels different. It feels like there's a plethora of emotions behind it.

He feels this, too.

He feels this deep connection we have, the comfort of being with each other.

Where he makes me feel at ease in my head, I calm his chaos.

"I want to feel you," I say, settling deeper onto his lap, and he groans. I move my hips back and forth slowly, fire building between my legs again. I don't know if this is normal to feel ready again this soon, but I'm chasing the high I feel with him. "I'm *ready* to feel you everywhere, Dallas."

He swallows, and I pull back, reaching for the hem of his shirt to pull over his head before I toss it to the ground behind us. I trail my fingertips down his broad chest, grazing over his rigid abdomen. His body shivers at my touch before he pulls me into him. My nipples graze his chest, and the warmth seeps into every part of my body from the contact. He buries his head in my neck, just holding me, breathing me in, committing me to memory.

I can tell he's holding back, but I want this. I want him.

"I want you, Dallas," I murmur against his skin.

He brings his face up to look me in the eyes. His brown eyes darken with desire, changing from warm flecks of amber until they turn a stormy brown. He lifts me off of him, and I stand naked and bare to him. I don't hide it, there's no sense. He's seen every part of me, touched every part of me. Looking me up and down, he stands, tipping my chin up with the back of his index finger, a smirk playing on his lips.

"I'm going to take care of you, Poppy. But I need you to understand one thing." I swallow, unsure of the next words out of his mouth. "You've already ruined me for anyone else. So I fully intend to ruin you in the best way possible."

I don't want anyone else, is what I want to say, but I don't.

I stay silent, reaching for his jeans to unclip them, but he stops me. "Lie down on the bed, Poppy. And spread those pretty legs for me."

I do as he asks. Anticipation is humming through my body.

He watches every move as I lie down, lifting myself on my elbows to see him and how slowly he unbuttons his jeans and pushes them to the floor. As he steps out of them, I bite my bottom lip. As his eyes trail my body, I slowly open my legs for him, and he hums in approval.

He leans down on the bed, holding his body up with one arm, still wearing his boxer briefs, and takes two fingers and swipes them through my pussy. My back arches at the contact, and he shocks me when he raises those same fingers and puts them in his mouth.

"So fucking sweet," he growls. "Your pussy is aching to be touched again, isn't it?"

I nod repeatedly.

"Tell me again what you want."

"You."

He shakes his head. "Tell me again what you want," he repeats, emphasizing each word slowly.

My cheeks flame with embarrassment. He means this—sex. He wants me to tell him what I want, when I don't even know what I want. I want to feel him inside of me. I want to feel the euphoric feeling of Dallas making me come. I want it all.

"I want you to take off your boxer briefs."

He smirks, standing up again and pushing them to the ground where the rest of our clothes lay scattered. He reaches down into the pocket of his jeans and pulls out a little square wrapper, tearing it open with his teeth before sliding a condom over his throbbing cock. Then he stands there waiting for me to tell him the next thing I want. He's giving me control while being in control.

Jesus, this is so hot.

I can't believe this is happening right now.

"Can you…tell me everything you're going to do to me. You know, show me?"

He brings himself up on the bed, kneeling between my legs, urging them open more than they already were. Leaning forward, with both arms caging the sides of my head, he leans down, only a breath away from my lips. "My fucking pleasure."

He kisses me, softly at first. But the moment I lift my head, meeting his urgency, he turns primal. His tongue dances with mine, my hands raking the skin on his back as I pull him as close as he can to me. My hips lift on their own, chasing the feeling of *anything.*

"I'm going to fuck you with my fingers, and then you can have my cock," he says, reaching between us, not waiting before driving two fingers inside of me. He stays hovering over my lips, our breaths mingling with one another as he drives in and out of me. "Ahh, yes."

It feels so good.

Too good.

"More, Dallas."

"Beg for my cock, Poppy. You know I'll give it to you, but I love hearing you beg for me."

"Please," I moan. "Please give me more."

Desire, anticipation, and excitement all run through my body at the same time. Never in my life did I think I would be the woman who would beg for it after avoiding it for so long.

But Dallas makes me feel empowered.

He makes me feel alive.

Like I've been sleeping for years, and he came barging into my life and woke me up.

He pulls his fingers out, moving his hand to his long, hard length, pumping his shaft a few times before he settles himself between my legs.

"Will it hurt?" I ask.

"It will be uncomfortable at first. I'm going to go slow and take care of you, I promise."

I nod and look down between my legs at where Dallas is gripping his cock, lining it up with my entrance. He slides the tip through, soaking him, and putting just the right amount of pressure on my clit.

"Mm-hmm."

"Remind me again, what you want, Poppy?"

I lift my eyes, meeting his. "I want to give you all of me, Dallas." I think about his words from just moments ago, asking me to beg. "Please. I want your cock inside of me."

"Christ," he draws out, pressing the head into my pussy. "That has to be the sexiest thing I've ever heard in my life."

My legs widen, allowing him the space to get in.

"Now watch me as I give you what you want, baby. Watch it slide inside of you."

My body trembles at the feeling of him pushing dangerously slow. I sit up as much as my body allows to do what he said and watch. I don't stop staring as the head of his cock disappears inside of me. I gasp at the mix of pain and euphoria coursing through me.

"Talk to me. Tell me how you're feeling."

"It hurts a little. But keep going."

"You're doing so good," he praises, sliding deeper and deeper.

I don't take my eyes off the way his cock disappears inside of me. Once he hits a certain point, I hiss in pain, my back falling to the mattress as I grip the sheets around me. My eyes are glued shut as I let my body adjust to his size, willing it to pass.

It's too much.

The pressure and pain combined are so intense that I feel like I can't breathe.

Dallas draws back before pushing back in, still keeping his movements slow and steady. Only this time, when he pushes himself back in, the feeling changes from pain to pleasure. A fullness settles between my legs, and I release a long moan, muffled by some other inaudible words because I can't think or see straight.

"Look, Poppy," he says, forcing my eyes back open. His gaze is settled on the spot where we're connected, so I follow it. "Look at how perfectly your pussy is taking me. Watch how my cock disappears inside of you. *My god*, it's like you were made for me."

I can't answer.

The feeling is so intense; I feel like I might die right here. It's a good kind of intense, though.

"How do you feel?"

"It feels so good," I manage to get out. "So good."

"Does it hurt anymore?"

I shake my head.

He sits up taller, resting both hands under my knees and pushing them up toward me. Then he looks down at where we're connected, biting his bottom lip and driving his cock in and out of me.

"Dallas," I moan his name, snapping him out of the trance he was in.

He leans forward, my legs on both sides of his stomach. The move only drives his cock deeper inside of me, forcing my lips to part. He captures all the air in my lungs when he crashes his lips to mine. Tongue swirling in my mouth, hips moving against me, and my hands clawing at his back.

He pulls back, hovering over my lips. "Now I'm going to fuck you properly, Poppy."

He moves his body just enough that he's able to hold himself up on his elbows, caging my head in between them. His fingers find their place tangled in my hair.

Dallas pulls his hips back and I feel the tip of his cock pull out of me just enough before he slams into me full hilt.

"Yes!" I scream.

Finding a steady rhythm, he moves in and out of me, doing exactly what he said he was going to do. I know I've never done this before, but I can't imagine it being any better than this. My body is on fire, electrifying every inch of my skin. His breathing is fast, but steady. The only noise is our breaths mingled together, and wet skin slapping against one another. He doesn't once take his eyes off me. He's watching me with such intensity that it makes everything between my legs build that much more.

"I...don't know how much longer I can last, Dallas. It feels so good. I feel so full."

"I know. I can feel your pussy squeezing me, baby," he says, barely able to get the words out from being so out of breath. "Come for me when you're ready."

"I'm ready," I practically scream. "Dallas! Ahh."

And my orgasm rocks me from the way he thrusts his hips into me, and the gruff tone of his voice. Everything about Dallas is enough to drive me to this point. I'm giving myself to him, and he's protecting it—protecting me.

"I'm coming."

"Yes"—thrust—"you"—thrust—"are," he says, barely holding it together himself. The way his body tenses, I know he's coming, too.

My arms wrap around his neck, pulling his head down to kiss me through it. I want his lips on mine, to breathe him in at this moment. I'm unable even to hold the kiss as I pant into his mouth.

"You're mine," he whispers into my lips, so low that I almost miss it. "God, I'm so ruined by you."

"I think I like being ruined by you," I reply.

He kisses me again, a silent confirmation as he stills inside of me. I feel the pulse of his cock between my legs, his chest rising and falling, but he doesn't move. He just keeps kissing me as if I'm the oxygen he needs.

Little does he know, he's been mine since the start.

When he finally pulls away, he lifts, slowly pulling out of me. "Don't move," he says, leaping off the bed and exiting the room. He emerges seconds later with a wet washcloth he found in my bathroom and places it between my legs. "Your first time is going to make you sore. You may even see a little bit of blood, but it's okay."

I just sit there and stare at his eyes, and the way he's taking care of me. I thought I would be mildly embarrassed by an older, more experienced man taking this from me. I don't feel an ounce of that.

I feel wanted.

I feel cared for.

"Thank you."

He shakes his head. "You never have to thank me for taking care of you. I love doing it."

I sit up and feel the soreness creep in between my legs. Settling on the edge of the bed, I take his hand in mine. "I like you taking care of me."

"Good." He looks from me to the door, pain written all over his face. "I fucking hate the idea of having to leave you tonight." His hands grip his hair as if he's frustrated with himself. "But I have Mitch and Ty back at the house, and I have to be there for Sage."

I stand, cupping his face. "Dallas, I get it."

He closes his eyes. "I don't want you thinking otherwise, honey."

"I won't."

"You promise?"

I nod.

We both move in silence as we get dressed. I wait for the negative thoughts to creep into my brain, the voice telling me that I won't hear from him again. But they don't come. They remain dormant and hushed, and I can't help but smile at the thought.

Once he's ready to go, he pulls me into him, wrapping his arms tightly around my body, holding me so tightly that a part of me wonders if he's going to end up staying.

"Good night, honey," he says against my hair, pressing a kiss to the top of my head.

I walk him to the front door, turning the front porch light on for him. Just as he steps down the last step onto the walkway, he turns around.

"I tossed the package that was delivered to my house somewhere on your couch. Don't you dare open it without me." He winks and turns around, walking across the grass to his house.

I fall asleep with a new soreness between my legs, and my mind consumed with thoughts of Dallas.

CHAPTER 32

POPPY BARLOW, ARE YOU IN LOVE?

POPPY

The smell of freshly baked muffins fills my senses the moment I step foot into Batter Up. Lily had texted me that she was going to have my favorite chocolate chip muffins ready for me today, and to stop by when I left the school.

"It smells so good in here," I say, and Lily snaps her head toward me and smiles widely.

"Between the new batch of muffins today, and Blair trying some random recipe she found online for glazed donut cookies, it really does smell sweeter than usual."

"Did you say glazed donut cookies?"

Blair emerges from the kitchen as if she's heard me. "Yep! You have to try them, Poppy. One of my sister's new clients told her about it and she immediately sent it right over to me."

"You know I'll try anything you two bake."

Blair reaches into the display case, pulling out the cookie that's almost the size of my hand, and puts it on a plate for me, along with the chocolate chip muffin.

"You're going to put me in a sugar coma." I laugh.

"The best kind." Lily winks. "How was school today? It was a half day, right?"

I nod. "It went by quickly. A fun Friday paired with a half day? The kids had a blast." I laugh.

Both Lily and Blair look at each other, and back at me, grinning from ear to ear. I cock my head to the side in confusion because they seem off.

"What?"

"Nothing," Lily says, shaking her head. "Something's different."

I look to Blair, who has one arm wrapped around her waist and the other resting on top of it with her hand by her mouth, deep in thought as if she's assessing the situation and trying to figure out what's different herself. And then her eyes widen, lips part, and hands fall to her side. She looks around to see if anyone else but me is in here before facing me again.

"You had sex," she blurts out.

Lily nearly chokes as her face goes white, staring at me, waiting for a reaction.

The only reaction I have is to look anywhere but at either of them, and I feel my cheeks turn hot. I know they are as red as a tomato right now, too.

"Poppy fucking Barlow," Lily practically shouts. "Is she right?"

I still say nothing, giving them the answer without giving them one.

"Oh my god." Blair gapes.

Lily hops up to the counter. "Ready when you are."

How do I even begin to explain the most perfect night to my sister? There are no words that can even come close to sharing how Dallas took care of me, making me feel comfortable and sexy at the same time. I spent days with an ache between my legs, the best kind of sore. The best part of it wasn't just the sex or losing my virginity to Dallas, it was that I didn't spiral after it. I didn't second-guess his intentions or stay up all night wondering if I'd hear from him the next day.

It was the opposite, I woke up to a *good morning, honey* text from him at five a.m. As if he knew that was the time I would wake up. Dallas has seemed to pick up on my day-to-day routine without me even having to tell him what it is. I woke up with the biggest smile on my face, again bringing the comfort to my mind that I've been so desperate for.

"Yeah, Blair is right," I settle on, letting a smile creep up slowly.

"This is the greatest news of my life." Lily beams, sitting up taller. "Did this just happen last night?"

I shake my head, biting the inside of my cheek. "It was last week."

"And it's taken you that long to tell us about this?"

"I don't know how this works," I admit defensively. "I didn't think to pick up the phone and tell my sister, *hey, I just lost my virginity*."

"Valid," Lily agrees. "How do you feel about it all?"

I shrug. "I don't feel any different. I guess I'm just…happy. But I was feeling that before this, too."

"I know I don't need to ask, but we're assuming it was Dallas, correct?" Blair asks.

I nod, smiling wider now.

"And he took care of you?"

I nod again. "I don't know how it is with anyone else, obviously, but he made me feel alive, and at the same time made sure I was okay. He made sure to tell me what he was doing, and never stopped asking if I was okay." I blush saying it out loud, because some of the things he said, oh my god…Things I can never repeat out loud because it would just turn me on. "It was really hot."

"I love this so much for you." Lily beams.

The front door opens, and we all turn our heads to see Nan walking in.

"Ahh, all my favorite girls in one place," she says, clapping her hands together in excitement. "And it smells great."

Lily looks at Blair and me in confusion. Nan is always nice, but she's got this look about her that says she's up to something.

When none of us respond, Nan laughs. "Let me take a gander, you think I'm here for something."

"Yep," all three of us say in unison.

Nan bends at the waist, gripping her thighs in laughter. "Y'all are funny. It's cute how well you know me."

"And there it is," Lily murmurs under her breath.

"But it's not for all of you. My question here is for Blair." Blair looks at her, confused. "Are you doin' anything with that tiny home of yours now that you're moved in with Griffin?"

"I don't know what I want to do with it yet. I'm not ready to give it up."

"Noted. If you change your mind, you know where to find me. I'll find someone just right for that place," she says with a wink, turning to face me. She does a double-take, and I look down to see if there are crumbs or chocolate on my shirt. "You look different."

"Same me," I choke out, forcing a smile so she doesn't pick up on anything. The last person I need to know I had sex is Nan.

"Nah. There's something about you," she says, stepping closer and lifting the ends of my hair as if to assess me before eyeing me head to toe. "Poppy Barlow, are you in love?"

My head rears back, eyes wide at how bold that question is. I blink a few times and immediately feel everyone's eyes on me. I don't know how to answer that question. I don't even know what love is outside of loving my brother and sister fiercely—the love I have for my family and Tucker. That's foreign to me.

There's no way I'm *in love* with Dallas.

There's a chemistry between us, but that's all it is.

Right?

Oh my god, is this what loving someone feels like?

No, there's no way.

I shake my head quickly. "No, definitely not in love here."

"Okay." She shrugs, brushing it off. *Thank god*. Then she turns to Lily, pulling out her wallet. "Well, I'll take a muffin to go, please."

Lily looks from me to Nan, cautiously, because it's not like Nan to brush off the thoughts she has. It's not like her not to speak up and say what's on her mind. Lily bags a muffin for her, and after she pays, she's out the door without another word.

"That was so weird," Blair says.

"Do you think she can sense that you had sex with Dallas?" Lily laughs. "Maybe that's why she thinks you're in love."

I scoff. "No way."

Just as I open my mouth to say more, my phone buzzes in my pocket. Pulling it out, I find it's a text from Dallas.

DALLAS
Hey, honey.

I smile down at my phone, reading his text.

Jesus, what's wrong with me?

"Looks like she got a text from Dallas," Lily tells Blair. "I'm starting to wonder if that's what Nan just saw."

"Me too," Blair agrees, and I roll my eyes, ignoring them as I type a text back.

Hey. How was your day?

DALLAS
It would be a hell of a lot better if I got to wake up next to you, but even still, it's not a bad day so far.

That's sweet.

DALLAS
That's sort of why I'm texting you. I don't want to ruin any plans you have, but I'd like to take you out next weekend. Just the two of us, if you're up for it.

My smile falls, because this is most definitely a date.

Another thing I don't know how to do.

"Everything okay?" Lily asks, and for a second, I forgot Lily and Blair were still in the room, watching me text Dallas.

"Yeah. Dallas texted me that he wants to do something next weekend, like a date. But I've never done that either. I guess we can just go out to eat?"

"First of all, I love that he's so attentive to your routine, and scheduling something for next week so you aren't doing something at the last minute. That's so sweet. And, no. Absolutely not," Lily says, jumping down from the counter. "You have to do something different. Something fun."

"I agree," Blair adds. "Going out to eat for a first date is standard across the board. Besides, it would be at Seven Stools. You two have already had drinks there before. This first date needs to be epic."

"Do you think I should just let him plan it?"

They both shake their heads.

"Oh!" Lily says, hands in the air as if telling us to stop everything we're doing. "The weather is getting warmer now that it's almost spring here. Why don't you guys do a sunset picnic by the lake?"

"Yeah. I guess we can do that," I say, looking down at my phone to text Dallas back.

I feel a hand on my shoulder, and look up to see Lily there with a comforting smile on her face. "I'm really proud of you, Pop. You're stepping outside of your comfort zone with grace. No matter what happens, we're here."

I nod, emotions thick in my throat as I start texting Dallas back.

> How would you feel about a picnic at the lake?

DALLAS

> You should already know by now, I'd do whatever you want to do.

Picnic by the lake it is.

CHAPTER 33
AND THEN LIFE LAUGHED AT YOU, DIDN'T IT?

DALLAS

> **CLARK**
> Are we still set for our meeting next month at the stadium?
>
> I'll be there.

"Daddy?"

"Yes, bug?"

"Are we even going to still be here for the first game of the season?"

I turn around in the driver's seat to face her, sitting in the back. "What do you mean?"

She sighs. "I've just been practicing really, really hard with the other kids. What if I'm not here to be on the team when the season starts? Will the team be short a player? It's been so much fun playing baseball, and I want to keep playing. I want to win a game with my friends."

I sit there in silence, staring at my daughter.

I've been so focused on the next step after leaving here and the future plans that I haven't even thought about what she'd like to do. She's different from the day we arrived. Or maybe she's not, and I just realized it because she's living with me now. Either way, she's grown here. She's made a whole new group of friends, which was inevitable because she's outgoing and friendly.

But it's more than that.

There's a sense of belonging in this small town. It's hard not to get sucked into the charm of it all and see yourself living here for good. I don't even know how that would work with April's job and my career being back in San Francisco.

"I don't know," I answer honestly. "Daddy still has a big decision to make next month. I have a meeting with Mr. Harris at the stadium while you're at your mom's."

She deflates, looking down at her hands.

I see the pain written all over her face over the fact that we might be going back. She wants to cry, but she's holding it together before we step out of the car and head to one of our weekly nights at the barnyard. We spend two nights a week here. Whether it's practice with the kids or hanging out with Griffin, Tucker, and everyone, messing around for a game of baseball.

She looks forward to these nights more than I anticipated.

"Let's have some fun tonight," I tell her, reaching back to give her hand a reassuring squeeze. "We can take this all one step at a time without making any quick decisions, and then see what happens."

She looks up at me, smiling, before she unclips her seatbelt to get out of the Tahoe.

As I'm about to get out myself, my own words stop me in my tracks.

I used to move fast, running on adrenaline and impulse. I was the guy who said yes before the question was even finished, and walked out a door before it was fully open. That guy? He wouldn't even recognize this new version of me.

Bluestone Lakes has not only changed my daughter, but it

chipped away the parts I didn't realize were holding me back. Slowly, in a way that rust creeps onto surfaces, I make less rash decisions now, and I think things through.

It's not like I went and became someone else.

I'm still me, just less chaotic.

And I think I like this guy better.

Smiling to myself, I exit my Tahoe. Hand in hand with my little girl, we walk to the barnyard where everyone waits for us. Tucker is the first to rush over to us, reaching for Sage first as he lifts her in his arms and jogs to meet up with everyone at the field.

Lily and Blair stand off to the side, laughing and drinking, while Griffin runs a hand down the side of the dugout he helped me build, as if he's assessing the work we put in together to bring this field a new life. Nan is on second base, with a glove open, while Sage giggles, running from first base to second, while Tucker follows her.

How in the world could I ever leave this?

How can I go back to the life I had, when everything I could ask for is right in front of me? A found family that my daughter and I are now a part of.

"So this is what happens on game night, huh?"

The voice behind me forces me to turn around, my body instantly on high alert that Poppy is now here. My eyebrows narrow in confusion, but quickly shift to something I can't quite explain.

Because she's here.

Poppy is here for the first time with everyone else.

I'm stunned speechless.

"Poppy?" Griffin says, now standing beside me. "What are you doing here?"

"I wanted to see what all the fun was about."

I feel him turn to face me, and then back to Poppy. I don't see it because my eyes are only on one person—only ever on one person. And she's looking back at me, silently telling me she's here for me. My heart rate picks up speed as if I were just running the bases with Tucker, but I haven't moved from this spot.

"Interesting," is all Griffin says before he retreats to everyone else.

I stare, still stunned. "You came."

"Lily and Blair have been telling me for a while now that I should come one night. I knew it wasn't for me, since I don't know anything about sports and stuff. But now that I don't miss a single recess anymore...I started seeing what all the fuss was about. Sage actually taught me how to hold the glove, catch the ball, and the best stance for batting."

"She did?"

Poppy nods. "She knows a lot about baseball. She shocked me so much, although I'm not surprised, being that she's your daughter."

I know my daughter loves the sport. She doesn't miss a game. I guess I just never considered that she was learning while watching, picking up on every little thing enough to teach Poppy how to do the basics.

"Are you okay?" she asks, with a soft palm on my forearm.

I clear my throat. "Yeah. That's just...I didn't expect that."

With her hand still on my skin, she steps into me, keeping eye contact and taking every bit of oxygen from my lungs. "Well, I skipped out on finishing a really fun baseball puzzle that my neighbor got me to be here tonight, so..." She pauses, smirking. "What do they say in baseball? Let's play ball?"

I turn to face everyone, and Tucker is spinning Sage around in a circle above his head. I lean down, pressing a kiss to Poppy's forehead, no longer giving a fuck who sees us or what they care about me falling for the girl next door. Because I have. No part of me sees a future without her. "Let's play ball, honey."

I wrap my arm around her shoulder, guiding her to where everyone else is at the barnyard. Lily and Blair's eyes both widen before they soften into a silent acceptance. Tucker now stands on third base, clapping his hands together and bouncing in place.

I don't even know what we are at this point, but Poppy has let me in fully. She's told me all the most vulnerable parts about herself and allowed me into her heart in the most intimate ways.

There's that uneasiness in my gut reminding me that I'm supposed to be leaving.

She makes me want to stay here in Bluestone Lakes.

Start a new life here…with her.

Lily raises a plastic cup filled with some kind of alcohol, I'm sure, and Poppy makes her way to where they stand.

Griffin comes to stand beside me, nudging me with his elbow. "I see she's let you in."

I swallow and nod.

"I told you once, but it's worth repeating. Don't fuck this up, Westbrook. I'll be forced to murder you and hide the body."

"I'll help," Nan adds quickly as she walks past where we stand, not stopping, just continuing walking to where the girls are.

"I don't want to fuck it up," I admit. "I have a lot of decisions to make. For the first time in my life, I don't know what's right or wrong."

My eyes land on my daughter, who has her arms wrapped around Poppy's waist, holding her as if she never wants to let her go, while the girls all continue talking.

"I had it all mapped out. Do my time here, and then go back to baseball. I wasn't going to form any attachments."

"And then life laughed at you, didn't it?"

"Yeah."

"Funny thing about plans is they never turn out the way you hope. I told myself I was going to be single forever because I liked my quiet, secluded life. I wanted to be alone. It was peaceful." He looks to where Blair stands and smiles. "Blair came in like a hurricane and changed my life."

I know the feeling.

Griffin places a hand on my shoulder, giving me a light squeeze. "Sometimes the detour is where the journey really begins."

I watch as Poppy throws her head back and laughs loudly with her sister and best friend, feeling deep in my chest that Griffin is right. Baseball may have been my life for as long as I can remember, but I'm older now—different. I've been so in my head about keeping the consistency of what I've always known, the one thing that's never let me down. When I stop to think about it, there are so many other things in my life that have never let me down.

Maybe the next journey I'm supposed to be on is here, in Bluestone Lakes.

"Think about it," Griffin adds with one more squeeze of my shoulder before releasing his hand. "Let's have some fun tonight."

I nod and follow him to where everyone stands in the dugout.

"You guys ready to play some baseball, or what?" Sage shouts.

We all snap our heads to where she stands in the outfield, arms out in the air with an impatient look on her face. It takes us a minute to notice if she's joking or not, and when her hand covers her face and she starts giggling, we do too.

And it hits me all over again.

I have no idea how I can leave this town.

"That's so out!" Nan shouts. "You've got to be kidding me. This is bull."

"His foot touched the base before the ball reached his glove. What don't you get about that?" Griffin argues.

"What he said," Tucker adds. "I'm like lightning. You can't get me out even if you tried."

"Ugh. I hate this game." Nan rolls her eyes.

Griffin does the same and turns to face me. "She's very competitive."

"So I've learned." I chuckle.

"This is the most fun I think I've ever had in my life," Poppy says as she jogs up to where we stand, hair pulled back in a ponytail, and wipes some dirt from her forehead. "Who knew baseball was this fun?"

Tucker, Griffin, Lily, Sage, and I all raise our hands, which forces her to giggle.

"It would be more fun if we won," Nan adds flatly, but then smiles and raises her hand. "But yeah, I knew baseball was this fun from the first night we all got together here for this." She turns to face me, smacking a hand lightly on my arm. "Thanks for coming into town and introducing us to this. It's keeping me younger than I already am."

I nod.

"Daddy, can we have cotton candy ice cream tonight when we get home?" Sage asks, joining us where we stand as she takes her glove off. "I think since I was on the winning team, we can have some."

"You ate the last of it a few nights ago, bug." I laugh, tugging playfully at the brim of her San Francisco Staghorns baseball cap. "And it's getting late. The General Store closed five minutes ago."

"I have some at my house," Poppy says.

"You have ice cream?" Sage asks, shocked as if other people don't ever have ice cream at their house. "What flavor?"

"Cotton candy. Someone told me it was the best flavor, so I bought some to keep on hand." Poppy shrugs.

My lips part, and my heart skips a beat. There's no way she bought some just for herself, right? No. She keeps it stocked for

Sage. The realization makes me lose my breath, and I'm unable to find words to reply.

"Daddy? Can we go to her house for some?"

I nod, answering Sage, but my eyes are fixed on Poppy.

"Yes! Now I can see your puzzle set up too!" Sage beams, settling herself next to Poppy with one arm around her waist. Poppy does the same, resting an arm around her shoulder. "Ice cream and puzzles after playing baseball? Wow. This might be the funnest night of my life."

Poppy giggles at my daughter.

"Well," Lily says, grinning from ear to ear. "*We're* going to head out. You three have fun." She wiggles her fingers in the air to say goodbye, and Poppy glares at her. "But not too much fun."

"Impossible," Sage emphasizes. "We're gonna have too much fun."

"Can I come have some fun, too?" Tucker asks.

"Read the room, Tucker," Griffin deadpans.

"We're not in a room."

"I can't stand you." Griffin shakes his head, gripping both of his shoulders to guide him to where his truck is parked. Lily barks out a laugh as she grabs her things, following them to the cars, leaving the three of us still standing on the field.

Nan stays back for a moment longer, looking back and forth between Poppy and me. Then a soft smile graces her lips before she tips her chin and follows everyone else.

"You're welcome to come over if you want," Poppy says softly.

I lean down, close enough so that only she hears me. "Are you sure? It's kind of last minute, and Sage will be fine if we can't. She gets over things pretty quickly."

"I'm sure, Dallas."

She takes Sage's hand in hers, and I watch as they walk to where we're parked. A piece of my heart, and the missing piece of the puzzle I didn't even know I was missing, walk hand in hand together.

CHAPTER 34
I'VE NEVER DONE THAT BEFORE.

POPPY

> LILY
> Have fun on your date tonight!
>
> BLAIR
> Oh my god, that's tonight? Have the best time ever.
>
> Thank you. I don't know why I'm so nervous.
>
> LILY
> Don't be. It's going to be perfect. You deserve that.

Change used to scare me.

It used to be so debilitating that it would send me into a spiral of thoughts, making me feel on edge and out of control.

But in just one week, everything has changed.

I've found a new normal with both Dallas and Sage. A routine that I actually look forward to. One night, Sage came over and helped me with the baseball puzzle that Dallas got me while we ate cotton candy ice cream on the couch. Another night, Dallas showed up to drop off flowers, nothing more, but ended up staying for hours. We talked, laughed, and ended up in my bedroom having explosive sex. The night after that, Griffin invited me over for dinner, only to also invite Dallas and Sage. It's not out of the ordinary since we've all had dinner at his house before with everyone.

What makes me feel comfortable around it all is that Dallas looks out for my needs, not just in the bedroom, but in all aspects of life. He doesn't want to ruin whatever routine I have. He never once judges me for the lists I have lying around my house, or that I'm constantly wiping down my kitchen counters, even if we don't eat on them. He understands me in a way I didn't think someone ever could.

So abandoning my plans for a Friday night to have a picnic by the lake with him doesn't make me feel like I'm stepping away from my normal.

Dallas has turned into a part of my normal.

More and more, I've been thinking about the future, though.

There's no doubt I'm falling for Dallas Westbrook. I'm in deep, and the crippling fear of him going back to the city is enough to make me lose sleep some nights. It's not something I like to think about, but he cares about me. I know he does. So there's a new voice in the back of my head telling me he's not doing all of this if it's a temporary fling to get him by while he's here.

The knock on the door pulls me from any other thoughts.

Opening it, I find Dallas standing there wearing a pair of jeans and a red long-sleeved T-shirt rolled up to his elbows, exposing his forearms that make me weak. His eyes trail me as he takes in the knee-length spring dress I settled on, pairing it with a cardigan for when the sun starts to set over the mountains.

"You look... God, Poppy. You look beautiful."

His words fall from his tongue as he steps toward me, wrapping one arm around my waist to pull me flush to him, with the other cupping the side of my face. His lips press to mine, soft and sweet, like it's part of a routine he can do for the rest of his life.

"Thank you," I say against his lips before I lean in to steal one more.

I step away, opening the door wider to let him in.

"I dropped Sage off with her mom for the weekend, and ran to the General Store to grab some sandwiches for us," he says, standing on the opposite end of the counter from me. He places the plastic bag next to a wicker basket.

"I put some snacks in here for us, too," I add.

He takes the sandwiches and places them in the basket, and hooks it in the crook of his elbow. "Ready?"

I nod. He extends a hand for me to take, and I do. Following him out the front door, where he only releases my hand to allow me to lock my front door. Like a true gentleman, he opens the passenger door of his Tahoe for me.

The ride there is quick as I guide him past the barnyard and Barlow Ranch. He has his hand over the center console, resting on my thigh the entire time. Every so often, I look down and smile.

There's a small trail I guide him down, and he looks at me curiously.

I giggle in my seat. "This is how we get out to the lake. There's another entrance about five minutes down the road, but everyone uses that. This one is on the Barlow Ranch property, so only Griffin, Lily, and I use it. Besides, the views at the end of this trail don't compare to any other part of the lake. Trust me."

"I do," he says quickly.

My stomach swirls with butterflies. I know he means more than just this trail.

He's offering me words of affirmation, my love language, without realizing it.

Looking forward, I sit up taller in the passenger seat, pointing to the open clearing off to the left. "Right there."

He turns the Tahoe and parks it in front of the smaller path that's only accessible by horse or on foot. He jumps out quickly, rounding the hood of the car to get the door for me again.

I smile up at him, gravity pushing me into his chest as I rake my arms around his neck to kiss him again. As much as I know he needs his lips on mine, I think I'm starting to feel the same.

He's intoxicating—addicting.

But the way he holds me and angles my head just enough to deepen the kiss, and it sends a fire right to the spot between my legs.

"Sorry," he says, pulling away. "I get a little carried away with you."

"I don't mind." I shrug.

He shakes his head and interlocks his fingers with mine as I guide him down the path to the lake. Once we get there, he stops, pausing as he slowly scans the area. I watch him while he takes it all in. His lips are parted, and his eyes barely blink.

"All this time, this has been on the other side of the ranch?"

"Yep. It's one of our favorite spots. Since it's secluded, we come out here and are able to enjoy this view of the mountains without anyone bothering us."

"I thought the view from my backyard was nice, but this... this is unreal."

I follow his gaze to the open lake. The water almost looks like glass tonight, quiet and calm, reflecting the mountains on its surface as if the world is folding in on itself.

We both stand there, just breathing.

No noise.

Just the quiet of the lake.

"It's been so long since I've been out here," I admit.

"But you brought me?"

I nod, still looking forward. "I forgot how peaceful it was out here."

"It's beautiful," he says, barely above a whisper.

Slowly, I turn to face him, and he's smiling at me. It's the same signature one I saw the very first time I met him. He's flipped my world upside down in all the ways I wasn't ready for —in all the ways I didn't know I needed until him.

For the next hour, we lay down the blanket next to a tree. We talk about school, the baseball team's improvement, and Sage. He even tells me about how Nan tried convincing him last week to join the pickleball team in town. We laugh the entire time, and neither of us thinks about anything but being in this moment together.

When I glance out at the lake again, I see the sun just barely above the mountain. The sky shifts as if it's ready to put on a show for us. Dallas notices and quickly puts away whatever is left over from our meal into the basket. Then he settles himself behind me, his legs on each side of me, and pulls my back to his front, holding me there with one arm around my chest.

We watch as the sky shifts to a golden glow, clinging to the edge of the clouds before turning to a delicate pink. As the minutes tick by, I don't move. No words are spoken between us. But finally, I settle deeper into him, as if I can't get close enough.

"Careful, Poppy," he growls into the crook of my neck.

The tone of his voice and the feel of his breath on my neck send shivers down my spine. I tilt my head further to the side, allowing him full access to me. His arms move from my chest to my thighs, where he gives me a light squeeze. The feel of his palms resting so high on my legs makes me squirm.

My legs tighten, as if I'm trying to hold back the tension forming between my legs. He trails a finger delicately up each leg, across my hip, and up my sides until stopping right under the swell of my breasts. My chest rises and falls with every inch he moves, my heart beating faster than before.

"You're in control here," he whispers against the shell of my ear. "Tell me to stop, and I will." With one hand gripping my waist, he trails his other hand up the sides of my breast, and my body sinks further into him.

I don't answer because I don't want him to stop.

He takes my silence and cups both breasts from behind. My

head rolls back onto his shoulder as he takes his thumb and index finger and rolls my nipple between them through my dress, pinching just enough to cause me to moan.

"You're so responsive to my touch, baby," he says before bringing his lips back to my neck, letting them linger over my pounding pulse. Letting one shoulder of my dress fall down my arm, he brings the top down enough that he can take my bare chest in his hands. It only forces me to moan more, my legs pinch tighter together, craving some sort of friction between them, with how turned on I am right now.

I trust that Dallas will take care of me.

"Your body is craving more, isn't it?"

"Yes," I breathe out, but my voice is hoarse from him still gripping my breasts.

"Spread your legs for me." I do, letting my dress ride up further on my thigh. "I want to see how turned on you are right now."

"I am. Trust me."

"Show me," he demands. "Touch yourself and show me how wet you are from me just playing with your nipples."

Lifting my dress higher, I reach between my legs, moving my panties to the side. The moment my index finger makes contact with my clit, my back arches, and I suck in a sharp breath. I'm about to show him like he asked, but he stops me.

"Play with it for me, baby," he says in a rough tone. "Rub your clit and pretend it's me."

Releasing one hand from my breast, he reaches down between my legs. I'm about to remove my hand where it rests, but he holds me in place with his hand on top of mine, forcing my back to arch. He starts moving my finger in slow circles, sparking my entire body to life. I squirm between his legs, but he holds me down. The feeling is so intense in this moment.

Not only are we outside where anyone can find us.

But I'm touching myself, and he's showing me without judgment.

The thought of the two things makes me exhale a moan, moving my other hand that isn't playing with my clit, to grip his thigh.

"Fuck, you're dripping for me, Poppy."

"Yes." I let his fingers guide me, moving faster and harder, as the pressure builds. It's not enough, though. "More, Dallas. I'd rather this be your fingers. I need you to touch me, please."

"I love when you beg," he growls, letting his finger replace mine, as he presses harder against my clit and I scream out in pleasure. "Wider. Spread your legs wider for me."

I do, and open as wide for him as I possibly can. He wraps his arm around my body to give him better access, and instantly, his fingers are inside me. My hips start to rock on their own as he moves his fingers quickly in and out of me while his thumb plays with my clit. My breathing grows faster, more unraveled.

"Dallas," I keep my voice low.

"Such a good fucking girl," he whispers against my ear. "As much as I want to hear you screaming my name when I fuck you with my hand, I'd much rather not share your noises with the world. They are mine," he grits out. "Every sound belongs to me."

"*I* belong to you," I pant. "Dallas, you have me. You have every part of me."

A rumble vibrates in his chest on my back, and he moves his fingers inside of me faster and harder than before, like a primal beast just released from its cage. And it's just enough for my body to tense up as my orgasm climbs. My hips rock against his hand, his erection pressed into my back, all of it's so much right now—so intense.

"Right there. Don't stop."

"I didn't plan on it."

Within seconds, my body quivers and shakes as the orgasm rocks my body. My vision goes hazy, and I repeat his name over and over again like a chant as I ride out the intense feeling of all of it.

As soon as my breathing slows, Dallas pulls his hand between my legs. I trail his movements as he brings them to his lips, sucking them clean. His eyes flutter closed as if he were eating some kind of dessert straight from heaven.

"That was...wow."

He pulls my back flush with his front again, holding me again the way we were before things got out of hand. I never want this feeling to end. Just having his arms around me is everything I never knew I wanted.

"Dallas?"

"Yes, honey?"

"Will you stay over tonight?"

"Are you sure?"

"I've never been more sure of anything."

CHAPTER 35
I LIKE YOUR LISTS.

DALLAS

Poppy's front door slams shut as I press her against it. We haven't been able to keep our hands off each other the entire ride from the lake to her house. Now that we're inside, they roam each other's bodies as if neither of us knows where we want to touch; we just want it all.

It's frantic and messy.

It's hot and desperate.

I reach down to lift her, and her legs wrap around my waist. She grinds against the erection behind my jeans, screaming to be released. She bites down on my bottom lip, and this new side of Poppy is something I will never take for granted.

She trusts me.

She's comfortable enough with me not to hold back.

"I need more, Dallas." She pants, bucking her hips into me. "I *want* more."

"Your wish is my fucking command, baby," I growl against her skin, carrying her to her bedroom. "I fully plan to make you forget your name tonight."

I stop in the middle of her room, she unwraps her legs, and

stands in front of me. I flip her around so her back is pressed to my front. Looking over her shoulder, I see the vibrator that was delivered to my house by accident sitting on an end table next to a mirror in the corner of her room. I angle her body until we're both facing it. She's looking at me through the reflection, and my heart thunders in my chest. I reach a hand around her, brushing my fingertips across her chest and then her collarbone. She shivers at my touch, but keeps tracking my every move. When I bend down to reach for the hem of her dress, I pause, silently asking if this is okay. She nods.

I pull it up her body and over her head before tossing it to the ground next to us, followed by her bra, leaving only her panties on.

"I'll never stop admiring how goddamn perfect you are, Poppy."

I reach up, brushing her long hair behind her shoulders, exposing her full breasts to me in the mirror, and then trailing my fingertips from her shoulders, down her chest until I reach her nipples. Goose bumps pebble across her skin, and she lets her head fall back.

"No. Watch."

Her head snaps up, eyes connected with mine again as she bites down on her bottom lip. Her one leg trembles slightly as she tries her best to hold it together. I cup both of her breasts once, playing with each nipple before trailing my fingers down her stomach, stopping at the hem of her panties.

"Please," she whispers softly and breathlessly.

"Say it again."

"Please touch me."

"That's my girl, but there's one thing before I do…"

I remove my hands from her and make my way to the end table to grab the vibrator. I go to turn it on and it vibrates to life in my hands. I lift an eyebrow and smirk. "Have you used this yet, Poppy?"

She shakes her head.

"Good, because I told you I'd help you check it off your list. And I fully intend on making that happen now."

She doesn't move where she stands, but shock is written all over her face as if she didn't believe me. I can't help but grin wider as I take my place behind her again, watching her through the mirror.

Reaching around her, I tug her panties to the side with my pinkie finger, before lining the vibrator up with her clit. The moment it makes contact, she sucks in a sharp breath, and one hand involuntarily reaches for her breasts.

"Fuck, that's hot," I say against her bare shoulder, pressing my lips against it. "Do you see how perfect you are?"

"Dallas."

"Watch," I order, reaching further around her as I slide the vibrator into her pussy. She's watching intently as it completely disappears inside of her, and I can't help but watch the pleasure on her face. The way her lips form an O shape. The way her hand grips my forearm for something to hold onto. The way her legs tremble from the intensity of it all.

"Oh my god," she breathes out, rapid and frantic, rocking her hips as if she's fucking the vibrator. I've never been so turned on in my entire life watching her. "More. I want more."

"You want my cock inside this tight little pussy?"

"Yes…please," she draws out.

"On the bed, Poppy. Hands and knees."

She does as I ask. I keep my gaze locked on hers as I turn the vibrator off, tossing it on the mattress before reaching into my back pocket. I put the condom packet between my teeth as I unbutton my jeans.

"Does it feel different without one?"

"A little," I admit, taking the condom wrapper out of my mouth. "But I haven't had sex without one in a very, *very* long time."

"I've only ever been with you."

Her admission is one I know, but hearing it again from her

lips sparks a feeling deep inside that I can't explain. This urge to protect her, claim her, and never let her go is overwhelming. She admitted earlier tonight that she belongs to me, saying I have every part of her. At the moment, I couldn't fully grasp what that meant, and I didn't want to. My only focus was on her pleasure.

You have every part of me.

Her words ring in my ear, making me want to give her every part of *me*.

"If you're okay with it, I can toss this to the side," I say, holding up the foiled wrapper in my hand. She nods, and my cock stands at attention, pre-cum dripping from the tip, the moment I slide my boxer briefs down. It's been craving to be inside of her since we were back at the lake.

Kneeling behind her, the mattress dips under me, and I lean forward to press a kiss to her ass before giving it a light smack. She jumps and makes a noise that's a mix of a shriek and a moan, and my dick gets harder if that's even possible. When I look at the mirror again, I see we're both still watching each other through it from the bed. I angle my cock up to her from behind, she arches her back, giving me better access, and I groan the moment the tip becomes soaked with her arousal.

"There's no way I'm going to last," I say, looking at her eyes through the mirror. And then I slide fully into her. "Fuuuck."

"Dallas," she shouts. I pull out of her slowly and slam into her. "Oh my god." She tucks her head down, arching her back more to give me better access.

"Eyes. On. Me," I tell her. "I want you to watch me fuck you, Poppy. I want to see those green eyes glisten as I take"—I pull out of her, thrusting into her again—"what's mine."

"Yes!"

Picking up speed, I drive into her over and over again, not taking my eyes off hers. I feel myself getting sucked into her through the reflection more and more. It's not just about the sex anymore; it's so much deeper than that with Poppy.

Everything feels deeper with her.

I feel things more intensely than I ever have before.

"Mine," I growl, driving into her quickly, my balls tightening, and I feel my own orgasm building. "You've ruined me, Poppy Barlow." I slow my movements, trying to control myself before this ends quicker than it started. "You've completely ruined me," I repeat, my voice lower.

And it's the truth.

I didn't come to Bluestone Lakes with the intention of feeling anything for anyone, but sometimes everything you didn't know you wanted doesn't show up loud. It slides into place like the last piece of a puzzle, and you wonder how you ever lived without it.

"I'm going to come," Poppy pants, pulling me from the heavy emotions taking over.

"Give it to me, baby. I want to feel you soak my cock."

I thrust in and out of her, letting her orgasm build. Pressing a hand to her upper back, I push her down lower, and I know I've hit the spot that will tip her over the edge when she screams my name like a prayer. Her pussy contracts around me, and it's enough to tip me over the edge, but I fight it off.

"Come with me, Dallas. Please."

"Fuck, Poppy."

"I'm on birth control. *Please*," she begs. "I want to feel it. I want to feel everything."

I growl, pushing inside of her as far as her body will allow me, forcing a shout from her. Driving in and out of her, our orgasms rock our bodies as nothing but the sounds of wet skin slapping together, and Poppy panting fills the air.

"Yes! Yes!"

I groan, feeling my abs tighten as I spill my come inside of her. Wrapping an arm around her waist, I still my movements inside of her—holding her as if I never want to let her go.

Truthfully, I don't.

It hits me that I don't know how this will work beyond my

time here, which only makes any decisions I have to make that much harder.

Once we both come down from our high, she moves to grab her clothes, but I sit her on the edge of the bed. Wordlessly, I leave to find her bathroom and a washcloth to clean her up. When I come back, I find her, naked, standing by her nightstand with a pen in her hand. Clearing my throat, she startles, the pen flying through the air as her hand comes up to cover her mouth.

"What are you doing?" I laugh.

"I—Uh," she says with wide eyes as she moves quickly to find the pen. "Nothing."

I look at the dresser and notice her list is sitting there. Three check boxes, but only two of them have words following them. It's her list.

When she finds the pen, she hides it behind her back. Smirking, I step closer to her, pulling her naked body into mine again. I'm instantly turned on again because I can't help it when I have my hands on any part of her. Dipping my face into her neck, her head rolls to the side. I press a quick kiss to her pounding pulse before snatching the pen from her hands and lifting it in the air.

"Dallas," she groans.

I move to the dresser where the list sits. I smile when I see "give a blowjob" which I already checked off. Clicking the pen once to expose the ink, I place a check in the box next to "try a vibrator," then I turn to face her again.

"What will the third one be?"

She shrugs, and her cheeks turn red. "I don't know yet."

Reaching up, I brush a sweaty strand of hair away from her face, then press a kiss to her forehead. "I like your lists."

"That's because you're on the receiving end of the things on *that* particular list."

"No." I laugh lightly, cupping her chin between my fingers. "It's because your lists make you, you."

"You…you mean that?"

I nod. "I don't know if you've picked up on it or not, but I like everything about you, Poppy. Now let's get to bed."

She doesn't bother putting clothes on as she climbs into her side of the bed. Settling myself behind her, I pull her back to my front and hold her the way I've been desperate to hold onto her from just moments ago when we were in the moment.

This time is different.

Everything with her is different.

"Good night, Dallas."

"Good night, honey," I say, pressing a kiss to the back of her head.

As my eyes fall closed, the last thing on my mind is how I could ever give this up if I go back to San Francisco.

CHAPTER 36
DO YOU NEED A TRAVEL BUDDY?

DALLAS

"You have everything?" I ask Sage, looking at her through the rearview mirror.

She nods and remains looking down at her lap, not moving to unbuckle her seat belt.

"What's wrong?"

She shrugs. "I'm sad that you're going back to the city. Because I know it means we all may be going back to the city."

I sigh. "I haven't made a definite decision yet."

"I wouldn't be mad either way, Daddy. I would just be sad."

My stomach has been in knots this entire drive to drop Sage off with April. I'm heading back to San Francisco tomorrow for my meeting with Clark and the rest of the board with my decision on what I want to do moving forward.

Not many people get the chance I was given.

In this industry, you're let go without a passing glance.

I like to think it's because of my relationship with Clark, and him being in my life for as long as I can remember. Everyone knew my situation, though. They knew I jumped into everything quickly after the accident. They knew baseball was what I needed to recover from that.

I guess I didn't know then what I really needed was a break.

"One step at a time, remember?" I settle on because I don't know what to tell my daughter right now.

She nods, finally unbuckling to get out of the SUV.

April stands, propped against her car, waiting for us. When she sees us round the hood of the car, she pushes off it and walks toward us. Her head is down, and my eyes narrow. She has this look in her eyes like something is up.

"Hey, baby." She smiles wide for Sage, putting on a mask. "Ready for a fun weekend?"

"Yep," Sage answers flatly.

April doesn't push it with her, but she's going to ask me about it in about three seconds after Sage gets in her car.

As soon as she does, she turns to face me, arms crossing her chest. "What's wrong with her?"

"She's upset about me going back to San Francisco. She has a feeling that we're all going back."

"And she doesn't want to go back?"

I shake my head. "Her words were 'I wouldn't be mad, just sad,' and it breaks my heart because I don't know what to do about anything." I feel my voice growing louder with every word, angry that I can't make a decision as easily as I used to. "I don't fucking know what to do about all this."

April pauses, eyes wide at my tone, before her features soften and a lopsided grin forms on her face. "You've changed."

I narrow my eyes, tilting my head to the side, figuring out what she means.

"For once in your life, you can't make a decision. You're actually thinking things through without jumping the gun."

I nod, my chest feeling tight.

"Talk through it with me," she continues. "Where is your head at? Is it because of Poppy?"

Things with Poppy have only grown over the months I've been here—it's easy. Steady. It's shifted from casual to something I look forward to. Even the quiet nights together of watching her and Sage work on a puzzle, their fingers turning puzzle pieces in their hand while we all talked about our day.

It's a normalcy I didn't realize I craved, or how she slips into my arms without needing to be asked. She's become part of my everyday routine, something to look forward to.

She's given me a reason to want to be better.

And that's something I didn't see coming, but I'm glad it did.

"She's part of it," I admit. "I told myself I wasn't going to form attachments while I was there. But I think I formed an attachment to the town. Bluestone Lakes has a charm to it that I can't explain, and it sucks you in—makes you feel a part of it even if you're technically not."

She nods repeatedly in understanding.

"I can't lie to you, I've made a few rash decisions since staying there, like coaching the kids' baseball team that didn't exist before I got there, and then rebuilding the barnyard."

"The barnyard?"

I smile, thinking about where it started versus today. "It's what a few of the kids used as a makeshift field. The kids had cardboard boxes as bases and a bench that looked like they picked it from the trash. I rebuilt it for them. It's not much, but it's enough to spark their joy for baseball even more."

And mine.

The realization slams into me that not only did the field spark *their* joy, but mine, too. Coaching a professional team wasn't what I ever planned, and I think I held a lot of resentment toward it because I wanted to play. There's a new feeling associated with coaching the kids and building a foundation for them to love the game and continue playing.

I think of Austin and Archie, and how they remind me so much of myself.

If they continue to work hard, they can undoubtedly make it to a professional team in the future.

"It helped me fall in love with the game again, too," I add, not even realizing that I'm smiling.

"I guess before you head back, we should talk about some things," she says, voice trailing off as she looks away from me. I say nothing, letting her continue. "I wasn't sure where your head was at before this conversation, and obviously, Sage is the determining factor for everything I do."

"For me too."

Her lips twist into a soft smile, as if she's been waiting for me to put Sage first all her life. Never again will I put her after anything. "I've been doing a lot of thinking. You already know I've met someone and got this job opportunity." I nod, remembering the conversation. "Well, this idea came to mind about possibly opening a practice. Closer to Bluestone Lakes in case you decided you wanted to stay."

"You can do that? Open your own?"

"Well, it wouldn't fully be my own," she says with a smile, chewing on the inside of her cheek. "My boyfriend. He's supportive of whatever decision you and I make regarding Sage. He said if we decide to stay, we need to be closer to Sage to make it work for everyone in her life. And besides, we checked things out and Bluestone Lakes has nothing less than thirty minutes away."

This…is so unexpected.

My brain is swimming with this information as I take it all in.

"You mean…we can stay here?"

She nods. "I think if *we*"—she tosses her finger between her and me—"decide this is something permanent, I don't want to keep up this travel in the city. If it's something we both want to do, then I say we stay. But I'll be moving closer to Bluestone Lakes, and I'll commute if we struggle to find somewhere closer to open something. I'd rather commute than be this far away from Sage longer than I have been."

I remain silent, shocked at everything she's telling me.

"I'm not telling you this to sway your decision, Dallas. I want you to do what will make you happy. If going back to San Francisco is it, then I have my old job waiting for me. If staying here is it, we have a plan. But please don't make your decision based on my opportunity."

I smirk. "So…boyfriend, huh?"

She scoffs, rolling her eyes. "That's all you got out of all of this?"

"No, but it does give me some things to think about. I want you to be happy, too, April. You deserve it just as much as I do. I've made your life a living hell for years—"

"No, you haven't, Dallas. Don't say that. I think the two of us just weren't meant to be, and that's okay. People fall out of love all the time. But you didn't make my life a living hell."

I nod, remaining silent because now I don't know what to think.

I'm not sure if her sharing all this information is making my decision easier or harder.

"I'm going to get going, though," she says. "Have a safe trip back to San Francisco, and let me know how it goes."

"Okay."

She hugs me, and I retreat to my car.

I really could use a drink now.

"Remember that stuff you gave me the first night I was here? I'll take whatever that was."

Griffin laughs. "You got it." Then he grabs a bottle from the top shelf, pouring me a glass and sliding it across the bar. "Everything all good?"

I shake my head. "I have to go back to San Francisco in the morning. I have a meeting with the Staghorns about my decision to go back."

Griffin stills, his face falling. "You think you'll go back?"

"Truthfully? I don't fucking know what to do anymore."

He swallows, wanting to say more, but Tucker coming up beside him, stops anything he was about to say.

"Did I hear Staghorns? How're my buddies, Mitch and Ty, doing?"

"Fine, I guess."

Tucker's smile falls from his face, realizing that I'm not laughing.

"What's going on?" Tucker asks, looking between Griffin and me. When neither of us answers, his eyes widen. "Are you moving back?"

I look down at the glass between my hands because I don't have an answer for him.

"You can't. You can't go back. Dallas, you need to stay here. You're my best fucking friend."

Griffin raises an eyebrow. "Did you steal that line from that comedian you're always watching?"

"That means my bullshit is your bullshit. And your bullshit is my bullshit."

Griffin groans. "I wish I weren't related to you sometimes."

I laugh. I can't help it when these two interact with each other.

"Hey, Tucker," Nan shouts from the front door, forcing all of us to turn our heads. "Guess who got the last bag of pretzel twists at the General Store?" She holds up the bag as she makes her way to us.

Tucker smirks. "You only got the last bag because I bought the other five they had in stock. I stood there and thought"—he crosses an arm over his chest, bringing his other hand to his chin—"maybe I'll be nice and leave Nan one single bag."

Nan glares at him before looking at me. "What's wrong with your face?"

"He's going back to San Francisco," Tucker answers before I can. "But it better not be for good."

"I'm only going back for the weekend. I have a meeting with the team about what's next for me."

"The weekend?" Tucker raises a brow. "Do you need a travel buddy?"

"Please take him off my hands," Griffin begs. "I don't even care if I have to work open to close, *take him*."

I laugh, thinking about it.

I could use the distraction for the sixteen-hour drive back and forth. Tucker isn't the worst person to be stuck with. He may drive me crazy at times, but I also think he may help things move more quickly.

"Are you going to be an obnoxious fan if I bring you to the stadium with me?"

"He probably will," Nan says flatly.

He stands up tall, lifts his chin, and holds up two fingers. "I'll be a good boy. Scout's honor."

I look back at Griffin. "You sure you want him to go?"

"*Please.*"

"Take him. More pretzel twists for me," Nan adds.

"Fine. You can come. But you get one hour *max* on music control for the ride, and you're not allowed to gush over my teammates."

"One hour?" He gapes. "Two. And they don't need to be consecutive."

I roll my eyes. "Fine. Be ready to go at four a.m."

"Jesus. Can we push it to five?"

"Tucker."

"Ugh. I'll be ready for four," he agrees reluctantly.

I slide a twenty-dollar bill across the bar, and Griffin pushes it back. "On the house. You're doing me a favor."

"Take it. You have to put up with him the rest of the night." He barks out a laugh, and I join him as I stand from my stool. "Thank you for the drink."

"Anytime, Dallas."

As I leave the bar, I realize there's one more person I need to see.

CHAPTER 37
TELL ME TO STAY, POPPY

POPPY

I smile when I hear the soft knock on my front door.

Tossing the puzzle piece from my hand to the table, I make my way to the door. Opening it, I find Dallas on the other side. He has an unreadable expression on his face, which makes my smile fall.

"Dallas? Are you okay?"

He stands there, not moving to come in, but a grin forms on his lips. "It's like déjà-vu."

"Huh?"

"The first night I showed up here…you said the same thing."

I have to think about his words for a moment, because I remember him showing up here, but I don't recall what I said. The fact that *he* does makes my heart thump in my chest.

He doesn't continue, and I don't know what to say.

Something is up.

"This would be a hell of a lot easier if you weren't you." He steps toward me, crossing through the front door and into my house. "I knew after first seeing you at the coffee shop that I wanted to get to know you more."

I stand there, shocked, as recognition hits me right in the face.

It's all the things he said to me the first night he showed up at my doorstep.

"My thoughts of you are still very unprofessional." He laughs, taking a hand and cupping my face. "I *still* haven't been able to stop thinking about you since the day I moved here."

I close my eyes, letting his words flow through my head.

"Ring a bell?"

I nod, unable to speak because all the old feelings I've had are coming rushing back. This feels like an end. It feels like he's ready to pull the rug from under me and pop the bubble of happiness I've found myself wrapped in.

He's leaving. He's saying goodbye, and that's the only thought I'm thinking.

Then his lips are on mine. Slow, as if he's committing me to memory like it's the last time his lips will ever be on mine. He pulls back too quickly, resting his forehead on mine.

"Can you do something for me?"

I swallow. "Yeah."

"Tell me to stay, Poppy. Tell me to make this my home for good."

Emotions are thick in my throat as each word comes from his mouth. I'd give anything to make him stay, but I can't do that. As much as it breaks my heart to admit, I can't be the reason he gives up a part of his life.

Because I know that if he does stay, it will be for me.

So I stay quiet, not giving him the answer he's looking for—that I'm begging to tell him.

Instead, I wrap my arms around his waist, pressing my cheek to his chest to hide the tears that are fighting to break free. His chin rests on the top of my head as he holds me back. Neither of us moves from this spot for what feels like hours. A cool breeze sweeps through my open door, pulling us apart.

"I have to get home to pack, I have to get on the road early."

I nod, it's all I can will myself to do, even when there are a dozen questions I want to ask.

My brain is screaming to tell him to stay.

Please, stay.

But the words don't come out. Nothing does.

He tips his chin, leaning down for one more long, drawn-out kiss. I let him, welcome it. Even if it means it's the last one I'll have.

"Good night, honey."

And then he turns on his heel, making his way across the lawn.

Closing the door, I let my back fall against it, sliding down and tucking my legs up to my chest, and I cry until my eyes finally close and I fall asleep.

When I wake up at my usual five a.m., he's gone.

There's no text on my phone.

The Tahoe isn't in the driveway.

And that's when I know...he didn't stay.

CHAPTER 38
I DON'T KNOW WHAT THIS MEANS GOING FORWARD.

DALLAS

"Is now a good time to tell you that I've never been to a city before?" Tucker asks, looking out through the floor-to-ceiling windows of my penthouse that's been vacant for months.

"Never?"

He shakes his head, turning around to face me, and shrugs. "Small town boy."

His tone is flat, and for the first time since knowing Tucker, there isn't a joke behind his words. There's no punchline coming, and it's an uncomfortable feeling, but I choose not to push it. If he wanted to tell me, he would.

"What time is your meeting?" he asks.

"Noon. You're coming with me, right?"

His eyes widen and quickly shift to the Tucker I've known since the day I met him. "I can go?" I nod, and he begins pacing. "Oh my god. Like, I get to see the Staghorns stadium? Are other players going to be there?"

There's the Tucker I know.

"That was my plan all along." I laugh, grabbing my keys from the entryway table and holding the door open for him.

"Let's get going, and I'll give you an official tour before my meeting."

He skips toward me with a smile on his face.

I close the door behind us, locking up, and I find myself pausing with my key in the lock. As I stare down at it, it feels foreign. It's been months since I've been here, since deciding to go to Bluestone Lakes when April was presented with an incredible opportunity.

It was for myself, too.

I needed to get out of here and away from the decisions that weighed on my chest.

I just didn't know being back here would make me want to go back to Wyoming and…stay.

I don't want to lock this over the top penthouse suite anymore. I don't want a view that overlooks the city with horns blasting in the streets below me. I never thought I'd feel this way because being here was for one thing, and one thing only.

Baseball.

Pulling the key from the lock, I stuff it in my pocket. "Ready?"

Tucker nods. "I was born ready for this moment."

We both laugh as we make our way to my Tahoe parked in the garage. Even driving through the city right now is bringing back all those same feelings. It's congested and busy. It smells like shit.

How have I never noticed any of this before?

The drive to the stadium is quick, and when we pull into my designated parking spot, I turn to face Tucker, who's looking at the stadium through the front window as if it's lit up for game night. There's a wonder in his eyes that reminds me of kids going to their first major league game.

"This is the greatest day of my life," he whispers to himself.

I wish I could say the same since I'm about to have a meeting that could possibly change my entire future—a meeting where I *still* have yet to come to a decision.

I sigh, exiting the Tahoe, and we both make our way through the stadium.

For the next half hour, I show Tucker the locker rooms and the dugout. He walks onto the field and takes in his surroundings, looking up at the empty stadium seats. The entire time, a smile never leaves his face.

"I can't believe I got to see the Staghorns stadium. Just... wow," he says, looking down at his watch. "Oh, you have your meeting in two minutes."

"Shit," I say, checking my own watch. "Are you good here, or what are your plans?"

He shrugs. "I have no plans. I never make plans for the future."

"Not even for the next hour?"

"Nope. I let life take me where it wants to take me," he says proudly. "But I do plan to walk around the main corridor of the stadium before I head outside to this bar I read about in a blog yesterday. The website told me that it was a little hole-in-the-wall joint that's a *must* visit when you come to San Francisco."

I nod, knowing which one he's talking about. "They shouldn't be too busy today, either, since it's the middle of the week and no games are happening."

"Perfect!" He turns to walk away, but stops to face me again. "And Dallas?"

"Yeah?"

"Thank you for showing me all of this. I'm lucky to call you a friend, and I want you to know that whatever you decide today in your meeting—which I know is weighing heavily on your mind, I just didn't want to bring it up. You can't get rid of me." He shrugs. "I'm still going to be your best friend. As someone who doesn't plan much in advance and goes with the flow, I hope you follow where your heart tells you to go."

I narrow my eyes because what the hell was that?

He barks out a laugh. "Yeah, that was weird even for me. Nan told me to tell you that."

Now it makes sense, and I smile. "Thank you, Tucker."

"Anytime, coach." And he turns to walk away, leaving me to think about how he just called me "coach."

As I make my way to Clark's office, championship banners and trophies from years before I ever joined the team line the walls. I find myself pausing as I look up at them, the way I always have since I first set foot inside the stadium.

Having my name attached to one of these cold, gleaming pieces of metal has always been the dream. I pictured myself lifting one over my head under the stadium lights, champagne spraying, the crowd screaming my name, and confetti raining down as everything finally comes to life. I used to look at these, and it would make me work harder—play harder. I did everything in my power to make it happen, and it never did.

Looking at them now, I don't feel that way anymore.

Everything has changed.

I no longer feel the strong desire to push for it like I did when I was playing, or the gut-wrenching pain of never achieving it after my career ended.

I realize in this moment, I don't want this anymore.

I'll always love baseball, but there's no way I can come back here.

Pulling my phone from my back pocket, I check for the millionth time to see if there's anything from Poppy.

Nothing.

I begged her to tell me to stay—to give me a reason to stay. She didn't, and I don't blame her. With how much I've grown to know her, she doesn't want to be the reason I make my choice.

Little does she know, she's every single reason.

She's changed my life in more ways than one. Without even trying, she's helped me learn that baseball isn't the only thing that matters in life. There's so much more out there than just this sport, and there are ways I can still keep it in my life.

A throat clears to my left, and I snap my head to find Clark leaning against the door frame of his office.

"Sorry, I'm late," I tell him, making my way to his door. "Got a little sidetracked."

"No need to be sorry, son. Come on in."

We both make our way into his office, and I take the seat across from his desk. My palms feel sweaty because even with all those thoughts and revelations since coming back to this stadium, I still don't fucking know what I'm doing here.

"Thanks for coming out here for this meeting. I know we're supposed to meet with the board today, but they had another meeting set up at the same time. I also figured you'd be better off with just me."

I nod.

"First things first, how was your time off?"

"It was…exactly what I needed."

He grins, because this was partly his idea, too. "That's good to hear. Did you find ways to keep yourself busy?"

"I did. My sole focus was Sage, of course. I never had the chance to be a primary parent for her, and it was nice to get that opportunity. She loves it in Bluestone Lakes."

"Do you?"

I swallow, because how do I tell the man who changed *my* life that the town I found online did the same thing in the short time I was there?

I lean forward, clasping my hands together and resting my elbows on my knees. "I'm going to be straight up with you, sir. When I left here months ago, I didn't want to do it. I didn't like the idea of a break, even though everyone told me I should. You know better than anyone else that baseball has always been my life. To the point that I put it before everything. My marriage. My daughter." I swallow past the emotions sitting thick in my throat. "And myself. Leaving all of this behind to go to a small town changed everything."

Clark sits there, shock written all over his face because he didn't expect any of that. Hell, I didn't either. His features eventually soften, and I see the corner of his lips twist into a grin.

"That's all I ever wanted for you."

"Huh?"

"Since the day I met you, you've been this incredible baseball player. I knew you would make it to the big leagues. I never thought I'd get to witness it and continue to work with you." He laughs lightly. "But it's been an honor. However, you've always been known for being a little reckless and impulsive. It's why I refused to hear an answer the day we lost that game. I didn't want you to keep jumping into something if it wasn't making you happy. I knew deep down it wasn't, even though you had baseball as the head coach, it wasn't making you happy, son."

"I don't know what this means going forward."

"It means whatever you want it to mean. You've clearly thought about this for a while now. And reading your face at this moment, you still don't have an answer." He pauses, and I remain silent. "Which tells me everything I need to know."

He's right.

Fuck, he's right.

I can't come up with a decision because there's a part of me that feels like I'll be letting my team, Clark, and my friends down. But the other part of me knows that my heart is stuck in Bluestone Lakes. It's found a home in the people there, the town, the scenery. All of it.

"I can't see myself here anymore," I tell him honestly.

He smiles, and this time it's laced with a profound feeling of him being proud of me. My heart hammers in my chest, and I know deep down that this is the right decision for me.

"I've always just wanted you to be happy, Dallas."

His words hit me like a brick to the face, because I can't remember the last time I ever considered my own happiness in any choice that's been presented to me. I've been selfish in many of my decisions, but I never stopped to think about what would truly make me happy in the long run.

With that in mind, I can't help but think of Poppy.

I know deep down that happiness doesn't live in another person. You can't just hand someone all the broken pieces of yourself and expect them to make it whole. That's not love, it's dependency dressed up in romance.

But there's something to be said about having the right person beside you.

Someone who sees you.

Not because that person or place is your happiness, but because they remind you that it's still possible. It's not that Poppy makes me happy, but with her, she sticks around and makes everything feel lighter.

She stays.

"Then I think it's time for me to go back to Bluestone Lakes," I finally tell Clark.

He smiles and nods. "I think it's time."

I stand from the chair, and Clark does the same, extending his arm out over the desk. Shaking it feels like the decision has been made, and I can't help but feel the weight of everything lifting off my shoulders.

It feels right.

I hate the idea of putting this team and stadium behind me, but it feels like what I need to be doing.

Clark rounds the desk, stopping briefly before me before wrapping his arms around my upper body, pulling me into him the way a dad would his son. My body stiffens for a moment before I return his embrace. "I'm so proud of you," he whispers.

"Thank you," I manage to get out through the emotions taking over. "For everything through the years. You've always been like the dad I never had, and I'll never find the proper words to tell you what that means to me."

He pulls back from the hug, wiping a tear from his eye. "Get out of here, son."

We both laugh, and I make my way out of his office. Stopping by the old trophy display once more to take in the life I've always wanted that's now in the rearview mirror.

I sacrificed so damn much for that dream—birthdays, summers, relationships, without so much as batting an eye, and constantly telling myself that it would be worth it when I had one of these in my hands.

But now? Now I see my daughter running around the backyard of our rental in Bluestone Lakes, laughing with her arms in the air as she spins in circles. I see Poppy standing in the doorway with a coffee in hand and watching her with a smile on her face.

There's a strange feeling of peace in realizing that the thing you chased for your entire life wasn't the thing that mattered the most.

The desire will always be inside of me to win a championship, but it's not everything anymore.

I used to believe that having a trophy would define me.

Now I know it won't.

It's focusing on my own happiness that will.

Strangely enough, that feels like winning a championship, too.

CHAPTER 39
WHERE ARE YOU?

DALLAS

> I'm at the restaurant you said you would be at, but you're not here. Where are you?

TUCKER

> Met someone.

> Be home late.

> Or early tomorrow morning. I'll update you soon.

CHAPTER 40
BUT I CAN CONTROL THIS LIST.

POPPY

I've spent the last few days stuck in my own thoughts.

Immersing myself in the classroom on Friday didn't help because Sage was missing. It was just another reminder that Dallas had left.

I miss Sage.

I miss Dallas.

I have no idea if it's for good or just temporary.

I didn't ask for more information, and I didn't tell him to stay. I picked up my phone at least a hundred times to send him a text to see how he was, what he's up to, or if he's coming back, but I couldn't bring myself to do it once. I was so fearful there would be a reply back telling me he and Sage aren't coming back. It's a pain I'm not ready to deal with right now.

When my sister picked up on the fact that something was off with me, she put two and two together when she realized Dallas wasn't in town anymore.

Now, I'm sitting outside of the barn at Barlow Ranch mid-afternoon with Lily and Blair, enjoying a glass of wine together. It's been so long since I've been out here to enjoy the ranch that I didn't know the peace this place brings was exactly what I needed.

"Talk to us," Lily says.

I sigh. "I don't know what's going on right now. My mind is a mess."

"We know, that's why we're here," Blair says. "This is the best place for clearing your head of whatever mess it's in. Plus, good friends and wine help, too."

I can't help but smile because she's right.

While everything in my head might feel like a whirlwind at the moment, being here with my sister and best friend brings a sense of comfort for me to think things through.

"He asked me to tell him to stay."

Both of them remain silent, letting me process what I want to say next.

"And I didn't say anything. I've been replaying the moment over and over in my head since the door closed behind him. I didn't want to be the reason for any decision he has to make. Part of me wishes I had asked him to stay, because I…" I shake my head, averting my gaze to the mountains in the distance.

"You love him," Blair finishes for me.

I don't know what being in love feels like, but this has to be it.

The feeling of becoming so connected with another person, wanting to see them at any chance you can, and missing them when they're gone. I feel all of those things with Dallas Westbrook. I feel those things with Sage, too. I've tried to deny it for so long because he had an expiration date here. I've tried to stop my heart from feeling anything, but I couldn't help it.

The fall was inevitable.

"I don't know how to navigate this," I manage to get out as emotions sit thick in my throat and tears threaten to break the surface. "Is that what you really think this is?"

"Oh, babe." Blair sighs with a smile. "It most definitely is. I had the same questions when I was falling for your brother. He was the last thing I expected to happen to me, the same way you didn't expect Dallas."

She's right.

I know she is, even if the voice on my shoulder, who's always feeding me the negative thoughts, tries to tell me otherwise.

A bell chimes not far away, forcing us all to turn our heads to face Nan, who's pulling up on her bicycle. She dings the bell on her handlebars with a smile on her face as she comes to a stop in front of us.

"Ahh. All my girls. I've been lookin' for you three."

"We're escaping reality, Nan," Lily says, sitting back deeper in her chair.

"Reality is overrated anyway." Nan waves us off, taking a seat at the edge of the deck. "But what are we all trying to escape from? I want to join y'all."

The three of us turn to face each other and start laughing.

"Oh, Nan," Lily says, shaking her head. "You don't need to worry about us."

"I always worry about you three, Lily. And when I saw Dallas drive out of town, I knew I especially needed to worry about this one," she says, hiking her thumb in my direction.

"Why?"

"I'm old, but I'm not blind. At least not yet." She shrugs. "You two have something going on. There's a visible chemistry between you two that no one can deny."

My head hangs as I look down at the wine in my hands.

"He will be back," she says with her chin held high, full of certainty.

"How do you know?"

"I have a feeling."

I raise an eyebrow. "And you trust that?"

She points a finger in my direction. "If it's one thing you should always trust, it's your gut. It gives you all the answers you need."

Lily barks out a laugh. "I don't understand you most of the time."

Nan swivels in her seat to fully face Lily. "What's not to get? When something's off, it will tell you. Let me tell you a quick story."

"Oh boy," Lily says under her breath.

"This one time, a friend of mine was giving off weird vibes. I knew something wasn't right, but I just sat back and let it play out. Later down the road, about a year later, her true colors shone. Everything I was feeling was right. Then there was this other time, I took a young man into my home who wasn't from here. Everyone around me thought I was nuts."

"We still do," Lily says. "But we love you for it."

Nan smiles. "Anyway, I helped him get his feet off the ground. My gut didn't raise any red flags. I knew it was the right thing to do, and guess what? I was right." She points a finger in the air. "He never once stole from me or tried to kill me either."

"I'm not sure my gut knows what to think, Nan," I admit. "I'm sitting around, wondering what's next, questioning everything. I mean, you're right, I *do* feel something for him. It's something I've never felt before, which scares the crap out of me."

"I think you're just going to need to keep yourself busy." Nan smiles. "You like lists, right?" I nod. "So do that. Make yourself a list of all the things you want to do to keep yourself busy while you wait."

"You sound like my therapist."

"I may as well be one for the town and all the problems y'all keep having." Nan laughs.

"Okay, ouch," Lily says. "But valid."

Maybe she's got a point.

Nan stands from where she sits, straightening her back as if sitting for too long made her feel stiff. She releases a stretch and starts making her way to her bike. "Oh, and Poppy?"

"Yeah?"

"You should know that he didn't turn in his keys before he

left," she says before mounting her bike. "So yeah, I got a feeling." Nan winks, buzzes the bell on her handlebars once more, and rides off down the road.

My mouth hangs open as I watch her disappear.

Maybe I just have to keep myself busy to avoid my wandering thoughts.

Pacing my living room, I haven't had it in me to take Nan's advice and make myself a list. It's not like me not to want to create one. I have lists all over the house of things I need to do, want to do, and items I need to buy from the store.

Lately, when I think of my lists, I think of the one Dallas has helped me with.

Everything seems to go back to Dallas.

I can't look in the mirror anymore without thinking of the night he was here. I can't look at my kitchen counter without remembering our moment there. I can't focus on a puzzle without thinking about how he got me one.

Everything is *him*.

This isn't just an attraction anymore.

It's not just the way I can't get him out of my head, or the way I'm replaying his voice in my head like a favorite song I can't stop listening to. It's not about how he's always finding ways to touch me by brushing hair away from my face. It's not the butterflies or fireworks I feel when he's around.

Yes, it's all of that, but it's so much more.

It took him leaving for me to realize. How I miss the way he laughs at anything and everything. The way the sunlight catches his eyes makes me smile without even realizing I am.

The way I feel for Dallas Westbrook isn't some casual feeling. It's a deep, tangled in my ribs type of feeling. I've shown him the parts of me I've never shown anyone else, physically and mentally.

I crave him in a way one would crave their favorite dessert.

I want his peace, his chaos, his *presence*.

I now know what this feeling is.

This is grounding, the feeling of finding a home in a person. It's the scariest feeling in the world, like standing on the edge of the tallest cliff, but knowing you'll jump anyway because every part of you wants to.

It's a feeling too big to contain.

The scariest part? I didn't mean to feel these things for him, but I did.

I love him.

Tears threaten to break the surface at my realization. The unknowns of everything feel like they're crashing down around me.

Picking up my phone, I decide to send him a text message.

I *need* to know what's going on so I can relax even a little bit.

> Hey. It's me. Poppy. I was thinking about you and wanted to see how you were. Are you coming back?

I delete the text before I hit send, tossing my phone on the couch and plopping myself down next to it. I sit and stare at the fireplace in front of me, yet another thing that reminds me of Dallas.

"Get a grip, Poppy," I say, picking up my phone to actually send a text this time.

> Hey.

And then I put the phone face down on the coffee table.

I keep it short and sweet, the invitation to hear back from him, and then I grab a blank piece of paper and start a new list of things for myself.

1. Wipe down the back deck furniture
2. Buy paint for the DIY bathroom project
3.

I can't think of a third one at the moment, so I move to stand at my back sliding door, noticing there's still sun left in the day, and I decide now is the time to get started on everything. My brain is a mess, and I realize I cannot control this situation even if I wanted to.

But I can control this list.

Stuffing it in the back pocket of my jeans, I spend the next half hour wiping down all the furniture on my back deck as the sun creeps behind the mountains, and then order paint colors online for the bathroom project that's been sitting on my saved tabs for months now. Next, I clean up the living room mess by fluffing my throw pillows and folding the blanket over the back of the couch in its usual spot.

Checking my phone, there's still no reply from Dallas.

My eyes land on the unopened baseball puzzle that Dallas surprised me with. A smile touches my lips, even with the sting of my text message going unread, it still brings me a small bit of happiness, mostly because I haven't touched a puzzle in what feels like weeks. I've spent so much time wrapped up in Dallas, getting out of the house more, Sage, and teaching. It's forced me to do things outside of my old routine before him.

And I was really starting to like the new routine we fell into.

I turn on the soft light over my puzzle table and get to work on it.

As day turns to night, I have all the edges of the puzzle pieced together to form the outer piece of what will be a baseball field.

As soon as I stand to get myself a drink, headlights illuminate my living room for a brief moment, forcing me to look outside.

That's when I see it.

The familiar Tahoe is sitting in the driveway next door.

I don't move from my spot looking out the window.

I can't move even if I try.

Watching through my window, I see Tucker emerge first from the passenger seat, opening the back door to let Sage out. My heart hammers in my chest when I see her. She's smiling and skipping with Mr. Marshmallow in her arms.

It's not until I see Dallas round the hood of the SUV that I release the breath I was holding. My body tenses, wondering if he's going to come over here. He has his phone pressed to his ear and looks deep in conversation. He stares at my house, but doesn't move to make his way over.

I feel my heart breaking little by little.

Was everything I felt one-sided?

No. There's no way.

Watching as he makes his way to his front door, still on the phone, my shoulders sag. I should go over there. Is that crazy?

God, I feel crazy right now, but I need to see him.

I find myself pacing my living room, one arm wrapped around my waist, with my elbow resting on it as I chew on my thumbnail, thinking about what to do next. I pull out the list I created earlier tonight, seeing what I've accomplished to keep my mind busy. I check off the two boxes of the items I finished.

The third line still remains blank.

Pulling a pen from the kitchen drawer, I write down the last thing I want to accomplish tonight.

3. Tell Dallas how you feel.

CHAPTER 41
I SAW YOUR CAR IN THE DRIVEWAY.

DALLAS

"Draw up the papers for me."

"You know, I had a feeling this would happen. They're already done and ready for you. I can meet you at Cozy Cup first thing in the morning to sign everything over," Nan says through the phone. "And, Dallas?"

"Hm?"

"Take care of my girl."

I nod, even though she can't see me, and remain quiet before I hear Nan hang up on the other end.

I've spent the entire drive in silence as Tucker slept. When he finally rolled into the penthouse around four in the morning, he said he hadn't gotten a wink of sleep from being up with a woman all night long. Good for him, but he wasn't enjoying the fact that I was ready to hit the road a half hour after he showed up. Truthfully? I would have hit the road right after leaving the stadium yesterday if it weren't for him.

I had to pick up Sage and get back here.

I *needed* to get back.

"Did she agree to letting you buy this place?" Tucker asks,

emerging from the hallway after being adamant that he put Sage to bed for me.

"It will officially be mine tomorrow morning."

Tucker grins. "Listen, I know this was a hard decision for you, but selfishly, I'm so happy you're staying. Sage loves it here, and I know you love it here. Bluestone Lakes has a way of changing people in all the best ways possible."

"That's very wise coming from you."

"Sometimes I can be wise when I'm not being stupid."

I scoff. "You're far from stupid."

He puts his hands on each hip, cocking his head to the side. "Yeah? Then tell me why I spent the best night of my life with the hottest woman ever, only to leave before she woke up like a coward."

"What?"

"Yeah. Riddle me that, Westbrook."

I walk toward him, resting a hand on his shoulder. "There's always another time. We can go back to the city for a baseball game, and maybe fate will play its cards right for you to run into her again."

He shrugs. "Maybe. But I'm going to head out. Is my bicycle still on the side of the house?"

"Should be."

"Perfect. And hey, thanks again for letting me tag along for your trip."

"Anytime."

Tucker leaves, and I make my way down the hall to check on Sage. She's sound asleep, hugging Mr. Marshmallow to her chest.

I need to see Poppy more than I need oxygen to breathe.

She texted me sometime during the drive, but I didn't want to risk taking my eyes off the road for a second to respond. I just knew I needed to get back here.

Back to her.

When I enter my living room, I hear a noise behind the front door—a soft murmur in a voice I recognize. Rushing to the door, I swing it open and see Poppy on the other side. Her head snaps up when she sees me, and her eyes widen. She's wearing jeans, a tank top covered by one of her many cardigans, and clutches a piece of paper in her hand.

We both stand there in silence for a moment as I take her in.

There was an ache in my chest while I was gone, and it had everything to do with the woman in front of me—the pain of leaving her and not letting her know what was happening.

"Hi," she says softly.

"Hi."

"I...uh." She turns her head to face my Tahoe before looking back at me. "I saw your car in the driveway."

I nod.

"And I don't know why I'm here." She sighs, straightening her spine. "No. I know why I'm here. I'm here because I created a stupid checklist today to keep myself busy. I've been going crazy the last few days, and finally today I made one. I didn't know what you were doing or if you were coming back," she says, rattling off everything in one quick breath. "I texted you, and you didn't respond. I thought the worst thing possible. So I went ahead and tackled my list." She reaches into her back pocket, pulling a folded piece of paper from her jeans, and then looks down at it. "I wiped down the furniture on my back deck and ordered paint for a bathroom project I'm planning. Then, when I saw you come back, I wrote down that I should tell you how I feel. I hate that it took you leaving for me to realize that I love you—I'm in love with you—but it happened." She finally looks back up at me. "Now I have this list that only has two things checked off. So I'm here to tell you how I feel. I'm here to tell you that I want you to stay. I should have said that before, but I didn't. I didn't want to be the reason—"

I cut her off by gripping the back of her neck and pulling her into me. My lips crash to hers, and it takes her a moment to register what's happening before her hands rake around my neck and tangle in my hair. Her body melts into mine, and I pull her into me with my other arm.

Poppy just told me she loves me.

It wasn't some loud declaration—it was mixed in a ramble of thoughts.

And because it's so her, I wouldn't have it any other way.

Pulling away from the kiss, I hover over her lips, smiling, and she smiles back. I let my fingertips brush her hair back the way I always do, tucking it behind her ear before cupping the side of her face. Her emerald eyes glisten as they stare up at me.

"I love you, too, Poppy."

"What?"

I pull her inside by interlocking my hand in hers, and close the door behind us. I guide her over to the couch and take a seat next to her. "When I left the other day, it was because I had a meeting in San Francisco to decide my future as the head coach of the Staghorns. When I last saw you and begged you to tell me to stay, I didn't know what my plan was yet. For the first time in my life, I wasn't jumping into anything without thinking." I bring her hand to rest on my thigh, tightening my hold on her. "The thing is, I couldn't make a decision. I knew then and there it's because this is where my heart is. Here in Bluestone Lakes with you."

"You want to stay?"

I nod. "I want to stay, honey. Not because you told me to, and not because I failed at being a coach in the city, but because this is my home. You've had me wrapped around your finger from the moment I first laid eyes on you in the coffee shop, and every moment after that, you only tightened the rope."

She smiles at that, looking down at where our hands are connected. "I love you, Dallas. I do. I'm scared of this feeling because I've never felt it before. I don't want to screw this up."

"You couldn't screw it up even if you tried."

Sniffles from around the corner force both of our heads to

snap down the hall, only to see Sage standing there, creeping around the corner.

"Sage? I thought you were in bed, bug."

"I heard Poppy's voice, and I wanted to come see her," she says, making her way to where we're sitting, settling herself on my thigh. "Are we staying here, Daddy?"

"We still have some stuff to figure out with your mom, but yeah," I say, pausing to look at Poppy and smiling. "We're staying, if that's okay with you."

"And will Poppy be your girlfriend?"

Poppy's cheeks blush as she averts her gaze.

"Only if she wants to be."

"I heard her say she loves you, Daddy. I think that's what married people say to each other."

I lean in to whisper in Sage's ear, but keep my voice loud enough that Poppy can hear the next thing I'm going to say. "Someday I will marry her, bug. Mark my words."

Poppy brings her fingertips to her lips and sucks in a sharp breath before her cheeks turn pink and she relaxes into a smile. *My girl.*

"I love that," she whispers back, smiling from ear to ear. "That plan is better than any ice cream date night ever."

"I think this deserves an ice cream night, huh?" Poppy says.

"Yes! Right now!"

"It's getting late, bug," I say to Sage. "And besides, Poppy probably has things to do before getting ready for bed."

Poppy stands from the couch, extending her hand for Sage to take, and she does. "This is exactly what I want to do tonight. I have cotton candy ice cream and a baseball puzzle that's almost done at my house if you want to come over."

"Yes! Can we please, Daddy?"

I shake my head in disbelief, smiling as big as Sage is before standing from the couch. "Only if you're positive, Poppy."

She holds Sage's hand, hooking her other arm in mine. "I've

never been more sure of anything in my life." And then she lifts on her toes and kisses me.

"Yay!" Sage cheers, forcing us to laugh against each other's lips.

I lift Sage in my arms, take Poppy's hand in mine, and close up the house behind me.

Because I too, have never been more sure of anything.

EPILOGUE
TWO MONTHS LATER.

DALLAS

"All right, huddle up," I shout to the team as they gather around me in a tight circle. Placing my hands on my thighs, I lean down to their level. I take each of them in and think about how far each of these kids has come since our first practice in the school gym. There's no more riding the bats like horses or running in circles. They shifted focus from snacks and juice boxes to learning the game.

This is my team.

"Listen, I know we didn't win our first game, and that's okay. We can't win them all."

"Yes, we can," Archie cuts in. "We have what it takes."

"I agree with you, but when it comes down to it, we may lose some, and I want everyone to know that's okay, too. But I love your energy, bud."

"We got this," Sage shouts.

"We do," I agree, smiling at my little girl who's loving this game as much as I always have. "If you all play the way you have over the last few months, I have no doubt we can win this one. Besides, we're at our home field."

"Duh. We play here every week." Ethan says.

"Exactly." I laugh. "Which means we know how this field works. We know every patch of dirt, every weird bounce the ball can take, and the way the sun glares. This field is ours and belongs to us. So do you know what that means?"

"We don't have to pay for hot dogs at the food cart?" Ethan says.

"No." Archie smacks the back of his hand against his arm. "It means we have the home field advantage."

"I still don't get it, but okay," Ethan agrees.

"It means we can win this," I tell them. "When you play where you belong, you fight harder. You play like you have the whole town behind you. And guess what?"

"What?" they all shout in unison.

"You *do* have the whole town behind you. We're up by one point, and if they don't score, we win. Now let's show them what a home field advantage looks like."

"Yes! Let's win!" they all shout in a half-organized cheer.

There are so many reasons beyond this one that make this field feel like home. And when I look over to the benches and bleachers we added before the season started, I see it.

I see her.

I came to Bluestone Lakes to figure things out and connect with my daughter. I never expected to meet someone who made me feel like I had been missing something all along.

This was only supposed to be temporary.

But then I saw Poppy laugh. Then she taught me how to braid my daughter's hair. She kept ice cream on hand for Sage and brought her puzzles because she knew she loved them. She opened up to me in a way that made me feel like we can trust each other.

I eye the crowd, and seated on the right side of one of the benches is my ex-wife and her boyfriend. Nathan and April have been seeing each other since before they decided to move right outside of Bluestone Lakes to a town called Bonneville. Nathan opened an OB-GYN practice where he and April will take turns working between there and the hospital. They'll commute every few days, but we've all fallen into a practice of doing what's best for Sage.

Sage has acclimated to the changes so well. She loves having two rooms at two different houses. The only thing she was adamant about was continuing school with her new friends in Bluestone Lakes.

Seated next to my ex-wife and her boyfriend sits Poppy. It's like they've been best friends forever. She's in the bottom seat in the bleachers, wearing *my* jersey. A San Francisco Staghorns jersey with my last name and number on the back from when I was the starting pitcher.

Every time I look at her, I remember that *this* is what home field advantage really means. It means finding where you're supposed to be.

"Hands in," I tell the kids, and they all reach into the circle. "Home run on three. One…two…three…"

"Home run!" they all shout before the group of kids filled with chaos and heart take the field.

I'm not worried about the way I used to be when I wanted to win a game more than my next breath. I know deep down, these kids got it in the bag.

I look to Tucker next to me, who looks deep in thought. "You all right?"

He nods, void of his normal fun expressions.

"I know now isn't the time, but if there's anything you want to talk about, I'm here."

"We don't need to get into it now, but I might want to talk about it later. But it's the date on the calendar. It's a hard day for me," he says, his voice somber, and I know it's something bigger than a conversation in the dugout between innings.

I clasp a hand on his shoulder. "Later then. We can grab a drink at Seven Stools. I'm here for whatever you want to talk about."

"I appreciate that."

The first batter hits the pitch Archie throws, and his brother Austin takes him out at first. Archie then throws a strikeout. I lean forward, placing my hands on my thighs as I watch the opposing team's best hitter come to bat.

One more out.

That's all we need for these kids to win this.

Archie's first pitch, the batter swings, and I swear time slows. I feel like I'm back at the Staghorns stadium and watching us lose our chance at a championship title. That's not what this is, I remind myself. These are just kids.

The ball flies through the sky into the outfield.

Gabe and Sammy, with her glitter shoes, run with their gloves stretched out in front of them, hoping to catch the ball. My jaw hangs open when I see Sage also running. Time stills even more. Tucker grabs my forearm as he watches, too, and any sound from the crowd is gone as I watch the ball fall directly into my daughter's glove.

She looks down to see if it's there, and turns to face me with a proud smile on her face, lifting the glove and ball in her hand.

Then the sound in my ears roars to life again.

Tucker is jumping up and down beside me before running toward the kids. They all pile on Sage, screaming and cheering. Poppy and April jump up and down, yelling louder than anyone.

We won.

We fucking won.

This might be a small town little league game with folding chairs, juice boxes, and paper scoreboards, but it feels like we just won the championship game under the bright lights of a sold out stadium.

My body finally reacts to the win, and I toss my baseball hat to the grass and run as fast as I can across the field to Sage. I dive into the rumble of kids and lift my daughter onto my shoulders. The kids all chant her name around me as I walk her to the crowd.

353

"You did it, Sage!" Poppy says.

"I'm so proud of you, baby," April adds, giving her hands a tight squeeze over my head.

"Amazing catch, Sage!" Nathan adds.

"I did it! I caught the ball!"

"Yes, you did, bug. And we won the game because of it." I tell her, setting her down next to us. "I'm so proud of you."

"I wanted this for you, Daddy. You're the best coach in all the land and deserved a big win."

"I agree," the kids chime in around us, rattling off their agreement at different times.

"The best!" Tucker adds with a fist to the air.

"This win deserves ice cream," Sage says.

"Did someone say snacks?" Ethan chimes in.

"All the snacks, dude," Tucker says, clapping a hand on his shoulder.

We all break out in laughter as the kids run off into the dugout to grab their things.

"I'll go help her," April says, leaving Poppy and me alone.

I step closer to her, cupping her face in my hands, and press a kiss to her lips before she can say anything more. As always, she melts into me, and *God*, I'll never get used to it.

"You did it, coach."

"They did it."

"Well, they had an amazing coach to help bring this all to life the last few months."

"I had some help with Tucker. I didn't expect it to go as smoothly as it did after he insisted on helping me. But it turned out to be better than I thought."

Poppy's features soften at the mention of Tucker. Whatever he was feeling before during the game, she knows, but I won't ask her. I want Tucker to be the one to tell me his story.

I hook an arm around Poppy's neck, pulling her close to my body and turning to face the kids in the dugout. They are still screaming. Gabe is trying to do a victory dance and ends up falling flat on his ass, and Ethan is asking everyone when and where we're getting ice cream after this. All the kids are running up the Sage, giving her high fives and hugs, celebrating her game winning catch.

At this moment, it's clear.

We won something way bigger than this game today.

We found home.

Don't forget...
Sign up for Jenn's newsletter to be the first to hear the news on new releases, announcements, influencer opportunities, and more.

http://jennmcmahon.com

ACKNOWLEDGMENTS

If you've read my acknowledgements in the past, you know I've thanked my readers and my team individually. From the ones who work hard behind the scenes with me, to my alphas, betas, editors, social media managers, and so many more. I'm so thankful to have had the same crew stick with me for every book I've published. They are my rock and support system when I need it.

I wouldn't be here without my readers.

I wouldn't be here without my team.

I also wouldn't be here without me.

I wanted to take a moment to thank the version of me threaded through every page, especially in Poppy—the character who carried pieces of my fear, my flaws, my fire, and my strength. She held the parts of me I was still learning to accept.

In building her, I found broken pieces of myself.

Mostly the strength I forgot I have.

From the tears I cried when no one knew, to the sleepless nights, to self-doubt, and to deleting the whole book and rewriting it right before my deadline. There was always that voice inside of me that said *keep going* when I just wanted to throw it all away.

I'd like to thank the version of me who refused to give up.

The version who kept breathing life into the story on the days where there was nothing left to give.

To that version I say:

I'm proud of you.
You did it.

ABOUT THE AUTHOR

Jenn McMahon resides along the shore in New Jersey with her husband, two boys, and three fur babies. She has spent years engrossed in romance books, to now writing her own and sharing them with the world.

When Jenn is not writing, she can be found reading, watching reruns of her favorite TV shows (Scandal, Grey's Anatomy and Friends – just to name a few), or doing puzzles. She also loves taking trips to the beach with the kids, Atlantic City date nights with her husband, and thunderstorms.

Scan Here to access my socials, Facebook reader group, newsletter sign up and everything you need to stay connected.

instagram.com/jennmcmahon.author
tiktok.com/@jennmcmahon.author
amazon.com/author/jennmcmahon

Printed in Dunstable, United Kingdom